Song of ABRAHAM

*The fascinating
life story of the man
both Arabs and Jews
call "Father"*

D0029984

ELLEN GUNDERSON TRAYLOR

ISBN 0-8423-6071-9

9 780842 360715

50595

ABRAHAM—

one of the giants of all history. A leader
who followed a different voice, whose
children changed the world and whose
name will live forever.

PHARAOH—

ruler of Egypt who conquered by divine
right in love and war—until he met Sarah,
wife to Abraham.

SARAH—

beautiful wife of Abraham, coveted by
Pharaoh but saved by her love, her integrity
and her faith; destined to star in a far
greater drama than the scene in Pharaoh's
chambers.

HAGAR—

seductive servant who came between an
aging Sarah and her beloved Abraham to
create the living sword of Ishamel.

LOT—

Abraham's nephew who loved earthly
delights more than heavenly promises; who
deserted Abraham for Sodom only to return
a lifetime later.

SONG OF ABRAHAM—an epic
story of one man, his family and his
faith. A story as important today
and tomorrow as it has been for
4000 years.

Song of
ABRAHAM

Ellen
Gunderson
Traylor

We Welcome Your Response
Choice Books of Ohio
14264 Hackett Road
Apple Creek, OH 44606

LIVING BOOKS®
Tyndale House Publishers, Inc.
Wheaton, Illinois

Living Books® edition

Living Books is a registered trademark of
Tyndale House Publishers, Inc.

Library of Congress Catalog Card Number 80-53501
ISBN 0-8423-6071-9
Copyright 1973 by Tyndale House Publishers
Printed in the United States of America

12 13 14 15 93 92 91

*To my husband, my parents,
and to all true seed of Abraham.*
Galatians 3:26–29

To this day he is known by many names . . .
Abraham the Patriarch, The Exalted Father,
Father of a Multitude, Father of the Faithful
. . . Abraham Khalil: The Friend of God.

CONTENTS

Now faith is the substance of things hoped for; the evidence of things not seen.

Hebrews 11:1

PART I

The Quest and the Call

~~~~~~~~~~~~~~~~~~~~~~~~~~~~~~~~~~~~

Thus saith the Lord God of Israel, Your fathers dwelt on the other side of the flood in old time, even Terah, the father of Abraham, and the father of Nahor: and they served other gods.

Joshua 24:2

Chapter I

c. 2086 B.C.

Ur was a foul city after dusk. Darkness hid the sick and outcast as they found their way inside the gated walls, seeking shelter from the cutting winds which blew off the Mesopotamian plains. Beggars in tattered clothes slept in dark corners, and small motherless children wandered among them in search of food.

A young runner from the Chaldean hills hastened through the great city gate and directed his steps toward the center of the metropolis.

He was aware of the sleeping bodies near the walls. He could not clearly see them, for at night the only light came from low doorways bordering narrow passages. But he heard the pleas of hungry men who woke as he passed, and he felt outstretched hands brush the hem of his skirt.

The packed-earth streets were still hot from the day. The boy felt this keenly through the thin soles of his leather sandals. More than once he glanced over his shoulder as he ran, and with any new or strange sound issuing on the night air, his young frame shivered. The shadows were alien to him.

Finding his way to the wide street leading to the central square, he stopped to rest. He felt more at home here. His master's household came this way to worship on holy days and to celebrate the festivals.

Ur's central square could be seen at the far end of the avenue. Adjacent to this, as large as he had remembered it, stood the temple. The moonlight behind the magnificent ziggurat set it off in monstrous silhouette. The staircases ranging on all four sides led his eyes to the top, where he could clearly see the columned altar house. On its apex the moon seemed to balance, as if watching him.

The sight threw his mind back to the last time his master's house had come to Ur. All the horrors of that day returned, bringing the story which had been retold in his dreams time and time again. As he gazed at the ziggurat, it was as if he could once more see the two priests escorting the girl up the front slope to the altar. He could hear the beats of the hundred drums measuring each step the three paced. He trembled as he recalled the bravery with which she followed and the horrified struggle she finally displayed as the priests strapped her down.

The top of the pyramid was so high and the drums had been so loud that the throng had not been able to hear the girl. But the boy, Dari, was sure she had screamed. He knew she had. It came in his dreams that way, and upon waking he had always fought to conceal his face in the bedclothes, as he had hidden it that bygone day in his mother's long sleeve.

He stood motionless, staring transfixed at the top of the temple, his mission almost forgotten.

Shamed by his emotions, the boy sought to cast off the thoughts which held him there. Following the instructions Hebron had given him, he left the wide viaduct and started up the moonlit hill which led to his destination, the House of Terah.

The great estate sat on the ridge.

Moonlight shone brightly through a cloudless sky, and the bleached brick of the merchant's domain was easily distinguishable.

Dari had heard often of Terah's wealth, and the impressive house was ample confirmation. Several levels terraced the hillside and spread in white beauty to the left and right. The broad roofs were laced with overhanging vines and flowered plants, the hues of which could be fully appreciated only in daylight. But Dari was sufficiently awed by the beauty and symmetry of the landscaper's art.

He could see less as he drew closer, for high walls surrounded the grounds. As he walked along the outside, Dari strained several leaps in frustrated attempts to see more.

He finally came to a large double-doored gate. Taking from under his belt a tightly laced leather bag, he pinched it to assure himself that the valuable paper was still contained, then called loudly for the gatekeeper.

The call was unanswered. Dari slammed the large brass ring hanging on the door. At last the gate was opened by a fine colossus of a man in a short white tunic, belted about the waist with polished leather adorned by a golden buckle. His black hair hung straight and was banded at the forehead with a leather thong. This was clasped in front with the symbol of the slave's quality, a small silver crescent moon.

The slave was clean-shaven, a sign of submission. But Dari knew he was worthy of great respect. Terah had bought him at a high price, for only slaves selected and sold by the temple priests wore the sign of the beneficent moon. Had the man not borne the symbol, however, his stature alone was enough to impress Dari to silence.

"State your purpose, boy," the gatekeeper demanded. "It is late and the master is retired. Why are you on the streets at this hour?"

"Sir, I have urgent news for Master Terah. I am Hebron's messenger boy. My news is for Terah's ears only. I must see him."

"Hebron is picking his runners young. How do I know he sent you? Where is your seal?"

Dari drew the leather bag again from his belt and opened it. Indeed, the paper was stamped with the seal of Hebron, but when the slave reached to inspect it, Dari drew back his hand.

"No one is to see this but Terah. The seal is Hebron's. The ram's horns are the symbol of his trade."

At this, Dari was reluctantly allowed to pass.

The man directed him to the entrance of the servants' quarters, where, he was told, he would wait until the master received him.

He followed the lane from the main gate to a low wing of the sprawling house. The brilliant moon lit the premises with majesty, and the boy saw that the home was composed of many buildings. Courtyards and breezeways separated unit from unit, each open corridor or yard landscaped with verdant lawns and floral gardens.

The domain ranged in terraced levels up the side of the hill, the main hall joining outlying buildings like the midpoint of an angle. The lowest terrace contained the stables on the left hand, the drill and training house for Terah's armed men on the right. The quarters of the armed men and the groundworkers' and attendants' apartments composed the two sides of the second terrace. Dari considered the work which must be the responsibility of the attendants, for it was well known that Terah owned the largest fleet of chariots and the finest military equipment of any merchant prince in all Chaldea.

The top level, the one closest to the main hall, housed the servants and their work area, and on the opposite side, the master's business quarters. Only the wealthiest and most progressive of businessmen in Ur entered the latter court.

The master's main hall, unlike the other buildings, was two stories high, the ledges and balconies surrounding it inlaid with carving and intricate sculpture. Dari feared entering this impressive home, so foreign to his own.

But suddenly the servants' door jarred open, and the gruff voice of a small but robust old woman ordered him to enter.

She escorted him with pride and great speed, complaining all the way that messengers had their nerve arriving so close to bedtime and with such of little urgency as he probably represented.

"You think you deserve an audience with my master, and yet you refuse to tell the gatekeeper your errand. To my way of thinking, you must be feeling the pride of your first job," she complained, and pointing a chubby finger, "That way is the master's hall. Enter with humility." At this she left him standing at the great carved door of Terah's chambers.

Quickly, for he had been delayed much too long already, Dari walked into the master's presence, facing the ordeal of his errand.

Terah stood in the center of the magnificently furnished room, his large cloudy eyes showing the trials of his advanced years. The past, which had provided him the wealth of a prince, had also brought heartrending divison to his home.

He had three sons. Nahor, his eldest, and Abram, his second, were still with him and were his happiness in old age. But the third son, Haran, whom he loved with that special affection which fathers often hold for their youngest, had left the great house many years before.

The family unit had been broken when Térah's wife died, though in reality it had long been unstable. Haran had been born to his parents many years after they had ceased to hope for more children, and to his mother he was a gift of renewed youth and vitality. But the old woman had so strongly loved him that her feelings ranged to the extremes of dominance and unquestioned possession, and upon her death Haran had shown little emotion but that of a young caged animal suddenly set free.

The next day, he had left for the Chaldean pastureland. The old father had seen Haran many times gaze out his chamber windows at the distant hills, home of nomadic wanderers and herdsmen, as he yearned for the romance and freedom of the wayfarer's life.

Haran had joined Hebron, a wealthy herdsman, whose journeys took him from end to end of Mesopotamia. Old Hebron, who had traded with Terah for many years, had often dwelt on tales of nomadic adventure when visiting the great house.

Many years had passed since Haran had gone. He had frequently sent messages to his father, but the old man's heart had never recovered the real loss of his son.

Terah broke the silence of the room: "A messenger from Hebron, they tell me." He cautiously turned from Dari as if to defend himself from the inevitably foreboding news. "What is this urgent message you bring me, boy? Does it concern my son?"

"Sir, I truly am Hebron's messenger. I am certain that if you will read the contents of this pouch, you will see why one so young was chosen to bring bad tidings."

"Master Terah," the letter began, "I hesitate to send news that your son has been seriously wounded. The Guti invaded our encampment last night. We had hoped to be spared their plundering, but they have dealt blows to herdsmen up and down the valley. We are certain they plan to attack Ur very soon. I am sending a boy to give you the news. All my men are armed and ready to ward off ensuing attacks.

"Your son is in mortal danger. Please come, and see fit to bring aid. Your servant, Hebron."

Terah's grey eyes grew hot with hatred. Anger and shock were etched on his face as he finished the letter and laid it on the heavy marble table at his side. The old man gathered his robes tight about him and sat down in silence.

The Guti invaders came from the region to the northeast of Chaldea. Little was known of them save their barbaric warfare and vicious plundering. Entire towns and small cities of Mesopotamia had been subdued by them, and when they rested, they found sport in spying out and overcoming trade caravans and nomadic encampments scattered throughout the hills.

Hebron's camp had been the subject of one of these assaults. The fact that he had lived to send word of it must mean that the attack had been instigated by a small band. The Guti were known for their cat-and-mouse sport of "playing" with their victims before finalizing a coup. When the time would come for their kill, they would bring an overwhelming force of men and arms to carry it out, and the comparatively small camp would quickly fall.

Dari stirred restlessly as he waited for Terah's statement. He watched as the princely man, his stature only slightly bowed with age, rose from his chair and paced the richly carpeted floor. Terah looked first out one chamber window and then another, his large hands clenching repeatedly.

Cool streams of night air from the hills wafted into the dimly lit room. Flames of the wall torches wavered uncertainly with each soft breeze, and the cool silver blue of the moonlight emphasized the chill of the evening. Terah walked through an archway opening from his chamber onto the surrounding balcony.

Dari hesitated to follow, but his curiosity would not let him stay. The balcony gave a view of Ur familiar to the boy. The hills which were his home provided the same sight, though from a much greater distance. The city stretched across a wide, flat expanse of plain hemmed by ambling highlands. Pale stone and brick buildings illumined it on a clear night like this. Lights shone here and there in shops and houses where people were still awake. The night sky cast shadows on the wide viaducts and very narrow back streets and alleyways. Flat-roofed buildings of one and two stories formed stairsteps on the horizon. To the far side of the city could be seen the mouth of the mighty gulf which brought wealth through trade from all parts of the East, and which had elevated Ur to a high pedestal of dominance among the empires of the day.

Ur had been one of the first cities inhabited by Man. The chronicles contained this evidence, though the memory of those early days had vanished. Along the west side of Ur flowed the immortal Euphrates, life-giver of civilization and keeper of the secrets of Man's beginnings. It joined its twin, the Tigris, which flowed far to the east, into the gulf.

From Terah's balcony little noise of the city could be heard. Only the occasional rumble of a wooden-wheeled cart driven by a late returning worker or the soft-stringed music of the taverns would drift up the hill to the mansion.

Many evenings had found Terah on this veranda breathing deep of the clean air which blew off the gulf, listening to the breeze and the music, as he pondered the wisdom of a business venture or a trade contract. From this vantage point, the old man surveyed the city as a lord overlooks his land holdings. And though Terah did not own Ur, he was the most prominent of those close to the governors and priests and carried more influence with them than any other merchant in Chaldea.

Tonight saw Terah in a different mood. He was the father of a wounded man. That thought alone possessed him.

He turned to the messenger boy, whose curiosity had brought him to the railing of the balcony at his side.

"How many men does your master have with him in camp?" Terah queried.

"About fifty, sir, but no more, and some of them are weak already from wounds and hunger. The invaders took most of our supplies, leaving us to starve. We would have moved on, but we could not because of the wounded. Master expects the Guti will return on their way to attack your city. The women and small children have little hope, sir. And the men are giving up what hope they still possess. Master says the Guti plan to dominate all Chaldea."

Terah's face was solemn, and he clutched the railing in silence. At last he spoke. "You are a brave boy to come so far through the hills. How far away are your people?"

"They are camped in the Wadi Saboth, about fifteen miles to the north, maybe less. I stayed low in the groves scattered throughout the hills. When I had to go through the plains or along hill tops, I ran with all my might. I saw no sign of Guti between Ur and Master's camp." Dari hesitated and seemed to tremble. A dewy sweat dotted his forehead. "Sir, the Guti killed our herds, just to see them die!"

The thought of needless slaughter and bloodshed and the ordeal of his errand had caught up with the boy. Terah hastened him back to his chambers and called for a servant.

The old woman who had escorted Dari to Terah's parlor answered the call, her attitude of indifference to the boy's errand dissolving as she entered.

Dari sank into a soft, round-backed divan, gradually ceased his crying, and in a few moments was calmed by sleep.

But the night held no rest for Terah. He would need the remaining hours before dawn to plan his efforts to rescue Haran.

His domain housed five hundred men, ready to be armed. They were trained to protect the caravans which his trade demanded that he send in all directions from Ur. But five hundred would not be enough. The small band of Guti which had threatened Hebron was only the beginning. When they returned, it would be in thousands, and as the boy had said, they would simply overrun the camp on their way to sack Ur.

The threat of Guti invasion was not new to the city of the moon, and the empire was certainly powerful enough to ward off attack, even of the magnitude for which the Guti were famous. But strange as it may have been, Terah knew he must go outside Ur for help.

The Guti was well known throughout Chaldea, but the final arbiter in all military affairs, the king of Ur, was unmoved by their threats. Sargon, for fifty-two years king of the city-state, was an old man. In his prime he had led Ur well, in the fashion of several generations of proud Sargonic governors, whose dynasty descended glamorously in the tradition originally set down by the conqueror, Sargon of Akkad, nearly two hundred years before. But now the once-great ruler, in his senility, set too much store by the enchantments and premonitions of the temple priests, who often took advantage of his readiness to accept their word and sought power for themselves.

Terah had been at council with the governors in Sargon's presence when the king had explained his lack of overt action against the Guti. Ur's high walls had been posted with guards at every tower. Defense stood ready to ward off invasion, but the priests warned that offensive action, taken in the form of actual attack on the foe, would be hazardous unless the moon was in his half-darkened stage.

Terah, and indeed all Ur, worshiped the beneficent moon god, Nannar, who was held responsible for all good gifts. Harvests of bounty, family happiness, new-born sons and daughters, productive cattle, success in battle, and any other good thing was given at his hand. Any ill was attributed to the myriad mischievous and demonic spirits which, in vain, warred with the moon and in so doing brought misery to his followers.

But Nannar was not totally generous. In return for his bestowals, he exacted human sacrifice, one of which young Dari had recalled so vividly on his errand to the great house.

The day of the council, the old king had entered after the governors were assembled. Withered with age, he came with the assistance of two menservants, each supporting him as he walked. The salutations of the governors showed the reverence they gave his position. But when the king announced his refusal to become involved in affairs which "the signs and the seasons warrant unnecessary," the councillors, who had been thirsty for war, questioned his wisdom and his interpretation of the priests' prophecies.

The old king left the council chambers without further discussion, and the city was left with little security.

Terah left the balcony and rested on the divan which had earlier cradled the messenger boy.

His faith had never been so challenged. Nannar could not mean to leave Ur defenseless. Something was out of joint. The priests were misguiding the king, to be sure. Yet how could this be, if they were Nannar's spokesmen?

In his wrestling, no answer came to Terah. He must deal with the problem in his way. He could wait no longer for Nannar's answer, as the invaders had brought the problem home. The dilemma was no longer Ur's alone. The Guti had harmed Terah's own son.

Small beads of perspiration stood on his forehead as he struggled with the reality of his decision. He was about to challenge his god and his king, and that rebellion would remain forever with him.

As the first rays of dawn sleepily opened the morning, when the room was still so dim that daylight was only a promise, the old merchant rose and quietly stepped to the washing bowl. The house was still. Not even the servants stirred. He washed his face in the cool, scented water, always fresh in the container.

Sleep had barely touched his mind. But by now his plan was formulized, and despite the agony it brought him to break with his beloved traditions, he hastened to carry it out.

He first went from his chambers down the hallway to the suite where his son, Nahor, lay asleep, as yet unaware of all that had transpired during the night. Nahor was the only son present at the time, as Abram had accompanied one of his father's caravans into faraway Egypt, where the special treasures of Chaldea were highly prized.

Terah had restrained himself from waking Nahor when he first received the message, as he knew his son would be a better aid with a full night's rest.

Nahor, Terah's first-born, was a strong and capable man, gentle-tempered and surprisingly wise for his age.

Very much devoted to his father, he had assisted him in many ventures and would not fail him now.

Nahor and Abram, the second son, were very much alike in many respects, devotion and great capability being among them. But Nahor had frequently been at odds with Abram, the more outspoken and forthright of the two, and he had often considered his younger brother coltish and foolhardy in his adventuresomeness.

Yet despite, or because of, this youthful and sometimes uncalculated exuberance, Abram had always been the most productive and aspiring of Terah's sons. The old father took pride in the successful and intelligent decisions Abram had made without his guidance, many of which had brought new fortune to the family. His assistance in the ensuing conflict would have been beyond price, but there was no way to send him word of the necessity in time.

Nahor's room was dimly lit by the rising sun. The thick red tapestries which usually blanketed the windows were drawn back with links of gold chain, and the sun's rays illumined the richly appointed room. Terah shook his son from sleep and, with urgency, related the dilemma.

"My instructions, Father? What are they?" Nahor asked as he dressed.

"You are to alert the runners," Terah answered. "Send them out in all directions from Ur to the merchants with whom we have good relations up and down the valley, from Eridu to Sippar. They will explain the need of the moment, and the merchants will send their mercenaries in full arm to meet my five hundred at the Wadi Saboth where Hebron is camped. The runners are to stop for no reason but necessary rest. They are to speak to no one before or after they speak directly to each master. While you do this, I will ready the battalion."

Nahor rushed to accomplish the errand but suddenly hesitated and turned to Terah. A handsome man, Nahor's grey eyes were like those of his father, full of intellect and vigor. Nahor was dark and robustly built, his black hair and cleanly trimmed beard showing the care he gave his appearance.

Like a servant about to ask a favor of his master, Nahor faced his father. "Sir, I will accompany you to Hebron, will I not?"

Terah slowly walked toward his son and placed his hand on his shoulder. Nahor was much taller than he, and Terah's wise face looked up into his son's as he faltered to find words with which to express his feelings.

The old man did not utter a sound, but his eyes related his gratitude and spoke for him that his heart would have broken if his son had not asked.

Chapter II

The day was hot already, though the sun had several hours yet to reach its zenith. It was morning, but it might have been midday for the heat.

The young runner Dari hastened on his way to a small village west of Ur, carrying Terah's urgent message to the wealthy merchant Masen. Dari had begged Terah to let him do this, so the wise man had sent him to the hamlet not more than sixteen miles away, while his older runners took on the longer distances.

Dari ran at a rhythmic pace, not as quickly as he might. He had learned always to run more slowly than he was able, thus conserving his strength for the length of the trip and not tiring before its end.

The wilderness through which Dari traveled was desolate. Hot wind blew across the plains and dashed sandy dirt in his eyes. At places the loose, powdery dust of the road was so deep it covered his feet and felt like beds of soft, hot ashes about his ankles. His rough brown tunic absorbed the rays of the sun and held them against his body. His uncovered arms and legs had been tanned by twelve years of exposure and remained comparatively cool as he ran. The only spot of color which designated him as more than a part of the drab landscape was his red sash, fashioned by his mother in the distinct weave of his tribe. It was to this that he had attached his message pouch.

Dari had traveled half the distance to Masen and was ready for a rest. As he ran, he lowered the mantle from his head and brushed a stray lock of damp hair from his forehead. Ahead he could see a very large oasis of ancient oaks near the roadside.

The grove was the stopping place for weary travelers

who had passed this way through the centuries. Relaxing in a patch of cool brush, he reached into the folds of his robe and drew out a skin of wine which Terah had given him to quench his thirst. The cool liquid shocked his parched tongue but refreshed his weary spirit.

The grove was peaceful, the hot wind of Chaldea rustling the leaves above him and rocking his mind quietly. Dari took out his small shepherd's pipe to pass a few moments with the music he so dearly loved. As Hebron's piper, he attended the flocks with his soothing melodies, and today he would have little time for such diversion.

But his alert eyes scanned the horizon in all directions. He had been trained from childhood to be wary of highway robbers, who were known to lurk in the most desolate of places in wait for rich caravans. The messenger boy carried no money but could be the victim of assault nevertheless.

As his eyes swept the far reaches of the wilderness, they took in rough plains, here and there dotted with low brush, dry and thirsty under the sun. At widely separated points on the horizon, craggy stones rising from the ground stood solitary, like lonely people. The constant wind blew the earth around about them, but they resisted, as they had for centuries, the erosion of the elements.

Suddenly his attention was drawn to a dark line midway on the great expanse. It had moved, he was certain. As he watched, the line grew longer.

He replaced the pipe in its fold. A small chill of fear ran up his back and tickled the hair on his neck. He knew what he saw was alive. It could be a group of riders on their way to Ur from some distant place, a pack of desert wolves running wild in search of food, a troop of bandits.

In any case, fear froze him, and he lay low in the oasis.

As the line grew more distinct, Dari could more clearly distinguish the shape. It was a caravan, vast in proportion, and his fear subsided as he took in the approaching splendor. Nearly three thousand animals composed it, camels, asses, and oxen, not to mention the men needed to command it.

Methodically the procession crept through the arid wasteland, stretching along the road like a long, lazy snake. Dari's better judgment told him he should circle far around the oncomer and be on his way again, but youthful curiosity held him. He had never been so close to a caravan. Only from the distance of his native hills had he watched trains pass over the plains and speculated as to their nature and wealth.

Dari scrambled behind a boulder near the spring which watered the oasis. He lay low, barely peeping over the top.

As the caravan was still a good way off, two scouts spied the oasis and, breaking from the ranks, headed toward it.

Dari now huddled even closer to the rock and watched as the runners circled the entire boundary of the green retreat and surveyed the grove, entering cautiously between the trees. Apparently pleased with what they saw, they returned to the road and signaled their approval.

Instantly, several dozen men with limp goat skins slung over their shoulders separated themselves from the caravan and dashed eagerly toward the desperately needed water supply.

Gathering shoulder-to-shoulder at the banks of the large pond, they dipped their empty vessels into the water and allowed them to fill. As they did so, they drank avidly and splashed the water hilariously on their neighbors in childlike abandon.

But as quickly as the skins were filled, the levity and laughter ceased, and the seriousness of their purpose there was recalled. Returning as quickly as possible to the oncoming caravan, they were greeted by the cheering hundreds who awaited the water. Covering the length of the train, they distributed the bulging skins among the attendants.

Meanwhile the caravan was coming on more quickly, and the first figure to catch the boy's attention was the rider of a large, two-humped camel, the finest Dari had ever seen. The gangly but uniquely graceful creature was decked with an intricately beaded saddle crossed under its girth, a harness shiny with gold and silver crescents and a regalia of streamers tipped with tinkling bells.

The master of this fine animal led the entire caravan. A tall man of majestic stature, he maneuvered his beast with one hand. Constantly aware of the responsibility he shouldered, he surveyed the landscape intently and frequently glanced at the train following him.

As caravaneer, he was undoubtedly wealthy but apparently not content to eat, drink, grow soft and white. He dressed in the typical fashion of the wealthy. A golden pendant, the size of a man's palm, hung from a long chain about his neck, and a large, sheathed sword was secured close to his body by a sash about the waist of his white tunic. A heavy striped cloak mantled broad shoulders.

His head was uncovered for the time being, and as custom dictated, his lustrous dark hair was longer than that of the servants who followed. His full beard marked his aristocratic birth and set him apart from the clean-shaven men behind.

A life of travel had exposed his arms and legs to the hot sun which daily burned over the open country of Mesopotamia. The wind blew his hair back, disclosing a ruddy, tanned face and neck.

Directly behind him rode three armed men, brass weaponry glistening in the sun. The center man carried a tall staff, the top elevated far above his head. A scarlet banner slapped the breeze at its pinnacle, and an emblem of strange design was laid against the brilliant background of the flag. One thick black line formed a circle, but the ring was not continuous. A small portion remained disconnected, and so the circle was incomplete.

As the caravan drew close to the oasis, the caravaneer began bringing his camel to a halt, and he raised his hand high above his head. As he did so, each group of men behind him, in turn, made the same gesture until the final member was aware that the train would stop. All movement ceased gradually, and at last no sound was heard as the caravan awaited instructions.

Now Dari could fully appreciate how enormous the train was. Ranks of men were positioned at intervals throughout. Between them were heavily burdened asses, captured wild and tamed to serve their captors. Bulky oxen drew small carts and wagons laden with bundles of precious ointments, juicy fruits, figs, dates, bolts of scarlet and purple cloth, bags of copper and beaten brass.

Under normal conditions of travel, the animals were easily restrained. In fact, the burros usually demanded frequent prodding with pointed sticks to persuade them to go on. However, the train had come farther than usual under the scalding sun without rest or drink, and the oxen and asses quickly were the first to recognize the proximity of water. The aroma was keen to them. Here and there the anxious creatures strained at their harnesses and bolted. The beasts' tugs jolted the wagons. Great vessels clanked within the vehicles, and wooden wheels ground with hot friction against their crude brakes.

Burros emitted pitiful cries, and oxen lowed repeatedly. Their drivers fought to restrain them from breaking rank and tearing in chaos for the pool. But everything must be done decently and in order. Many of the animals were unhitched, several dozen at a time, and led to the water, while others drank from pails filled by their attendants.

Meanwhile, the men were allowed to go to the grove. In their excitement, all formality was forgotten, and they tore feverishly for the shade. Many flung themselves full-length into the cool, damp grass. Others sat complacently under the trees, resting against the trunks. Most of them, however, headed directly for the pool.

With unrestrained abandon, they indulged their thirsts and cooled their parched bodies.

But at last the reverie gradually tapered to a sleepy silence, men here and there dozing in the shade.

Until this moment, Dari could not have left without being seen, but he could slip away now. He knew he must be going, so he began to crawl through the tall grass behind the boulder, toward the trees which hemmed the oasis. Once blocked from view, he would continue his run from the grove.

His departure came to a sudden halt, however, when a commanding voice pierced the silence.

"Enough of your idleness!" it shouted. "We will eat now and be on our way."

It was the voice of the caravaneer. Dari wanted to return to the boulder to get one last look at the handsome man in authority. But he continued hastily crawling through the grass. In a moment he would be free of the strangers.

The voice was obeyed instantly. Drowsy men stirred quickly. Each sat erect, legs crossed. Several came quickly with wineskins, bowls of fruit, plates of bread and cheese, each man taking his fill.

By now Dari had come to the edge of the grove, and he got off his knees, running in a stooped position until he thought he was out of view.

Meanwhile, one of the armed men had come again to the spring for water. Bowed over the clear pool, he ceased his drinking and looked toward the grove. He had heard a rustling among the trees, and he stood to get a better look. There he saw the young boy dashing from the grove onto the road.

Like lightning, the man rushed from the pool, through the grove, and toward Dari. The boy ran quickly but he was no match for his pursuer. The man firmly grasped his arm. Dari tried, painfully, to wrench away, his rough tunic splitting at the sleeve as he kicked viciously against his opponent. The stir brought several more men running from the oasis.

It was no use. The big men easily overcame the boy and brought him back to the grove, thrusting him into the middle of their group.

All eyes were on Dari. Angry men stared down on him, but the frightened lad did not cease to struggle. Soon several servants began to laugh derisively at his efforts for freedom. His captor planted his foot on the back of Dari's neck, holding his face to the dirt. "What do you see now, little spy?" he roared.

Gradually Dari ceased his fighting, and the men split the air with raucous laughter.

But then, as if suddenly muted, the crowd was silent. The heavy foot was lifted from Dari's neck, and he sat up. Wiping the dirt from his mouth, he raised his head, looking for the answer to the crowd's sudden docility.

There above him stood the caravaneer. The man stooped over Dari, and his large arms supported the boy to his feet. "Since when does it take four strong men to quell one small boy?" the handsome man ordered, his face flushed with anger and his dark eyes flashing tempestuously at the cruelty of his men.

The servants shamefacedly looked at the ground. The man led Dari aside, and then, with a kind but stern voice, demanded of him who he was and his errand.

"I am not a spy, sir," Dari insisted, his voice shaky with fright.

A fleeting look of anger crossed the caravaneer's face. "Do not lie to me, boy," he commanded. "What is your tribe? What is your errand? You must tell me. It will do no good to hide the truth."

The man was hard in his questioning, but his eyes betrayed a kind spirit.

Straightening his shoulders and raising his head high, Dari said, "The merchant ordered that none of his runners should speak of this to any man until they reached their destinations. But if you mean to hold me unless I talk, I will have to tell you, sir, as I must be on my way." Breathing deeply, he said, "I am Dari of the tribe of Hebron the nomad—"

The caravaneer anxiously interrupted. "Hebron! I know him well. What is your errand?"

"Master sent me to Ur last night to tell a man the Guti had invaded our camp, and to ask him to bring aid. It was most important I tell him his son had been badly wounded. The kind man proceeded to send his runners throughout Chaldea in search of aid. I was sent also. And so, you see, the need is urgent, and I must be going."

With the boy's explanation, a look of agonized shock had suddenly imprinted the caravaneer's face. He knelt down eye to eye with the boy, placing firm hands on Dari's shoulders, and with urgency in his voice, he asked, "Son, please, who was the merchant of Ur?"

"Terah, sir."

The man searched Dari's eyes as if hoping to see some joke there. Finding none, he rose.

"Terah is my father."

"Sir!" cried Dari. "You are Abram?"

"Indeed, I am, boy."

"Oh, sir! This is beyond belief that I should find you. Master Terah needs you badly."

"My father has taken his forces to aid Hebron?"

"Yes, sir."

After receiving precise instructions to Hebron's camp, Abram turned about hastily.

"Bowman!" he shouted. "Our stay here has been cut short. Take charge of the train. Return it safely to Ur. I must go to Hebron's camp. Half the men will come with me. Half will guard the train home!"

A bulky man stepped to the front. He was not tall, but powerfully built, and he wore a band about his head clasped with a silver crescent moon, just as Terah's gate-keeper had.

Swiftly the company organized itself into two units. The bowman shouted commands rapidly. Within min-utes, the caravan was ready to move on, and a sizable armed host awaited Abram's lead.

The dark-eyed caravaneer expressed his deep gratitude as he grasped Dari's hand warmly. He then ran for his camel and, at a command, the host made speed in two directions.

The messenger watched briefly as the handsome Abram led his unit speedily down the road. The slow caravan behind gradually became a speck again, and Dari also was lost to sight as he resumed his run to Masen.

Chapter III

Long shadows of dusk stretched like taut ribbons across the open plains. Rocks and plants slightly raised above the flat, broad expanse joined their lengthening shades with the sandy surface. The huge ball of sun dipping behind the western rim of the Mesopotamian valley cast red rays, like fingers, into the foothills and across the floor as if to leave its mark before retiring.

The broad uninterrupted plains were, as always, unendingly quiet. The small creature Man had, within the past centuries, built up large towns here and there in the fertile crescent of the bowl, where the mighty twins, Tigris and Euphrates, had deposited a rich alluvial soil. Man had succeeded in crisscrossing the valley floor with the thin cut-out lines of trade routes, and these connected his precious empires, giving him a spindly web with which to reach his neighbors across the lonely miles.

He had altered the courses of Chaldean streams to water his miniscule garden plots. He had hewn temples to worship his gods, and he had hewn the gods themselves, out of foothill stone and brick.

Man had provided well for himself from the resources of his valley, and he had taken pride in all his doings, saying, "I am a wondrous creature of untold abilities." But the vast miles of undulating plains, ribboned sparsely with shining blue streams—the scalding sun, searing the atmosphere—the wide avenues of foothills and mountains hemming the region—all these laughed at the antlike inhabitant and told the true size of his impression.

Today several large black birds swooped, dipped, and then rose again and again above a sizable band of men below. The leader, Merchant Terah, who directed his battalion from the height of a great dromedary, glanced apprehensively at the setting sun. He hoped to reach Hebron's camp before night.

It was not much farther now. The young runner had told him the camp lay in the Wadi Saboth.

To the east across the plains, his son Nahor spied a deep crevice in the hills. It was difficult to distinguish it from the other hilly creases, but Terah struck out away from the highway, knowing they had found the spot.

Cool air settled into the valley as soon as the sun disappeared. The extremes of temperature, hot during the day, very cool at night, were typical of the wilderness. No cloud cover held the heat in the atmosphere after sundown, and so, save for the warm ground, the entire valley was bitingly cold. Icy winds whistled down through the gorges as the men approached the foothills.

Terah drew his robes closer about him and got down from his camel. He called for a runner to check out the crevice, who soon returned with news that Hebron's camp was positioned just to the left of the stream's source.

Quickly Terah's company rode into the hills. When they had come to a high ridge, they saw the light of the campfire, cleverly hidden from any lower vantage point.

Terah was grateful for the night which hid his face from the other men. Doubt clouded his eyes and apprehension nudged at his spirit as he thought of what he might find in the camp.

When they were still a good way off, a deep voice split the chill air and ricocheted off the walls of the gorge. "Halt! Who goes there and what is your purpose?"

Terah, aware of the unwritten code that anyone approaching a camp without warning was in danger of his life, returned, "I am Terah, of Ur! My five hundred are with me. May we pass?"

"Send an unarmed man, quickly, with your seal!" the voice demanded.

After due inspection the band was allowed to pass,

and Terah's men, looking above, noted several armed guards positioned at various points along the mouth of the gorge. As they came to the camp, the entrance to the large central tent was thrown back. A man, old as the merchant but short and stocky in stature, ran excitedly to meet the group.

"Blessings on thee, Terah. How I have longed to see this hour!"

It was the nomad Hebron, and he greeted his guest with oriental fervor, grasping the tall man's shoulders and planting firm kisses on each of his cheeks.

"Friend, I came as quickly as possible," said Terah, "and we have sent for help from all Chaldea. We hope to have enough aid to meet the Guti in force."

The nomad rubbed his plump hands together excitedly. "Blessings on thee, Terah, for thy foresight and bravery. I know of Sargon's refusal to battle with the offenders. Perhaps we will be their stumbling block."

Terah, scarcely hearing the little man, looked toward the main tent quizzically.

"Haran is faring ill, my friend," said Hebron in answer to the unspoken question. "Come this way."

The nomad's tent was surprisingly warm inside. Small lamps hung from the ribbing, giving off heat as well as dim yellow light. A young woman knelt over a blanketed figure on the floor. She held a bowl of steaming mixture, at intervals spooning it into the wounded man's mouth.

Now, trembling with emotion, the old father ran to the bedside and knelt with the girl. Looking into the face of his son, all feelings of estrangement disappeared for him, and the years seemed to peel away, time standing again at a point of past union and understanding.

Terah sought a look of recognition from Haran, but the son only lay on his crude bed, eyes closed, breathing heavily.

"Son, my son!" cried Terah in broken tones. Rivulets of salty tears coursed down his cheeks and into his beard. Unashamedly, he bowed over the figure and wept.

After a time, the young woman at Terah's side spoke. "Master, you are Terah, my father's father?"

He slowly raised his eyes to her. "Milcah? My grand-daughter?"

"I am, sir. How long I have wished to meet you, my grandfather! Father has spoken so often of you." And then, with a saddened expression, she gazed at the wounded man. "If only my father could know you are here. He has been in a deep sleep since his wounding. He neither speaks nor recognizes any of us."

"Child, I have often pictured you. Haran's messages over the years have praised you." Terah said no more then as he took in the beauty of the face before him. The girl was of marriageable age. Thick auburn hair hung loosely about her face and shoulders. A deep complexion set off large dark eyes and thick lashes. Her full lips wore a sad expression as she anxiously tended her father. She was a small, delicate girl. Terah found himself remembering the first time he had seen his wife. Milcah bore such a strong resemblance to her.

"Child," he whispered, as if not to disturb the picture, "where are Iscah and Lot?"

The young woman pointed to a dark corner of the tent where a small girl lay asleep on a bed of goatskins. Terah had not noticed her.

"That is Iscah. She is eight years my sister. Lot, my brother, is with the men on the hill."

The old man pondered the strange hand of events which had deprived him of three grandchildren and his youngest son. Desire cried out in him to turn back time and rearrange it all. As he looked at the sleeping Iscah, a stranger to him, as he thought of the young man Lot on the hillside, whom he had not yet seen, as he considered the girl before him, who should have grown up in his house, sadness, like a bitter liquid, poured over him. Somehow he felt like an intruder before his own kin.

The wounded man moved his head slightly and his eyes opened. There was a fleeting hope that he might regain consciousness, but this went as quickly as it had come.

Hebron, the nomad, entered the tent with a look of anticipation. There was something about this little man that somewhat lifted the heaviness of the room, though the anxiety of the recent battle and the desperation of his people bore heavily on him. He was a likable fellow, very short and round, his brown face crinkled with smile lines. He had a brief, pointed beard and was dressed in a rough woolen robe, tied with a sash like Dari's. His head was mantled with a flowing hood secured about the forehead with a thick cord, and his sandals only served as soles for his feet, which were wrapped in warm bindings to keep out the chill.

As he came into the tent, his eyes were excited and his plump hands clamped together tightly. "A stream of torches is seen in the valley, Terah! They come from the south."

The tall merchant rose from the bedside and walked into the cold night air with Hebron. Nahor, who had been with Terah's army, joined them. Everywhere men were stationed along the ridge, ready at a moment's notice for any encounter. Tension filled the atmosphere.

From the surrounding tents the muffled cries of hungry children could be heard. The camp was destitute, stripped by the invaders. Hebron was quiet, stroking his beard nervously. He looked from tent to tent, fervently wishing to satisfy those cries. One large tent housed other wounded men, and women tended them through the long hours, as Milcah did her father.

As they walked through the camp, Terah bore a distracted look, preoccupied with a new thought. "I did not expect help so soon. I sent your runner Dari to Masen early this morning. He is the closest ally in the valley, but it should have taken even him much longer to arrive."

The three men came to the ridge, which commanded a vast view of the valley floor. The full moon lit the huge bowl and a sharp wind whistled up the heights. There, as Hebron had described, was a long line of yellow lights winding like a tiny luminescent worm through the flat expanse.

In a whisper, as if hesitant to hear his own question, the plump nomad at Terah's side said, "You fear they may be Guti?"

"Friend, as you said, they come from the south, and they angle in from the west, unlike the Guti. Be calm, now. Possibly it is no more than a night caravan." But Terah's voice betrayed a disbelieving spirit.

"Master, what caravan would travel at night? And see how they seem to have left the highway for these foothills?"

Terah looked steadily at his companion. "Keep your courage, Hebron. You have long been a devoted ally. We will not fail one another." Then he raised his eyes to the moon which pierced the night sky. "One blessing is on us. Nannar shines to guide us."

Chapter IV

The winding lights did not bring Guti. When word came that it was Abram and his host approaching, Terah's spirit was renewed.

Silence is sometimes more poignant than words to express feeling, and such was the greeting of the old merchant as he clutched his son in disbelief and gratitude.

"Father," said Abram after a prolonged embrace, "we returned early from Egypt. Our business there went easily, so we hastened home. Near Ur, my caravan met Hebron's young runner, who told us of the invasion. We came as quickly as we could. How is Haran? Please take me to him."

Father and son went to the central tent, but before entering, Terah hesitated. Again he looked high above, a reverence covering his face. Abram studied his father. The moon emphasized the furrows of the forehead and lit up the lines written on that beloved face by years of anxiety. Abram saw, as never before, the old man's age, and as he noted the respect Terah gave the moon-deity, as he read the pride his father took in his arrival, his love for the old merchant came into sharp focus.

Abram laid an arm across the old man's shoulders. "Tell me, Father—what do you think of?"

"The moon which has so blessed me tonight, son. Do you see?"

Abram longed to see. He had seen how Nannar was worshiped for good gifts, how Nannar also demanded precious lives. He had closed his mind to that dark side of the moon, just as all Ur had, and as the ancient Sumerians had before him. He had fallen down in worship to Nannar, but not in certainty. Doubt had lodged in his mind once, and he would never shake it.

Love for his father restrained his tongue, which would have voiced his lack of faith many times.

"Yes, I see."

The next hours were trying ones. Haran's condition grew worse, and Dari did not arrive with Masen until later than was expected. But they brought four hundred men, and the spirit of the camp rose.

It was past midnight when a message came that many more armies were approaching.

Excitement ran up and down the camp. The crowd which had collected in this niche of the desert foothills now rushed as a body to the ridge. Terah and Hebron, along with Abram and Nahor, climbed to the peak of a jutting, rocky pinnacle to scan the valley floor.

A dull hum ascended the slopes, a most awesome and deliberate droning sound as thousands of soldier feet tramped toward them across the vast waste. The distance separating the approaching armies from the Wadi Saboth reduced the noise of their marching to a monotonous undertone, which grew only gradually louder. In another region, perhaps, no sound would have been distinguishable, but the blank openness of the valley carried it easily. The effect of such a hushed, stamping vibration was one of heightened excitement and tension, as when a bow is drawn across a string.

The point Abram had selected as a lookout opened to his view the entire stretch of wilderness from as far north to as far south as his eye could see. To the south lay Ur, hidden in its hemming highlands, to the north, the great city-state Sippar. Between were vast miles scattered with low rolling hills, occasional smaller cities interrupting the loneliness. Kish, Issin, Erech were among them.

At widely separated points in this vista were seen tonight dotted lines of torchlight, long, spindly, creeping.

Looking at the spectacle was like viewing a black

vault of the heavens whose stars were arranged in ordered rows rather than haphazard sprinkles.

The torchlit armies, nearly thirty in number, were
following the well-traveled roads which connected city
with city. Far to the north a barely visible line of light
was emerging from the direction of Shuruppak. A twin
to this could be seen far to the east, from the small town
Kazallu, and between these emerged the others. Winding through gullies and hills, like glowworms at night,
they came. From whatever direction, however, they invariably merged into the highway which cut centrally
through the floor.

Ground is covered slowly on foot or camelback,
especially with heavy weaponry. Several hours passed
and it was nearly dawn when the first army began its
trek up the gorge to Hebron's waiting camp, and for
three long days troops poured into the Wadi.

By the fourth day it appeared that the last of the
forces had arrived. The gorge and the flat at its mouth
were crowded with camps. The men who had come
numbered nearly seventy-five hundred, and added to
this were Terah's five hundred, the largest single unit.
An impressive force had congregated in this fold of the
hills.

The general attitude of the battalions was one of alert
rest. Tents had been erected, and men sat in their
shade. Small chariots cast patches of shelter from the
sun, and men rested there. Anywhere shade was, men
were. The heat was fierce.

Abram rode in a two-wheeled chariot through the
masses of campsites. Except for the distinguishing banners which flew from the largest tents, only slight varia-
tions in speech, dress, appearance, or differing tent
styles showed that this group was of Umma, this of Nip-
pur, this of Lagash, and so on.

But Abram was well acquainted with the distinctions.
His father's trade had sent him throughout the eastern
world, and no group of men gathered here was foreign
to him.

He was as well known to them. Everywhere in the camp men saluted him with respect, and invariably he inquired for the master, asking each to council at Hebron's tent within the hour.

Chapter V

The Guti were coming.

They were angling down the east side of the Euphrates between the foothills and the great river, on the way to Ur. Hebron's messengers determined that it might take two days for the mercenaries to reach the region near the Wadi Saboth.

The large tent at the top of the gorge was crowded and almost stiflingly hot as the merchant princes gathered in council to plot the best strategy for meeting the oncomers.

The geological structure of the foothills, which extended for miles on either side of the wadi, provided a fine military fortification. The hills were quite high and steep, and numerous smaller valleys, similar to the Wadi Saboth, provided convenient hiding places for large numbers of men.

Abram and the leaders whom he had called to council in the tent had not failed to recognize this. It would play a strong part in their defensive and offensive measures. The central issue at present was the choice of a chief to lead the armies. The question was a mere formality, however, as all eyes seemed to look to Terah without hesitation.

Terah assumed the role easily, though he had never led such a sizable host. Abram was proud of his father, whose very confidence seemed to pervade the narrow tent and seep through the men gathered there. He had admired and emulated his father all his life and was much like him. In appearance both were big-boned, rugged men, but refined to a degree by their aristocracy. In temperament congenial, cultured, they were yet leaders of men in any situation. Like all greater men throughout time, to those who watched them they were symbols of dignity, security, and confidence.

This was the picture drawn of them. What feelings dominated beneath the surface of their personalities were known only to themselves. It was difficult for Terah to keep his mind to the task before him. His wounded son kept crowding into his thoughts. Unanswerable questions plagued him. If his son died, what possible reason would there be to continue with the plans? Questions rushed at him. What purpose would there be? Even defense of his homeland would be no reason if his own god and priests denied it was right to do.

Nothing fit together properly. All was out of focus. How could a god demand obedience and in return ask the sacrifice of a son? How could he claim the love of a land and give it up to marauders? And if this was not his nature and the priests were misrepresenting him, how could he allow this?

"Nannar, how can you torture me so with doubts? Benevolent one, I trusted in you. I am left with no choice but to disobey, and yet I will carry the stain forever." It made no sense to Terah. His mind was a mass of confusion, anxiety, bombarding questions, and feverish guilt.

"A man of weak faith—this is what I am. But faith in what? In a god who demands human sacrifice? What is faith if it is never rewarded but in fat cattle and newborn sons who will be taken away?"

And here he stood, leading others against the wishes of his god. All the men present, believers in Nannar, felt similar confusion—the confusion of choice between survival and blind obedience. They had chosen to follow Terah and survival, but such apostasy he never would have thought possible in himself. Religion was the very fount and fiber of Chaldean life. All activity revolved around it. It was not simply a passing thought or the hobby of a few. Individuals and dynasties plotted their courses on the motions of stars and planets and the shadows of the moon. A man was no less a man for his reliance on the supernatural. And now, when he most needed Nannar's reassurance, he knew he could not even ask for it after having betrayed him. "Nannar shines to guide us." The words which he had spoken to reassure Hebron as they had watched the streams of lights in the valley now echoed hollowly in his head.

Abram caught a slight glimmer of anxiety which had unwittingly escaped Terah's eyes. No one else in the tent saw it, but Abram was keen to the emotions of his father, for much of the same confusion had often been his. And in the light of present circumstances—a dying brother, a wayward priesthood, a divided family—the feelings of doubt were stronger than ever before. He knew what his father was feeling.

The Guti were forced to pass along the valley floor between the Euphrates and the foothills. There were no highroads along which troops of their number could easily or safely progress. To come to Ur from the north necessitated a risk, and the Guti were forced to take it. But they, knowing of Sargon's edict, had no reason to expect ambush. The seventy-five hundred men were divided among the thirty or more large gullies which ranged on either side. The plan of attack was clever. Terah felt confident in it. There were not enough of the expensive camels to be used in the skirmish, but chariots were plenteous, and the best military leaders from each camp were ready to carry out the maneuvers which had been plotted in Hebron's tent the night before.

The Guti were boisterous as they marched. They were tremendously confident in their pursuit of Ur and had good reason to be. They sang as they came; they laughed and joked; they brawled and squabbled. Their minds were far from worry. But their seeming indifference would not make Terah less wary of them. They never had been known for their formality in military matters. They were barbarians, crude and lusty and merciless. But what they lacked in discipline they made up for in enthusiastic savagery, and their very appearance struck fear in the hearts of their enemies.

When the first visible sign of the Guti crept over the horizon, tension grew and the men's throats tightened. Timing was all-important. Terah and Hebron felt this keenly, and they strained their eyes in the direction of the northernmost fold where the first battalion was stationed. Men for this group had been chosen by lot, for theirs was a nearly suicidal mission.

Abram, in typical style, had volunteered to lead this mission, and if successful, would then take the leadership of the entire campaign. His brother Nahor stood with the supporting company of men in the wadi to the left of him.

As the Guti came within the range of vision which allows a man to make out the size and general bearing of his enemy, Abram turned to his men and gestured that the time was very near. His men were a strange crew, of every tongue and appearance known to the fertile crescent within two hundred miles of his homeland. Here were the well-dressed men of Ur, dark-complected and aristocratic, fishermen, shippers, and merchants; here the smaller men of the poor regions to the north, away from the rivers, men whose principal livelihood came from herding, men who worshiped gods of the elements, or of the animal kingdom. All were men who, from time to time, had known quarrels and even battles between their tribes and cities, and bigotry against one another's creeds and ancestries.

Strangely, it had taken a common hatred to bring them together, just as a mutual hatred and mistrust had divided them before and would again after this interlude passed.

Abram did not think of all this just now. None of them did. Abram's eyes were on his father far at the pinnacle above the wadis. The old man stood straight and tall against the sky with his vision fixed on the oncoming horde.

When the tramping of many feet could be heard, and even the rude laughter of the barbarians, every muscle of the men awaiting orders tensed, and their bodies stiffened for action. Foreheads tightened and pulses pounded erratically. Abram, sensing that the time was seconds away, did not take his eyes off his father but gestured for his men to ready their weapons. Silently spears were fixed and swords were loosed from their scabbards.

Then Terah determinedly raised his hand and swiftly brought it down to his side.

Abram's chariot plunged forward at his command, and the men leaped from the wadi onto the flat surface between the foothills and the river, directly into the left flank of the Guti.

The blow stunned the unprepared barbarians, and the element of surprise was Abram's most effective weapon. The Guti were wild-eyed and off balance. Several would rush at one of Abram's men, and their strength was used in awkward ways, without forethought or plan.

Abram's forces dealt awesome blows to the enemy as they penetrated the flank. But the Guti were quick in overcoming their awkward position and soon rallied like the savage force rumor had said they were.

Now the supporting allied forces began to maneuver. As planned, each group was to come into play at a particular point in the battle. Nahor was next to lead his men, and following him, a group circled the Guti and struck their right flank. Repeatedly the value of shock counted in favor of the allies. Over and over, even though the groups numbered fewer than their foe, they were unexpected, and this proved to their benefit.

This is not to say the Guti were easy prey. They were savages in war. Possibly their single greatest weapon was their awesome, grotesque appearance. These men from the northeast of Chaldea were not physically softened by urban life. Their social structure was based on a hunting economy. They were not city dwellers but lived in tribal units, bound together under the same leader. Manhood was based on cleverness and brutality, the combination equaling savage cunning.

It naturally followed that since their lives revolved around the hunt and depended on the game animals, their religion was a simplistic worship of the desert wolf, the most cunning of all hunters. They employed the wolf's tactics in their fighting. They looked just as frightening as he. They were large-boned men, not tall but deep-chested, with thick muscles and stocky limbs. They wore hides and fur pelts for clothing, with no distinct style or pattern. Their shins and calves were covered with peculiar heavy leggings of leather bound with cords of hide.

The most frightening aspect of their uniform was the use of wolves' heads for helmets. The lower jaw was removed and the remainder was placed atop the Guti soldier's head, with the massive wolf skin draped behind like a cloak over his back.

They did not use chariots but did all their fighting on foot and were surprisingly quick for their husky builds. Once their enemies got over the initial shock of their appearance, the next surprise was Guti weaponry and fighting style. Abram's men principally used long spears and double-edged swords for close combat, while the charioteers and men on the hillsides employed the bow and arrow or sling with deadly accuracy. But the Guti, while using all these methods, introduced their most awesome tool, a massive two-edged ax, wielded by their strong arms like playthings and aimed primarily at the legs of their enemies. They had learned this method of attack from the wolf, who repeatedly dives for the forelegs of his victim, breaking them and thus incapacitating him.

The allies had never encountered this torturous system in battle and so were unprepared for it.

Abram's blood ran cold as he watched men around him chopped cruelly down, their bones shattered and splintered by the blows. He ordered more troops from the wadis, and again the enemy was on the defensive. The allies wasted no time in placing the charioteers in front of all maneuvers, and behind them rows upon rows of shielded men marched and replaced one another like ocean waves. In this manner, fresh men were always up front and the undisciplined barbarians began to lose their vitality.

As the troops saw the Guti diminishing, they were already celebrating victory in their minds. They called for Abram to order more men into the conflict so they might make a quick and total end of the enemy and then sack him.

Abram's confidence was tremendous and he waved his father to send in the remaining forces. They would overrun the Guti and revenge would be complete. Terah and Hebron were equally secure in the victory and immediately obliged Abram. The remaining men, about two thousand, stormed from the gullies at Terah's command.

The old man smiled triumphantly as he watched Abram and Nahor lead the armies across the body-strewn plain, forcing the Guti into the foothills.

"Hebron, my god has blessed me. He is pleased with me. He is not angry with me!" Terah shouted. "All my doubts have been resolved. Nannar is not displeased with his servant!" Lifting his hands high above his head, the old merchant said, "Nannar, you have avenged me! The corrupt priesthood has been undone, and your face shines favorably on me!"

Hebron watched reverently as his friend praised Nannar, who was his god also. And then, as the two surveyed the battle, they saw the remaining Guti break and run for the foothills with the allies following in pursuit. As the forces scrambled over the distant ridge, they were lost to view, but the two old men standing at their pinnacle rested in the assurance of victory.

The allies laughed and shouted as they drove the wolfish Guti up the slope. They proudly waved their banners and shields in the air and clasped each other wildly in their excitement.

But just as they reached the military crest of the hill's backside, another round of laughter ascended to meet theirs. Abram raised his hand for the forces to stand still. There, to the horror of the allies, stood unnumbered Guti, covering hillsides and gullies, thousands of them, spears and axes raised, mouths open in hideous grins, hyenalike laughter piercing the very souls of their unwitting victims.

The allies were totally disadvantaged. The great majority of their forces were still coming up the hill from behind, unaware of the grotesque turn of events which had just greeted the front lines.

Whether these Guti had lain in wait throughout the battle, having known of the allied plan and using their first troops as a decoy, or whether they had only recently arrived to support their dwindling forces was not known. There was no time to speculate on the matter as Abram ordered retreat and sent his men back down the slopes to the valley floor.

The surprised soldiers who had not heard of the new enemy joined their friends in the downhill retreat, asking no questions and needing no answers.

Terah's elation turned bitter as he and Hebron watched their heroes skirmish down the heights and onto the plain, not as victors, but as victims.

As they reached the plain, the fresh Guti horde virtually overran them, for the allies had wasted all reserve troops in premature celebration. The exhausted men were easy prey, and in only minutes thousands had fallen. The chase left behind scores of bodies, broken and lifeless, butchered by the bloody axmen.

Abram's eye was caught by the flash of an overturned chariot. It was his brother's. One of the wheels had caught in a rut and thrown the chariot over, tossing Nahor onto the ground. He scrambled to his feet, but not in time to escape a Guti warrior who was soon upon him.

Abram saw him aim for his brother's legs. Nahor put up a strong struggle, but his sword had come unsheathed in the fall and lay several feet away. The Guti crashed a blow to Nahor's calf. At the sight of his wounded brother, Abram cried out in agonized anger, his mind a frenzy of hatred.

From the height of his chariot he had good aim on the warrior. He raised his spear and drove it deep into the Guti's back.

Those who escaped the enemy were few. The allies had been sadly defeated. Terah and Hebron looked on in astonishment as their men, those who remained, dragged themselves across the field and into the foothills. So sudden had been the reversal that the two old leaders at the pinnacle had barely time enough to let the reality of what they saw penetrate their minds.

Terah seemed frozen to the ground on which he stood. The enemy was now enjoying the spoils of war, rushing from one body to another across the field, ripping anything of value from each corpse. Here was a pendant, there a carved leather scabbard, there a well-turned sword. The Guti were engrossed in their sport to the neglect of the few allies who were silently escaping to Hebron's camp. Many who were too badly wounded to move were carried by their comrades, but those who were not reached in time were soon greeted by the axes of their merciless strippers.

Nahor was gashed badly, though not so much as to lose his leg. Abram tore a remnant from his cloak and bound up the wound tightly. But as he bent over to lift his brother into the chariot, he saw a younger man racing across the fields to him, leaping over the dead men in his haste.

"Sir, let me help you!" he called.

Abram wiped the sweat from his forehead and stood

erect. While all the other men were heading for the camp, this fellow was coming back to the middle of the field to assist him.

"Certainly," Abram greeted him, rather perplexed. "But, why—"

"Sir, we have not met before, as I was working in the hills when you arrived, and then I served with a flank battalion. My name is Lot. I am Haran's eldest and your nephew. I could not run to safety while both my uncles were still in danger. This entire affair was begun on account of my father, was it not?"

"Thank you, Lot," Abram replied. "Here, you support his right side."

Chapter VI

It was not until the next evening that the crippled entourage of seven hundred wounded fighting men and a small host of women and children arrived at the gates of Ur.

It had been rumored throughout the city that Terah had taken his men to fight the Guti, but few fully believed it until they witnessed his unseemly return.

The downcast merchant made his way through the streets amid the jeers and taunts of scabby beggars who never would have dared speak to him before. Lepers from the caves shouted, "Care to join us, Master Terah, Master Nahor, Master Abram? Care to join us?"

From windows city women called, "Praise the fearless warriors who break the laws of the priests! Now the priests have broken you! Wealthy sons of Terah, what will your father's wealth do for you now?"

At one point in the long trek up the hill to the great house, a motley harlot poked her head out a high window and spat upon Terah. Abram, in unthinking anger. took out his sling, when Nahor grasped his arm. "Brother, think! Do you want to play into the hands of this crowd? Put up your sling!"

Lot called for Dari, Hebron's young runner, and sent him ahead of the crowd to prepare Terah's servants for their arrival. Dari's young mind had barely been able to take in all he had witnessed and lived through during the past few days. There had been little he could do but keep out of the way. A boy his age was not allowed to fight in battle, and he had thought himself useless and helpless. As he ran now, he felt his feet were lead, so great was his eagerness to accomplish his errand.

When the huge company finally arrived at the house,

the servants were prepared for the worst. Beds were ready for the leaders in the guest house, and the soldiers' quarters had room enough for the many wounded. The women helped the servants in tending them, while the exhausted children slept on small pallets. The house was a bustle of movement and noise as servants hustled about on their errands and the wounded cried for help from their beds.

Terah and Abram carried Nahor into the family parlor. The huge pit fireplace in the center of the room was a welcome friend. Terah had asked that Haran be brought into this room for nursing, though the battle which had been waged in his honor was unknown to him. He had lain in his feverish state of unconsciousness since Terah had arrived at Hebron, and he had been carried to Ur, all without knowledge.

Milcah, Iscah, and Lot were with him when Hebron brought him into the parlor, and Dari proudly carried his medicines. The small, intimate group knelt in front of the fire to wait. Wait for what? They did not know, but none of them wished to leave Haran.

Terah had said little on the long, slow journey to Ur and had not spoken a word as they passed through the jeering mob in town. His mood was not one of self-pity, but deep sorrow. Everyone in the dim-lit room recognized and respected his feelings.

Dari had not played his pipe for many days. Though it was not to be a light-hearted tune, he felt it might ease the minds of his friends to hear the music. He looked at Abram, the heroic caravaneer who had filled his young mind with idealistic admiration. The fact that his idol had failed in battle made his friendship only more attainable, and did not bring him down.

Directing his attention to Terah, then, Dari took out his little pipe and began gently. No one spoke. Except for this, the crackling fire, and Haran's deep breathing, the room was silent.

The haunting melodies which poured from the boy's pipe mellowed and eased the atmosphere. Abram looked at the faces around him. The fire lit up the weary lines imprinted on them all. There was his father's dear friend Hebron, nearly asleep with fatigue; the pretty, delicate Milcah and the girl Iscah, so young for such unhappiness; his nephew, Lot, too soon thrust into the manhood required of him; his brother Nahor, who had given so much of himself; and his father—the man whose sorrow was his and whose heartaches were so great it was a wonder he survived them.

"If only I might ease your pain, Father," Abram thought. "If only I could, in my power, ease your pain—"

Then his attention was caught by a movement from Haran. "Brother!" cried Abram, "Are you awake? Do you see me? It is I, Abram."

The music ceased, Terah was at Haran's side instantly, and everyone crowded about to see if the wounded man were conscious.

"Son!" shouted Terah. "Son, do you hear me? It is your father!"

Then a single, slow, rasping, deep word came from the lips which had not spoken for weeks. "Father—"

Terah leaned over Haran and cradled his head in his lap. "I love you, Father," Haran whispered. "Forgive me the sorrow I have caused you."

"Hush, son. Don't speak now. You are going to be well. Just rest."

The old man cradled that head for hours, throughout the evening and into the night, and his face wore an expression of peace it had not known in years.

As the small group in the chamber kept silent vigil around the reunited couple, young Dari's eyes were caught by a banner leaning against one wall, fluttering in the night breeze. He recognized it as a flag of the House of Terah, of the same design Abram's men had carried the day he met their caravan on the road to Masen. A small, incomplete circle lay against the red background, and now Dari knew the meaning of the emblem.

Carrying the banner over to the fireplace, he picked up a piece of charcoal, and knelt down in front of Terah. The curious group watched as with one small, dark line he closed in the open portion and completed the circle.

Terah smiled at him.

About midnight, something woke Abram. There was a strange, hideous silence in the room, and an atmosphere he could almost touch closed around him.

What had awakened him?

The fire was dead now, and the room was cool. When his eyes adjusted to the darkness, he strained to see what he could now only sense, something heavy with gloom. Everyone in the room seemed to be asleep, but when he looked more closely, he saw that his father was not. Terah's face was ghastly, pale and lifeless, his eyes staring straight ahead into the blackness. The old man barely breathed as he clutched Haran to his chest and sat motionless.

Abram could scarcely stand the sound of his own voice. "Father," he whispered, "what is it?"

Terah did not respond but only sat, holding Haran, looking at nothing. Abram crawled to his side and stared in disbelief. Haran was dead.

How long had his poor, lonely father sat there holding his dead son, refusing to accept his death, refusing to awaken anyone?

Abram lifted Haran from Terah's arms and carried him to a divan. Then he lit the wall torches and quietly woke the others.

"Father, come outside with me. The night air will do you good."

Nahor's leg was in such pain that he could not accompany Abram as he walked the docile, silent old man out into the hall and opened the archway leading to the courtyard.

A group of the disillusioned allied leaders who had returned to Ur with Terah sat in the yard talking, apparently unable to sleep. They asked about Haran, and Abram told them of his death.

With prize-winning callousness, one of them walked up to Terah and with an ugly grin said, "This is what comes of disobedience to your god, Master Terah, and of leading others against him."

At this the old merchant prince looked as if he had been physically knocked down. His face was a stunned horror of shock. He stared wildly at the group gathered there and then, after a slight hesitation, clutched his coat as if in pain. Abram reached for him, but he fell against the garden wall, then tore himself away and ran for the gate, disappearing down the moonlit avenue toward the city.

Abram grabbed the sharp-tongued leader and slammed him against the stone wall. "My friend, your head, as well as your heart, are made from the same stone. And I would grind them to a powder if I did not have the dignity my father had handed down to me!"

Then he released the man, who slumped to the ground, and he ran out the gate after his father.

Far down the road, he saw Terah hurrying as quickly as he could for the city center. When he reached him, the old man was doubled over with pain.

"Father! Father, where are you going? Let me carry you, wherever you wish to go!"

"Take me to my god," Terah whispered.

Abram tenderly lifted his father and carried him through the city, passing houses, taverns, and shops until they reached the central square.

He went directly to the temple, silhouetted high above all the other buildings of Ur. The slabs of sundried brick which formed its many steps led to the altar house at the top, where the sacrifices were made.

When he had reached the foot of the huge structure, which took in more than a full city block at its base and towered awesomely above, he and his father knelt on the first step. Abram's heart beat rapidly from the run, and his breath was wild and heavy. The blood rushed to his ears and drummed loudly. At first he barely understood his father's words.

"Nannar! Forgive me!" Over and over his father cried loudly, "Forgive me—forgive me!" Abram watched the gruesome spectacle, as his father, once proud and strong, lifted his hands like a slave to beat against the heavens and wept aloud.

"Father, please!" Abram tried to console the old man, tried to raise him to his feet and to his full manhood again. But his repeated efforts failed as his father continued in vain petition to cry out his grief.

Utterly confounded by the whole spectrum of recent events, the pageantry of his once-proud household's downfall, his family's losses, and his father's rapid decline, Abram could not pray as Terah would have wished. He stood up and stared fullfaced at the moon, which seemed to grin disinterestedly at him.

The heavens shone its thousand diamonds across the limitless vault of velvet black. Far, far below, in a city place between the Tigris and the Euphrates, in the openness of the moonlight, were two antlike figures at the base of a strange pyramid, darkly attempting to open the ears of an indifferent god. And while one, bowed down, mourned, "Forgive me!" the other, arms lifted high above his head, cried out, "Help me to understand!"

Chapter VII

Dawn found father and son in an exhausted sleep at the foot of the temple. Only the morning noises of the waking city finally stirred Abram, who got rapidly to his feet and woke Terah.

"Father, come. Quickly. Let's be getting home."

Terah rose, looking pathetic and worn. Abram supported him as they hurried through the shortest route to the great house, hoping to avoid the gawking crowds. He would not have his father further humiliated or mocked.

When they reached the house, there was an uneasy silence about the place. Servants and guests busied themselves in all sorts of errands, undoubtedly to stay out of their way. Apparently news had been spread of the foolish leader's biting comment the night before and Terah's reaction to it, and so the entire household waited for a more opportune time to give their condolences.

Once in Terah's chambers, Abram let his father sleep again. Nahor, barely able to walk, joined him, anxious to know of Terah's health. "Abram, how is Father? Is there anything I can do?"

"Just now I think it best to sit and talk with him when he wakes, Nahor. We must restore his pride somehow. He's convinced this has all been the punishment of Nannar. He has enough grief to contend with." And then, thinking of the night before, he said, "Guilt will rob him of his mind."

Nahor gave a perplexed look and walked to the window.

"What are you thinking?" Abram asked.

"I don't know, exactly." Looking over the city, he was deep in thought. "Abram, like so many things, this doesn't seem right, but how do we know it is not the wrath of Nannar? After all," he said very gently, "Father did disobey, and you know what the priests have said is the consequence of—"

"Nahor! No!" Abram lashed out, in stunning ferocity.

"Brother—" Abram began again. "I am sorry. Forgive me. I didn't mean to challenge you. But—" Abram paused, fighting to find words. "Somehow it's so wrong. If Father deserves punishment, don't we all? Don't you and I, and every man who allied with Father? Why is he so much more to be resented than you or I? What was his sin? Loving his son and his city too much? Was his sin perhaps the beginning seeds of doubt? Was it the— the questioning of his god?"

"Abram! If that was his sin, it was—heresy, was it not?" asked Nahor, confused at his younger brother's outburst.

Abram was not surprised at Nahor's question. He knew it amounted to that—"heresy." He had only avoided the use of the word, the most unforgivable of Sumerian transgressions. Abram was silent for several long minutes and then, gathering all his reserves, he turned to Nahor and said very slowly but deliberately, "Yes, Nahor, perhaps it is heresy. And if so, I am the chiefest of heretics, for I have doubted long and solemnly." Gaining the courage of his convictions, Abram continued, "Brother, yes, I have doubted—I have doubted in this: a god who demands loyalty, and then leaves his people to suffer without a purpose; a god who allows a sick priesthood to represent him; a god who, above all else, above loyalty, or even obedience, demands human sacrifice. These are my doubts, Nahor. And if the god of my father wishes my loyalty, he will have to give me understanding of all this!"

"You ask Nannar to bend to *your* desires of him, Abram?"

"No, Brother. I do not wish Nannar were different so much as I wish to understand him. This is all I wish. If I could but know him and understand. In all my upbringing, no one has offered me a why or a how or a reason. I only wish understanding!"

Nahor was paralyzed by the force of his brother's words. "Blasphemy, Abram! Who are you to question our god or to demand of him a reason?"

Now Abram let loose the words he had so long withheld. "Let me be quick to correct you, Nahor. He is *your* god, not mine. And who am I to question? I will answer that. I am a *man,* Nahor."

"A very *proud* man, Abram!"

At this Nahor turned to leave but stopped abruptly, seeing Terah had risen. "Father! Please rest. We did not mean to wake you!"

Terah did not seem to hear. He walked toward Abram and did not take his eyes off him. Abram was sick at the thought that his father had overheard his denial of Nannar. He, who was usually so fluent and well-spoken, was now speechless. How could he have hurt his father so?

Terah seemed in a daze, his eyes cold and glazed. He wore an expression neither son had seen him wear before. The sight of it reminded Abram of the wild look he had seen once in the eyes of a wounded wolf as it struggled to free itself from a briar into which it had fallen, its thick, matted fur tangled about the thorns, driving them into its flesh at each movement.

Deep from within Terah a rumbling, agonized, protracted groan finally found expression. "Blasphemy!" An awesome, hideous sound, "Blasphemy, Abram!" He blurted out his feelings in a geyser of words which seemed to rip apart his very soul. "You, Abram! You, too, have left me? Will you also now deny your heritage? Will you now renounce your father as well as your god? Yes, *your* god, Abram. Are you somehow exempt from the domain of Nannar? Are you immortal or divine that you may question Nannar, that you set yourself up as his judge and prosecutor? If I am punished, it is for giving birth to a heretic! Do I know you, Abram? Who are you? I do not know you!"

And then, taking a large whip from the wall, he raised it over his head and let it fall rapidly across his son's shoulders. Abram was temporarily numbed to the pain by the simple bewilderment of what he witnessed. He lifted his arm to stop the biting blows, but his father was a wild man, using all his strength to beat out his agony upon him.

"Fool, do you think you can stop the punishment of Nannar which is now given at my hand?" screamed his father in lunatic tones.

Nahor rushed to Abram's aid, but his father was too quick. "Do you defend him, Nahor? Do you side with him?" Terah shouted.

"Father, stop! See what you are doing! Abram is your son!" Nahor cried.

Terah raised his hand again to wield another blow, and Abram covered his head. By now Terah had driven him into a corner, and Abram, even for all his strength, could not restrain the whip which his father dealt with seemingly superhuman power, but he would not have struck his father even if he could.

"Cower like the dog you are!" shouted Terah.

Nahor finally succeeded in stopping the whip, and Abram slowly stood up, in stinging pain from the stripes driven into his neck and arms. Both brothers carried their father to his bed and watched as he lay there writhing in agony. "Lick the dust of the floor, Abram!" he cried out. "I am Nannar! I have willed it!"

Nahor and Abram looked at each other, aghast with what they heard. Their father's mind had broken, as well as his heart.

Abram was ill. He was no longer the proud man Nahor had said he was. His humiliation was immeasurable. Looking about for a way to escape, he ran out the nearest door and into the streets, and kept running, nowhere, until his legs could no longer carry him.

Chapter VIII

Abram was somewhere near the western river when he woke from the stupor in which he had wandered countless hours. The sun was setting, and beautiful golds and reds ran together in the water like dye.

His wounds were not bleeding, but huge welts stood up on his arms and neck and he winced under the pain. In oblivion he sat, his mind a confusion, thoughts bumping against one another without form, when a voice from the grove caught his attention.

Someone was calling for him. He slumped down in the high reeds, fearful that he might be recognized in this condition.

"Master Abram?" the voice called. "Abram—can that be you? Do you hear me?"

Now Abram recognized the voice. He was awkward and clumsy in his efforts to hide. He could not let her see him like this. Almost humorously, he attempted to disguise his large frame in the brush.

"Are you all right, Abram? Please do not play games with me."

From the seclusion of the grove a woman walked out onto the marshy bank. Stunningly graceful, she seemed a natural part of the scene, willowy as the reeds which grew resplendently along the river.

Abram peered through the grass and lay as low as possible, but this did not dissuade her. Apparently she had seen him fully well.

Finally, resigned to it, he stood up, gathering his clothing around his neck and arms so she would not see his wounds, and grateful for the dusk which might disguise them.

"Good evening, Sarai," he said weakly.

"Why, Abram, you have never hidden from me before. Are you all right, sir? What are you doing out here?" Her inquisitive dark eyes were playful. "I know," she brightened. "You were walking and saw me in the grove, and you thought to capture me by surprise! That's it, isn't it?"

Grasping at the straw, Abram replied, "Yes, of course, Sarai. That's it. But you found me out, didn't you? And now my joke is up and I'll be going."

He turned quickly to leave, not wishing to stay longer, for fear Sarai would ask questions. But she called after him, "Abram, do you mean to leave so abruptly? How cruel you are," she teased.

Abram knew he had no choice. He turned back so as not to offend her. How ironic, he thought. How many times he would have given a fortune to be with this woman, for she was indeed lovely and much to be desired. She was, as her name implied, a princess, one of Ur's aristocracy, and her family was close in social standing with Abram's. And now when she was begging him to stay, his one desire was to escape her.

"Come here, please," she beckoned. "Abram, you are not yourself tonight." And then, with a startled look, she grabbed his arm.

"Sarai, please—"

"Abram! What is this? You are hurt! Oh, Abram, what has happened?"

"Just a scuffle with some measly beggars in town," he offered.

"No, Abram. Tell me the truth. You would not get involved in something so beneath your position. Why, Abram!—someone has beaten you! I have seen marks like those only on slaves." Her eyes were moist with the beginnings of tears. "Poor Abram. Please tell me the truth. I must know."

Abram attempted haughty masculine scorn. "You are a most headstrong woman, Sarai. You are most stubborn. By all the gods, you are one to be reckoned with!"

"You flatter me, Abram. But it is only concern for you that makes me so."

"Most forward, too," said Abram. "Have you not learned your place, woman?"

"Forgive me, sir." And with this she assumed a most beguiling docility, which only worked in her favor.

"Oh, Sarai. Do not look so. You know I cannot keep the truth from you. I never have been able to, have I?"

"No, sir," she smiled.

Their thoughts were of more youthful days, when as students in the courts, Abram's attraction to her was more obvious than he had wished. More than once he had been caught by the schoolmaster with his mind wandering from his mathematics as he watched her with the rows of regal young women walking through the temple square. "Master Abram," his instructor would call out. "Yes, sir. What is it, sir?" "I have called on you twice to solve this problem. Are your thoughts on the lesson, or on that young lady?" At this the class would break into unruly adolescent titter. "Sir," Abram would rise, red-faced. "I am sorry." "Yes, Master Abram, as always, you have good reason to be sorry." And then Abram would lean over, while the muscular attendant, usually a temple slave, would administer justice in the legal district.

Abram's weakness for Sarai had never diminished, and now, many years later, it was even more powerful, though it had never found overt expression. Since he had taken to caravaning for his father, his stays in Ur had been infrequent, and this had offered little time for more personal pleasures, though no other woman, in all his travels, had attracted him as she did.

"I suppose you will not let me go until I fully explain myself, Sarai, though I don't know what power you have to make me stay."

Sarai's eyes sparkled with pleasure at this. "Sit with me, Abram," she said.

The night breeze was descending off the hills and swept without obstruction across the flat expanse of the

city on the plain. For a long time Abram was silent, and
Sarai caught some of his mood. She did not speak but
waited for him. Finally he got to his feet and paced the
bank. "You know of my family's disgrace, Sarai?"

She reflected for a moment and said, "I know of your
battle with the Guti, sir."

"And the defeat?"

"Yes, sir."

"And would you not call defeat a disgrace, woman?"

"Begging your pardon, sir, no. I would not call anything your family endeavors 'a disgrace.' "

"Then the citizens would call you a fool for your loyalty."

"A fool, sir?"

"Yes, Sarai. Have you not heard of the reception the
fine people of Ur gave my father?"

"The 'fine' people, as you call them, were beggars
and harlots. None of your friends have turned on you."

"No? Sarai, you are quite innocent to believe that.
Even Father's allies have rejected him."

"That cannot be, Abram!"

"But it is. And now—" Abram grimaced. "I cannot
stay, Sarai."

Sarai hastened after him. "Abram! Please. Don't go."

She caught up to him and held onto his coat. Abram
wheeled around to free himself but Sarai clutched at
him with a pleading look. "Abram, please! You were
about to tell me something. I know I am a foolish
woman, and forgetful of my humble station, but I cannot let you go without knowing what has pained you
so."

Abram was captivated by her face. There was such
tenderness there, something he badly needed. He spontaneously held her to him in silence.

"Sarai, my own father feels that I have deserted him.
Last night my youngest brother died, and something inside Father died with him. He feels he is being punished
by Nannar."

"Abram, I am so sorry," she said softly. "But that does not explain these bruises."

"I am ashamed to tell you, Sarai. My own father feels I have deserted him, and in his broken state of mind, he lashed out at me with a whip."

Sarai looked at Abram in horror. "Terah? But what could drive him to that? Abram, you are not telling me everything."

"By the gods of mortal man, Sarai! I have told everything!"

Sarai waited as Abram walked toward the river. Finally he spoke again. "Dear woman, do you ever doubt? Do you ever question the teachings we have received since childhood?"

"What do you mean, sir?"

"If I told you—" Abram hesitated. "If I told you that I had lost my faith, would you still cling to me as you just did?"

Sarai looked at him without understanding. "I would try to help you, sir. I would do all I could to help you."

"No, Sarai!" Abram blurted. "No! If I were beyond help, would you stand by me?"

Abram searched her eyes for an answer.

"Yes," she replied without a pause. "I would never leave you if I felt you wanted me."

Finding some relief in those words, Abram received the courage to continue.

"I have doubted for a long time. Do not be offended, Sarai, as I tell you this. Please bear with me.

"When I was first in Egypt, I saw other temples and other gods. I saw temples to the sun and stars and planets, the Earth, and animals, kings, and the great river of that country. I visited the nobility with whom I traded, and I heard them speak of their gods. I even spoke with Pharaoh, and he told me of his beliefs.

"For many months I thought about this. Who was to say that my god was *the* god and theirs were nonexistent or of a lower nature? This ate away at me until I went back this last time. Sarai, when I was there I did what I could not have done under the watchful eyes of my priests. I visited their temples and consulted their wise men. And do you know what I found? I discovered that in many ways their worship is like ours. Now, Sarai, how can it be, if the moon is *the* god, that the sun or the stars or the Earth or the river can be theirs?"

Sarai was perplexed. "I can only speak with the words of faith, Abram."

"But, Sarai, Man was given a mind. Faith should be intelligent if possible," Abram paused. "My brother calls me a proud man. Possibly I am, but if so, let Nannar take me. I *will* question him! I must have understanding, or my life is death. I cannot go on as generation after generation has gone, blindly following, blindly obeying—blindly dying!"

Sarai watched and listened wide-eyed, as the man she so admired spoke disparagingly of all she held dear. "Abram, I have never heard such talk," she said.

"Bear with me, Sarai, or if you wish me to go, I will." He could easily see she wished no such thing.

"While I was in Egypt, Sarai, I learned much of astronomy. We of Ur are well versed in this, but it is not so exact as in Egypt. And I learned from my studies that the sun, the moon, the stars, the planets all have orbits and order, paths to follow without varying. I learned of an order to the universe which I had never dreamed existed. Now, if not only the moon but also the stars and sun have order, this seems to speak to me that they are only parts of a much greater whole, a greater force than them all."

Abram looked at Sarai, expecting a rebuttal but receiving only awed silence.

"Sarai, we were not put here to live like the puppets we played with as children. We are men and women with a purpose, or our lives are meaningless."

The lovely woman slipped her hand into his and looked toward the sky. "I am frightened and bewildered by what you say, Abram. You take my mind on flights of fancy that it has never imagined. But something speaks to me of solidarity and wisdom in your words. I cannot argue with them, for my arguments are weak and empty now."

"And my life is weak and empty, Sarai, without understanding." He looked at her moonlit beauty. "Even to have you, Sarai, would be empty without a purpose. Can you understand that?"

Sarai knew what Abram meant though he had never spoken the words. She knew he loved her as she loved him.

"Abram, go seek the understanding you need," she said gently.

Those were the words he most needed to hear, and as he walked away from the city into the Mesopotamian plains, he looked back at her only once.

Chapter IX

The fire warmed only a very small area of the narrow cave into which Abram had crawled for the night. He had no bedding or food and the clothes he wore were his only protection from the cold, damp walls.

He could not sleep. He left the cave and walked onto the small flat at its mouth. The night was beautiful in these hills. Below, the great Euphrates glistened like a bright ribbon under its dark canopy, as it made its slow, laborious trek to the city at the mouth of the gulf.

Abram had never felt so totally desolate and alone. As he listened, the night sounds seemed to mix with his feelings. He could hear the flowing, gushing river, the chirp of crickets, and far away on some equally lonely hill a young male wolf whining long and mournfully at the moon.

"And here am I," Abram thought, "also whining at the moon. Why am I here? Abram, wealthy, educated Abram. Such a place for you! Have you no home, no family? Why are you not enjoying the luxuries of your heritage?"

Abram laughed audibly. The novelty of his condition, nearly sick with fatigue, hunger, and humiliation, seemed somehow humorous. "Such a scene, such a setting for this 'proud man.' If my elder brother could only see me now!" But his laughter was hollow.

"Only the mad speak to themselves, Abram. Did you know that? Perhaps you are mad like your father. He was once a proud man like you."

Abram's heart beat with painful, heavy throbs at the thought of his father. He had never known such agony. He had known unhappiness and even sorrow, but agony was something else. It was a physical as well as spiritual torture. It could break the heart and kill the spirit of a man. He was now learning this.

Abram could not sit and think. He had to walk, for only walking allowed his body to breathe without mental effort. He tried desperately not to think, for the sorrow it brought was so tangible it seemed to tighten itself around his throat so that the only relief came with tears, and Abram did not wish tears.

Scenes kept flashing through his mind no matter what effort he made to shut them out. He saw the crowds closing in on his family, screaming and laughing; he saw his dead brother and his father's lifeless face as he held him; he saw the temple and Terah bowing and scraping and moaning for forgiveness; and then—he felt the horror, again, of that whip and saw his father's grotesque expression as he wielded it.

"Stop!" he cried. "Stop your torture, you bloody, infamous fiend, Nannar! Curse you! Curse your priests and your worshipers! May your temple be desecrated at the hands of bloody men!" Abram raised his fists to the sky and spat out a profusion of blasphemies to Nannar, in loud abandon. "May you eat the filth of your own temple, Nannar! The lovely, virginal priestesses who sell their bodies for your profit, the corrupt priests who buy and sell men like cattle, the oozing blood of freshly slaughtered human bodies!

"By your own bloody spirit, Nannar! You are not worthy of my praise! My prayers are too good for your ears! If you have ears—do you have ears, Nannar?"

Abram was exultant, free as he ran from hill to hill shouting and screaming in his frustration and his bitterness. Such a spectacle he made, one solitary man, mad with gaiety and sorrow, strange mixture as he tore through lonely, empty hills, leaping unconsciously over boulders and ridges.

Finally, in exhaustion, Abram fell to the ground, half laughing, half crying, in a state of mind akin to hysteria. He did not hear his own next words, words which now broke through the bitterness and pride he had carried so long, words which came from deep inside him.

They were no longer curses, or revelries or pleas for recognition. They were not even the demands for understanding which he had craved so long. Abram had reached the bottom, with no more pride of any kind, with no more demands or claims.

His words came in a whisper, slowly and brokenly. "Help me."

"Help me, please."

Something happened in that instant. Abram was conscious of something. He was conscious that he was not speaking to himself or to Nannar or to any human being. But he was whispering, "Help me. If you are there, please help me."

Suddenly a strange mysterious silence overtook the hills and valleys. The crickets ceased chirping. A desert owl which had been crying in the night was now quiet. The lonely wolf was not to be heard. The whole of nature seemed suddenly muted, as if some strange power held her in its sway.

An uneasiness crept through Abram. An incredible fear lay hold of him. With scarcely perceptible movements, he slowly, carefully raised himself, every muscle tense with dread. He got to his knees in wide-eyed wonder.

What was it? He could actually hear and feel the silence. For countless, unending minutes it continued, and Abram knelt there, a frozen stone.

Perspiration began to break out all over his body as he waited—for something. Each muscle screamed for a change of position, but Abram did not dare move.

It was uncanny how the whole of nature seemed to have ceased motion. And then Abram felt something beyond his understanding. It was as if, suddenly, the entirety of the universe were focusing on him, as if the very stars themselves were looking at him, and somewhere, from the cosmic range of infinity, a Personality was reaching out to him.

Abram felt compelled to look above him. His eyes involuntarily strained through the openness of space, carrying his thoughts upward, upward, upward past worlds and worlds, through ages and infinities to still other infinities. His head swam with the mystery of it all, that no matter where he might draw a line for his thoughts to cross over, there would always be another destiny beyond that point, and—

"Endless," he whispered.

"Thou art endless."

The awe of that moment shook him violently, and he cowered again to the ground, trembling. He could not speak, his fear was so great. And even his thoughts hesitated to ask the question, "Who are you?"

And then, just as quietude had wrapped itself around the hills, another silence began working within him. As if in answer to his unspoken question, a balm of peace began to pour itself through him.

The calm he felt did not come suddenly, but slowly, like a gentleman who enters a room, and as it did, it wiped out the fear within him. For long moments he sat drinking in the sweet savor. He would never be able to describe this quietness, this security. It was warm and all-encompassing, with a tangible, personal affection.

No longer afraid, Abram got to his feet and looked heavenward.

"I know You now," he said in awed reverence. "I have sought You long and hard, and all those years You were bringing me to this hour, this point. My Lord and my God, how I have longed and yearned for Thee." Large, joyous tears flowed unashamedly down his face and he delighted in his revelation.

He could feel the smile of his Creator and knew a peace he had never known. And then a feeling of gentle expectation grasped him, as he again waited—for something. His ears pounded, straining for—he knew not what.

The intimacy of his God was sweet and overpowering as He audibly reached His Chosen Man:

"Get thee out of thy country and from thy kindred and from thy father's house into a land that I will show thee. And I will make of thee a great nation, and I will bless thee and make thy name great and thou shalt be a blessing, and I bless them that bless thee and curse him that curseth thee; and in thee shall all the families of the earth be blessed."

PART II

The Wanderings

∞∞∞∞∞∞∞∞∞∞∞

By faith Abraham, when he was called . . . obeyed; and he went out, not knowing whither he went.

Hebrews 11:8

Chapter I

All those things which might otherwise have hindered Abram's return to Ur were meaningless to him now. Despite the reception he would receive and the idiocy which his revelation would undoubtedly seem to all concerned, it was with a sense of strength and purpose that he turned his face homeward.

By the Sumerian law of obedience, a son was bound to honor his father, and Abram could not leave without attempting a reconciliation.

As he entered the great city gate, he knew this was the last time he would do so. But there was no sentimentality in his feelings as he walked through the familiar streets past boyhood haunts, the court where he had been educated, and the temple. He went quickly, wiping from his mind the childhood memories of the festivals. He tried not to think of Harvest Moon, when once a year from infancy, he had watched as the loveliest virgin priestess was chosen for the cherished and highly honored station of Bride of Nannar. She must join the god by leaving the mortal body, and this was accomplished only through her death in the altar house, at the hands of the priests.

The spectacle had always been gruesome, for though only one woman was given the honored title of Nannar's queen, many more joined her to ensure his pleasure and the continued blessings of the god. Abram had watched year after year, from childhood to manhood, as scores of fresh and youthful virgins were led ceremoniously into a special vault dug into the temple square, where they self-administered poisoned drinks and waited to die—isolated by the heavy door which was slid and locked securely over them. And then, amid the frantic pounding of drums, the great golden image of the god, five times the size of a man, towered over the crowd as slaves carried him on their shoulders up the hundred steps to the altar house to claim his bride. Only once a year were they privileged to see him, and the crowd would go wild with dancing and raucous celebration, which went long into the night and usually lasted several days, deteriorating into a mass orgy of sexual and gluttonous debauch.

Again the crowds descended on Abram as he made his way home. But with eyes fixed straight ahead, he pushed through them without stopping, closing his mind to their taunts and ordering them aside with the sheer force of zeal to accomplish his errand.

Somewhere during the journey, a gentle voice reached his ear, and Abram, half-consciously, turned to find Sarai pressing her way to his side. Since early morning she had waited expectantly at the city gate for him to return, and would have done so day after day until he came back.

Abram put his arm around her slender waist and nearly swept her off the ground in his haste to get through the crowd. When they had finally come to the bottom of the hill leading home, the crowd gradually tapered off, and Abram hurried her to a quiet corner.

"I can see something in your eyes," she whispered. "Something happened in those hills, didn't it?"

"Yes, Sarai."

"You found your answer, Abram?"

"Yes. I cannot hope to make you understand. But—" he hesitated, "if I leave Ur, will you trust in me, and come with me?"

"Leave Ur?" The sudden introduction of the thought was a shock to Sarai. She had been brought up in the finest fashions of the great city and from childhood had been nurtured in luxury.

Abram studied her incredulous face, and with a pang of rejection, he whispered stoically, "Sarai, I am leaving. If you must know why, you do not trust in me."

Sarai turned urgent eyes toward him, fearful of losing her one opportunity to hold him. "Oh, sir, no—please —I find it a hard thing to think of, but only because it is so new to me. I will not ask why, Abram. I would leave my family and everything I have for you!"

Abram could see that Sarai's words were honest. He held her tenderly and raised her face to his. His kiss was warm and gentle, and Sarai knew his love was enough for her.

As Abram approached the great house, his apprehension grew. But, remembering the words of his God, he took courage and entered the gate. Going straight to his father's chambers, he asked to enter.

Nahor greeted him, a look of relief mixed with disappointment crossing his face—relief that his brother was returned safely, and disappointment that he could have hurt their father so.

Abram walked to the center of the room, bowing himself to the floor to show Terah he came in humility and reverence.

The old man stood at the window, too proud to acknowledge Abram's presence, and too proud to show how glad he was that his son had returned. But when he finally turned and saw his son's honor for him, he could not restrain the emotion he felt and, running to him, lifted him to his feet.

"Son!" The old man blinked back the evidence of his happiness.

"Father, you are well?" Abram asked shakily.

"Yes, son. Now I am."

Deeply surprised and grateful for his acceptance, Abram and his father embraced each other in silence. For a long time, no words were spoken, both men reconciled by a much deeper form of communication.

But Abram knew he must speak. "Father, I have brought Sarai with me. May she enter?"

"Why, of course, Son, but why—"

"Sarai," Abram called, "come and hear this."

She entered and Terah, rather bewildered, greeted her. "Child, how pleasant to see you."

But Abram interrupted, anxious to get to the point, and with a blunt note of urgency he announced, "Father —I am leaving Ur."

Terah stared at him blankly, the full impact of the words slow in taking conscious form. "For a journey, Abram? To collect your thoughts?" he asked, attempting to bring such a seemingly vacuous statement within the realm of reason.

"No, Father. For good." Abram went on. "I am leaving my homeland."

His father's face was a mirror of incredulity, and Nahor listened in stunned silence. "But, Son, why?" Terah groaned.

"Sir, while I was away, I learned something which you could never understand," Abram proceeded. "You would think me mad if I told you. You would say it was hunger or lack of sleep, but I know what I know—and I must follow."

"Sit and tell me what you learned," Terah offered, his voice full of great horror and his heart perplexed by his son's strange behavior.

Abram began, at first with hesitation, to explain his experience. And Terah took it all in quietly. The conviction with which Abram spoke did not allow total disbelief, and when he had finished, he said, "I have found my God, Father. I do not know His name, but He has known me forever. I am a man of worth and dignity in His eyes."

Terah sat in awed silence, not knowing what to think, his own faith so badly shattered that he scarcely had grounds to criticize. "I cannot say that your revelation is unreal, Son," he said at last, sadly, his head still reeling with Abram's first announcement. "I am totally without foundation. And when I hear your words, I wish to feel as you do—and yet, something boils inside me to speak in defense of my god as you propound this strange doctrine."

"Father, my defense is based on experience, not guesswork or the words of other men, as my belief in Nannar was. It would do no good to debate with me."

Terah walked to the balcony and looked over the city.

"I have no more defenses," he said hopelessly, his mind deluged by cruel memories. "In my fitful dreams I see my temple and my city in desolation. I see the altar house thrown down and Nannar's image destroyed. I see the priests murdered and Ur burned to the ground."

Abram stepped close and spoke gently. "Father, perhaps you are being prepared with me. Won't you come? Leave Ur with me, Father. As a member of your house, I am bound by law to obey you. But I have received a higher law and will leave without your blessing."

Nahor walked to his father's side as if to defend him from the sting of those words.

"But where will you go, Son?" Terah sighed in resignation. "And what of Sarai? Can you go without her?"

"I do not know where I am going, Father. But Sarai will come with me," he said, turning to her. "She has promised that."

Terah turned toward the balcony again, his shoulders stooped by the too-harsh miseries of his life. With a heavy heart he said, "Nannar has left me nothing to live for but you and your brother, my son. If I lose you, I will die with my city. He leaves me no choice but to stay or go, and somehow that has destroyed my faith in him, for he has contradicted himself in leaving his worshipers to be destroyed with no hope."

Abram gently touched Terah's shoulder. "Father, my God is hope."

Chapter II

The day Abram left Ur, a large company went with him. He had finally convinced his father that there was no reason to stay. Though it was the hardest decision Terah had ever made, he faced it with dignified resignation and, as the head of the house, took the position of leadership in leaving the city.

Terah had not ordered the members of his house to follow but had left them to their own decisions, and many had, in loyalty to their master, decided to join him. Among them were over fifty servants and devoted slaves, most of the armed men who had survived the Guti battle, Hebron, the young Dari, Iscah and Lot, and Milcah, whom Terah, following tradition, had given to his elder son, Nahor, as his wife.

Nahor came out of devotion to his father only, and not because of any acceptance of Abram's new ideology. In fact, his disappointment in his brother had only grown steadily more intense as he watched him follow his wild dreams.

A group the size of Abram's did not usually go unnoticed passing through Ur, but today was different. A mood of fever held the city in its grip. People ran madly to their homes and families, and women ushered children to places of seeming safety, for it was finally upon them: the Guti were approaching.

Clinging tenaciously to the commands of the priests, which forbade the faithful to flee, most families would remain in the city, despite the holocaust soon to be upon them.

Sarai walked dutifully with Abram, who commanded a strange entourage of choice cattle, sheep and goats, and a bevy of wagons loaded with valuables of every description, from silks to rings of gold and brass, the currency of the day. Before leaving the city, the company came to the spacious home of a city aristocrat, where Abram paused and asked entrance. Well known to the slave who greeted him at the door, he was begged to enter, but Abram told him that, strange as it might be, he wanted access to the outer yard of the premises, rather than to the house.

"Of course, sir," the slave replied in bewilderment.

With this he swung wide the gates, and in gawking silence watched as Abram led the cattle and wagons of goods into the yard. Then, turning to leave, Abram said, "Tell your master that these are from Terah's son Abram, in exchange for the hand of his daughter, Sarai. And tell him that I am claiming her in this manner as my bride. Tell him that I require no dowry, and that he is not to grieve, for Sarai will be in good hands."

Then Abram hurriedly left and escorted Sarai from the gate to which she was clinging sadly.

The simple group of wayfarers then made their way quickly to the city gate and passed out of Ur, never to return.

Once outside the walls, Abram looked at Sarai, knowing he would see the look of apprehension and sadness she wore upon leaving her home and family. He reached tenderly for her hand and held it to his face. "Dear one, it was the only way."

With a tremble she whispered, "I know, my lord."

Abram's company avoided the marauders by cutting away from the well-traveled roads and heading to the relative safety of the hills. The heat beat unmercifully upon them as they strained up the slopes, but their eagerness to find sanctuary overcame their weariness, and they were prodded on by the echoing sounds of the approaching Guti.

When they were a sufficient distance from the city, they stopped to rest.

The Guti were visible now. As they watched, thousands poured through the delta at the mouth of the Gulf, swarming like disorganized hornets toward the great walled city.

When the horde was within a mile of the gate, the cries of the citizens blared throughout the valley. A wrenching, distorted sound, the screams and high-pitched wails of Ur's women and children echoed through the hills.

As if signaling their predetermined victory, the noisy cries inspired the Guti to an even hastier attack.

Terah could not stay seated to simply watch his city's demise like a vulture on a branch. But like the others on the hill, even he could not tear his eyes away from the spectacle. Standing, he paced the forehead of the slope, once, twice, over and over, as he sorrowfully witnessed the Guti storming the massive walls.

Abram walked to his father, who stood alone some distance from the group. Even during this moment of crisis, Abram could be glad for one thing: his father was once again the statuesque, dignified man he had been before that horrible night. Abram could scarcely believe the rapidity with which his father had resumed his old self again. The pride Abram had felt as he watched Terah the day of the war council in Hebron's tent was still there today as he saw the silence with which his father bore what he witnessed now, and in light of the journey ahead, he only hoped his joy at the old man's recuperation was not premature.

The company did not speak for long minutes. Dari, in manly silence, stood apart from the crowd, sensing the sudden maturity demanded of him. Small slave children clung to their mothers' skirts in terror, and Sarai ran to Abram, burying her face in his heavy cloak.

"Son," Terah whispered.

"Yes, my father?" Abram bent his ear close to Terah's lips.

"This is what I saw."

"What do you mean, sir?"

"In my dreams—they stormed the walls and burned my city—and we will see the temple fall."

Still respectful of the old man's lifelong faith in Nannar, Abram placed a strong arm around his beloved father's shoulders and slowly led him away from the scene. "No, sir. We will turn our backs and be going before I will allow you to see that."

One by one, the group on the hill tore themselves from the spectacle as they hastened to follow their leading men, but Terah was apprehensive.

"Son, let me stay," he proposed weakly.

"Nonsense, Father. Do not look back. Look forward. We have a new life now."

"But, Abram, I am old. An old man can have no future and surely no new life."

"See a new life in mine then, sir," Abram said softly. "Am I not an extension of yourself?"

Those words seemed to bring a hint of a smile from Terah, a pleased expression which Abram had not seen from his father in many long days. And the tiny caravan crept down the backside of the range, away from Ur.

The acrid odor of grey-black smoke filled the Chaldean valley. Large, unnatural barges of burning debris floated into the gulf at the city's mouth.

Slaughtered specimens, once living bodies, lay in wild array throughout the back streets and all around the central square. In their haste to reach the governmental quarters, the Guti had shown no mercy to those in their way.

Women here and there lay half-naked, their clothing ripped violently from them. Small children cried helplessly for their parents, and the majority of Ur's remaining populace cowered in the ruined shells of the city's homes and shops.

Within a matter of moments the invaders had won dominance over the citizens, and now the Guti leaders stalked the palace hallways in quest of Sargon, Ur's aged king.

In the temple square the marauders awaited their leaders' return and raucously displayed their booty, material goods, and human captives alike.

The palace hallways and chambers were silent save for the echoing tramp of Guti feet, while servants and slaves hid out of sight, fearful to breathe lest they be caught.

Sargon's ministers had led him to a relatively remote sanctuary, but it took only a few short minutes before one clever Guti spied the disguised doorway which gave the clue.

Roughly the Guti dragged the king from his stronghold, and his ministers, attempting to stop the abduction, were quickly eliminated.

Out in the courtyard, barbaric soldiers roared their approval as the old king was thrown ruthlessly onto the palace steps and left to struggle to his feet in wild-eyed fear.

"Men, this is Sargon, king of Ur!" one Guti shouted sarcastically. "And we now have a bargain to fulfill!"

The crowd laughed and cheered uproariously, knowing what was to come.

"Bring forth the good men who have aided us so well this day, that we may repay them the debts we so humbly owe!" cried the blustering wild man.

Again the crowd cheered, and from somewhere in the ranks, five well-dressed men came forward amid loud applause.

Sargon's face turned pale with disbelief. So this was how it had been. He watched in utter desolation as the five men, his trusted priests, the men who had counseled him to avoid offensive attack on the Guti, rose to the platform, beaming with triumph.

Again the Guti leader spoke. "These men gave us the keys to Ur and have been our trusted guides. We have promised them a share in all our earnings, and we must be men of honor," he smiled, a devilish glint in his eyes.

The priests were now sure of their cut in the division of booty and power, and their conviction was further assured when a Guti soldier approached the platform with a large chest. Thinking it full of jewels for their hire, they smiled broadly as the leader took it and walked ceremoniously toward them.

"Good men, take this with my humble gratitude," he said, bowing low. Then calling five of his own men forward, the Guti asked them to dip into the chest and distribute tokens to the priests.

Obediently, the soldiers reached in, and then, upon the cue of a loud shout from the mob, they turned and plunged five crude daggers into the hearts of their unwitting victims.

This was the moment the crowd had awaited. Rushing from the courtyard and storming the temple, they ran as a body up the hundred steps until they covered the ziggurat like bees on a hive. And then, clearing a broad descent down the slope, they shouted their exultation and triumph as the great image of Nannar was thrust down the steep-staired incline from the altar house, tumbling over and over again until it reached the stone floor, where it lay dismembered and deformed, crushed like the city which had worshiped it. And under the crushing weight of Nannar's shattered form lay the barely recognizable body of King Sargon, trapped there as a symbol of all who had been trapped in the betrayed city.

Far away in the hills, the echoing vibration of that thunderous overthrow reached the ears of Abram's people.

Terah let go one unsuppressed shudder of horror as he heard it. But he never looked back.

There was no reason for anyone to look back, though they knew that sound echoed not only the demise of a god but also the death of an entire civilization.

Chapter III

The small group of travelers was unused to the strenuous labor of caravaning. Even experienced leadership was little consolation for them as they trekked day after day farther up the Euphrates away from Ur and all they loved so well.

They knew they traveled toward the fertile land of the Canaanites, but other than this, their destination was unknown to them. Morning by morning they rose early and pushed on, never asking where they were going or when their journey would end. After leaving the hills, they followed the trade route northwest from Ur, which bore along the west side of the great river. They made only infrequent stops for rest and nourishment or to barter their goods for food at the small villages and camps scattered along the way.

But their simple faith in their leaders could not hold their tongues forever. They knew they had been given the choice to come, and therefore they began questioning the wisdom of their own decisions. Would life under Guti rule have been preferable to this? they wondered.

Their distaste for traveling was not related to any lack of life's necessities. Terah's wealth provided well for them. But not knowing their final destination ate at them day and night.

Abram sensed this keenly, and even when his bride looked to him with inquisitive eyes, he was unable to answer her.

One evening, after an unusually hot and weary day, the caravan came to the lights of a small inn. Since they had left Chaldea, nearly thirty days before, they had traveled half the distance from their home to Haran. Nearly seven hundred miles northwest of Ur, this was

the homeland of Terah's ancestors, and in keeping with
tradition, he had named his third son for this city. In a
sense, then, it would not have seemed unusual for
Abram to seek refuge there for his people. But the con-
nection was ancestral only, and though he had traded
there, Abram had no intention of seeking sanctuary in
Haran, the largest center of moon worship, outside Ur,
in all the fertile crescent.

When the caravan settled at the inn, they were well
received, as the family of Terah and the names Nahor
and Abram were well known wherever they traveled.

Abram's recent purchase of several large, awkward
camels had managed to keep the minds and talents of
the servants busy whenever they stopped for the evening. It had taken several days, but gradually the men
were getting used to handling the mean-tempered
beasts, matching wits with the clumsy creatures as they
tended them. Kicking at the legs or knees of the headstrong camels to make them lie down, the men could remove the saddlery, but curses flew thick and fast as the
stubborn animals fought their masters, and onlookers
stifled the laughter which the scene inevitably evoked.

Inside the crude hostel, Abram and Sarai sat alone.
Abram's face was full of weariness and his thoughts far
from his bride. Sarai touched his hand. She knew what
he was feeling. "Abram," she whispered.

But he did not speak. Shamed by his own lack of direction, questions filled his mind. Where were they
going? Where was he leading his people?

Sarai sensed his feeling of helplessness but could not
give him any answer of her own, and after a prolonged
silence, Abram rose and left her side. Wandering to the
door of the inn, he breathed the cool, fresh air of the
plains.

Outside, the servants still struggled with the camels,
and a smile worked its way across Abram's face. But as
quickly as it had come, it was gone, for he had caught a
glimpse of his father sitting alone against the wall of the
inn. He studied the old man's face. The journey had

taken toll of Terah, and it seemed now that his health was failing badly. Waves of guilt hit Abram as he considered that it was his fault.

Nahor entered the courtyard. Resentment clouded his face when he saw Abram, but he did not speak. He walked quickly to Terah's side and leaned over him with a comforting gesture. Try as he might, it had become increasingly hard for Nahor to hold back his feelings. The affection he had always felt for his younger brother was being replaced by a confused animosity. Abram sensed this and turned helplessly back into the hostel. Perhaps he could cheer his bride in some way.

But how? Hadn't he done Sarai an unforgivable injustice? He had taken her from her natural position just as surely as one destroys a flower when ripping it from the sod, and all in the name of his dreams and convictions.

Without a set direction, how could he convince anyone that his revelation had been true?

He fought back the next inevitable question. Had his revelation been true, or had it been the product of a crazed, bewildered mind?

Just as he was about to enter the hostel, Lot called to him.

"Sir, may I have a word with you?"

Sarai came silently near the doorway to listen.

"Of course, Lot. What is it?" Abram answered.

His nephew was awkward as he fought for the appropriate words, for he knew he might offend Abram with his question. "Sir, if I may have your counsel—I have been asked by several of the company—"

"Yes, Lot."

Sarai was rigid with apprehension.

"I have been asked by several of the company—if I might approach you with a question?"

Abram's weariness had lent a certain brevity to his temper. "Make yourself clear, Lot!" he snapped. His reaction seemed to catch the attention of the entire caravan, and silence filled the camp. Lot looked about him.

He had hoped his coming to Abram would not attract attention.

"Uncle, sir, I—we wish to know where we are going," he said at last.

That was as plainly as the question could have been put, and Abram knew Lot had spoken for everyone there.

All eyes were on him now, and he felt the anticipation of the crowd as they awaited his answer. He saw the weary faces before him; he saw his father, half-ill with the journey; he saw Nahor's restrained disgust; and he felt the pressure of the occasion.

What could he say? What alternatives were there? Surely, he thought, they should not go to Haran. Surely, if his God had called him out of Ur, he was not now calling him to another city of Nannar. But what answer could he give the people?

"My God," he wondered, "are You real? What am I to do?" But it seemed no answer came just then.

Under the strain of the moment, Abram laughed openly, as if the answer were ridiculously obvious. And as if the very question were a surprise to him, he said, "Why, my good people, where did you suppose we were going? Where but to Haran, of course."

His broad smile was a relief to the crowd, and they broke into a celebration of laughter. Of course; where but to Haran?

But Abram's smile had been a lie, and instantly, when their backs were turned and when the demanding pressure was gone, he felt the guilt of it set in.

He saw his brother give a look of bitterness and turn into the hostel. Abram's casual facade had not fooled him. And from the doorway he saw Sarai's face. For the first time there was doubt in her eyes.

Looking at her briefly, he turned and walked into the night to be alone with his own thoughts.

Sitting in the quiet of the desert gave him solace to listen to his heart.

Guilt plagued him feverishly. He had never intended to go to Haran. He knew it was just as perverse as Ur had been and that it was an unwelcome home for any beliefs such as he held.

"My God, I am filled with fear—fear of my own failings and most of all, fear of You. What was I to do? Where were we to go? I know I have acted in haste. But I had no answer from You.

"I am humble, Lord. Do not mistake my words. I am not blasphemous, but filled with fear and doubts. My Lord—You are real, are You not? That night, when I heard You, I did hear You, did I not?"

Abram sat in loneliness, looking and feeling very much deserted. Doubts flew at him. He had not known his God long and did not know Him well. He had not been able to overthrow his upbringing in an instant and tended to view his new Sovereign in the light of his previous teachings of Nannar.

Fear was his principal emotion, and with it came frustration and doubt, for he had been brought up on fear. He had once felt so strong and proud in his newfound faith, but now he felt inadequate and almost foolish.

Perhaps it had been a hoax, he thought.

Cradling his head on his knees, he sat huddled like a lump of clay.

A lonely time passed before he began to feel a working on that piece of clay. A vague light of understanding began to shine through his thoughts.

Of course, it had not been a hoax! Would a hoax lead him and his people away from Ur, the very day it was to be destroyed? Would a hoax reunite him with his father and give him Sarai?

Could it be that this God worked in a life without forever shouting instructions or filling the eyes with spectacular visions? Was his God bound to work in one way only? Could it be that he had been given an answer and a direction when he needed it most and had simply not recognized its source?

When there were no other routes to take, the one remaining was the answer he had searched for. Perhaps he had been avoiding Haran because it did not seem the proper answer to him, and not because his God wished him to detour around that city. Perhaps he had been molding his own directions to suit his limited idea of the Lord.

"And all the time, You were molding me," he smiled.

Chapter IV

Time often shields its subjects from the fear of the future by blinding their eyes to things which lie ahead. Had Abram known what sequence of events was held in store for him, he might never have ventured on.

The large commercial city of Haran, which lay on the Belikh River sixty miles from its entrance into the Euphrates, was on the busy caravan route connecting with Nineveh, Asshur, and Babylon in Mesopotamia, and with Damascus, Tyre, and Egyptian cities west and south. Like its notorious neighbors, it was renowned for its bloodlust and ritualism and for the general decadence of its moral structure. Like Ur in many respects, it nestled among foothills, these of northern Mesopotamia, and part of its wealth was attributable to its river, which supplied it with agricultural bounty.

From the first moment he and his people set foot in Haran, ugliness plagued their steps. Though he had been in Haran before, he would never forget his feelings when the small caravan entered the central gate, for the first thing to catch the eye was the inevitable temple to Nannar. His stomach sank at the sight of it, and he turned his face from it instantly.

The first day in Haran, Abram and his people, exhausted from their journey, hungered for sleep. They had arrived late and there was no hostelry available, so they found it necessary to camp outside the walls of the town. There they were forced to join a motley crew of Bedouins from the hills, with their goatshair tents and stinking animals, as well as homeless beggars and lepers from the town proper.

The dignified and aristocratic people of Terah's household found it more than difficult to adjust to their station, but they recognized their lack of choice and settled down silently for the evening.

The noise of the city died down, and the Bedouins sat camped around their fires. The party from Ur followed suit and pitched its shelters in a rude circle.

Abram saw to it that his father was comfortable in his tent and then came to Sarai, who patiently waited in theirs. "Abram, you are so weary. Sit by me, here," she softly whispered.

"I've had so little time for you, Sarai," he smiled as he knelt beside her. "Such a wedding feast for my bride. And you have been so understanding."

Sarai drew Abram to her. "Tonight, my lord, you are mine," she answered, "and all the fathers and brothers and caravans in the world will not keep you from me."

Abram kissed her warmly and for the first time since they had left Ur, they were truly alone.

The next morning found the homeless ones somewhat refreshed from their journey. Abram went to his father's tent and found Nahor tending him.

"Abram, may I have a word with you outside?" Nahor asked.

They walked several feet from the tent and Nahor, with a look of anxiety, related his concern for their father. "He is growing worse, Abram. The journey was so much for him that I am afraid he will never recover."

Abram's forehead was knit with heaviness. "I will go into Haran today and find lodging for us, Nahor," he said. "I am known in the courts here as Terah's son, and the governors will make us at home. We must find Father a comfortable resting place. He is still a strong man and, with time, he will regain himself, don't you think?"

Abram looked at his brother but found little encouragement there. Nahor could not resist the thought that his father's condition was solely the result of Abram's strong will. Abram sensed this, and at length, unable to look Nahor in the eye, he asked, "Would you have had us stay in Ur, Brother?"

Nahor did not answer immediately, looking at the ground. "Speak your mind, Nahor," Abram pressed him.

"It is not the journey which has hurt our father," he answered at last, suspiciously sullen. "You know what I am saying. We did not leave Ur to escape the Guti, but to follow your illusions, and that, my dear brother —that is what is killing our father!"

This cut Abram like a knife. Even the day Nahor had called him a proud man, he had done so without being cruel, and Abram did not know how to respond to this new twist in his brother's usually gentle character.

Falteringly he sought words to help Nahor understand. "Please, listen. I know how wild and incredible my beliefs must seem to you," he began. "But, Brother, that is because they are not only beliefs, but also realities. During the past weeks while we have traveled, there have been many times when I questioned them myself and had strong doubts. There were even times when I wished I never had heard what I heard or witnessed what I witnessed. But, Brother, it is all true. There is no way to convince you, but with my last words I will witness, 'It is true. I know my God is real!' I do not know Him well yet, but I learn more each day. And He speaks to me in many ways you may not understand."

At this point a distraught Nahor interrupted. "But, Abram, if your so-called god is not an illusion, what makes him so much more to be desired than Nannar?" And looking with bitter eyes on his younger brother, he said, "Is he not requiring the life of your own father?"

At this Nahor quickly walked away, only turning when he had almost reached Terah's tent and, with an expression Abram had never before seen him wear, shouting, "You are a madman, my brother—a sick, confused madman!"

Suddenly Abram felt as he had the night his father

had whipped him. Stumbling in the dark, stunned with the blow, he leaned alone against the great wall of Haran like a numbed animal.

Sarai, who had overheard Nahor's rebuke, ran feverishly to Abram and threw her arms around him. Abram held her close and hoped she would not see the tears which flowed silently down his face.

As the months passed, Abram and his family became more familiar with Haran. Though he hated going into this city, so much like Ur, Abram found it necessary to trade for food and goods inside the walls, and as he had promised Nahor, he had gone to the court to find help. He had been welcomed warmly by those who knew him or had heard of his father and of the tragedy of Ur. Soon they had been settled in comfort, and Terah spent several days in peace.

But Nahor had grown more and more distant, and now Abram sensed that his brother's feelings were no longer based solely on his father's failing health but on the beginning seeds of jealousy. It had become apparent throughout the journey and during their stay in Haran that Abram was the leader, though younger than Nahor. And Nahor, even though he had always been known for his patience and even temper, had become increasingly irritable.

The oriental custom of the right of the first-born extended not only to birthrights and material inheritances, but into the realm of leadership as well. Abram's zeal in his faith and his inborn personality greatly overshadowed Nahor's position and only added fuel to the elder brother's ever-growing fire of animosity. Nahor's feelings evolved in expression from sullen silence to more and more frequent faultfinding.

By way of unconscious revenge, Nahor often now sought occasion to bring his brother into open quarrels, hostile and vindictive.

The tense situation was especially difficult for Sarai,

who had grown much attached to Milcah, Nahor's young bride, and to Lot, her brother. There were few young people in the household with whom Sarai felt kinship, and she clung to what family she could find in her displaced position.

One afternoon when Abram returned from the marketplace with Lot, where they had made purchases of cattle and camels, Nahor greeted them at the gate of the villa.

"This one is meager-boned, Brother," he goaded, pointing to one of the two-humped camels. "Perhaps I should go with you the next time."

But the hot-tempered Abram had taken the final insult. "You have called me proud; you have called me mad," he said. "You have blamed me for my father's illness. You have watched me with the eyes of a judge and prosecutor! Will you also now teach me my trade, Brother? Who has spent his adult life traveling from Mesopotamia to Egypt with his father's trains, you or I?"

And with a sneer, knowing he now had Abram at a disadvantage, Nahor retorted, "You never were one to warm the fires at home, were you?"

"Perhaps you could have used a fire to warm your ambition, my docile brother," Abram returned.

"Ambition is something you trade well in, Abram. Or is 'pride' a better word?"

Abram was enraged. "It is time, Nahor, we saw which of us has the most reason to be proud," he shouted, raising a clenched fist to his brother's face.

Lot restrained Abram and shouted for the two to stop their quarreling.

Nahor was about to retaliate when Sarai came running from the hostel. "Abram, Nahor—come! It is Terah; he is calling for you!" she cried, her face white as harvest wheat and her eyes wild with desperation. "Oh, Abram, your father is—"

Ceasing their squabble, Abram and Nahor looked at one another shamefacedly and ran madly for the room where Terah was lying, entering cautiously, afraid of what might wait for them.

There he lay in a well-appointed chamber, fitting for the wealthiest merchant prince of Chaldea. Looking more ghostly than manly, he raised a hand and motioned for his sons to approach.

Abram and Nahor came near the bed and knelt by their father's side.

"Please, rest. Do not try to speak, Father. You are very tired," Abram insisted weakly.

Nahor sat on the couch and held the old man's hand.

Terah whispered inaudibly and then more distinctly, "Sons, I heard you quarreling."

Abram and Nahor glanced at one another, both feeling the guilt of that moment unlike anything they had felt before. "No, Father, we were not quarreling," Nahor tried to convince him.

"My brother is right, Father. We were discussing my purchases. Nahor knows a poor trade when he sees one."

Terah was too weak to discuss what he knew was untrue.

"Sons, listen well. My time is here, and I cannot leave without seeing you reconciled." He hesitated, a shudder wracking his body. Turning to Abram, he said, "Your God is with you, my son. I do not know Him well, but I trust the son I have raised and trust his God to bless him. And," Terah stopped for a long moment, contemplating the import of his next words, "Nannar is no longer my god," he said falteringly. "You said you were but an extension of me once, my son. Perhaps— perhaps you should have said your faith has been extended to me." And then he paused, tears blinding him momentarily, as if his eyes were witnessing a tragedy. "He must exist, Abram. I know it, for I felt it on the hill the day Ur was destroyed."

Terah then turned to Nahor, who held fast to his wasted hand, and said, "Blessings on you, Son. All of what you claim is yours, for you have inherited the greater part. But do not destroy what I have left you with hatred for your younger brother." And then looking at them both, he said, "You are all I have in the world and in my life, my children." The old man could only whisper, and closing his eyes, with his final breath he said, "Do well with what I have given you—"

The sudden and unexpected aura of death hung in the air, and Abram, looking incredulously upon the beloved one, laid his head on his father's chest and wept. Nahor sat stunned, cold and heartbroken, his face expressionless as he stared, stonelike, at the hand he held.

And when Abram raised his head to comfort his brother, the face which met his was alien.

"No!" Abram thought to himself. "Do not do this!" And with a hesitant whisper he sought a response. "Nahor?"

But his brother's eyes were glassy with unforgiveness.

Chapter V

There now seemed no reason for Abram to remain in Haran, the city he so despised.

Upon his father's death, Nahor, as custom dictated, received a double portion, or two-thirds of the estate, while Abram received one-third. Though the major portion of the family fortune had been destroyed with Ur or confiscated by the Guti, Terah still had left a handsome inheritance to his two sons, both monetarily and in reputation, for the trade contracts still stood and the means of reacquiring that fortune was at their disposal.

This may have made Abram feel he was to stay permanently in Haran, but Nahor's attitude gave him more reason to go than remain, as he knew he could never work side by side with his brother as long as Nahor felt as he did.

Abram sensed alienation, not only from Nahor, but also from many of those who had come with them from Ur. Most of the household had followed out of loyalty to Terah, their master, and not out of devotion to Abram or his beliefs, though he had always been loved and respected by them. But now that Terah was dead, the majority of the servants were obligated to Nahor, the legitimate heir, and even if they had been given the choice, would have stayed in Haran rather than go into yet another new place with Abram, whom they were beginning to question.

On top of all this, the words of Abram's God frequently came to him now, "Get thee out of thy country and from thy kindred and from thy father's house." As long as he remained, he felt he had not yet fully broken with those old ties.

Yes, he had left his country and the kindred Chaldeans and his father's house, but he knew that ultimately God required still more of him. He knew that ultimately God was asking him to leave *all* he had once held so dear, and that the bonds of loyalty he had been temporarily allowed to maintain had been largely dissolved with his father's death.

All this left him little reason to stay in Haran. But as he walked outside the walls of the city, he felt lonely, dispossessed, and homeless. Questions gnawed at him.

Why had his God impressed upon him the necessity of coming here at all? He had certainly not wished it himself.

Why, if he had been directed to come here, was he now feeling he should leave?

And why, if he should leave, must he be compelled to go without being reconciled to his brother?

Abram always did his best thinking alone. It seemed he was forever questioning his God, and yet he felt totally unable to answer his own doubts and confusion. Hesitantly he asked, "Why, God? Why did You bring me here? Only to see my father waste away and my brother turn against me? Before I even ask where I am to go, I will ask why I was to come here at all. Lord God, be patient with this weak man. I know You want me to leave, and I do not wish to stay here. I despise the temple and the filth of this city, as I grew to despise Ur. But, Lord God, my brother is here—my only remaining brother—and I still love him. Am I to leave like this?" he sighed emptily.

Abram hardly noticed the camps he walked through, so deep were his thoughts. But lepers and Bedouins made way for the handsome man with the furrowed brow, and at last he rested his body against one of the jutting walls of the city.

So vast was his concentration that he barely realized the presence of a man who had approached from the gate. Thinking him to be a beggar, he reached inside the folds of his robe and pulled out a purse of gold, handing the man a piece without looking at him, in hopes that he would leave.

But as Abram put out his hand, the man said, "It is not gold I want, my brother."

"Nahor?" Abram whispered in amazement. "Why are you here?"

Nahor was silent as he held out his hand to greet Abram's. "Brother—forgive me," he said, brokenly. And with those three words, Abram read a book in Nahor's face which said, "I have been foolish. I know you loved our father."

Abram's mind flashed to scenes of their youth when they had been as close as any brothers could be, and he felt almost that same unity now, though this confession came so unexpectedly that he hardly knew how to take it.

"Oh, Nahor, I am the one who should ask forgiveness, not you. For I am the one who has been proud."

His brother smiled broadly and they walked toward the gate, their arms about each other.

Abram looked above and silently thought, "God, thank you." And then, just as quickly, he added. "Help me to tell my brother You want me to go."

But before he could say anything, Nahor had stopped, his face betraying a desire to speak.

"What is it?" Abram asked.

"Abram, I have nothing now. Even two-thirds of my father's estate means nothing without a purpose," he said hesitantly.

Nahor left his brother and walked a few paces out into the night. "I can no longer believe in Nannar. When Father rejected him, much of my trust was destroyed, and even though I find it difficult to admit, your words about your nameless deity have truly confounded me."

Turning to Abram, he continued, "I am so lonely—something I cannot tell anyone but you. Brother, in my heart I have always known you are not one to fabricate an incident—you are not one to lie. If your god is real,

will he speak to me as well?" he asked, emotion crowding his voice.

Abram was awestruck. "Oh, Nahor! He will speak to
you! He is speaking to you now."

Nahor walked out, far onto the plain, and Abram did
not follow him, for he knew his brother was as proud as
he and preferred to be alone with his innermost feelings.

Abram waited several minutes and then returned to
the hostel where he had closed his father's sunken eyes
in the moment of death. The vision of that final scene
had impressed itself indelibly on his memory, but now
joy for Nahor somewhat took the place of mourning.

Abram did not yet see the purpose in coming to
Haran, but if he could have looked into the future, he
would have seen how the unborn generations of that
city, and indeed of all upper Mesopotamia, would trace
their faith in the One God to his brother's influence, to
the impact of their forefather, Nahor.

As he reached the gate, thoughts of a different sort—
insightful thoughts of his father, his brother, and himself—struck him simultaneously.

"How strange," he said, "that we must all be brought
to nothing before we hear You speak to us, my God."

Chapter VI

The day Abram departed from Haran, he did not leave all he had ever known, for he had traveled with the caravans for his father throughout the eastern world. But he had never felt as he did today, as if he were stepping out into dead space with no particular foothold or goal.

The entire household accompanied him to the gate, the oriental parting fervent with sincere sorrow. Abram and Nahor, knowing they might never again see one another, clung to each other for several long seconds, and the separation was torturous for Sarai, who was once again being torn from her family.

When the last good-bys had been said, they turned from the gate and the small company started on its way.

As Haran slowly became a small dark spot on the horizon, Sarai hung tightly to Abram, and in her silence, her face spoke her fears. Abram tried to reassure her. "Sarai, trust me," he said. "View all of this as the true beginning of our lives together. I know how you feel; I am leaving all of my people, and that is not an easy thing—" Abram broke off into private thought and Sarai slipped her hand into his.

The company was silent with them as they trekked farther away from Haran, when a servant ran up to Abram. "Sir, someone approaches on the plain!"

The group turned to see a young man and a boy riding camelback in long, fast strides after them. "Uncle! Abram! It is I, Lot!" the master rider called when he was within hearing distance.

Abram's eyes sparkled with excitement. "Lot! You mean to come with us?"

"Yes, Uncle—if I may." Lot's face was feverish with anticipation.

"But, Lot, are you sure? And who is this with you—Dari? Young Dari?"

"Yes, sir. I know what I am doing, sir. I cannot stay behind," Lot said, catching his breath. "And Hebron gave Dari leave to come, asking that you accept his eager desire to be with you."

Abram smiled widely. "But you may want to turn back," he hesitated.

"Not I, Uncle. I will trust you wherever you lead me."

"And I, too," the boy added urgently.

"Uncle," Lot said, looking at the ground, "since my father died, I have no one, really—"

Abram smiled warmly and Sarai reached for Dari, embracing the youngster who had grown so close to them.

Abram grasped Lot's hand, holding it fervently. "I am proud to have you, Lot." And looking at Dari, remembering the day the lad had so bravely faced him at the oasis, he smiled again and said, "What was I thinking of to leave you behind, young man? You have certainly proven yourself invaluable in times past."

Dari beamed with exultant pride.

The slaves and freemen whom Abram had bought or enlisted before leaving Haran had been specifically chosen for the type of travel the company would be engaged in.

Though Abram was still a caravaneer and would continue the trade in which he was so well versed, he was not now so certain of his future and how soon he would return to civilization. Before he had left Ur, his travels had been well-routed and planned to bring him into large centers when restocking of supplies and food was necessary. Now he would need a second source of sustinence on which to fall back. And so, despite his wealth, he assumed the role, if not the poverty, of the nomad, the wandering wayfarer.

He was prepared for any contingency. Knowing his God desired him to leave all behind, he took up, temporarily at least, the Bedouin existence. Though happy he was not a member of that despised race, he was ready to live in any fashion his new life required of him. With the nomadic economy he was free from the bonds of profit and trade, though not to be completely severed from this income unless necessary.

His future, then, would find him a strange combination: the famed and wealthy son of Terah, who could enter the courts of kings, and the humble plainsman, who accompanied sheep and goats.

Of course, it was a crucial adjustment for him, but much more so for the pampered Sarai, raised with luxurious finery. She found it often necessary to work side by side with the women whom Abram had gotten for her, and sometimes, though not often, she felt bitterly displaced.

The tents had to be raised and lowered each day, which fell to the women by custom, and the goatshair fabric was rough and heavy. The two- or three-room tents, each room separated by flaps, provided little privacy, and the furnishings, though of fine quality, were only the barest necessities. The floor was covered with mats and cushions, a few in the servants' tents, but many more in Abram's and Sarai's. A large circle of intricately carved leather, spread upon the floor, served as eating space, and small lamps and lanterns, hung from the poling, provided light.

The women slept apart from the men, though Sarai's tent was adjacent to Abram's.

Her husband had not given her a poor existence. The life of travel made simplicity necessary, but Abram's people were extremely well-to-do in relation to those of other nomadic tribes. In fact, wherever they went, Abram still was honored as the aristocrat he truly was. And their tents, like all else about them, suited their position. Their "tabernacles," as they were called, were nearly twice as large as those shared by groups of servants.

Large, colorful embroidered bolsters, carried by the pack animals during the day, were strewn upon the tent floors in the evening. The dim lamplight softened the mood at evening, and the gentle incense which filled the lamps would have been equally appropriate in the wealthiest of city homes, giving a distinctly pleasurable atmosphere to the quarters.

And so, as they traveled the many-day journey from Haran west to the Euphrates, the band was not typical of the clans which traversed Mesopotamia, Egypt, and Palestine. They had more camels and single-humped dromedaries than other groups, and this alone distinguished them as being wealthy. Abram, Sarai, and Lot rode their tall "ships of the desert," and many of the servants had colts to ride, an unheard-of luxury for such societies. Their sheep and cattle were the finest, and even the slaves were handsomely, if simply, attired.

The camels added color and music to the little band. The tinkling of their harness bells lent a cheerful note to the sometimes depressingly lonely sound of the desert wind, and their brilliant red and gold strapping and blankets, fringed in many colors, enlivened an otherwise monotonous landscape. Many times, too, Dari's pipe filled out the hollowness of the wind, soothing and caressing the evening air.

When they reached the river, which was much narrower in this part of Mesopotamia than it had been at the broad mouth of the Chaldean gulf, they were faced with the nomadic problem of fording.

The animals swam across, their bundles divided proportionately among them and piled evenly on their backs. The men and women floated across on makeshift barges supported by inflated goatskins. They chose the shallowest and smoothest spot available, the strong-armed men standing on the shores and directing the floats safely to land by means of heavy ropes. The animals had no problem, the sheep ignorantly but fearlessly risking the more dangerous currents.

The land beyond the river was steppe country, lovely grassland perfect for grazing. Abram took his people and his flocks through this region, which led southward toward Damascus, nearly three hundred miles. This was their current destination, mainly because the natural lay of the land led that way, but also because the dry season would be upon them in about three months. Damascus was the last major city before the Jordan River of Canaan, which was the favorite nomadic rendezvous and the link for world trade between Egypt and Mesopotamia.

Like all herdsmen, then, Abram followed the custom of necessity and went where his animals and people would best survive.

Often he considered how strange it was that his father had vaguely intended going to Canaan after leaving Ur. The entire family probably would have gone this way, had his father not died. But their business in the fertile Jordan area would have centered much more on trade than his life now would. His father would have been surprised, if not disappointed, had he seen his son in his new nomadic role.

The trip to the Damascus area was, of course, very slow. Sheep do not travel quickly, nor do they graze quickly. Many days and weeks elapsed between villages or towns. Aleppo, Hamath, the site one day to be called Carchimish—all these were welcome stops when they came into view. But the days were long, and fortunately Abram felt no need to travel more quickly than they could to reach Damascus before the dry season.

The slow, simple journey afforded him a great deal of time to meditate on his God and his calling. More and more the reality of his Lord's leading impressed itself upon him. This journey struck him as none of his others had.

The steppe country was a narrow ribbon of grey

green which slipped unobtrusively between a vast, arid expanse of desert on the east and the Palestinian forests on the west. As Abram traversed this country, a parallel to his own life caught his thoughts many times.

"I was like that desert, Sarai," he told her one night. "And all my old life was like it; Ur, Nannar, Haran, my childhood—all of it seems empty, like that desert. Mesopotamia—" He stood up and walked to the tent door, the cool steppe breeze blowing his hair.

Sarai listened intently, her large dark eyes filled with admiration for her husband and his words.

Looking across the steppe, Abram could make out the edge of the flat expanse under the moonlight. Turning again to Sarai, he said, "And now, the steppes—I am like the steppes now. I am neither fertile enough for forests, nor am I as dry as I was. I am between the two, and at times when I look west to the mountains, I know that I—you and I, Sarai—will one day be like them, tall and proud and abundant with good things."

Sarai was a bit perplexed. "I know you speak of your God, but—does He wish to use me also?"

He had expected her to ask this and he was ready to respond. "Sarai, my God promised me a great name among all the families of the earth. How can that be without you beside me, and without our children to carry that name for us?"

This was the first time they had really spoken of children, and the first time Abram had ever told Sarai the words which God had given him that lonely night long before.

"Abram," she smiled, "When you returned to Ur, you told me you had found your answer. You also said I would not understand then. Do you think I am ready to understand now?"

He held her close and they walked to the tent door. By custom, the women of the day were rarely confided in as Abram was about to confide in her. Women were victims of their class position, primarily tools of child-bearing and enjoyment. Infrequently did a man look on his wife as Abram looked on Sarai, as a secret-sharer, confidante, as more than his "woman."

Yes, he thought, she was ready to understand. She had patiently endured seven hundred miles of travel from Ur to Haran and was enduring more now; she had left two families and watched her father-in-law die; and she had taken on a new life style, all in the course of a few months, without complaint. She was ready.

"Sarai," he said, cradling her head on his shoulder, "that night, my God came to me. Why? I do not know. All the universe stood still in that instant when He spoke to me. My ears still tingle when I recall His words. He said I was to leave my home and my family, that He would bless me and make my name great and that all the earth would be blessed through me—Sarai, do I sound like a madman?"

"Oh, Abram, your voice proves your sincerity and assurance. You are no madman, my lord. If the One God has chosen you, it is because you were ready to be chosen."

"I cannot say, Sarai. I don't know why He chose me; that alone humbles me. But I know, beyond doubt, that He is real; that is all-important. And you, Sarai—you are one with me."

One with him? Men did not often say such things, at least not that Sarai had ever heard. She looked across the steppe, and the thought illumined her face. Was she so dear to him, when many wealthy men even went so far as to take symbolic status in the procurement of many wives? Her face was radiant, and she felt a kinship and an alliance with her husband that she never knew a woman would be allowed to feel. From that moment she began to know something of the personality of Abram's God through the love of her husband.

And she watched silently as Abram cast another look at the faraway desert, whispering, "Mesopotamia—may I never be recalled to you."

Lot proved an invaluable aide to Abram. The able-bodied young man was vigorous in his enthusiasm for Abram's new way of life, and since he had been born and raised in Hebron's tribe, he taught his uncle much about Bedouin existence.

Abram found himself relying greatly on Lot's experience as a herdsman.

"My brother Haran taught you well, Lot," he would often remark.

"Yes, my father was a good and great man," Lot would reply, his voice deep with reverence for his memory. "The nomad's way of life is a hard one, but my father loved it. He was also a great warrior, and the Guti—" his voice trailed off. "The Guti had a difficult fight on their hands with my father," he smiled bravely.

Often Lot told how Haran had spoken highly of Abram, and frequently he compared the two. As time passed, Abram and Lot were bound by a cord of affection as strong as that of father and son.

Sarai was happy to see this, as it gave her a family again, and she was glad her husband had companionship in his lonely profession.

One service Lot performed for the tribe was the gaining of contracts from local inhabitants of the areas through which they traveled, allowing Abram to graze his sheep along the way. He was exceptionally good at this, having learned from the old nomad Hebron, who had a prickly temperament when it came to business dealings. Lot had learned to squeeze a contract out of the most obstinate of patrons through sheer force of will and perseverance.

One afternoon, far north of Damascus, Lot and Abram brought their herds to a village in the volcanic hills of the range separating the Canaanites from the Amorites. The rolling region provided good pasturage, despite its rocky nature, and Abram was anxious to secure grazing rights near the settlement. But the Amorites were not known for their generosity, and Lot prepared for a difficult session.

The caravan settled on the outskirts of the hamlet and waited while Abram and Lot entered. The two men came to a small, square hovel made of rocks and muddy clay, and Lot called toward the low door, "Keeper of this house, may we speak with you?"

They heard shuffling within, and an incredibly old woman, half-blind and bent with age, came to the doorway.

"If you be from the east country, as your speech betrays, we'll have none of you here," she spoke sharply, pointing a gnarled finger to evict them.

Lot would not be put off that easily. Continuing in her tongue, he replied, "We are from the land between the two rivers. We will stay only a short time. Where is the head of this house?"

"My son is in the hills. He will not give you pasture. Continue to Damascus—Bedouin." She said the last word with a tinge of condescension and with decided emphasis, typical of any village or town dweller's attitude toward such nomadic wanderers. But Lot caught onto this and used it to gain support.

"We are not Bedouins, madam," he smiled, bowing low. "We are only recently come from Ur. My house is the house of Terah, merchant of Ur, and this is my uncle, Abram, his son."

"I do not know this Terah or this Abram," she snapped, unimpressed. "We care not for your ways or people, Bedouin."

Lot, still undaunted, looked for yet another answer, and with a gleam in his eye, he held out a ring of gold. Too blind to see it, she held it to her mouth and bit down hard on the rim to test it. Satisfied it was genuine, she still objected. "How am I to know you have more? Will you sit all day while I nibble your gold?" she asked wryly.

Lot laughed an empty laugh, and turned to Abram, shrugging in frustration.

Then another gleam came to his eye, and Abram watched, at first confounded and then amused, as Lot took the old woman by the hand and said, "Here, Mother. This may prove our wealth to you." And he led her from camel to camel as she felt each one's nose and counted them.

"—six, seven—oh, my lord! You have many camels!"

"Many more than you've seen before, I'll warrant," he laughed.

"Oh—well, yes—I would say so," she mumbled, and then, hardly able to restrain herself, she shouted with surprising volume, "Haniel! Haniel! We have guests!"

From over the distant ridge, a very tall, large-boned, slumping man, with a giant belly, came leading a measly flock of goats. Lot smiled slyly at Abram, for they knew the bargain was sealed.

On the return to the caravan, when they were out of earshot, they looked at each other, and unable to control themselves any longer, doubled with roaring laughter at the thought of the seemingly helpless little blind woman whose eye for business had never been dulled, and whose hulking son hid in the hills while she tested the customers.

Chapter VII

At the end of the Syrian cascades stood majestic Mount Shenir. Over nine thousand feet high, it could be seen for one hundred twenty miles, so vast was its leap into space. Its three snow-capped peaks stood like beckoning fingers to lure the weary travelers to its jewellike footstool, the magnificent city of Damascus. Abram and his party approached Damascus from the northeast across the flatlands of the desert area adjacent to the city, the sparse tamarisks, acacias, and thorny plants of the arid wasteland contrasting sharply with the verdant abundance of the shining city.

Damascus lay on the fertile Abana River and was the natural crossroads for traffic east and west. Three great roads led in separate directions, and the city basked in economic security.

On a broad plain between the eastern desert and the western range, thirty miles from Shenir, it was a garden spot, saturated with the cool, rapid waters which ran down from the snowy reservoirs.

It was surrounded by some of the most fertile pasture land in the eastern world. Grass and bushlands, wheat and barley fields, olive groves and vineyards dotted the area, the cool ocean breezes descending off Shenir to meet the dry desert winds, forming an almost perfect climate.

The city's founders, who had come from the Haran region, were largely Semitic and therefore distantly related to the line of which Terah and his people had been members from old time.

The people of both Haran and Damascus traced their ancestry to a common figure, Aram, therefore calling themselves Arameans, though the city itself was influenced by many different cultures.

The Amorites of the region across the Jordan and
scattered northeast, the Assyrians from the east, and
especially the Phoenicians and Canaanites of the coastal
areas greatly influenced the society and beliefs of
Damascus.

Shamash, Molech, Milcom, Hadad—many names
were applied to their god and his consorts. But the most
popular was Baal, the son of El, the chief of gods. Baal
worship had grown out of the ancient rituals of sun
worship, whose origins were lost in antiquity. He was
also related ancestrally to gods of grain and fertility,
and his counterpart, Hadad, the god of storms, provided impetus to his strength.

When the caravan entered Damascus, they were not
surprised to see the primeval sanctuaries of Baal worship scattered throughout the hills. Baal was worshiped
in "high places," and the city was surrounded by craggy
hills of volcanic stone, used to erect his altars.

On the day Abram's party settled in the city, they
were confronted with one of the many-day festivals of
this god, and as the family passed through Damascus,
seeking hostelry for the night, they were forced farther
and farther up the incline, which led ultimately to Shenir
and the priestly temples of Baal.

The major streets directed them into the riotous festival area, and there they were greeted by sights more
horrible, more brutal in many respects, than any of
those ever accompanying the orgies of Nannar in Ur.

Ear-shattering music, licentious dancing, and the
seemingly senseless slaughter of sacrificial beasts satiated the lusts for blood and sexuality which the festivals
inspired.

Abram, Lot, Sarai, and their servants had witnessed
much in Ur and Haran, but Baal worship was far
beyond the most desperately frightening sight any of
them had ever known. Many of the Damascus citizenry,
half-crazed with the sensuous frenzy of their festival,
lay exhausted from the orgy, which already had lasted
four days and nights, and in inebriated delirium they

now slept uninhibited in alleyways and along the streets.

Booths sprinkled about the marketplace sold charms, sacrifices, and wine, and in the open areas groups of priests, surrounded by beggars waiting for remnants of the charred meat, drank the blood of animals.

The addiction of Baal worship prospered on prostitution. There was nothing hidden or secretive about this. High in the foothills, lines of men awaited entrance to the temples of sacred harlots and female impersonators.

As Abram viewed all this, he anxiously looked for a way out, Sarai clinging to him nervously. "My lord, I am faint. Please find me a place to rest," she shouted above the din. Abram found a place under the shade of a tree beside the temple, and there they sat numbed to the maniacal pageantry weaving itself about them.

Abram surveyed the scene, wishing desperately to conceal all this from his wife, who trembled with awed fear at what she witnessed. But in his accounting, he could not help noticing one group, possibly Arameans, who seemed to stand apart from the crowd. During the entire festival they had apparently not sampled any of the celebration, and he wondered who they were.

"Abram," Sarai said, "Ur was never like this. Never —like this!" He held her close to him, and recollections of the Nannar festivals flashed through his mind. He did not wish to destroy her memories of her city, but indeed the orgies of the moon god had been this brutal, this bestial, every bit this transparently gross. Perhaps, living there, they had grown callous to their surroundings, seeing other cultures as far more primitive or senseless than that of their nativity.

As he thought on these things, Abram noticed that Lot was not reacting to the festival as he was. In fact, his nephew seemed engulfed in thoughts foreign to his own. Lot's eyes followed avidly the celebration all around him, and his face betrayed a desire to become involved. A group of sparsely clad women descended the temple steps and received customers. Several of them seemed to notice Abram's party, and their faces gleamed in the light of such wealth. Lot, with dark and handsome youthfulness, especially interested them, and as one of them made a move in his direction, he turned to go with her. Abram could not believe what his eyes told him.

"My God," he whispered. "Not my nephew! Not Lot!" And before he could think further, he was on his feet, racing to Lot's side, grasping his arm roughly and wrenching him backward.

"Uncle! What is it?" Lot cried.

"No, Lot! Not as a member of my house!" Abram shouted roughly.

"But, Uncle—why?" Lot responded, incredulous of this strange behavior. "What do you mean, sir?" he asked blankly.

"Ha! What do I mean, you ask? As a member of my house, you will serve my God, and not Baal!" Abram demanded, his dark eyes flashing madly.

"Serve Baal? I do not intend to serve Baal!" he answered. "I merely intend to go with the priestess to her chambers."

Abram could see that reason would not hold him back, but he still clung to his nephew's arm tightly, as the harlot came closer.

"Do we have a quarrel here?" she asked slyly. "Now, now, gentlemen, you shall both enjoy me," she smiled with a toss of her head, and then starting up the steps, she expected Abram and Lot to follow.

"Uncle, I mean no disrespect, but I will go with her!"

"No, Lot! You shall not or you shall leave my house!"

Lot hesitated and with a shaky voice inquired, "But sir, have you never visited the temple priestesses of Ur or of any other city you have visited in all your journeys?"

Abram looked at Sarai, who sat with Dari under the tree, and he could see that she, too, desired to know the answer to Lot's question. Her large eyes seemed fearful of whatever that answer might be, and she sat rigid, waiting.

Abram saw, as never before, his life, and he remembered the many such opportunities which could have been his. The thought struck him for the first time, that despite all his journeys and years in the courts of false gods, he had never taken advantage of the harlotry available.

At a time in history when most viewed it as a matter of course to visit women of the temple, and indeed, considered it a form of worship, he could only recall the odd revulsion and utter disgust which had always been his at the thought of lying with them. This unique quality could not be attributed to any lack of masculinity on his part. Nor was it that the priestesses had found the strong, rugged caravaneer undesirable, or that he had not come in contact with their wiles. His appreciation of a pretty face was like that of any other man.

Why, then, had he not consorted with them?

A vague smile lit his face. He realized why. In all his travels, even when he had had no reason to believe it wrong, his God had kept him separate, apart from that tainting indulgence. His God had chosen him and had guided his decisions long before he had met Him, not allowing him to become, like so many lesser men, bound, addicted.

Three words came from his lips at the thought of that loving Guide. "No—thank God."

"Truly?" Lot inquired again.

Abram loosened his grip on Lot's arm and answered, "No, Lot. In all my life I have never done what you are considering. I thank God for that, Nephew, and I am certain you do not doubt my manhood because I have not visited harlots."

Lot looked at the ground. "Of course not, Uncle— but I still cannot say I understand—"

"The One God has shown me, Lot, that righteousness and true happiness go hand in hand," Abram urged. "I cannot hope to make you understand, Nephew, if you do not wish to. However, the knowledge is in you and in every man here, if he will be honest enough to uncover it—to let the filth of his surroundings step aside long enough to hear his own soul speak. My God has given all of us this knowledge."

Abram caught a gleam of comprehension and guilt in Lot's eyes. But as quickly as it came, it was superseded by other thoughts.

"Are you coming?" the harlot called.

Lot looked at Abram, and at his aunt, Sarai, who pleaded with her eyes that he not go. Then, looking at the priestess, he made his decision and turned to follow her up the steps, with each pace the weight of his uncle's words falling away from him.

Spurred by white-hot indignation, Abram hurtled up the stairs after him and caught him by the shoulder. "If you do not know what is right for you, I shall make your decisions for you!" he roared, and nimbly slung his nephew down the broad banister.

With this bold struggle, the crowd's attention was caught, and the noisy throng became suddenly muted. All eyes were on Abram, and he looked about in astonishment to see the drama he had created.

Sarai stood with a badly battered nephew on the edge of the breathless crowd and watched anxiously for Abram's next move. The harlot, dumbfounded, stood numb on the steps behind him.

Abram knew the crowd expected an explanation. Desperately he looked around him at the eager faces. A strange gathering, many different cultures were represented today, all here for the festival, and he had not intended to attract attention. His heart was in his mouth. "God, what shall I say? Give me words for these people," he whispered.

The throng pressed close but Abram stood tall, looking more confident than he felt.

"I—I am Abram, son of Terah, of Ur," he began. A hushed vibration ran through the crowd. Many knew that name. Some of them had even traded with Abram and remembered the striking face.

"I have left Ur. My father is dead. I no longer trade for him. But this does not explain my entry into your city or what you have seen today," he continued.

Gathering courage from their attentiveness, he cried loudly, "Look about you! Who is Baal that he is to be worshiped in such debauchery? Your god, you say, is a god of many consorts. He enjoys and demands the perversion of all that is truly manly or womanly, all that is —human dignity!

"What is the body?" he demanded. "A plaything, a creation for the senses only? What are you? Who are you? Do you call yourselves men and women? What is your purpose, your function? To fulfill bodily desires, or to fulfill a noble position on this planet?"

The crowd was silent, listening to every word, nor was there any movement from them to threaten him.

Continuing with words which seemed to roll from him without mental effort, words which were not his alone, he shouted, "Such deviant inhumanity! Or shall I call it 'humanity'? For perhaps this is all Man is meant to be. Am I right? Is this what Man is meant to be?

"Look around you! I do not ask if this is what Man *is,* for the answer to that is plain. He *is* this! But—what is he *meant* to be?

"Who is Baal? Is he no more than you or I? If he calls for this display and nothing more, nothing higher than physical pleasure, he must be nothing higher than what he calls for. He must be no higher than you or I, and therefore not deserving of our worship! For worship of him calls for no thought or true service, only appetite, which even the animals we call beneath us do not indulge in so vilely."

Walking higher up on the steps, he cried out, his voice rending the air, "I suggest that Baal is *nothing!* He is no greater than you or I, because he demands nothing great or high of us!"

The crowd was growing uneasy. Abram saw that on

the steps behind him an ever-increasing group of temple women, and what appeared to be male prostitutes, were crowding toward him.

Beads of perspiration stood on his face and neck, and his hands were dewy with sweat, the perfume of the impersonators nearly suffocating.

"God, give me strength," he whispered, and pointing to the priestesses and the perverts, he asked simply and deliberately, "Are these what we admire and desire to emulate? Men who are no longer men and women who trade their bodies for gold and silver? Look at them! Who are they, in their bestial, scented flesh, that we should admire them? What do they offer that the beasts of the field do not already have? Look at the rounded pillars placed around this city, and in the hills, everywhere you walk. Symbols of 'masculinity,' you say? What of 'humanity'?" And gathering all his reserves in profuse indignation, he roared, "Give me a symbol of Man's *purpose*."

The crowd was now enraged. A loud murmur flooded the marketplace, and several of the deviants lunged at him, but Abram jumped back and threatened, "Do not corrupt me with your pink hands!"

The crowd heard this biting but all too appropriate insult, and many of them laughed uproariously, admiring Abram's gall, though not necessarily agreeing with him, and at this they shouted, "Let us hear what the man from Ur has to say! It is not often we hear such things."

Abram continued quickly, leaning toward the crowd eagerly. " 'Not often,' you say? I take that to mean you have heard it at times. And I'll warrant those times were when each man here was in a thinking posture, alone, or at night when others were asleep and he was closed in with his own mind.

"That is when the knowledge of good and evil awakens all of us. When there is no noise or tumult to impose itself upon our consciences—that is when we evaluate our lives, our actions."

Abram became quiet for a moment and looked deeply into the faces of the men and women there. He saw the guilt each one experienced at his words. Even the priests, who had been impatiently straining to eject him, cringed with the truth they heard, but then one of them, in brilliant red and gold garments, stepped forward, laughing. "Tell us, Abram," he called up to him, "how can you say Baal is nothing, when the god of your homeland demands equal worship?"

Abram took this cue and responded fervently, "My God is the One True God!"

The crowd bellowed at this. "Nannar?" they shouted. "He is only one among many gods, and Baal is the son of El, the chief of gods!"

"I do not speak of Nannar!" Abram shouted to be heard. "I do not speak of Nannar!" And the crowd grew silent again in bewilderment.

The priest who had challenged him demanded with a sneer, "Oh? Then who, may we ask, is your god? Is he a new god, Abram, and have you carried him here in your pocket?" The audience applauded, but Abram went on with growing confidence.

"My God is not new. He has always been. He created the sun, whom you call El; the moon, whom my people call Nannar; the storm, whom you call Hodad; and all the elements which Man has labeled and worshiped.

"He made us and all we see around us, yet we worship His creations and not the Creator!"

The audience was divided in confusion. Some began to leave in disgust, but most stayed to hear, either out of curiosity, for the sake of entertainment, or because of genuine wonder at the words of Abram.

Among those who stayed were the people whom Abram had noticed when he had entered the marketplace, those who had only stood by and not entered into the festivities. Of all those who listened, these showed the most interest. Dressed in simple garments, they were apparently Aramean, but not of the same group which mostly inhabited this city.

He continued, "I have traveled perhaps more than any other man here. And I learned early that every nation and culture has its own deity or gods, and without exception these are personalities attached to planets, moons, stars, suns, rivers, birds, animals—every created form imaginable. Those here today know I speak the truth, for Nannar and Baal are only two gods out of many hundreds."

Pacing the temple porch, he went on, "When I visited Egypt, I studied with the royal priests the movement of the spheres and learned they have perfect orbits. I wondered, 'Is this their own doing, or the doing of a mastermind?' Why do they follow rigid courses if each has his own personality? Why does the flood rise and fall regularly, the sea ebb and flow? Why do the seasons rotate each year and the moon wax and wane?

"Because they are creatures in the hand of a Creator, I reasoned. One never created, One Who has ever been and ever will be."

Abram folded his arms and stared intently at his spellbound audience. "I know Him," he said now, reverently and softly. "He has called me to be His own, and every man should be His. He has a purpose for us, more than to fulfill the perverted desires of our bodies. He gave us desires, but we have twisted them somehow. And they, like all else, are His creation, intended to serve us and Him—not to make us their slaves, however attractive that slavery may seem on its surface."

Abram began to descend the steps, but before leaving, he said once more, "This God of whom I speak has talked to me, to my father, and to my brother. And the guilt you feel now, which makes you burn in hatred for me, is a result of His speaking to each of you."

What more could be said? He was finished, and as he walked through the silent crowd, they stepped back to let him pass.

When he reached the city gate, the throng became more restless. Some threatened to stone him, the priests murmured their hatred for him, but others, mainly the strange group of individuals who had stood apart from the orgy, wished to hear more and followed him until he passed beyond the city wall.

Chapter VIII

The caravan from Ur was not welcome inside the borders of Damascus now. Abram knew the priests would see to it that he did not stay there long.

But it was with a sense of accomplishment that he took his people to find a campsite that night. After they had pitched their tents, Lot approached his uncle in an attitude of deep humility, saying, "Sir, may I speak with you?"

"Of course, Nephew."

"I am sorry for the trouble I have caused you today. I told you I would go with you wherever you went, and now I have brought degradation to you and Sarai." He paused. There was so much more he wished to say, but he did not know how. "Your words struck me deeply today," he continued at last, "and I understood what you were saying. Can you forgive me?"

Abram placed a hand on Lot's shoulder and said, "Of course. But it is not for me to forgive you. Nevertheless, I love you like a son, and all I wanted was to—protect you. Do you understand?"

Late that night, Abram and his company were awakened by the sound of voices in the camp.

"This must be his caravan," one said.

"Well, awaken them, then!" demanded another.

Abram was up and dressed when the first voice shouted, "Abram of Ur! Come out!"

"Who can it be?" Sarai asked nervously.

"Men from Damascus, undoubtedly," he answered.

"Master Abram, son of Terah! You must come out!"

they called more rudely than before. "It is ordered by the high priest that you present yourself!"

"Not just men of Damascus, Sarai. The royal priest-hood wants us," he smiled, unimpressed. "Well, shall we see what they want?" he added, throwing his cloak about his shoulders.

He drew open the tent flap and walked into the center of camp. One by one the men and women of Abram's company came out, sleepy and bewildered by this night visitation.

Outside was a large company of priests in brilliant garments, embroidered in gold and silver. They carried torches, and several slaves accompanied them with spears and shields.

"Why are we honored with this friendly call?" the Man of Ur asked.

"The high priest wishes to speak with you, Abram. He has ordered that you return with us."

"Hasn't your priest the courage to face me during the day?" he laughed. "And why do you feel it necessary to come armed, as if I had force to use against you?"

One of the priests ordered the slaves to move forward and take Abram.

"You needn't manhandle me," he laughed again, wrenching his arm from one who grabbed him. "I will go, most willingly."

"And I too," said Lot, stepping up beside his uncle.

Abram and his nephew were taken into the city and brought quickly to the temple. As the priests escorted them up the steps, Abram caught a glimpse of a stranger hiding within the shadows outside the temple gate. The man saw Abram look at him and briefly stepped out, giving him a signal of some kind. But before Abram could determine who he was, he and Lot were ushered inside the sanctuary.

They were moved along so quickly that they could see little of the building, but it was arrayed in finery, unsurpassed by the temple of Nannar. And they were brought to a dimly lit chamber, long and narrow, with a high pulpit at one end, beneath which was a golden altar, smoking with heavy incense.

Behind the tablelike pulpit sat a man, gaudily attired, with black hair and the flowing beard typical of his station. His sinister face, with a sharp jutting nose and piercing eyes, was frightening in every respect.

"These are the men of Ur, your Holiness," one of the priests said, thrusting them forward.

The high priest stood up and left his bench. "So, you are those who disrupted our festival today!" he demanded, his arms crossed in obvious self-confidence.

"Yes," Abram returned simply.

"Do not speak!" the man retorted. "We all heard your foolishness this afternoon! The people are displeased and upset. We are asking—no—we are ordering you to leave Damascus by morning, you and your entire company," he scowled.

Abram straightened his shoulders. "We intended to leave in the morning. Of that you may be certain. But as for your people, I thank my God they were displeased, and as you say, 'upset,' " he returned.

The high priest ordered silence, but Abram only smiled as the demagogue stepped down and confronted him.

"Master Abram, this new god of whom you speak is not wanted here! Whoever he is, he came with you and he will leave with you. We will hear no more of this!" he sneered threateningly.

The priest now turned to go to his chambers, confident his point had been successfully made, but Abram called out, "Let me ask one thing of you! What is frightening in what I say—so frightening that it makes you come to me at night with armed guards? A lie would not be so disturbing, your 'Holiness.' Despite your facade of authority, you tremble inwardly at my presence because you fear the truth I bring. You come to me at night because you fear the people may follow that truth, and you do not wish them to see the folly into which you have led them. You know they would begin to doubt you if they saw your fear."

But the priest would hear no more. "Take him away!" he ordered. "Remove him and his people from Damascus—at once!"

The guards took hold of Abram and Lot, ushering them roughly toward the door. But before he left the room, Abram remembered where he had seen the mysterious figure who hid outside the temple gates. He was one of the Arameans who had stood apart from the festival that day, and Abram turned, shouting, "All your people do not believe as you do! There was an element of malcontents in this city before I came, was there not —your 'Highness'?"

The high priest raised a fist and cried, "Remove him!"

The slaves tightly bound Abram and Lot and took them through the streets until they reached their camp outside the walls. There they threw them to the ground, and a priest who had accompanied them warned, "Be gone by morning, or it will not be well with you and your women."

When the men had left, Abram and Lot were untied. "Tell us what they said," Sarai asked shakily.

"They told us to leave by morning," Lot answered. "Uncle, will we do as they say or remain here?"

"We have no choice, son. We may as well get ready to leave now. None of us will sleep before morning."

The members of the caravan had begun to make ready when Lot noticed someone at the wall. "We are being watched, sir." And pointing to the gate, he showed Abram a man seemingly spying on the caravan.

"It is the Aramean," Abram whispered. "I saw him in the crowd today and later tonight by the temple. He gave me a sign of some kind, but I could not tell what he meant."

"Who is he?" Lot asked.

"I cannot tell, but he and his friends did not partake in the festival."

As they discussed him, the man by the gate moved out from the wall slowly, looking behind him as he came. When he got closer, he raised his hand and gave the same signal he had given earlier.

"It is a sign of friendship, isn't it, Uncle? His palm is turned toward us."

"Yes, I think so."

Cautiously Abram walked out to meet him.

The man came forward quickly. "Sir, do not let them see us," he said softly, looking repeatedly over his shoulder, urgency in his mien.

The man was younger than Abram had thought him to be. In fact, he was not much older than Lot, but he had a certain dignity which belied his years. He was dressed in very simple robes, so that Abram could not tell his class position. He was not a slave, for his light brown hair was long and his beard full. He had intelligent eyes and a deeply serious face, which seemed to say he had been forced to grow up quickly.

He introduced himself softly. "Master Abram, I am Eliezer of Damascus. There is no time to explain now, sir, but will you trust me and come with me?"

Something about the young man's sincerity struck Abram favorably, but he was still wary.

"How do I know you mean us no harm, and where do you mean to take us?" he asked.

"I cannot explain further, for I was being followed when I came." The young man continued anxiously, "But I will tell you this: I am your kinsman. I mean only good for you, and I think you can help my people." He paused. "Will you come? We have lodging for you."

Abram pondered his words in surprise. Kinsman? How? He knew of no family ties with Damascans. But the young man's urgent attitude seemed to insist there was no time for doubt.

"This lodging, is it inside Damascus?"

"Yes, sir. I know you are to leave, but believe me, you will be safe with us, and we need to talk to you."

Abram and Lot agreed to go, though they wondered seriously if they were making the right decision.

Chapter IX

When Eliezer brought the people of Ur to the gate, Abram wondered how he would pass them under the watchful eyes of the guards in the high towers on either side. The company was surprised when the young Aramean looked up at the guards and gave the same signal he had given Abram earlier. The sentinels signaled back and then disappeared from sight. After a moment they returned, and one called out just loudly enough to be heard, "All's well!" and then motioned them to pass through.

Who was this strange young man, that he had league with the guards of Damascus and could find entrance for outcasts?

Once inside the walls, Eliezer led the people from Ur with catlike stealth. Through dark, narrow corridors and streets, around a seemingly endless maze of alleyways, he took them until their directional senses were confounded.

Finally they came to the back door of a very large, wealthy home, and here the young man knocked quietly."It is I, Eliezer," he whispered. "The people from Ur are with me."

The door opened quickly, and Abram and his people were guided inside, through a dark passageway until they came to a great, heavy door set in the wall at the end.

"Through there," Eliezer pointed.

Abram opened the door and light flooded the narrow passage. The opening now exposed a huge, warm room with magnificent furnishings, much like those of Terah's home.

"Where are we?" Sarai questioned.

Eliezer motioned to them to seat themselves and then, in obvious relief, he began to give them some answers to this mystery.

"Master Abram, my father will be here shortly. He is Jubah, the head of this house. Perhaps you have heard of him."

"Why, yes, I believe I have. Yes, now I know. I have traded with the men of this house in years past—but are you his son?"

The young man smiled, "I see you are surprised at my clothing. Yes, I am his son, though there are times when he might wish it otherwise."

"Not so," a voice came from outside the room, apparently in response to that statement. The chamber door opened and an old man, bent with age, entered. "Though I do not always understand, I am proud of my son," he smiled. Greeting the company, he said, "I am Jubah, master of this house. Let me be quick to explain why you were brought here."

He paced the room and began. "Today my son, his friends, and I heard your speech in the marketplace, Master Abram. Your words were startling and new to us, and we were moved by them. We have asked that you come here to explain further what you were speaking of."

Abram was still confused and curious about many things. "Why are you so concerned with my beliefs? They are alien to your city's, and surely you risk punishment by housing an outcast," he said suspiciously.

"Yes, but we are also alien to our city's worship," Eliezer spoke up.

"Let me explain further," Jubah continued, twisting a strand of his beard between his fingers in contemplation. "You may have noticed that there was a sizable group of people at the festival who did not join in."

"I did. They were dressed like Eliezer."

"Right. And that is for a special reason," Eliezer interrupted.

"We, whom you saw there today, feel that the worship of Baal is somehow—" here Jubah paused and looked at his son. "What do you call it, Eliezer?"

"Meaningless," he answered. "Foolish, actually. We believe in Baal, I suppose—though even that, I am beginning to question—but we feel the festivals are not a good thing." Eliezer rose and walked back and forth, looking for words to express his feelings. "I can't really explain, but we simply know, well, that something is wrong—something, somehow, is wrong."

Jubah went on, "Whenever we attempt to explain, we come up against a wall," he said. "And we have been ordered to defend our strange behavior and position many times."

"By the priests?" Abram asked.

"Yes. Of course, you can see how they would feel. The high priest even fears an uprising."

"And we may well give it to him," Eliezer said hotly.

"I fear my son and I do not always see eye to eye," Jubah smiled. "But I am an old man, and the future is with the young. Let me go on, for this is not all the story. Eliezer told you we are your kinsmen?"

"Yes. I am not at all sure I understand that," Abram replied, trying not to sound too bewildered.

"We believe we are if you are the son of Terah, for isn't it true that his family ties are traced back to the region of Padan-Aram?"

"You mean Haran?" Abram asked.

"Yes."

"Ancestrally we are related to those of Haran," Abram said. "My youngest brother was even named for that city."

"Then you are Aramean."

"Yes. But this is not new to me, and that is a very vague link with your family."

"But Abram, that link was strengthened today. There has always been a small group of Arameans in Damascus and throughout Mesopotamia who have traced their lineage even beyond Aram."

Things began to become clearer now. Abram recalled from his boyhood and from his travels that there always had been, scattered here and there, a few people who called themselves "Semites," and who traced their heritage back to Shem, from whom Aram was descended.

This distinction would have meant very little except that these people insisted that the legend of Shem was valid and therefore gave them a special position in the scheme of Man's history.

Shem was a figure connected with the ancient tale of a flood which had once covered the entire world. He was said to be one of three sons of the hero of the tale, known by various names but principally as Noah, who built a large ship to escape the rising waters.

The flood tales of Ur and Mesopotamia—of the whole eastern world, in fact—had been so embellished or changed from the original that the legend in its purest form had been nearly lost to the world. Little remained which was recognizable as the true incident. In his travels Abram had heard so many different versions of the original tale that he had given it up as mere mythology. But according to the Semites, who claimed to have the true story, Shem was the favorite son of Noah, and Noah had promised him a great inheritance, so vast that the whole world would feel his impact. His sons, the legend told, would rise to a place of supreme importance in the world.

"You are Semitic?" Abram asked, attempting vainly to disguise the sneer which came involuntarily to his face.

"Yes."

"Well, I do not understand what this has to do with me," he shrugged in some indifference, thinking he had made a mistake to come here. "Perhaps I am distantly related to those who put so much stock in the legend of Shem, but it would surely be stretching the tale to suppose I am in any way connected with the fulfillment of that legend."

Jubah rose and walked toward Abram.

"Would it?" he smiled rather secretively.

"Certainly," Abram objected. "My God is not the god of legend."

"Ah, but that is where you are wrong. Forgive an old man, but do you think this God of whom you speak has never dealt with other men in times past?"

Abram rose and walked toward the kindled fire in the center pit of the room. For long seconds he thought. Abram had never considered this. "No," he said at last. "Do not think me so self-important that I could even hold such an opinion, but I have simply been so engrossed in learning new things about Him that I have never thought of the past in that light."

He walked across the room. Deep in concentration, he said, "Of course, my God must have spoken to others before me. Or why would mankind worship any deity at all? But—" he paused, "how does this relate to the tale of Shem?"

"The tale of Shem is not just a story of a flood and a man who was saved by the gods, nor is it the story of how the gods gave the secret of shipbuilding, as the Phoenician sailors claim. No, Abram, the tale of Noah and Shem is more than all these. It is the story of a man who followed—one God."

"One God?" Abram interrupted, his eyes lit with sudden interest.

"Yes. And according to the story preserved by our little race, that God sent the flood to punish the evil of men. That evil," he paused, "is described in our legend as much like that of Damascus today."

"And in Ur, I am sure," Abram reflected.

"My people believe," Jubah continued, "that this story is much more important than the majority would like to think. Everyone at one time knew the true tale, but it has been so corrupted by time and rumor and by the designs of selfish men who twist it to serve their ideas of deity, that it is barely recognizable. But my people have preserved it." He paused. "Do I sound too boastful, Abram?"

"No, Jubah. You speak with conviction, and if what you say is true, you should be proud. But what of the blessing promised Shem?"

"We have pondered that for many generations. Many Arameans, who have not recognized the importance of their Semitic background, have come and gone. Many nations have risen and fallen, but the promise has not come true. Only recently the younger Semites, including my son, have shown a great urgency in wishing to solve the mystery of the blessing."

Eliezer interrupted, "That is because the worship of Baal has lost its meaning—if it ever had one. There must be something more than what we have."

Abram smiled, for Eliezer's words echoed the thoughts he had had for so many years before the night his God spoke to him.

"This is one reason the priests are so indignant at our refusal to join in the festivals," Eliezer said. "Semites have always been a minority with little impact, but lately we have symbolized a rebellion against established custom, and we are gaining a following. Not only do we symbolize a break with religious practices," he explained, "but we cut across social lines also." Pointing to his robe, he said, "We dress alike, and even you, Abram, were surprised to see the home in which I live."

"Yes, I was," he grinned.

"All of this confounds our royalty and the priests," Eliezer said, perhaps a bit boastfully.

"They fear it?"

"Yes. The blessing promised Shem must be gained," Eliezer insisted. "And we intend to find a way. Even the gate guards, as you saw, are in league with us."

Jubah began again, "Concerning this blessing, Abram, it must come through a Semite, and today, when we heard your words—"

Abram sat down now. "I am beginning to see." For a long period he was silent and then said, "Jubah, all you say fascinates me. It comes so suddenly, though, that I am unprepared to accept or reject it. But I do not see my purpose as that of a political revolutionary."

Jubah walked to Abram's side. "We thought you would feel this way. But please, do not be hasty. Will you not at least stay with us for a few days? Neither do we know your purpose. We only know that your words stir us, like the fresh stirring of long-slumbering chords from the ancient past. They give our people hope, for you are our brother, one of us."

Abram and his people remained in Jubah's house for three days. Of course, they could not venture outside, but their time there was uniquely rewarding. They came to be very close to these citizens of Damascus, growing to love and admire them.

Except for the legend of Shem, which taught of one deity, Jubah, Eliezer, and the other Semites had no concept of the personal God Abram had come to know. They were therefore anxious to learn all they could from him, and late into the night they would listen to Abram tell and retell of his revelation. Indeed, their appetite for knowledge was a great hunger.

Finally, late one evening when Abram was ready to retire, Eliezer took him aside.

Abram felt a great affection for this young zealot, whose youthful sincerity so equaled his own. Eliezer only looked at him with intent, awe-filled eyes, and said, "Sir, I truly believe you are the chosen one who will fulfill the prophecy."

Abram did not know what to say, and when Eliezer had left him, he walked down the corridor to join Sarai.

That night he could not sleep. "Abram, you are disturbed?" Sarai asked.

"Confused, yes. I believe these people mean what they say, but how can I know this is right? That the legend of Shem, which has meant nothing to me before, suddenly should mean everything? How do I know the promise and the call I received are parallel with that given Shem—if that story is true at all?"

"The only way to know is to seek your answer as you did so long ago," Sarai urged.

"I will," he answered, and after Sarai had gone to sleep, he paced the floor long into the night. It was well past midnight when he walked to a casement window, peering into the street below. A heavy darkness shrouded the city, and yet he had not slept.

"My God, I believe You brought me here," he whispered. "Now give me an answer, I pray."

Suddenly, in the court below, he saw torches. The priests again! They were coming to Jubah's house, and within seconds the building echoed from their beating upon the door.

Abram stood back from the window and watched out the corner. Sarai awoke and ran to him trembling. "My lord, what is it?"

He pointed to the priests. "Listen," he said.

A servant had answered the door. "We are to see Master Jubah!" they ordered roughly, pushing their way inside.

"The master is abed."

"Well, awaken him!"

"Yes, sir."

But Jubah had already come downstairs. "What is it? Why are you here at this hour?" he demanded.

"There are rumors you are housing outcasts, the people of Ur, who interrupted our festival!"

Jubah smirked and motioned them to leave. "Rumors, indeed! If you believe a rumor so easily, it gives me all the more reason to question your teachings."

The priests would not be put off that easily, and they ordered their slaves to search the house.

Sarai clutched at Abram. "What are we to do?"

Suddenly the chamber door opened. Abram and Sarai sunk back into the shadows. "Keep still," he whispered.

"Abram?" a voice called softly.

"Oh, Eliezer! Is it you?"

"Yes. Come quickly!"

He hurried them to the ladderway which led to the flat roof of the house.

Quickly they squeezed through the narrow opening, Abram reaching down to pull Sarai up. Lot and the others of the caravan followed one by one, and within what seemed mere seconds, the entire family was huddled together under the stars.

They could hear the priests searching the house. One royal slave came down the corridor just after the trap door had been closed behind the ladder. He had heard the scuffle of their escape and now stood directly under the exit.

The company on the roof felt the inevitable discovery approaching.

The slave below raised a hand to open the trapdoor. No one but he suspected the hiding place. He had hold of the latch, and then—a strange expression lit his face. He lowered his hand, stood for a long, painful moment in lonely silence, and then turned to leave.

A fellow slave entered the corridor, and the company heard him call, "Have you seen them?"

"No. I checked the roof, but there's no sign."

The next day Abram made preparation to leave. He knew they could no longer stay, as their presence would only endanger Jubah and his house.

"My son wishes to go with you, Abram. I have given my consent, if it stands well with you," Jubah said as the company was about to depart.

Abram was pleased to hear this, but he asked, "Couldn't he be of more help here in Damascus?"

"I know my son, Abram," the old man sighed wistfully. "He is a serious activist. He deeply wants to learn from you and—I feel he should experience this."

Abram thought and, turning to go, said, "Very well, then. He is more than welcome." But before leaving, he turned again to the dear friend he had grown to love in three short days. Jubah's face was marked with anticipated loneliness, and Abram placed a warm hand on his shoulder. "You have made a selfless decision, sir. We will take good care of your son," he smiled.

They had to leave at night, rather than risk being seen, and as they passed through the city under Eliezer's direction, the same way they had entered, they encountered no difficulty.

When they left the city gate, they were met by a very large group of men, women, and children, almost seventy-five in all.

"Semites?" Abram asked.

"Yes, sir," Eliezer said, strangely shy. "Sir, I did not know there would be so many."

"It was kind of them to come to see you off."

Eliezer glanced away. "They are not here to see me off, sir. They wish to come also."

Sarai stepped close to Abram, whispering, "This must be your answer."

And the Man of Ur, son of the ninth generation descended from Shem, only smiled broadly.

Chapter X

From the earliest records of Man's voyage on earth, rivers have filled a special place in his destiny.

The fertile crescent mothered his civilizations, and its rivers maintained their potential and abundance. Major cities evolved, without exception, where water ran free or could be channeled without great interference.

Of all the rivers in the ancient world, the Jordan served a very special function. The valley bordering this great river had been the arena of many skirmishes, battles, and even wars over its lush and desirable land.

Long before Abram was to bring his people into the Jordan area, it had been recognized for its strategic importance. Separating the coastal ranges of the Phoenicians and Canaanites from the arid expanses of Syria and the great eastern desert, the Jordan flowed through its deep gorge, weaving with each dip and turn a background for history.

Out of Damascus the caravan, now swelled with members, crept up the arduous, sometimes treacherous incline of the Shenir range. Finding the simplest route into Canaan had been the task of generations of nomads and caravaneers, and the centuries had seen a well-worn road developed, which led through alpine regions resplendent with green.

When Abram stood with his followers on the Shenir pass, nearly three days after leaving Damascus, and first saw that glorious valley as a called Man of God, he did not realize the intimate relationship his name would one day hold with that country. But the panorama had never failed to thrill him.

The company rested when it reached the western slope. The shades of Shenir alpines sheltered the most

abundant variety of plant life the Mesopotamians had
ever encountered. The dark, rich soil was covered with
a mossy undergrowth, and down the slopes, where the
warming sea breezes provided a temperate warmth, an
almost tropical maze of color dominated.

Hardy, sponge-leafed anemones of pale pastels nestled in the crevices of rocks and clung tenaciously to the
roots and trunks of cedars and pines. Delicate alpine vi-
olets, purple and blue, virtually carpeted the less-trod-
den areas and gave royal splendor to the hillsides, as if
cloaked in the robes of a King.

The company ate its noon meal under a great canopy
formed by the spreading arms of ancient oaks. Nearby a
mighty cascade, freshly turned from snow to frigid
water, tumbled unrestrained off Shenir and vaulted
thunderously down a colossal rift in the mountain wall.

From this point the source of the Jordan could be
seen as it might not be seen from anywhere else. The
cascade just described was one of many feeding four
tributaries which descended off Shenir and formed the
River Jordan.

The lay of the land at the foot of Shenir caused the
four cascades to merge, rather than allowing them to
meander in separate directions. The Jordan originated
at the head of a great cleft in the earth's surface, called
El Ghor, which began in the Shenir foothills. Along this
Ghor the Jordan dived and rolled through twenty miles
of fertile mountainous slopes bordering its sides, until it
began to slow, almost ceasing near the thicket called
Sibke, as if to rest before its further trek through the
hotter southern regions of the Chor.

From where the caravan stood on the slopes of the
pass could be seen the city of Laish, later to be known
as Dan, set in the mountains, and drawing its subsis-
tence from fishing and trade. The only other major city
to be readily reached was Hazor, south of Sibke.

Abram chose to go toward Hazor, as it was set on a
plain and more easily accessible. Thus the caravan
would enter Canaan near the thicket.

The trek down the western slopes of the Shenir range exposed a world busy with floral beauty. The rain forest of the northern Ghor was lush enough to nurture the most fragile flowers. The iris and orchid, so rare in more intemperate climates, flourished here.

Near Sibke, where the personality of the river changed from a snow-fed, rapid, swelling stream to a meager, meandering, almost stagnant pond, Abram's company came to rest. With the seventy-five from Damascus, the caravan now numbered nearly one hundred. This was an impressive congregation, though not by any means rivaling those of the pack trains Abram had accompanied in years past.

The Semites of Damascus, in joining Abram's company, had become "his people," their animals his, and all their possessions. No easy decision, then, had accompanied their leaving home. Abram was their master now, though, of course, he did not hold them in any sense against their will, and had they decided to leave, repossessing their goods, they would not have been restrained.

All the respect due the patriarch, the father figure of a tribe, was Abram's. His new people, who had fallen in love with him the day of the festival, willingly followed and obeyed him, and their sense of affection was only strengthened by his liberality.

In all of this, Abram had undertaken a responsibility which would have overwhelmed lesser men. Partly because of past experience as a tradesman, but more due to his innate qualities of leadership, the task had not, so far, offered more than an enriching challenge.

The region near Sibke was not a pleasant place to stay. Not only did the rapid drop off Shenir leave it humid and insect-infested, but it was also littered with debris and trash from generations of itinerant wanderers. This was a stop-off on the way to Hazor and cities farther south: Jericho, Salem and others. Wealthy and poor

alike had camped here for multiplied hundreds of years.
It was like an international crossroads, with diverse cultural references scattered about the grounds. Old pottery
shards were trampled into the ground; bits of scrap
cloth and rope were left behind from tattered tents;
myriads of strange altars, mostly awkward piles of
stone, had been erected in hollows and niches. To the
uneducated eye, each altar was like any other, but to
those who built them, their distinctions were as pronounced as those of the gods to whom they were raised.

When Abram's caravan entered the camp, the bustling activity of many other tribes pervaded the grounds.
Here and there the odor of campfires and roasting meat
greeted them.

By custom, travelers were obliged to treat one another with courtesy, though this often served only as a facade for suspicion. One never knew whom he might encounter along the way, and so he must be on guard. But
the Bedouin custom called for at least the show of hospitality.

The nomad never rejected a fellow traveler in need.
If asked for help, he was bound to give it, even to taking
the stranger in for an established number of days, after
which time he was no longer obliged to care for him,
though he often did.

A visitor received the warmest and most liberal of
blessings from the host. Always a meal was prepared,
and a strong brew, akin to coffee, was offered and gladly accepted. Conversely, the visitor was expected never
to question the contents of the offering and was to return the favor if and when the future posed the opportunity.

In accord with custom, therefore, Abram's company
was greeted by its closest neighbor in camp, the merchant owner of a Phoenecian caravan.

"I am Arphadad of Tyre," the tall man introduced
himself cordially. "I perceive by your speech that you
are of Mesopotamia?"

"Yes. Abram is my name, but most of these people

are from Damascus, as you may have noticed," he answered pointing to the distinctions in dress.

"Then you are a Hebrew?"

The term "Hebrew," or "Habiru," was not new to Abram. It was in common use in these parts, meaning "caravaneer," and designated especially those who traveled in trains, engaging in trade, but who neither were nomads nor claimed a specific citizenship.

"I am," Abram acknowledged. "For the time being, we have no home."

The man of Tyre was undoubtedly a sea merchant, probably inland for only a short time to secure goods. Tyre, a bawdy, brawling sea town was known for its hard-dealing merchants and often ruthless populace. But the tall, slender Arphadad, with his strange pointed, black beard, seemed benign enough.

"My caravan will be here only tonight," he said, "but we have plenty to share. Will you join us?"

Abram was grateful, for he and his people were famished from their journey. They had come all the way from Shenir to Sibke in one day, and now it was very late. The women were too tired to prepare an entire meal adequately.

The conversation was not deep. Arphadad was entirely engrossed in himself and his own dealings. Abram learned much about Tyre and its neighbor, Sidon, that evening, about its industrious shipping market and wealth, about Arphadad's family and aspirations.

When after three hours the host paused, for the moment tired of talking, no word had been asked of his guests as to their purpose in Canaan, or their destination. Abram made ready to leave, bowing low as custom dictated, and saying congenially, "Your hospitality has been most welcome and appreciated. May we do the same for you some day."

Arphadad accompanied him to the door, never guessing at the nature of Abram's journey or the place he would one day hold in history.

"The conversation has been most inspiring," he said. "I am glad you were my guest."

The next morning Abram woke early and rose even before the women, who were generally up and cooking the morning meal before anyone else stirred. He wished to have his people out of the Sibke region before the heat of the day.

In the foggy light of dawn, Abram tiptoed through the camp until he reached the far side of the campgrounds, where he had noticed a semipermanent village of Bedouins. There he hoped to get directions to good pasture for his flocks. The company, having been forced to leave the lush fields of the Damascus area, was now faced with the hard necessity of finding a new home for at least the worst three months of the dry season. Within days that season would be fully upon them. Already, hot winds marked the beginning of each new day.

Near the pond he noticed piles of dried, stripped papyrus plants from which the Bedouin women made a crude paper. The beaten reeds, glued together with resin and rolled flat, became a valuable commodity, which sold for a good price in the cities.

The Bedouin camp was filthy, and a stench rose from the field behind it, where garbage and excrement filled a large, open ditch. The Bedouins themselves were not any more inviting than their surroundings.

Abram came upon a group of young boys tending a herd of lean goats. As he approached, their naturally friendly grins exposed unhealthy teeth, yellowed by the thick, almost pastelike brew so cherished by their race, made of rancid combinations of bitter herbs. They raised their hands in greeting and Abram signaled back.

"Where is the head of this house?" he asked. "I would like to ask directions of him."

The group stood in silent awe of the well-dressed caravaneer. They were not often approached by such as he. For several seconds no one answered, and Abram was about to walk on when one replied, "I will get the master."

He turned quickly, and ran, looking back several times to be sure Abram was real, and then continued until he entered a tent at the edge of the camp.

"Father!" he called loudly enough to awaken the entire camp. "Come and see! A rich merchant, so rich, Father! He wants to see you!"

From inside the tent a grumbling, displeased voice snarled, "Go away, Manata! No more of your idle daydreams. Mama, what shall we do with the boy?"

But something in the lad's persistence must have convinced the father that there was at least a visitor, though not necessarily a wealthy one, for after many long minutes he emerged from the tent and, clearing his eyes of sleep, stumbled into the center of camp.

"Where is this stranger?" he roared. "Who wakes me at this hour?"

But when he fully comprehended that Abram was indeed real, and when he saw the fine woolen clothing he wore, the Bedouin suddenly changed his tone. In a new attitude of submission, he walked shyly to the handsome Man of Ur.

He bowed low, almost scraping the ground, and said, "Welcome to my humble home, Master. How may I be of service?"

Abram had received this gesture before. The wealthy were used to such deference, but the Bedouin's sudden change of voice and behavior somehow struck him humorously, and he smiled warmly, saying, "Pardon me for waking you."

"Oh no, no, sir. Why, I have been up for several hours—yes, I was, in fact, busy with some harnesses in the tent."

"Well, I merely wanted directions for my caravan," Abram said. "We have flocks which need pasture, and very soon."

The Bedouin's look was one of surprise. "Flocks?" he said, wide-eyed. "You have flocks?" Obviously his sleepy mind could not associate such finery as Abram's with herding and flocks. "Ah," he finally mused, "Hebrews, and very wealthy at that," he smiled.

"We are going toward the south. Can you suggest pasturage there?" Abram urged. He wanted the information quickly, for the morning was already coming on, and he was becoming annoyed at the inquisitive Bedouin.

"You would be from Mesopotamia, perhaps Ur?" the Bedouin continued, rubbing his scrubby chin. "You will want to be by a city, I suppose?"

"Perhaps. Do you know of a place?"

The Bedouin had a gleam for profit in his eye.

"Are you prepared to make contracts with a Canaanite?" he asked, looking at Abram's shining pendant.

"If necessary," was his reply.

"My brother has pasture thirty miles north of Jericho. Have you heard of Shechem?"

"Yes." Abram knew of the place, though he had never been there.

"Good pasture. He will rent you a field."

Abram asked his brother's name and then turned to go. Relieved to be leaving the stench of the village, he looked back once to say, "Thank you," and saw several tent flaps close quickly to conceal the faces of Bedouins who had been curiously spying out the wealthy visitor.

Chapter XI

It had been nearly half a year now since Abram had left Ur, and Sarai had become quite accustomed to her role as governess of the train. Her temperment, so docile with Abram, showed a blunter, more commanding aspect when she was overseeing the women of the caravan and displaying her ultimate authority over them. She was more decisive, more exacting under this responsibility than she was in any other role. Mistress Sarai had earned the respect of her servants through quick, sound decisions, and never did the women under her take advantage of her ingrained gentility, for they had learned she had a sharp tongue when necessary.

The people from Damascus did not always mix well with those acquired from Haran. Their interests and sentiments were different, for it is to be remembered that only a few had come from Haran out of loyalty to Abram. Most had come as slaves or hired tenants.

As a result of the differences in ideology, sharp arguments and disagreements sometimes arose, calling for steady, diplomatic interference on the part of Abram and his wife.

The Man of Ur watched in admiration at the strength of will and character Sarai gained from her experiences. Toward him, however, she was never less than respectful and dutiful. This was not her attitude out of obligation, but out of the tremendous love she had for him. He evoked only pleasant feelings from her.

Abram's way with Sarai was equally tender. True, as leader of such a host, he was sometimes necessarily hard and demanding with his followers. His word was law on the train, as surely as if he were a king. The patriarch of any such tribe was the undisputed one, the final arbiter. In joining him, the people had realized this would be so. Not that he was harsh or unyielding, for Abram had learned early in life that to be the true leader of a caravan demanded fair play and devoted ears, ready to hear grievances, and if possible, to rectify injustices. This he did with uncanny wisdom.

But with Sarai, Abram was not the same one who led a caravan, who mastered the respect of strangers, and who preached from the steps of city temples. With her, he was warmer, gentler, more easily influenced than with anyone else life had brought his way.

Sarai realized this. Many times she had looked up from her work at the ovens, where she and the others baked matzo cakes, or from the three-legged kneading troughs, where they prepared the pastelike flour, and there he would be, with a secretive smile, watching her. The daily routine of churning, grinding, and mending then took on a new dimension, a more liberated aspect —a new freedom.

When the train arrived at Hazor, their supplies were running low. But this Canaanite city had a splendid marketplace, and the company went eagerly to barter.

This afternoon, Sarai took her women to the textile merchant. She had been longing for a new bolt of silk and was anxious that she not miss this opportunity to get it.

Leaving Abram and trading on her own was a new experience for Sarai. At home in Ur, servants had handled this, and until now she had relied mainly on Abram's judgment, but she was mastering her position as mistress of the train and her duties as a wife, one of which was, by custom, to select clothing for herself.

There were many merchants in town that day. The marketplace, typically oriental, was boisterous with men and women "calling" their goods.

Sarai, though a bit confused at first, quickly caught on to the tricks of the trade. An easy learner, she soon pointed out the most likely stand for a good bargain and directed her keenest companion to begin. Walking to the small booth, the servant girl began the dealing. Keeping an eye on her mistress, she began by holding out three rings of copper.

Pointing to a high shelf, she said coolly, "This should do for that rather loosely woven purple there."

The short, dark Canaanite who squatted on the ground at her feet rubbed his bearded chin and slyly chuckled, "No, no madam. That is as tightly woven as any you'll find between here and Phoenicia itself. And the dye, why the finest scarlet, from Tyre, mind you." Then, "Six rings at least," he insisted.

The sharp-witted maid looked at Sarai, who stood with her back to the man about three feet away, her arms crossed in feigned disgust.

"Humph," said the servant. "I see you do not wish to sell today." She turned as if she were going to leave, and the merchant spoke again.

"Well, I see you have traveled far, and for such a lovely mistress as yours," he grinned, casting a gleaming eye at Sarai, "I would be cruel to ask more than five rings."

It would have been beneath Sarai's position to converse with the man, so she showed her disapproval by throwing back her raven head in scorn. Her jet-black hair, held up in intricate braids, intertwined with scarlet and gold, glistened in the noonday sun. Such a haughty, regal disdain showed how severely she disliked his offer.

"Mistress will not buy for more than four rings," the maid warned.

The merchant was about to expostulate on this statement when Sarai, realizing the time was ripe, walked forward.

"May she handle the material?" the maid asked.

The merchant, seeing he was about to have his sale, stood up and took the bolt from the shelf, handing it to Sarai. "The finest in Canaan, I'll warrant," he added, his nose crinkling in his sly grin. "You'll find none better!"

Sarai unwound the bolt and held the red-purple transparency to her cheek. Her lovely face peered through it like that of a goddess through clouds at sunset. Draping the material around her bust and slender waist, obviously pleased with the textile, she nodded her head and laid the bolt in her maid's arms.

"Mistress will give four rings," said the servant.

"Four and one bar," the merchant offered.

"You shall have your sale," the maid smiled, and handed the heavy currency to the merchant's scribe, who weighed it in a balance.

While this transpired, Sarai walked away a few feet, still retaining her dignity, but once sufficiently distant from the booth, she asked the maid for the bolt and for long minutes held it to the light, smiling and expounding on its beauty.

During the entire episode, the male eyes of Hazor had watched and admired the princesslike aristocracy of the Chaldean woman. Her olive complexion, fine of texture, her snapping dark eyes commended her to all of them.

And when Abram walked to her side, he was conscious of the good fortune he had in her.

Chapter XII

Leaving Hazor and traveling still south, the Jordan became rapid and free and then slow and sluggish again, emptying after ten miles into the fifteen-mile-long Lake Chinneroth. This vast reservoir, later to become famous as the Sea of Galilee, nestled between pleasant hills and valleys, still fertile but not so resplendent in green as those farther north.

From the elevated slopes above the lake could be seen mighty Mount Tabor, like a sentinel at the southeast boundary.

Dropping off from the hilly regions surrounding the lake, the land led easily downward until Abram's company skirted the very edge of the azure water.

Evening of the next day was near when the caravan came to rest under palms clustered by the lapping water. Abram was physically worn. The responsibility he shouldered, added to the sheer exertion of travel, had chafed his nerves and blunted his enthusiasm.

He left the tent where he had just told Sarai, "I am going out for a little while. Would you like to walk with me?"

Sarai could see the weariness written on his face. She knew he asked her out of love and that he really wished to be alone with his own thoughts.

"No, my lord," she answered. "Please go alone, if you don't mind. I'll just rest here; I'm so weary."

He went several hundred feet up the beach and found a shady, solitary spot to sit. Looking back at the train, his fatigued mind was somewhat shaken by the load of responsibility it symbolized.

From where he sat, the train looked peaceful enough. The camels, freed of their cumbersome saddles and harnesses, lay in the cool sand, occasionally letting out one of their strange, unearthly bleats, this time of contentment and not of their usual ill temper. The saddles were piled neatly in colorful stacks, the crimson and gold of the blankets and harnesses adding a glow of color. The central tents had been erected; first those of Abram, Sarai, Lot, and Eliezer, and around these, in a crude circle, the others, now being lifted.

The pack animals were at rest. The evening was lazy and the soft music of Dari's pipe lent a somewhat languid, slow note to the air.

But as Abram watched his people build their fires and saw the women busily preparing the evening meal, the many children hanging on their skirts, deep thoughts filled his mind.

He felt very much alone. Even if Sarai had come with him, he would have done the speaking and she the listening, as always. But tonight he had nothing to say. For the first time, he felt the need to have her equal partnership in faith. He had always led her. Now he wished she were independent enough in the knowledge of God to bolster him, but this was not yet probable.

He stood and walked to the lakeside. Picking up a handful of pebbles, he skipped them, one after another, across the water. Scarcely conscious of his action, he thought of his people, his destiny and theirs.

A warm sea breeze blew off Chinneroth. Often those breezes became sudden gales, abruptly turning the serene lake into a churning storm of water. But tonight, the sea was warm, gentle as a good woman. The pipe's tune, blending with Abram's thoughts, suddenly took on a rather sad, lonely, and haunting note, much like— what was it? He tried to recall where that feeling had been evoked in him before.

Yes, the lone wolf—the one he had heard wailing the night of his Call . . . that was the same sound.

At least this was how it struck him, though the young piper may not intentionally have inspired his music with that quality.

Nearly ten days had passed since the party had fled Damascus. They had traveled almost one hundred miles, and that through steep uplands with flocks and children. This was tremendous speed, but it had been necessary and would continue to be so if they were to reach a permanent camp before the dry season.

This urgency had allowed little time for real communication between him and his people. With the squabbles between those of Haran and Damascus, he had done little but arbitrate since entering Canaan.

The evening was young, and he knew that if he were to lead the caravan intelligently, he had to be alone for a while.

His was a singular mood. Partially because of fatigue, the strangest sense of depression had come over him. It was a feeling akin to loneliness, he thought, much like what he had felt when his father died and he had known he must leave Haran.

His mind wandered back to Ur. Somehow it seemed as though years and years had passed since he had left there. How could six months be filled with so much to change a man's life, his philosophy, his dreams?

Had it all really happened? Had the Guti come? Had his father beaten him? Had he seen Terah a crushed and broken man at the temple steps? Had his brother Haran died? Had his father—was he gone?

And what of Abram? Had he once been a citizen of Ur, a devotee of trade and profit, a follower of Nannar?

All this was like another life to him now, not so long ago in the sands of time, but unbelievably distant in thought and portent.

How alien and strange would his present circumstances have seemed had he seen them through some vision years before. A great gap now separated him from that life, as surely as the mountains and plains separated him from Ur. But as he recalled the past, and then looked at his people now, he felt as one might feel who had stepped into some great void in time, a warp in space, a vacuum with no sure foothold.

Those people over there: were they really depending on him? Who were they and who was he? Was he doing right to gain the trust and devotion of two young men like Lot and Eliezer, leading them in his paternal footsteps, when he had questions of his own? And what of the youth Dari? Abram sensed his trustful worship from afar, like that of a little shadow afraid of interrupting the image he simulated.

This was the root of the loneliness he now felt. It was that unique emotion common to those few, selected from among the millions born to Earth, who are destined to lead. It was an awesome, soul-shattering feeling, a sense of unworthiness, of inadequacy known only to the greatest among men.

It was that feeling which tested them, which separated them from those who only fancied themselves leaders, but who by their false sense of security and self-pride never developed a true courage.

It was a feeling of fear, the fear necessary to purify and temper a leader, fear which brings him to his knees in humility, realizing that he is unequal to the task, but that his willingness is the threshold of his strength.

As Abram stood alone at the edge of the lake, the sun slowly rolled down the western ridge behind him, leaving a red glow on the surface of the water. Abram felt an urgency to isolate his feeling of dread and depression, to categorize it neatly in his mind so he might understand and thus overcome it.

"Lord," he whispered, "I am so lonely, fearful of the future. When I remember my father, my brothers, my homeland, I feel deserted, solitary, empty. Thank You for Sarai, God. Without her, I could not go on. But the others, those whom You have given me, add strangely to my loneliness, instead of filling the void I feel. And even Sarai does not understand my feelings for You. She relies on me for her faith—if only she might know You as I do." He dwelt on this for some time. If only Sarai might fully share his feelings, at least he would be able to talk out his doubts and receive a measure of support.

"God, how can I feel lonely if You are real?" he said, a thick lump in his throat. "And here I am, again, questioning Your reality. Oh—help my faith, my God!"

Disgusted with his doubts, Abram could not understand the all too human aspect of himself which demanded frequent reminders that God is real. But his God understood, and waiting for those last words, "Help my faith," began the process.

Abram found his thoughts suddenly transported to the scenes of success and providence which had recently been his. The escape from Ur, the words of his brother Nahor—"Will he speak to me as well?"—the gathering at the temple steps for his speech in Damascus, the seventy-five who had joined him, and of course, the first words of his God on a similar night months before.

Abram relaxed a little. The tension was going. He was stepping out of that warp in time. But something still was missing. The picture was not complete, for he did not know *where* to step.

He envisioned trackless expanses of wasteland. In his mind flashed scenes of continual travel, like the wandering of the ghost ships spoken of in Phoenician legends.

"God, this is my feeling of loneliness. It is the wanderer's feeling. What good is a purpose if it is a homeless, groundless one, one with no end in sight, but to travel and seek its fulfillment forever?"

This was it. His feeling was a fear, an insecurity based on a sense of aimlessness. He knew his purpose, however vaguely; he knew, perhaps, his destiny—but not his home.

"Man needs a home, God. Even a Hebrew needs a home," he sighed sadly.

Above him, the warm Personality which had reached him long ago seemed to smile and say, "I know, Abram of Ur; I know. I was waiting for you to ask."

Chapter XIII

It was not to be long after this that Abram's fear of eternal wandering would be somewhat calmed.

Leaving Chinneroth, the company was obliged to travel about forty miles through hilly plains before reaching Shechem. There they would secure a long-range contract with the Canaanite to whom they had been directed and would pitch their tents on the plain of Moreh, famed for its strange grey humps of sandy earth and abundant grasslands.

On leaving Chinneroth, the southern view exposed the whitish slopes of the Carmel range, over which armies had entered and left Canaan for centuries, looting and conquering, leveling and raising civilization upon civilization in their conquests. Then came the boundless tracks of plains, and after three days, such a welcome sight Shechem was! Once no more than a nomadic stopoff, it had grown to a sizable town, though still mainly populated by transients. It was situated midway between Chinneroth and the Great Salt Sea, the ignoble end of the River Jordan. But here at Shechem, before emptying into that vast mineral bath, the Jordan meandered, fourteen miles wide, through the odd, dunelike protrusions of dusty earth.

The Jordan here was swampy, thicketlike, with jungle undergrowth in profusion along its shores. This area, while not aesthetically pleasing, was the most ideal herding land in Canaan. The Zor, as this region was often called, provided calm waters in abundance and miles of uninterrupted grassy plains.

The day the contract was signed was a busy one. The camp must be entirely settled, each servant and member undertaking his duties efficiently, before this could be savored as "home," temporary as that apellation might be.

Directly to the southwest, not more than a mile from Abram's camp, was Mount Gerizim. Upon establishing a home base, the shepherds of Abram's tribe took the flocks into the gentle foothills of that mountain and thus began a many months' homesteading of the area.

It was approaching noon of the second day when Abram felt everything was running sufficiently smoothly that he might walk to Mount Gerizim and survey the region.

Leaving Lot, Sarai, and Eliezer to oversee further activities, he took a long staff and began the hike. The sun would have been intolerable save for a cooling breeze which blew in from the direction of the sea.

Abram passed his flocks, taking in the pastoral serenity like a balm. The sheep were not all white. There were some reddish and some black, and the rams bore long horns. Here and there speckled or striped sheep grazed, though these were few in such a fine selection as his wealth allowed.

Low trees provided food, the sheep and goats often preferring the succulent leaves to their normal diet of bristly grass.

Abram's shepherds were accompanied by dogs, medium-sized for the most part, and of no particular breed. But they were well trained in herding and maneuvering the sheep.

The Canaanite's field was provided with a sizable sheepfold, four low walls with no ceiling and an open doorway, across which one shepherd lay at night, his body serving as a barrier to any intruder.

The shepherds were of all ages, but many young boys were employed, and as Abram passed, one group waved happily, obviously content with their task.

Near the group, Dari stood on sentry duty, his staff in his hand. His bread sack, tied to a short pole, rested on a rock nearby. Under his left arm his long, crescent-shaped water bottle was slung by a shoulder strap.

Abram had placed him in control of all the young shepherds because of his experience and reliability, and of this Dari was very proud.

"Good to rest at last, isn't it?" Abram called, and all smiled in agreement.

Abram was at peace today. Something in what he had asked of the Lord that night at Chinneroth comforted him. He had received no answer, no revelation, just a calm—a peace in his heart. Still, he longed for a home, or the knowledge of a place destined to be his. "Man needs a home," he had said.

But no longer did those words ring hollow in his ears. They seemed to be pregnant with fulfillment, and he knew, as surely as he was walking to Gerizim, that his God had an answer for him. He was not even anxious to know when and how that answer would come. The sure knowledge that it *would* come was a comfort.

And so it was not with a sense of anxiety that he climbed the slopes this noonday. His mind was, in fact, void of concrete thought of any kind. He was simply savoring the freedom of his hike, his strong legs carrying him higher and higher toward a ridge where he would see a good vista.

"Ah," he sighed, resting on a jutting ledge. The hike had felt good. The sun seared the vault of blue above him, and a circle of crows or blackbirds hovered and dipped over the river. In deep silence Abram sat, lightly musing at the vast resources still untapped in the giant hollow below. So this was Jordan Valley proper.

His eye took in the splendor of the green Ghor, the silver ribbon stretching through it limitlessly until lost to sight within the folds of the northern hills. The Salt Sea, variously known as the Dead Sea, the Sea of the Plain, or the Gulf of Arabah, could be seen on a clear day such as this, but even so, only the uppermost tip was visible.

Long moments of solitude passed. The beauty of the Creator's handiwork awed him. But as he surveyed the panorama, a strange sense of inexplicable anticipation seemed to grip him, an almost physical urgency rushed his heartbeat. Only seconds later, a snapping noise, like the footfall of some creature, jolted his keen hearing. A chill ran up his spine. Fearful to make a sudden move, he sat riveted to the ledge, only slowly turning his head.

"Abram," a voice spoke softly.

This was no illusion! Abram jumped to his feet, sending a small avalanche of rocks down the mountainside.

"Who is it?" he called hoarsely.

He saw no one at first. The voice and sound of the footstep had come from higher up on the face of the slope. He strained his eyes upward, bracing himself against a ledge so as not to lose his balance.

Yes, there was someone up there, standing near a clump of mountain berry vines. He was a tall, strong person, and from what Abram could see at this distance, he was clothed in undyed wool, though this was not clear.

"Who are you?" Abram called. "Did you speak my name?"

The figure on the hillside came a few steps downward and then seemed to motion for Abram to draw near.

"Not so, unless you identify yourself!" he called.

The stranger above stood quietly for several long seconds and then, leaning forward, placing his left hand on one knee to brace himself, he brought his right arm across his chest in a wide arc as if to span the entire valley.

Abram had not taken his eyes off the stranger, but so compelling was this gesture that he could not keep from turning to view that expanse with him.

But while Abram stood alone, gazing at the valley, the stranger came a few feet closer and said, "Abram, unto thy seed will I give this land."

Abram wheeled about. Had he heard that right? Who was this man—? Straining his eyes to the spot he had last seen him, Abram was chilled with fear.

There was no one there, and no place he could have gone.

Abram's knees grew weak. His flesh tingled with a strange sensation of dread, his hands suddenly blue with chill, despite the noonday heat. He took two rigid but hesitant steps backward. His legs, barely able to support him, sank shakily to the ground, and a tumult of emotion whipped at his mind. Could it be true, what he had seen?

Awe and a strange, all-pervading wonder flooded his soul. But dread was dominant, and it was only after many minutes, and with slowly returning strength, that he hiked with great but halting strides to the place where the stranger had stood. Trembling in fear of approaching too closely, he simply stood, his eyes fixed for what might have been an eternity on the vacant and hallowed ground, allowing the realization of what had happened to dawn on his receptive mind.

And from deep within the recesses of his soul came one sound, barely audible, "Lord?" he whispered, as if to recall Him with a word. Tears began slowly, flowing uninterrupted down his face and into his beard, his arms outstretched pleadingly before him as a thrill of incredulity surged through him.

"If only—no—it cannot be," he reasoned. "If only I had gone to His side when He called me," he whispered, "I could have seen Him more clearly. I could have—"

A shudder wrenched him. "I could have touched Him!"

His heart pounding audibly, his body quivering with fear and devotion, he did the only thing he knew to do. In solemn ceremony, he picked up one large rock after another, placing them silently atop each other until he had erected a low, crude altar. And when he had finished, he bent over the stone monument, embracing it in humility and awesome love, and there he unashamedly wept.

As the intimate silence slowly lapsed, Abram's spirit was gradually quieted and uplifted. No longer fearful, but still awed, he rose and looked again on the place of the encounter.

Straightening his shoulders, a new freedom, a sense of liberty, and magnificent enthusiasm gripped him. He must tell someone! He must shout it to the world, to the universe—"I have seen God!"

Turning to fly, he left the scene, looking back only once, as if to preserve forever the mark of that experience indelibly on his heart. And then the wonder, the inscrutable, incomprehensible wonder of what had happened—the urgent desire to tell it—bore him like an arrow, down, down the mountain; now sliding on a bed of shale, oblivious to bruises, cuts; his robes catching and tearing on the jutting rocks; his cloak slapping wildly; the wind whipping his face and hair—he ran exultant toward the valley.

With each step, each leap over the obstacles in his path, his heart and mind echoed, "I have seen Him! I have seen the Lord!"

From the valley floor, the group of complacent, gentle shepherds looked up in astonishment. "Look! It is Abram!" Dari shouted. "Look how he runs!"

"What can it mean?" asked another. "Is he pursued?"

"I see nothing behind him!" one offered.

"But see how he waves his arms!"

Abram was propelled past them by the sheer speed of his descent, and as they followed in chase, burning with curiosity, he shouted, laughed, exultant and free, "Praise God! Praise Him, all you people! For this land is ours!"

They had no time to question, following at an absurd pace, sweeping up a larger and larger following from the fields.

Lot and Eliezer jumped up from their work in camp, hearing the onrushing mob, and shock etched their faces at the strange sight of their beloved uncle and master.

By the time Abram reached camp, the entire congregation was gathered in wild confusion.

"What is it?" they cried. "Abram, what has happened?"

And with the concern of a son, Lot ran to Abram. "Uncle, is anything wrong?"

Eliezer clutched his master's sleeve. "Sir, what is it?" he pleaded.

Abram's face told only of his joy and ecstasy but they quickly caught the electrifying fever of his zeal, even though ignorant of its source.

Barely could he find his way through the jostling mob which reached for him from all sides, hungry with curiosity.

Finally, he saw his objective—

Sarai stood alone on the edge of the crowd, and when the people saw that Abram would not speak until he found her, they let him pass.

The mob was now silent in anticipation, Lot and Eliezer holding them back.

With radiant face Abram, in complete, joyous exhaustion, knelt at Sarai's feet, and flushed and jubilant, embraced her legs.

She bent down to him, holding his face in her hands, and listened in awe.

"Sarai, I have seen Him—I have seen the Lord!"

PART III

Famine
ฬฬฬฬฬฬ

If any of you lack wisdom, let him ask of God. . . .
But let him ask in faith, nothing wavering. For he
that wavereth is like a wave of the sea driven
with the wind and tossed.

James 1:5,6

Chapter I

After three months had passed, the field Abram had rented was nearly devoid of grass. It seemed a peculiarly arid season, even for the time of year—much drier than usual.

When the contract expired, Abram decided to take his people farther south toward the Salt Sea. At least there would be more chance of streams and waterholes nearer the lake. He also had heard that there was unclaimed land to be had freely there, if one sought it out, and this he intended to do. If God had promised him this land, he would no longer sign contracts unless necessary.

The day they took up their tents to leave, the spirit of the camp was at a zenith. Ever since Abram had returned from Gerizim with his news, which, of course, ultimately concerned all his followers, a keen sense of destiny and purpose had pervaded the company. Old and young, man and woman had been rewarded in the promise. They had new confidence in the providence of their decision to follow Abram. And· they had taken new hope in the legend of Shem, which had promised an inheritance beyond measure to his descendants.

As they passed through Shechem for supplies before going into unknown parts, they came to a large, brilliantly colored tent on the outskirts of the village. Here was the home of the famed sorcerer of Shechem.

Abram had heard of his wizardry and fortunetelling for many years, though he had never been here in his travels. The old man was reputed to be uncanny in his ability to see the future.

Perhaps the people of the caravan would have stopped to seek him out, had they not newly come out of Baal worship. But he was a Canaanite of Canaanites and attributed all his powers to that dark diety.

They passed his tent door without so much as slowing, except for a few servants of Haran, who looked that way in curiosity, hoping to see him.

The tent was indeed a masterpiece in attraction. Embroidered on the sides were strange emblems symbolic of the stars, the sun, and the deities associated with them. These, for the most part, were done in heavy black tapestry, while the banners flapping in the breeze atop the tent were scarlet and gold. The tent itself was woven in wide stripes, each of a different color.

When the company was nearly past the tent, the sorcerer, hearing the trampling of feet, came to the doorway and pulled back the flap. He was an awesome figure, though very, very old, and was dressed from head to toe in heavy, ebon robes.

He instantly caught the eyes of some in the train, and they stopped, staring in silence. Slowly the entire company, realizing some of its members were missing, came to a halt.

It was too late now. Even Abram could not stop the servants in time. Responding to the sorcerer's beckoning, a group of them went to his tent.

He smiled keenly and nodded his covered head in approval, the golden tassels on the edge of his hood shimmering as he did so. He bent his wrinkled lips to the ear of one servant and whispered something. Whatever it was, the servant became white with apparent fright.

This was all that happened. The Wizard of Baal then disappeared into the dark cave of his tent, and the servant rejoined his gawking friends, walking back to the caravan amid pleas of, "Tell us what he said. Oh, tell us, tell us! What did he say?"

Abram anxiously pushed his way back to the group of servants. "That will do!" he shouted. "On this train there is no consorting with false gods! Baal is not to be entertained here!"

But, the servant had already told his friends the message, and they stood speechlessly numb, looking pale and barely hearing Abram's words.

"But sir," one of them finally responded. "Don't you wish to hear what he said?"

Abram could see by their faces that the wizard's words concerned himself. For a moment he hesitated, curious and indeed a bit apprehensive of what the news might be. He had more reason to believe the sorcerer had powers, than to disbelieve. It was all too commonly known that the Wizard of Shechem was a diviner of some magnitude.

And even Abram, who believed in the One God, had no reason to think there were not other powers in the universe, lesser in strength but not powerless.

But he answered at last, "I will not listen to the voice of the demon Baal, who would establish himself as a god! There is but one God, and if there be other powers, they are subordinate to Him!"

Abram turned to leave, but the servants ran to him and one anxiously pleaded, "Master, may I inquire, are we going very far south?"

Abram stopped and looked at him quizzically. "Speak, man! What kind of question is that?"

"The Canaanite—" he paused, fearful of being rebuked.

"Speak! Get the nonsense out once and be done with it, if you must," Abram demanded, knowing it would be voiced eventually anyway. "What did the Canaanite say?"

"He said, sir, that 'to follow Abram'—he called you by name, sir—how would he know your name?"

"Go on," Abram was now curious indeed.

"He said, 'To follow Abram is to follow the way to—to death.'" With this the servant shuddered again.

Abram thought for some seconds, his mind a frenzy of conflicts. God was his leader, but the sorcerer was not of small reputation.

However, Abram at last lifted his head and straightened his shoulders, saying loudly, "People, hear me!

My God leads us! We will not bend the knee to Baal, to hear or heed his words! Our God needs no spokesman of Baal to carry His messages."

A murmur went through the camp, all eyes on the Master of Ur as he walked again to the front of the company, and it was in doubtful silence that they resumed their journey southward.

Chapter II

The land of the Canaaites extended all the way along the western border of the Dead Sea. It was not going to be easy to find uncontracted land. It was not until nearly a week after leaving Shechem that Abram at last received directions to a small town called Hai, on the west side of which, he was told, would be free territory.

Hai was a hamlet set in the mountain country of the Dead Sea plateau. One of its distant neighbors was the infamous Jericho, strangely a stronghold of moon worship in this land of Baal. Abram's company would not need to have dealings with the city, however, if they could find their own sustenance.

And happily they did.

Outside Hai, on the west, was a delightful, sloping grassland which blended into the heights of rocky ridges ribboned with wadis. After due inspection Abram brought his caravan to this field and established his property.

The right of primary claim made it his as long as he sojourned there. If challenged, however, he would have to defend his property to the point of combat or give it up to a stronger claimant. It was not likely that his right would be challenged, though, as this was back country, not heavily populated, and should other tribes pass by, they would have to be sizable to challenge Abram's one hundred.

When the company settled here, their fears of the sorcerer's warning began to subside. Such a pleasant domain this was, with a shallow but clear stream flowing through the rocky gully, and cool patches of grass robing the ravines. It was a refuge of fertility in an otherwise semiarid land, and higher on the slopes, the

grass was more abundant than below. Small scrub oak
and leafy bushes completed the scene, the shepherd's
ideal of pastoral beauty.

Here, then, they pitched their tents in a circle, forming a sheepfold at night, and during the days the shepherds took their flocks far back into the hill country,
where the stream watered the parched earth.

The terrain of this camp was much more rugged than
that of Shechem. Erosion had eaten pockets and rifts
into the earth's face. Its beauty was of a different sort
from that of the forestlands of the upper valley or the
rolling hills near Gerizim, but there was a mountain,
and it was to this high ground that Abram took his people the day of the settlement. In gratitude for their new
homeland and for pastureland, the one hundred followed Abram's lead and watched as he repeated, sym-
bolically for them, the building of the altar and instruct-
ed them to thank the Lord in prayer.

This had become customary for them ever since his
return from Gerizim. They would gather in a group at
the foot of an incline, much as they had at the temple
steps that day in Damascus. Abram's God was no
longer Abram's alone, but more and more surely theirs,
individually, personally, and they looked forward to the
altars of prayer. The first few times he had led his congregation in this fashion, they had only watched him
and then awkwardly followed his example, raising their
hands in adoration and repeating after him: "The Lord
our God is One God; there is none other besides Him."

Their ceremonies, in outward form perhaps similar to
the altar rituals of Baal, Nannar, or a thousand other
deities, grew to be a much-anticipated source of renewal
and reenergizing. They were simple rites, but rich with
meaning for these men and women. In childlike faith
they knew God was the only God, real and living and
with a purpose for them.

And how else could they worship Him but with the
form of custom and hearts of human love? Their faith

consisted in no more or less than this, and was as tangible as the flocks they accompanied.

Over the period of nearly four months since Abram had taken his caravan out of Damascus, he had grown to love and live for his people. He was truly the patriarch of the tribe, and though only very vaguely related through blood ties, he was as surely their father in spirit as any tribal chief. All ages and personalities composed this group. There were some older ones for whom leaving Damascus had meant leaving more than half a century of experience . . . but these were few. The caravan was made up mostly of young, independent-minded Semites, men and women, many with families, eager and zealous for the reformation of their city, but convinced that Abram's words were words of truth and life.

It was this youthful enthusiasm which bolstered and encouraged them and which won Abram's heart. Heavy was the load of responsibility he shouldered, but it was always rewarded in their growth and devotion to himself and their Lord.

Lot and Eliezer were among those who blessed Abram most, and Abram daily grew closer to his nephew and the young leader from Damascus. With a kinship of heart as strong as any father's, Abram would think of them as sons until blessed with his own.

Sarai, of course, held a special place in God's purpose. The land had been designated the inheritance of Bram's seed, and if the promise were to be fulfilled, she would mother that nation. Before, on the steppes north of Damascus, Abram had spoken to her of their children, and that night she had seen a fragment of God's love in Abram's words, "You are one with me."

Since his experience on Gerizim, however, her faith had become even stronger, more surely grounded than ever before.

One evening after the camp was settled, she came to Abram, her face radiant with happiness.

"What is it?" Abram smiled.

"Oh, husband, I have been alone by the brook, meditating."

"On what?"

"I was watching the women of the train with their little ones, and I began thinking of the sons we will one day have, and of the daughters we will cherish." Her eyes beamed with feminine fervor.

She sat by him and nestled her head on his arm. "Do you remember the night you told me we would one day be like the forests of Palestine?"

" 'Abundant with good things,' didn't I say?" he reminisced.

"Yes, my lord."

He was surprised she had held so tenaciously to those words.

"Oh, Abram," she went on, "the Lord has blessed me tonight. When I was alone, I thought of our little ones, our children." Her eyes brightened at the word.

Such a precious possession children were to the people and cultures of the ancient world. Words would have been inadequate to paint a picture of the desire and value placed on them and especially on sons to carry on and protect the family name.

A child was likened in value, so said their proverbs, to much fine gold, or youth in old age—to the very essence of prosperity and the very meaning of life itself.

A man with no children, or a woman who bore him none, was shamed, marked, and even suspect. And so barrenness in women or impotence in men was a curse more surely dreaded than death itself.

But such joy children brought with them! The moment of conception was sacred and tender; the moment of birth hallowed and revered; and the moment of death, a cause for passing on of blessings and legacies to the younger and future generation.

The vision of the time lay with the future, the hope with the children, and a man's life, no matter how vile, was not without worth if he had left children to carry it on, to right its wrongs, and to remember him.

"Children—" Sarai whispered again. "My lord, I have never felt as I do. I am sure I feel nearly as you did the night our God first spoke to you. I feel He has spoken this night to me as well."

Abram cradled her head on his shoulder in silent gratitude. Communing with his Lord, he thought, "Thank You. How many times have I longed for this moment. At last You are *our* God, and not mine alone."

Chapter III

There were seeds of discontent lying dormant, untouched as yet by the rains of adversity which would bring them to life. For all the manifest faith and devotion which the people of Abram's train sincerely felt, there were still those who harbored doubts from the words of the Wizard of Shechem. It was not soon to be forgotten that he had warned against following Abram. While the tribe had rested in plenty for several weeks at Beth-El, their campsite, it would take only a hint at that prophecy's fulfillment to shake the trust of many, for this was the encampment of a very new and very spontaneous faith.

Even their leader's trust in God relied more on spectacular revelation than he realized. This company's faith, then, was that of the newborn, dependent on the milk of experiential evidence, not yet challenged by the tough meat of distress.

And the meat which was finally laid before them was privation, a famine which came to sift them like wheat, to separate the chaff from the kernels, the truly faithful ones ready for maturity, from the weakling infants who would not long survive a spiritual drought.

The unusually dry season did not relent even when the rains should have begun. Several weeks passed and still the rains did not come. It seemed that the dry spell which had forced them out of Shechem was now about to leave Beth-El a parched and barren wasteland.

Day by day the shepherds took their flocks to the still waters of the brook, which seemed to grow more and more shallow, sluggish, and niggardly. Like a slowly wasting invalid, it subsided, until the stream bed hung out from its sides like wrinkled tissues, hungry for its life's blood.

Abram watched with deep apprehension the decline of his property. Each morning would find him up at dawn pacing the pastureland, seeking fresh grass for his hungry flocks, looking high above him for signs of rain, and then returning, downcast, to his waking people.

One morning Lot joined him. He had seen the growing fear in his uncle's eyes but had never verbalized his awareness. He knew Abram was hoping for a reprieve in the weather and that he feared exposing his doubts to his people lest they should grow needlessly anxious.

But it could no longer be hidden. The circumstances were no less real because they were not voiced. Lot must go to his uncle to ease the burden, if only with a listening ear.

That morning he left the tent and walked across the broad field. He thought he saw Abram far off in the grey morning light, at the far end of the pasture.

Passing the sleeping shepherds, he waved to the few sentries who stood their watch. "Is that my uncle?" he called very softly, pointing to the dark figure far away. Receiving an affirmative nod, he made his way there.

Abram did not hear him approach. He had never known a man like him, so much like his own father, but, and this was difficult to admit, even more admirable.

His uncle was bent over, studying the grass, running his fingers through its parched blades as one might pass them through the hair of a dying friend. He stood up now, holding a clod of dry dirt in his hand, crumbling it into dusty, lifeless fragments and wiping the residue on his cloak.

"God," he mouthed, "what are we to do?"

Lot, fearful of interrupting his uncle's solitude, stepped forward quietly and said, "Uncle, good morning."

Abram turned in surprise. "Oh, Lot," he smiled, as if

to cover up his thoughts. "Such an early riser. Did you sleep well?"

Lot feigned humor. "You speak of early risers as if you sleep until midday." He walked about for a few seconds, breathing deeply. "What a morning, Uncle! I'll have to join you each day to see the world before it wakes." Then turning to him, he asked, "I suppose that is why you are out here—to see the dawn?"

Abram's face was intent. "Of course."

"Uncle," Lot opened, "I could not help seeing you study the grass."

"Yes," Abram answered.

"You are concerned with the conditions," Lot interjected.

Abram hesitated. With a sigh, as if somewhat relieved to discuss finally what he had borne alone for many days, he said, "It will do no good to hide my fears, Lot. You have grown up and lived among nomads. You have seen the destruction and torment of famine. You know our land is suffering—deeply suffering, don't you?"

"Yes, sir," he sighed.

"Do you see any hope here, Lot?"

"Uncle, I have seen dry spells which seem interminable, and which suddenly break in a torrent. Perhaps—"

"I have hoped for that, Lot. I have hoped and prayed for that for weeks now, and—you see the results."

Lot looked for words of encouragement. "Sir, could it be that we are to move on?"

"Toward the south?"

"Yes, sir."

Abram smiled. "You don't fear the words of the sorcerer?"

Lot grinned broadly. "I believe your God is mightier than the words of a Canaanite spokesman for a false god," he beamed.

Abram placed his arm around his nephew's shoulder, and they returned to camp.

"Let's hope the others share your faith, Lot," he smiled.

But that hope was ill rewarded. When Abram called his followers together that night to inform them of his plans to go into Egypt, a murmur of fearful apprehension coursed through the crowd.

"Do you place your faith in the words of Baal?" he demanded.

The audience, confused, only responded in silence. But one, more outspoken, finally stepped out from the gathering and challenged, "Abram, we do trust in the One God, but has He led you to choose the southlands? If He has, say so, and we will not question you further."

Abram, feeling suddenly very much alone, looked at Eliezer, Lot and Sarai, who stood to one side. Gaining confidence from their trust, he stood tall and continued, "The northern reaches have already been closed to us. This plot of land is also dying, and I would be a poor patron of my people to keep them here with no sign of renewal. I believe our God can speak as eloquently in silence as He does in thunderings."

The crowd was mute. The man who had challenged him stepped quietly back into the congregation, and Abram said bravely, "We will leave in the morning. We will go into Egypt. God is with us!"

Chapter IV

The first step in the two-hundred-fifty-mile journey to the land of the Nile was the outpost of Beersheba. They were some miles from the town and had traveled for four days, but Abram was determined to reach it before nightfall. Along the road he found his train blending with a stream of many other urgent travelers fleeing the famine. But with the lights of the city came apprehension. This was the last populated area on the way to Egypt. Beyond lay two hundred miles of Negeb, a little-watered no-man's land, good in normal seasons for grazing but probably quite worthless now.

If they did not secure enough supplies before entering that expanse, their chances of survival were dim. Dozens of caravans had been through Beersheba before Abram's that day, and the supplies were extremely low. Merchants who had set up booths in the marketplace were profiting well from the trade the famine brought.

Like so many vultures, they sat perched behind their wares, eagerly making the most of the demands. Their prices had been doubled and tripled, and of course they kept sufficient supplies in reserve so their own families could fold shop and make their escape from the drought in due time.

The market was abustle with patrons from all over the eastern world, and the plaza rang with the incomprehensible chatter of a hundred dialects. The mood of the throng was not, however, typical of the usually festive gathering place. A tone of anxiety underlay all bargainings, and the pleas of hungry children, the wailings of thirsty infants tightened and irritated every nerve.

Even Abram's wealth brought only meager rations. His servants had done their best, but even he and Lot had not been able to secure more than a third of what would be comfortable supplies.

That evening, Lot, Eliezer, and Abram figured and refigured the rations, and when they retired, it was in strained faith that they smiled, "God is with us."

Abram went to Sarai's chamber. His eyes were vacant and she reached for his hand.

"My lord, things are not well, are they?"

He only shook his head.

She mused to herself how much he really needed her —her husband, so capable and strong. And yet now he felt the load of the world pressing him, though he would not wish her to know it.

She drew him to her and kissed him warmly.

The rains did not come. On the anniversary of his call, Abram's people were somewhere in the depths of the wastelands one day to be called the Wilderness of Judah.

They had traveled for weeks on sustenance ample enough to keep them and their flocks alive, but no more. Besides the incredibly small rations they had bought at Beersheba, desert herbs were their only food.

The terraces of the wilderness which dropped off toward the Dead Sea provided little watershed in good season, to say nothing of these circumstances. The fruits of the earth in the ancient world depended so directly on the few large springs and small rivers available that the slightest withholding of seasonal rains was sufficient to throw entire nations under the paralyzing hand of starvation.

The limited supply of water now left was not even enough to irrigate the level lands, and so the large cities, as well as the small towns and wandering Bedouin tribes, were feeling the awesome inescapability of drought.

Even if there had been localities of abundance, the inefficient methods of transit were so awkward and slow that it would have been impossible to relieve those devoid of sustenance. All of Canaan, then, was gripped in the grim jaws of famine, which would last for many months.

The place of Abram's encampment now was on a rolling, treeless plain, crowned with bare rock, ripped by canyons, gorges and strange, jagged protrusions of stone. Abram walked through the camp alone, feeling much as Hebron must have felt the night he walked through his circle of tents listening to the groans of the Guti victims.

A wailing wind split the night air, an eerie cry, which moved Abram to draw his robes tight about him even though it was not cold. His hair stood up in gooseflesh at the morbid sound, as though it spoke the helplessness of his people.

As he walked, he took account of the rations left to them, running the desperate quantities through his mind again and again as he had a hundred times already. They were dwindling, so meager that his heart ached with the thought.

His poor people. Egypt was still nearly one hundred miles away, and they could not travel with such weak flocks faster than a few miles each day.

As he passed one tent occupied by a young family, the husband one of his staunchest supporters, he overheard voices. Unaccustomed to eavesdropping, he still could not help being drawn to listen when he heard his name mentioned in low tones.

The young wife was crying softly, her husband trying to comfort her.

"Marla, God is with us," he would say over and over again.

"Oh, possibly He was at one time," she said. "But look at our children. They are so hungry. Tonight one asked me when he would see home again."

"I know, Marla. Abram is doing all he can . . ." the man answered.

"Abram! He brought us here!" she moaned. "Is

Abram the only wise man in the world? We received fair warning!"

"By a prophet of Baal, Marla!"

"But warning, even at that!" she cried. Then standing and pacing the tent, she said bitterly, "What good does it do to serve a god who lets his people starve? Dead bodies can do him little good, I'm certain. Oh, how I wish we had stayed in Damascus! Perhaps Baal is punishing us for leaving him. Perhaps this fool god of Abram's is the false one!"

Abram walked away from the tent, shattered by what he had heard. Hunger was gnawing at his ribs also. He had eaten two cakes of meal and drunk one cup of water today. On this he had traveled fruitless miles, and his deprived body ached from inanition.

Still, the words of the woman hurt him more than his hunger. He had known this would surely happen eventually if the famine did not correct itself. It was only to be expected that the people would turn from him. What had he given them?

"Fine platitudes!" he said. "What good are exalted beliefs on an empty stomach?"

And raising his hands above him, he prayed desperately, "My God, give us more than words and revelations. Give us food for our bodies! What am I to do for these people?"

But nothing—nothing but the desert wind, crying like a starving wolf, answered his prayers.

Chapter V

The days went on relentlessly. Mile after weary mile passed, but so slowly that the rations were not holding out as the three men had optimistically hoped. The tribe could not go more than several hundred yards before resting again, if their frequent stops under the broiling sun could be called rest.

The cracked earth beneath their feet provided only scant quantities of herbs and greens, enough for the evening meals of gruel portioned in half-full gourds. The women tried to make the sustenance palatable but as the food supplies daily dwindled, they lost the ability and the concern. Several meals had called for goats' milk, scalded to remove the impurities of disease, and herbs and dried meat—but the meat supply was now so low it had been rationed to one portion every two days for each member. The weak goats, moreover, had little milk to supply, and what milk they did give turned rapidly sour under the sun.

Conditions were more desperate each dawn. Abram had traveled through the Negeb before, but he gave up attempting to calculate the desert miles to Egypt. Rocks, outcroppings, and streambeds with which he was familiar were the only sources of bearing he had to go on now. They indicated the approximate distance of the train from the Nile Valley boundary, but the news they afforded was so discouraging that Abram rarely contemplated it.

Life had become a staggering, empty thing for his people and for himself. One foot in front of the other became the sole aim, the only objective of their existence. Even muscles toughened by previous months of nomadic existence throbbed with pain.

The camels and asses, angry and sick, refused to budge each hot dawn when their masters came to them. Infinite patience was necessary to raise them up, and when they did finally stand, the pitiful, bony creatures bellowed and groaned under their loads.

At first his faith had sustained Abram, but now that faith faltered and waned. Even the glories he had experienced seemed insufficient to keep him.

The reliance of his people, mingled with their obviously fast-fading trust, weighed on him just as surely as the great burdens of these animals weighed on them. And he staggered under the load.

They now had nearly twelve days' journey before reaching Egypt, and that only if their supplies held out, which did not appear likely.

They had long ago resorted to killing several of their prize rams for meat, and they saved their female goats for what little milk they could still provide.

Abram passed through the camp of his passive, starving people each night. How could they keep going? What measure of strength it had taken for them to come this far!

They barely slept for hunger. Tempers which had spontaneously and frequently flared along this journey were quite calm now. There was little energy, even for squabbling.

The adults, so young and once so full of enthusiasm, were the ones who had trusted in him. But the children were the most pitiful of the sights which greeted his helpless and now nearly hopeless eyes.

But young or old, all his people sat in the doors of their tents as he passed, some barely awake with weariness, some nodding a word of subdued greeting as he passed, others not even acknowledging his presence, their sunken cheeks and swollen bellies testifying their misery.

There were those who still hoped against hope that Abram would deliver them, that his God was truly their

Guide. But the majority only clung stubbornly to the lives they felt slipping from them.

Sleep did not come easily that night, nor was it meant to come. A cry was heard in the camp, a young shepherd boy calling for Abram. Ignoring convention, he now burst hysterically into his master's tent, his face contorted with fear.

"It is Dari, the piper! Master Abram, do you hear me? It is Dari! Come quickly!"

A crowd gathered in the center of camp. They all loved the boy who had lent so many soft notes to their lives, whose welcome smile had lifted many loads. What was it? What could the shepherd mean?

"My shift was relieved only moments ago, Master," he explained, "and when I came to sleep, I heard crying in the darkness of our tent."

The crowd followed Abram's lead to the sheepfold far out in the valley. "I did not know anyone else was in here, so I lit a lamp and there was Dari, in the corner. See!" the boy pointed.

There lay the young form so familiar to them all. The people pressed in until Abram had to send them away. Kneeling at Dari's side, the sight of the once plump and healthy boy, now sallow-cheeked and virtually lifeless, gripped his throat like a tourniquet.

"Boy," he whispered, "it is I, your good friend."

Dari opened his dim eyes and briefly smiled. He tried to speak, saying nothing of himself. "I was in the hills, sir. My sheep are starving—"

Abram bent over the boy and whispered, "Hush, now. Sleep, son. The dawn is coming and you will feel well tomorrow."

But his voice lacked conviction. He wondered how long the boy had suffered from exposure and hunger before leaving his sheep and creeping, undetected, into this dark tent. As he watched him sleep, Abram took up his small hand and pressed it to his own weathered face.

He remembered the day long ago when he had first met the brave runner of Hebron's tribe, how he had nobly struggled against the cruelty of the men who held him to the dust.

"Struggle now, as you did then," Abram thought. "Never was there a braver soldier than you."

Dari briefly stirred and smiled up at his long-admired friend, saying, "I will play for you in the morning."

When dawn was about to light the day, Abram came out of the tent and walked past the people gathered at its mouth. He bore a strange, deliberate expression, one which awed and frightened them, and they made no move to question him. With long, masculine strides and a flintlike face of purpose, he went far out onto the plain, and when he could no longer be seen by the people, he lowered his mantle from his head.

Raising his arms, he cried, "My God! Where are You? Why do You withhold Yourself from me?"

Pausing as if to await a thundering voice—a vision—a flash of lightning—Abram stood tall against the sky and was greeted by the silence.

Three days passed. Egypt came slowly closer, but Dari's condition did not seem to improve. He lay in a damp, sweaty stupor all that week, being carried on a pallet by alternating shifts of men. Daily Abram visited him and came away with little hope.

One member of the train took special interest in Abram's reaction to this. Lot's faith, which had bolstered Abram at Beth-El, when the grass was dying and the way was unclear—that faith relied much more on Abram's strength than either had realized. His uncle, his father-figure, was also his measuring rod, his line of communication with the Almighty. And that line, so dependent on another, could not long remain unbroken if its source was not unerringly strong.

Lot grew as Abram grew, and would falter as he faltered. Though he did not realize it, without Abram's aid he would easily fall away, as he almost had the day of

the harlot's temptation. And once fallen, he might, in
his disillusionment and dependency, never fully revive.

Lot, now more than ever, needed the assurance his
uncle had always given. Doubts concerning the leading,
even the existence, of his God plagued him.

But when Abram was not busy, he was with Dari.
Sarai personally tended the boy day and night, with little result, and Lot watched as his uncle trekked into
the plain night after night, to pray, the nephew thought.

But Lot had no idea of the tormenting doubt which
gripped his strong uncle. If he had ever seen Abram in
his moments of solitude, he would have known something of his humanity. Abram—not the leader, the great
patriarch, or the one called of God—but Abram the
man stood alone on the desert each night, without a
breath of hope, with only dejection, waiting for a sign.
When no voice or vision, no answer came, he would return, more uncertain than ever that his God cared—or
even existed.

Dari did not play for Abram again. His lifeless body
was buried on the plain thirty miles outside Egypt, a
week after he had taken sick.

The camp knew of the death when Abram emerged
from the tent, white with disbelief, his eyes untouched
by sleep for days, staring at them blankly. Lot, unable
to restrain his approach longer, ran to his beloved uncle
and grasped him as if to shield him from the blow, in so
doing unconsciously pleading that his uncle reassure
him. But Abram only walked stiffly into the desert, his
nephew following after him.

"Uncle, what can I say? What can I do to help you?"
he cried.

Abram turned to him, the one he loved like a son,
but only said, "You should have helped me long ago,
Lot, when I began to live for this God of mine. You
should have tamed my fevered mind and shown me my
error. You should have told me I was mad!"

Lot watched speechlessly as his master then walked into the night staring at the moon, and he listened with incredulous ears to Abram's echoing laughter.

Chapter VI

Somehow their supplies held out until they caught their first glimpse of that "gift of the Nile," the isolated five-hundred-fifty-mile strip of black earth which ran south from the Mediterranean. Averaging only twelve miles in breadth, the mighty empire of Egypt, more than seven hundred years old, was a stronghold strategically safe between the deserts of upper Africa on the west and the Red Sea on the east. Only the narrow no-man's land of the Gaza Strip on the northeast corner afforded entrance into and out of the land.

Under normal conditions, Abram's party might have found it difficult to pass through this area between Canaan and the Land of the Pharaohs, being challenged by the warriors of the many Bedouin tribes who often swept down on rich trains. But his was not rich, nor were the desert dwellers free from the famine themselves, or capable of exploitation.

Abram bypassed Gaza, the garden spot of the coastal lands, usually dotted with olive and sycamore groves. Even it would have nothing to offer him now.

Egypt was the goal. Its coffers were rarely drained; its granaries almost limitlessly capable of supporting the masses who poured into it from the dry paralysis of the east.

The nearer the caravan came to the boundary, the more travelers they met. Large and small trains, individual families, nomadic Bedouins, all were eagerly seeking the same sanctuary, and thousands poured into the valley each day. It seemed that all parts of the eastern world from the Syrian range west were represented in the cavalcade. Haran and Ur and other city-states in the Tigris-Euphrates valley were not so hard hit by the

famine and were thus not represented, but such a con-
glomerate gathering there was! From the coastal cities
of the north, Tyre and Sidon, to the cities of the plain,
Sodom and Gomorrah, all tongues, costumes, customs
were here, making Egypt a true kaleidoscope of cultures.

The suffering immigrants, some having traveled from
as far away as Phoenicia, brightened with renewed hope
as they reached the land of plenty, their fears of starvation ending.

But mere survival or even comfort was not all Abram
could think of. What of the dreams he had built for his
people, the promise of a purpose? His responsibility toward them was grave, borne of a love which had not
been dimmed, from the heart of a father. A desperate
guilt plagued him, knowing that they need not have
been put through all this, and fearing he had led them
on a fool's errand.

Scenes of their suffering—of the small, dying Dari—
impressed themselves upon his mind again, and as he
saw the gates of Egypt before them, he was helpless to
know what it would hold for those who had forsaken all
to follow him.

The shadows were lengthening as they came to the
Princes' Wall, the ring of fortifications which stretched
all along the eastern frontier of Egypt. A barrier to invasion, and an entry point for all such immigrants, the
Wall had been built many centuries before and had seen
millions pass through its portals.

Sarai drew her robes close about her slender body in
an effort to shield out the icy night wind. Her camel, led
by a servant, afforded some warmth, but she wished she
could be beside Abram. She stayed a proper distance
behind her husband, however, as they came to the outpost treasury where he was to register his people.

The group hung tightly together, following Abram
like so many frightened sheep, but even at that they

were jostled, pressed, sometimes separated by the crowds, all anxious to pay their toll and find shelter for the night. The camels bellowed and the donkeys whined in apparent discomfort. Lot and Eliezer directed the servants to control the unruly creatures, but the noisy throng so frightened the animals that they only bolted at restraints.

The gateway to the Princes' Wall was flooded with light. Torches and lamps brightened the street and plaza of the small official city like sunlight. Ahead, in large booths at either side of the mammoth entrance were the tax-collectors and registrars. Dozens of them, behind sturdy tables, were half-crazed with the influx of immigrants, and though they were relieved by alternate shifts, they could barely keep up with the time-consuming progression.

Here a large, jovial family greeted acquaintances and relatives from other towns, there a small child wandered about in tears, apparently separated from her mother, and throughout the crowd food vendors plied their trade and merchants set up wares while waiting for the slow line to move on.

Along the walls row upon row of beggars sat cross-legged, their bowls in their hands, or the blind wandered out from the fort-city seeking coins from generous donors.

But the generous were rare in this crowd. Those who had money would have to pay entry tax with it and were not willing to part with that precious commodity.

Everyone must be accounted for; even the smallest infant had his price.

Those who could not pay would be sent to work in the fields or placed on the many work projects for which the Pharaohs were so famous. The grand pyramids, the Sphinx, the temples and palaces, all had been the product of immigrant and slave labor. The immigrants of other times had, in fact, often been sold into slavery, and this could well happen at any time, though the extent to which this practice was carried out varied with each Pharaoh's administration.

Under the eighth dynasty, the man now on Egypt's throne was not known for extensive slave trade, and he especially gave amnesty to the men and women of the wealthy and powerful centers of the east, Canaan, Damascus, Phoenicia, Ur, and Haran, for diplomacy was strategic even for such an empire as he ruled.

So, if Abram ever feared enslavement, those fears were not strong. Being of Ur was one point in his favor, and he did know Pharaoh. Perhaps he could rely on the fact that the names Terah, Nahor, and Abram were well respected here.

But now his previous wealth could do him little good. It had been spent on the depleted provisions necessary to bring one hundred across the Negeb. And as much as he would have used its influence, he would have little opportunity to do more than be herded through the registry with the throng.

Above the registration booths were railed balconies on which the guards stood duty, watching for any who might try to slip into the country without due process.

Earlier that day a young boy and his sister had been spied doing just this, and the ready bows of the archers had been instantly raised. With two speeding arrows the children had been felled in their tracks, and no one tried illegal entry after that.

Among those so stationed on the balconies were several richly dressed men whose gold-tooled belts and bracelets, embroidered tunics of fine linen, and heavy leather headpieces marked them as princes of Pharaoh. These governors, whose luxurious apparel suited them well, were appointed many titles, Keeper of the King's Court, Keeper of the King's Cup, Keeper of the King's Chariots, and so on. Pharaoh had many such "princes," all his sons, the offspring of his many wives. He had a harem unsurpassed in the eastern world for quantity and quality, each woman selected for her exceptional beauty. Nearly five hundred women graced his grounds,

and since the first years of his early manhood, he had
made use of them.

In fact, one of the most important positions held in
the governorship of the Pharaoh's court was Keeper of
the King's Wives. There were several young men appointed to serve under this office, their sole responsibility being to travel the land up and down in quest of
fitting women for their master-father.

The women came from every station, from peasant
families to the aristocracy of the day. Even slave women
whose beauty recommended them were not barred from
procurement. Often women of other countries were en-
treated to join the selection or were offered as the diplomatic gifts of their rulers.

In any case, Pharaoh must be pleased. It was the
dream of many Egyptian families that their baby girls
might one day grow up to be taken to Pharaoh's
chambers, as the women were blessed with incomparable luxury and ease, and the families bestowed with fine
gifts and often immense wealth in return for their
daughters.

Many times, however, that dream was not realized
even when a woman's family was visited by the king's
men. Pharaoh always had the final say in the selection,
and often, when presented with a young beauty, he dismissed her through sheer capriciousness or ill humor.
And then the woman, perhaps having been brought
hundreds of miles and decked, at her family's expense,
in the finest silks and jewels, was returned shamefaced
to her parents, her only glory being that she had been a
"candidate."

This night there were many such princes on the balconies, overseeing the duties of the registrars and the
guards, but more particularly watching for suitable
women to fill positions in Pharaoh's chambers.

As Abram neared the registry, he looked above in
time to see several of these officials gathered in what appeared to be an intriguing conversation. While he could
not make out the words above the din, he noticed that

they seemed to be pointing toward someone in the crowd.

Looking in that direction, a sudden terror gripped him. They were watching Sarai!

He should have thought to conceal her in the riding tent atop one of the camels, but it was too late now. His mind was a frenzy of confusion. He must not allow them to take her!

But—wasn't she his wife? Abram reasoned. Of course, that was protection enough. But as he looked jealously at Sarai, he remembered the stories of men whom Pharaoh had ordered killed for their wives.

Now a new fear seized him, fear for himself. And with little reliance now on divine providence, with a faith shattered and debilitated by the misery of their journey, he saw himself a man—only a man—subject to the whims and calculating passions of other men, however evil their designs.

He looked again at the strategists on the balcony. Pharaoh's appetite for beautiful women was inhibited only by the institution of marriage, so highly respected and honored in Egyptian society. But Pharaoh would have his desires, regardless of convention, or despite it. What would Pharaoh do when another man stood in his way, when the wedded state of a woman blocked him? Far be it from the King to be caught in adultery. Such a beggarly crime was beneath him.

Murder was far more honorable, more fitting to his divine calling as a monarch, than the sordid condition of adultery.

Sarai, innocent of the drama taking place, shuddered as a night breeze cut through her silk shawl. Her face, concealed by a filmy veil, was somewhat protected, but as they neared the registry, she reached up to lower it.

Abram knew, with masculine instinct, that if the men saw her face, the decision would be final. With his heart pounding in his ears, he pushed through the crowd toward Sarai, not wishing to attract more attention to her

or to himself but nonetheless jostling and forcing interference aside.

"Sarai!" he called anxiously, and more loudly than
he had meant to, "Sarai! Stop!"

In surprised confusion she looked at her husband.
What could he mean? She had never seen such a look in
his eyes. It frightened her.

She took her hands from her veil and waited for him
to reach her.

"Leave your face covered!" he shouted.

This command came with such force that it startled
and further alarmed her. Abram had never spoken this
way to her.

Leaning down from her high seat, she asked, "My
lord, what can it be? What has troubled you?"

Realizing that he was handling this poorly, Abram
changed his tone. Smiling to disguise his internal struggle, he placed a gentle hand on Sarai's knee and said,
"You are too beautiful to be suited to this crowd. The
poor registrars will lose track of their duties if you torment them with your face."

Sarai smiled weakly. He had flattered her feminine
ego, but it was only too obvious that Abram was deeply
troubled, and not by something so light as he proposed.

"Abram, please tell me. It concerns me?" Sarai trembled.

Abram had never been able to hide his thoughts from
her. Even the night he had fled from his father's home
with the marks of the whip on him, she had gently pried
the secret of his pain from him.

Abram lifted her from the camel's back and ushered
her into a more secluded spot, away from the eyes of
the princes, who had still been watching her.

"What is it, Abram?" Sarai pleaded again, her bewilderment and fear increasing with each mysterious second.

"Sarai, did you see those men, the princes of
Pharaoh, standing on the balconies above the regis-
tries?"

"No, my lord. I was not aware of them."

"Well, they were aware of you, my wife. They were studying you. Don't you know why?"

"No, my lord," Sarai said, her wide eyes betraying her innocence.

Abram carefully but quickly explained to her the urgency of the dilemma, and she grew pale, clutching at her shawl.

"Abram, I am so frightened!" she whispered. But then looking at him confidently, she said, "My lord, you are my husband. Surely they will respect that."

"Oh, you don't know these men, Sarai! You don't know the Pharaoh's deviousness. He lets no man stand in his way."

"But you have told me the Pharaoh knows and respects you. Surely—"

"No man crosses the Pharaoh, Sarai, not even those closest to him," he said, tense with apprehension and impatience. "More prestigious men than I have fallen prey to his whims—don't you understand?"

At this Sarai was filled with a fresh fear. Could Abram mean that Pharaoh might—"Oh, my lord, surely you cannot mean—"

Abram read her thoughts. "Yes, Sarai. Any man might be his victim."

Sarai's ears burned with this revelation. Could it be that this was the same Abram who had charmed her with words of faith many months before, who had filled her imagination with glorious words of promise, of a plan for them, of a living, personal God? Was this the same man who had claimed he had spoken with God, had seen Him? Who had claimed the allegiance of one hundred people on the steps of Damascus?

It flooded over her now, the tangible reality of the past few days since Dari's death. Abram's hurt was more than a passing thing.

Sarai probed the depths of Abram's spirit with her words: "My lord, will not God shield you?"

Abram turned from her. He could not look at her.

His degradation was too painful. From the heights of Gerizim to the depths of the valley of famine, his faith had followed his circumstances, and was, it seemed, lost to him irretrievably.

He felt alone—desolate in a crowd of thousands. His palms were cold with sweat. He felt as if he were on the edge of a boundless chasm; he could not reach out to be saved from falling, for he sensed there was no hand to cling to.

He looked above him through the street lights, up to the limitless reaches of the heavens. Something nudged painfully at him to cry out again, "God, my God—help me in my trouble!" But he was silent, remembering the fruitless prayers he had thrown heavenward on the plains.

His heart was a heavy stone, and he turned to face his wife, who waited fearfully for his answer.

Her lovely face turned pale and lifeless at the words which seemed to come from an unfamiliar tongue: "Say, I pray you, that you are my sister, that it may be well with me for your sake, and my soul shall live because of you."

Chapter VII

Since Abram's party lived the Hebrew existence, their flocks rescued them, in a sense, from further hardship. Since their self-employment would bring them a comfortable life here, they avoided having to work in the Egyptian fields or on the Pharaoh's projects for a livelihood. Cheap labor forces were submitted to the crudest form of living in this land and were given only the barest of life's necessities until such time as they could return to their countries.

But the nomad was independent of such attachments. Once he had been registered and taxed, he was allowed to enter the fertile valley of the Nile.

The area the nomads leased was not privately owned but was grazing land reserved by the Egyptian government for just such itinerants as they. For a nominal price they were allowed to use the pasturage under the watchful eyes of the Keepers of the King's Lands, and when it appeared that their sojourning there was no longer necessary, they would be asked to move on, or would be charged a larger fee from the profits they realized.

This was a beautiful pastoral area. The people were fed and their strength was returning.

Like rich carpeting, the grass robed the rolling, velvet valley. Small white and purple flowers danced under a peaceful sun, and the sound of the streams blended musically with the soft breezes. The green hills and the deep brooks which watered them were some consolation for Abram, though his faith still sat on a rocky bed and did not yet take new root.

Eliezer accompanied him into the shepherds' hills several days after the company had settled here. It was unusually hot this day. They wandered far back into the grassy slopes, which afforded a glorious view of the vast green blanket of the valley.

Each in his own way hoped that the worst was over, that the vision of the future might once again prove itself, but they did not speak of it for fear that too hearty a grasp on it might make it flee their hands like the down of a thistle.

What conversation they did engage in was superficial, but it represented the desire to touch their souls together once again. In the proud ways of men, they discussed everything else but what they felt—saying perhaps more poignantly than they could in any other way, "We need each other."

Before suppertime they began their way home, and as they came to the last hill, the sounds of loud voices ascended from the camp below.

The men were too far away to make out the words but it sounded as if the entire tribe were in a general uproar. Hurrying over the ridge, they saw a large group of Egyptians on camels, and with them they had brought an entire train of wagons piled high with goods, flocks of sheep, and herds of fine cattle.

The tribe was gathered around a tent at the center of camp, and suddenly Abram's blood froze.

From that tent now came cries of "Abram! Abram!"

The patriarch looked wildly at Eliezer. "Sarai! That was Sarai!" he cried, and like a bolt he was off, his young companion following after.

"Sarai!" he cried. He had never run faster, numb to the jagged rocks which cut through his sandals and tore his feet.

He must not let them take her! What had he done? Was there no salvation in heaven?

"God!" he screamed. "Sarai! Sarai!"

But he could not reach her in time, nor could the noisy throng hear his cries from the hill as he ran madly down what seemed an endless course.

The leader of the train had her now. He emerged from

her tent with the frantic woman twisting violently in his grasp, her slender arms pounding feverishly against him, the men of the camp helpless to save her, as the guards stood over them with poised bows.

"Your brother has been paid handsomely for you, and Pharaoh will treat you well," the strong official laughed. "You should feel the honor of your selection, my beauty!"

Sarai was nearly faint with the struggle, but still she cried with her last energy, "Abram! Help me!"

Hot tears coursed down her face as the official handed her over to one of the riders, who pulled her roughly into the saddle behind him.

"Do not bruise her, fool!" the captain shouted. "Do you forget the bounty on her head? Pharaoh will be displeased with a blemished chicken."

The camelman laughed heartily. "Spirited, isn't she? Never seen one put up a fuss at going! Most of them would give away their own families to be chosen."

The official roared approvingly at this. "Yes, Pharaoh will like this one. She'll be a challenge for him!"

The Egyptians now took leave of the camp, Sarai struggling helplessly, the crowd held in check until she was well out of the way.

But as the guards were about to mount, Abram's voice pierced the din.

"Sarai!" he screamed, hoarse with terror. Anger replaced fear, however, as he pushed like a wild man through the crowd, and defying the spears of the sentinels, grabbed several at one bound, knocking them from their feet and tearing across the plain after the Egyptian princes.

"Sarai! Sarai!"

The panic-stricken woman sat up at that beloved voice, and struggling against her captors, she cried hysterically, "Abram! Help me—oh, for God's sake—Abram!"

Her huge, lucid eyes were wild with the fear of a

trapped animal, her arms outstretched, her white gown slapping the breeze as the camel of her kidnaper ran forward.

And still Abram pursued her, his muscles burning with stress, his lungs explosive with the pounding pressure, his stomach a knot of constriction.

"My God!" he cried, his breath coming in raw, throaty sobs.

But Sarai's captor clutched at her, and he laughed and shouted to his allies, "Never saw a brother care so much for his sister!"

"Pretty good pay for Abram, though. He'll be glad when he cools down. They always are. Heard he was a merchant, a special friend of Pharaoh's. It's beyond me what could make a man like that turn to sheep trapping."

The Egyptians laughed uproariously at this, their distaste for the Bedouin way displayed in lusty tones. But as they indulged their ribald humor, Abram stumbled and rose and stumbled again, his legs able to carry him no farther.

"My God!" he cried, raising himself to his knees and staring through tear-dimmed eyes in frantic horror as the Egyptians and their helpless cargo passed out of sight.

"My God—" he groaned again, and slumping onto the grassy plain like an offcast garment, he lay, a mute testimony to his own selfish folly.

Chapter VIII

The gates of Memphis, Pharaoh's capital, were nearly as high as the Ziggurat of Ur, and were fortified with enormous towers and guard stations. All along the wall walked the men-at-arms who hourly watched over the distant, flat plains which surrounded the city. From their positions toward the west could be seen the three mighty Pyramids of Gizeh, with the awesome, human-headed Sphinx surveying the empire at its feet.

To the east flowed the eternal Nile, its black, sandy loam banks rich with the fat of the land.

A broad, palm-lined avenue, nearly a mile in length, led from the gate past evenly spaced and squarely drawn city blocks, and perfectly perpendicular to this avenue were more streets, narrower, but nonetheless comfortably broad, with cedars and palms flanking them in cool, green splendor.

Even the simple folk lived well in Memphis under the wealthiest society of the day. It was a beautiful, easy way of life here. Public arbors and lagoons filled with tropical birds and crystal pools stocked with fish were in all parts of the golden city.

Memphis was forever busy, bustling with the trade brought by the great shipping lanes next to it. It was a port city and yet an agricultural center as well. Giant silos, their rounded tops reared toward the sky, housed limitless supplies of grain. And onions, chives, apples, pomegranates, olives, figs—the delicacies of kings—filled the marketplace.

But Sarai was unconscious to the beauty around her. Had she been interested, it would only have represented to her the product of generations of selfish, ambitious

men, the likes of which had torn her from her simple
home and loving friends.

When the Egyptians who had taken her reached the
central courts of the city, they dismounted and led her
toward the palace. They were in a huge, walled enclosure which housed the public halls. Ringing all sides
were colossal, pillared buildings, everywhere decked
with statues of deceased kings and queens, gods and
goddesses, grotesque to her eyes. The heads of men were
appendages to the bodies of jackals, great birds, and
cats. Or the heads and feet of bulls, alligators, or dogs
matched the bodies of men and women, and infinite
combinations stared down on her as she was ushered
through the temple square.

Her head spun with the alien surroundings, leaping at
her unprepared mind like scenes from some hallucina-
tion.

Great mosaics and tapestries adorned the fifty-foot
walls with scenes of legendary heroes, sacrifice, war,
and death. Carved on each stone, it seemed, were the
names of kings and queens, or poetry inscribed to the
great deeds of their deities.

Had Sarai come under different circumstances, she
might have been awed by the presence of such splendor,
which used gold and silver as if it were found in the
streets. But such was her fear that she could think of
nothing save what was to become of her.

Finally they reached a great, four-story building
columned within and without, situated alongside the
Pharaoh's palace. A multicolored tile porch, broad
enough for a large chariot to traverse, surrounded both
buildings completely. At each corner stood great marble
and gold likenesses of the bull god Osiris, symbol of the
Nile. And in the courtyard which ran between was a
mammoth statue to the king of all Egyptian gods,
Ra—the Sun.

Forty fountains of ascending size and intricate color
and design raised their heads to the pedestaled deity
which rose in golden glory above the polished floor.

Ra's falcon-shaped head was formed in gold, his breast in ebony, his feet jeweled marble, and a great, bronze serpent stood out from his forehead, symbolizing his supposed unearthly dynamism.

Between the fountains lay minutely raised steps, hundreds of them ascending in purple and scarlet embossed tiles to the altar at his feet. His haughty face, cold and unyielding, looked down on all worshipers from a mighty height, and when confronted by him, one could not help looking away in blinded awe.

Sarai was led quickly toward the smaller of the two buildings and into what she soon learned was Pharaoh's House of Wives.

"Sit here," her principal captor directed, leaving her guarded while he entered a closed room whose elaborate golden doors closed austerely after him. The hallway in which she now waited was floored in purple and white marble, the walls curtained in light blue and silver brocade. Huge polished slabs of copper were set into the walls, reflecting light like mirrors into the windowless corridor. And everything, every column, every tile, each archway, each vault was inlaid with precious stones, intricate carving, and gilding.

Sarai shuddered as the door again opened and the official entered with a buxom, silk-clad woman.

"There she is," he said and then left with the guards.

Sarai stared at the floor, her hands folded in front of her. She did not cry, but her face told her misery well enough. The woman introduced herself in a husky but gentle voice. "I am Atrisha, matron of the Pharaoh's chambers. You are undoubtedly hot and weary with your journey, but you have finally reached your destiny. Only one thing remains before the glorious day when you will go before Pharaoh, and that is to prepare you so he will not be displeased." She looked at Sarai, somewhat bewildered at her silence. "Nervous, I presume. After a good night of rest in your apartment, you will feel the joy of your selection. And," she smiled, "I do

not say this to every woman—but from the appearance
of you, I am certain Pharaoh *will* select you."

She then laid a gentle hand on Sarai's elbow and con-
ducted her silently into the grear parlor of the harem
chambers. The room was buzzing with feminine voices.
Throughout it were low, plush lounges and pillows,
each one strewn with beauties in velvet and silk gowns,
all laughing, gossiping, arguing, and teasing one another
in general ease. None of them seemed to notice Sarai at
first. There must have been at least fifty of them in this
room alone, and Sarai knew there were nearly five
hundred on the palace grounds all together.

They must have become quite used to seeing new
women ushered in and out day after day.

Perfume filled the room. Small tables ranged
throughout, laden with alabaster jars of ointment and
cosmetics, silver and gold-handled looking glasses,
combs, and brushes.

On each wall were many mirrors, each polished brilliantly and casting almost perfect reflections. On the far
side of the parlor was an open porch, columned and
filled with statuary to the glorious queens of the past,
each an ideal for the women of the harem. Beyond the
porch were white marble steps leading to the women's
gardens and bathing pools below.

The matron stood with Sarai in the center of the
room, and gradually the women around them became
quiet, all eyes on the matron and her charge. A flurry of
whispers now flowed through the crowd. "Who is
she?" and "Can it be—"

The matron raised her hand for silence and then, taking Sarai by the arm, presented her. "Women of the
King, this is Sarai, the princess of Chaldea. She is the
sister of Abram of Ur, the son of Terah. You have all
heard of her by this time, no doubt."

A low buzz of excited voices followed this statement,
and the women looked on her with envious and admiring eyes.

"Oh, she is beautiful, indeed," a young one sighed, and the others laughed.

"Of course," the matron smiled. "We are all to make her feel at home here, and leave her to herself for the present. As you can see, she is tired—aren't you, my dear?"

Sarai smiled weakly at the woman and looked again at the floor. Her mind was heavy with fear, and her heart with sorrow. She tried to restrain the tears which forced their way up at each thought of her husband. Never once did she hold against him the mistake he had made in assigning her to this torment in a moment of weakness. She could think only of his love, of the wounded cry he had made as he ran after her on the plain, and she wondered if she would ever be in his arms again.

Now hot tears began to flow unchecked down her face, for try as she might, she could not restrain them.

"What is wrong with her?" one of the onlookers asked.

The matron quickly ushered her into a private apartment and ordered a pitcher of cool water brought to her.

"Here, my dear. Wash your face now. Many women react as you have, but it is only the excitement of the moment. Rest here, and we will wake you in the morning."

Sarai lifted a sad head to her keeper and tried to brush away her tears. "How did the women know me?" she asked.

"Oh—" the matron smiled in surprise, "you are the talk of the courts, my dear. Since your brother came— poor man, such a pity he has come down so—he was quite a favorite with Pharaoh, you know—anyway," she continued, "since you were first seen, preparations have been going on to bring you to the King. Why, the Keeper of the King's Wives says none like you have graced our land since, well, for many years, and Pharaoh must have a look at you." The matron laughed now, "Oh, the women are envious indeed, but they know when they have been outdone, and it should not surprise me at all if you gain the throne beside His Majesty."

When a servant girl came to help prepare her bath before retiring, Sarai's emotions had reached the breaking point.

"Oh, leave me! Please, all of you! Leave me at once!" she cried, her face flushed and her knees weak with her misery.

In amazement the matron and servants assigned to her fled from the room. Sarai's body became chilled and numb, she grew faint and seemed to tremble. Sitting on the edge of her fine linen bed, shaken with fear and anger, her lovely face contorted with anguish and humiliation, she raised her voice in torment.

"Oh, Abram, Abram!" she wept. And flinging herself on her pillow, she cried herself to sleep.

Chapter IX

The news of Abram's betrayal of Sarai had spread quickly. When the Egyptians had taken her for Abram's sister and the servant in charge had denied this, saying, "Abram is her husband," they had only laughed at him for what they considered a feeble attempt to retain his sister.

Eliezer seemed to understand the spirit of despair which must have led his master to deny her. Lot, though, had suffered the final blow to his weak and flimsy faith, so dependent on his uncle's strength.

It was Eliezer who ran to meet his master when he returned from the plain where he had knelt in solitude for long hours after Sarai's capture.

"What are we to do, sir?" he had asked. "Is there any way I may help you?"

But in low, bitter tones Abram had only answered, "We will rend heaven with our cries, and when we are done petitioning, the very stars will bleed for our pain!"

Eliezer had then stepped back as Abram passed through the camp, his young heart already bleeding for him. And as Abram had come to Lot's tent, his eyes meeting his nephew's, Lot, no longer able to bear the sight of his fallen hero, had turned his face to the ground.

Abram had looked at him for some seconds, reaching out for help. But, ashamed to say a word, Lot had only turned into his tent, pulling the door behind him.

Abram walked to an isolated stream which flooded a nearby wadi. Sitting in solitude, he reeled internally with conflicts. What was he to do? If he were to go now to Pharaoh and tell the truth, he would surely be killed, and Sarai with him. The king could not forgive such deceit in man or woman. But what was he to do? The decision he had made which brought all this about had been based on a fear that God was nonexistent or did not care. Now, ironically, God's help was the only solution—if there were such a boon in heaven.

Not since the night his father had beaten him, when he had run through the hills of Chaldea crying out his torment, had he felt as he did now.

Self-hatred welled within him. Hadn't he known that his selfish decision would serve only a destructive purpose? He had only added danger to another, the one he loved more than life itself, for eventually the king would learn the truth. He had not even saved himself, for what was life to him now? And had he been forced to die for her, the struggle might at least have rescued her from her torment.

In disgust he thought on his lie and remembered how, outside the walls of Haran, Nahor had said of him, "Brother, I know you are not one to fabricate an incident—you are not one to lie."

Guilt bombarded him, anger welled in him, but the questions which had been his for so many days during and since the famine now no longer seemed to matter.

Whether or not there was a God who cared, Abram was compelled by desperation to cry out, not in curses, but in pleas.

"I have lived too long without You. I have drunk the cup of sorrow too long. Life is Death without You. Though I do not understand all things, I would rather be a fool with You, than a wise man without You, my Lord! Oh, God—if there be compassion in heaven, hear me! For I am consumed with my sin."

Chapter X

The next morning, Sarai rose early, having slept very little. The matron had sent handmaids to prepare her for the king.

She was led to a dressing room, where she bathed in water spiced with myrrh and jasmine. Her hair was let down and then piled intricately high on her head, surrounded by small, tight curls. Golden twine was laced throughout it, and from a cluster of shining braids crowning her head, a pastel veil fell about her shoulders.

Finally, she was robed in purest linen, symbolizing her supposed virginity, and a great drape of purple was hung loosely over one shoulder and gathered about the waist with a broad sash. Jeweled sandals were placed on her feet, rings and heavy bracelets high on her bare arms.

The princesslike pride with which she bore herself through all this was insufficient cover for her feelings. She loathed it all. The palace and the glamor which was the youthful dream of many women held nothing for her.

But, having no choice, she was obliged to see it through.

The Pharaoh sat at the far end of his mammoth receiving room.

Sarai was dwarfed and overwhelmed by her disproportionate surroundings. Immense arches led her eyes up to a vaulted ceiling inlaid with mosaics of shell, pearl, and ivory, and columns laced with intricate sculpture bordered the broad passage which led to the throne.

A thick blue rug mantled the aisle and ascended the steps at the king's feet, muffling her footfalls which otherwise would have rung throughout the marble walls of the echoing hall.

Now led to the center of the room, she could see her intended clearly. A tall, slender man, the Pharaoh was unmistakably of royal blood. Mature, haughty features, a refined nose, and clear eyes suited his position with precision. Well-worked and developed muscles showed under a very dark skin, typical of his Nubian ancestry and this royal body was decked in kingly style. His torso was bare, save for a heavy collar which covered his shoulders and breast. Molded of gold strips separated by intricate linen tapestry, it was studded with multicolored gems. His skirt, similarly designed, hung over his hips from a wide belt, and his sandals were laced to his knees. A broad headdress of scarlet and white fell to his shoulders, and banded about his head was the symbol of his divinity, the Python.

His face bore none but the most austere of expressions, the upper lip almost imperceptibly curled in a slight sneer of superiority. Nor did his face change as he raised a hand in a gesture of reception.

The matron stepped forward and presented Sarai to the Chief Keeper of the King's Wives, one of the highest-ranking princes, and the Pharaoh looked down on him with cold, heavy eyes, calculated to chill the blood with reverence.

"Pharaoh, Mighty Ra, God of all the Earth, Father of Osiris, the Nile, we offer the woman Sarai, daughter of Terah, sister of Abram of Ur of the Chaldees, a princess of Ur according to her name, born of aristocracy. May she please you."

With this lengthy invocation, the prince bowed low and Pharaoh motioned him to leave.

Sarai was alone now. Tension filled the room as the princes who had recommended her looked on, wondering what mood their master-father might be in today. For what seemed endless moments, Pharaoh sat on his throne, neither moving nor altering his expression, only staring stonily at Sarai. No one could guess what his thoughts might be, so cleverly did he conceal them.

At last, with a flick of the hand, he motioned the entire assembly to leave him.

Sarai was rigid. Did this mean she had been selected? Following his beckoning, she approached him.

"A woman of Chaldea," he spoke finally.

Sarai was silent.

Pharaoh left his throne and stepped toward a curtained antechamber behind him, directing her to follow.

"Sit there," he said, pointing to a plush stool beside a great reclining lounge. He then walked to a low marble table and poured her a goblet of wine.

"No, thank you, sir," she said, looking away as he handed it to her.

Pharaoh held the chalice in silent contemplation and then laid it aside. "Ah, we can endure such rejections from a beautiful woman," he said.

Pacing the room in silence, he then turned to her, saying, "I perceive you are not pleased to be here, Sarai."

Again she was silent. Pharaoh was somewhat angered at this, but he continued to tolerate her indifference.

Sarai glanced at the royal figure, who now walked to the archway overlooking his city. His rich dark skin, oiled and smoothed by the valets of his chambers, his clean-cut face, not a mark of shame in Egypt, his grand attire—none of this drew her.

"A pity Abram never told me of his lovely sister," he said, after some moments.

A chill went through her at the word "sister," so foreign to her ears.

"We should have been introduced long before," he continued, awaiting the response which did not come. "Abram has spoken often of me, I suppose." Pharaoh said confidently.

But Sarai, unimpressed with his obvious joy in himself, said, "Sir, he has told me of his visits here."

"Ah, yes," he smiled, apparently satisfied with that. "Your brother was a great favorite in our courts," he went on, "a rather strange man, I often thought, so caught up in lofty discussions with the priests whenever he came. But one tolerates such eccentricities in those one is fond of," he offered condescendingly.

"Yes, sir, I suppose one does," Sarai responded, ruffled inwardly at his self-importance.

Pharaoh shook his head. "So sad what has become of Abram."

"What is that, sir?" she said in confusion.

He gave her a bewildered look and answered, "Why, his decline, his loss of position."

"I do not know what you mean," she responded.

"Ah," he winked, "the true pride of an aristocrat never fails with misfortune. But I admire pride in a woman, especially in a beautiful one," he bowed.

Sarai ignored this, her mind still on the ludicrousness of his previous remark, and defensively she said, "If you mean by 'loss of position' my brother's new work, why—"

"Oh, that is how you say it," he smiled patronizingly, "'new work.' Of course, but tell me, do wealthy merchant princes, the caravaneers who enjoy the blessings of the Pharaoh's court, do they often turn to sand-rambling?"

Ire welled within Sarai at his impertinence.

"Ah, she does respond," he grinned catlike. "But, my dear, I have been cruel, and all the wisdom of the past teaches that even a monarch must not risk the wrath of his favorite subjects. Now," he said, changing the subject, "tell me, did you leave Chaldea because of the Guti invasion?"

Sarai hesitated. "Partly, sir."

"Partly? There is a mystery about her then," he winked, his eyes gleaming with intrigue. "You did not lose your wealth to the Guti?"

"No, sir."

"To what, then?"

Sarai restrained her anger. Pharaoh's temper was an edgy thing, or so his reputation had it. She dared not tempt it.

"To the famine, sir," she answered.

"But the famine did not reach Mesopotamia," he prodded.

Sarai felt his interrogation closing in on her. She had said too much already. She feared speaking of Abram further, lest her tongue should give up her secret inadvertently. "You would not understand, sir, or be very interested, I am sure," she said uneasily.

This did not satisfy Pharaoh; it only whetted his curiosity. But he did not pursue the question further, seeing her growing animosity. "We shall accept that for now," he said. "Still, it is a mystery how a man of Abram's stature—"

"Sir, my brother is a fine and good man," Sarai interrupted. "I can do nothing but honor him in my heart."

Pharaoh bowed low in deference to her wishes, saying condescendingly, "Of course, and so it should be."

Placated, he reclined now on the sofa, gazing in obvious admiration at her. "You know," he said, "it is not every selected woman who enters this chamber."

Sarai's face grew warm with fear.

"I see you are pleased," he smiled.

Sarai bit her tongue to retain the bitter words which almost spilled forth, and as Pharaoh leaned forward, she pretended not to recognize his beckoning gesture.

The king's brow now bore a trace of indignation. "Coyness in a woman is another admirable quality— provided it does not strain the admirer," he said in a tone of impatience.

Sarai sighed deeply and checked the tears which rose within her.

Pharaoh left his divan and walked toward her, caressing her bare shoulder with a solicitous hand. But, as if by reflex, Sarai wrenched instantly from him.

Pharaoh's eyes flashed.

"I have dealt bitterly with women who paid me more mind than you have tonight, Sarai!" he warned in an angry voice.

But still she sat tall and defiant, saying, "Yes, sir, I am sure you have."

Pharaoh glared at her in frustrated, angry pride. He placed his drink on a low, ebony table and walked to the archway again.

"Your three days of purification will commence tomorrow," he said with a flick of the hand. "By then you will find yourself in a more endearing mood."

Sarai rose, "I am to go now, sir?"

Pharaoh wheeled about, his eyes aflame with wounded ego. "By all means—go!" he shouted, pointing an enraged finger.

Sarai left the room quickly, almost running through the cold, lonely receiving hall, her tears no longer restrained.

Pharaoh walked onto his porch. The moon lit his city like a torch, and as he surveyed his domain, his seat of power, his anger turned to fierce arrogance.

Of course, the woman would be his, not by edict alone but by helpless adoration of him. It was inevitable.

Chapter XI

Sarai soon learned that the days of her purification involved near isolation. Only two servants remained with her and did not leave her chamber during those long days. Forced meditation and almost hourly bathing were prescribed as prime ingredients in the ritual. She may as well have been slowly tortured, so great was her ordeal and her dread anticipation.

Her soul panted and cried for Abram. Were the glorious promises of the life she had dreamed of to be culminated in the bed of Pharaoh? She could not endure the thought. When she was sure she had cried her last tears, that her eyes could not possibly weep more, again the agony came fresh upon her, and the evidence of her sorrow fell forth in a torrent.

Daily she was led in solitude to the prayer chambers of the Egyptian gods, where she was expected to invoke their blessings on the forthcoming marriage, but when the doors were closed and she was alone, she prayed to another God, the God of Abram. Nor did her prayers cease when she emerged from those confines, but continually she petitioned the hand of Salvation.

Her prayers blended with her husband's, for Abram neither slept nor ate in all that time, as he lived in the hills surrounding his camp, neither coming down nor showing his face to his people.

On the fourth day Sarai was taken with great ceremony into the bridal chamber, a large, ornate room, lined with frescoes reaching to the ceiling and depicting scenes of royal courtship and romance. Two huge glazed ebony cats with eyes of lapis luzuli guarded the chamber door against intruders, and a curtained

balcony gave privacy, despite its commanding view of
the king's empire.

Sarai was ushered to the entry and was left in the
charge of the king's guards. Holding the great doors
open, they waited for her to enter, but she stood rigidly,
her face pale with the finality of it all. At last one of the
guards took her by the elbow and said, "His Majesty
grows impatient. You had best not delay."

Pharaoh sat in a broad-armed easy chair, his back to
her as she came in. The lights were low, the warm reds
and golds of the chamber casting a moody light on her.

She stood silently, some distance behind him, wondering what she was to do, and at last Pharaoh said,
"Well, approach. We are not a biting dog tonight."

Sarai came closer but did not confront him. Finally
he rose and turned to her, his stony eyes suddenly soft
with the sight of her.

He did not draw near quickly, sensing that she needed time to adjust to him. "The shyness of a virgin—so
lovable a quality in a woman," he smiled. "And still,"
he paused, "it surprises me greatly that one of your age
—you are not a child, Sarai—that a mature woman of
your rare qualities has not been taken by some other
man by now." He reflected for some moments, and then
a smile lit his face. "But perhaps you, too, looked for
rare qualities, the kind found only in the arms of
Pharaoh."

Sarai cringed as he approached her and folded her in
his embrace. She was unbending and rigid as he did so,
and he held her again at arms' length. "You are so cold,
Sarai. May I get you a shawl?"

"Sir," she said, "I am not cold, just—"

"Oh, you are fearful, my lamb," he soothed. "I shall
not rush you, but do not put me off for long, as I grow
restless."

There was a certain tenderness in Pharaoh's eyes that
surprised her. It was not typical of his reputation. She
sat down on a small stool as he walked to the portico.
In a low voice he asked, "What do you think of me,

Sarai? Am I so wretched as the legends would have me?"

Sarai's face burned with bitterness. "I am surprised that you should ask me, sir."

"How is that?"

"Why, I am but a purchase, a thing of sale and commodity. It surprises me you should wish my opinion," she said, her voice sharp with long-suppressed antagonism.

Pharaoh was stunned at her biting words, and for a moment royal anger gleamed in his eyes, but then just as quickly, a note of admiration replaced it.

Looking fondly upon her as he might have admired a spirited colt, he beamed, "Well said—ah, how I enjoy a woman of strong words!" Pacing the floor, he sighed, "Oh, but how I tire of the flimsy females who are daily brought to me with mooning eyes and whispering ta-tas. But you, Sarai, you are different—a woman with fight in her—perhaps you knew I would find that a challenge."

Sarai rose and turned from him, her fists clenched tightly. "Nothing I do is calculated to please you, Pharaoh!" she said angrily. "I am not a reed to be bent to your will!"

Facing him with dagger-eyes, she cried, "I despise your egocentric approach to the world, as if all women —and men—lived only for your pleasure! I resent the inhuman culture which breeds those who can take a woman from her home and family without their consent or hers—and I resent your continual approval of everything I do and say, as if it were all to your credit!"

Tears of freedom now rose to her eyes—the freedom of expression she had given vent to.

But Pharaoh was silent as she dried her face, and when she looked at him, her blood curdled to see his expression. There he leaned against a pillar, a smirk of enjoyment covering his face, his arms folded casually across his breast, and when she regained herself, he applauded.

"Again, well said. Oh, Sarai, you are a rare jewel! One to adorn my crown!" Then, sidling up to her, he whispered, "Do you suppose, my beauty, that by attacking my name, you sully it? It is true that from other lips, those words would become death knells to the originator. But, from you, Sarai—they are gems, true gems."

Smiling triumphantly, he turned now and walked to the balcony, directing her to follow. She did so, shakily. Was this torment he had for her, this, his way of breaking her—to frustrate her every rebellion with complacency? If only he would strike her, lash out at her! At least then she would be satisfied in the knowledge that she had wounded him. But he was too clever for that.

Beneath lay the gardens, acres upon acres of them with brooks and fountains, arboretums, and ponds. Beyond the walls lay the city, splendid under the setting sun, which reflected off it like the gleam of a cut ruby.

"See—there flows the Nile, Sarai," he pointed to the eastern border. "I am its keeper, you know. I am called 'Ra,' the divine incarnation of the blessed deity. My queen, Sarai, would be empress of all she surveys here," he said softly, placing an arm about her shoulders. "All this—"

Sarai turned quickly and fled back into the chamber.

Pharaoh grew angry now. He could not understand her obstinance, her flightiness. Surely by this time she should have been his.

He followed her, about to cry out his indignation, his wrath which had meant the end of other rebels, but his heart was woven too tightly around this Chaldean beauty, whose likeness in form and spirit he had never before encountered.

"Sarai, I am at a loss to reach you," he sighed. "Have I not been kind to you? Have you not been treated well here?"

Sarai's face was wet with tears. Pharaoh could not understand. "Of course, sir. You have been kind—in your own way—in your understanding of kindness, you have been kind. But, don't you see—you should not tear a woman from her—"

"Her family," he whispered. "But, Sarai, Abram has been made wealthy for your sake. He has more now than he did when he was—well, before the tragedy of Ur. Don't you see? Your family, your brother has been blessed by all this. Daily, since you were brought here, I have sent him royal gifts."

Sarai shuddered to hear Abram called her brother. Desire cried out in her to scream, "He is not my brother! Abram is my husband! And twenty times the man Pharaoh is!" But she restrained herself. She could not be so foolish as to incur the wrath of Pharaoh on Abram for one moment of vengeance.

"Abram does not need your—your tokenism! Your regalia of gifts! Abram needs none of what you have!" she cried in a bitter outburst. "My people lack nothing which freedom to be their own masters would not bring them!"

At this, Pharaoh stepped back in wounded outrage.

"Do not test me, woman!" he shouted, pointing a forbidding finger in her face.

Sarai trembled but held her ground. She had scored a point. "Wound me, kill me if you must, mighty Pharaoh! I would rather die than be your slave!"

"I shall not wound you, Sarai," Pharaoh replied in an angry and suspicious tone. Sarai feared his next move; his eyes were so strange. He laughed scornfully and said, "You may challenge Pharaoh's will, my maid! I shall not wound you, for then we would both lose our pleasure. I shall have mine, Sarai! Despite your rebellion, you will be mine. You may suffer at your own hands if you like, for in refusing Pharaoh, you only refuse your own comfort. But as you endure your self-torture, I shall have my pleasure. One of us, at least, should gain from our relationship!"

Grabbing her ruthlessly, he threw her on the bridal bed, and Sarai scurried from his grasp. But he was too quick for her.

"My God!" she cried. "Deliver me!"

And just then, a scream was heard in the hallway. Pharaoh stood up in anger.

"What was that?" he stormed. "By the gods above— there it is again. What is this?"

He looked wildly at Sarai and ran to the door of the chamber. Throwing it back angrily, he shouted, "Guards! What was that?"

"Sir, we do not know! It came from the princes' quarters."

"Well, for the sake of the gods, see what it is!"

Still the screams continued. They were masculine, deep and fearsome cries which shook the palace and seemed to come from every room.

Sarai came out of the chamber, shaking in horror at the cries vibrating through the building. The women of the harem ran en masse from their quarters, crying to know the source of the bedlam.

"By the blood of the Nile!" shouted a guard.

"What is it?" Pharaoh cried, running down the hall toward the dormitory.

Suddenly he stopped short, staring madly into the quarters which housed his many sons. Sarai pushed her way through to a view of the calamity.

There stood the young men, some in pain, others mute with fear, all with hard, red lesions upon their faces, necks, and bodies, the product of inflamed boils which had come upon them as suddenly and mysteriously as a grass fire on a dry day.

Chapter XII

Sarai went back to her apartment in the women's quarters, but there would be no sleep this night. The plague of boils continued to spread all that night and throughout the next day.

Like a great, creeping hand, the plague held the house of Pharaoh in its grip. First each of the princes, numbering in the hundreds, was afflicted, and then the epidemic leveled its ugly finger at the women of the harem, as one by one they succumbed to the fiery pain.

Strangely, only the courts of Pharaoh were affected. No family, no individual outside those gates was touched, but inside no segment was spared. Servants, slaves, priests, charioteers, guards—all felt the dart of the enemy, some to a greater degree than others, but all painfully.

Save Sarai. She alone was unaffected, her smooth olive skin unblemished by the disease. As one by one those around her fell prey to the red lesions, she was spared, and finally she realized the power of her God.

At last, taking leave of the chamber, she ran to Pharaoh's hall but could not find him. From room to room she asked for him, but no one seemed to know his whereabouts.

At last she came to a secluded hallway, far away from the main wing. At the end she saw two guards and recognized them as Pharaoh's. She ran to them and begged them to let her enter. "No, madam. The Pharaoh is ill. He will admit no one," they said, both on duty despite the hand of the plague upon their bodies.

But Sarai would not be put off. With a quick movement, she pushed past them and opened the door on a darkened room.

There in the shadows sat the mighty Pharaoh. She could not see him well for the gloom, but he cried, "Who is there? Send the intruder away! Guards!"

"It is I, Sarai," she whispered before she could be ejected.

Silence followed and then, in a note of strangled pride, Pharaoh pleaded, "No, Sarai. Go away."

She approached the shadowy figure softly.

"Sarai, please, come no closer," he groaned, his voice trembling with humiliation. "Come no closer."

Sarai stood still, but as her eyes adjusted to the light, she saw more clearly the object of her previous hatred and antagonism. The once proud and regal man who had shown her his empire, who had so proudly demanded her adoration, sat now, bent over in pain, sheltering his burning eyes from what little light entered the room, huge swollen blisters festering on his magnificent Nubian skin.

Sarai's heart was no longer hard toward him. In that moment, she felt nothing but compassion, pity for the vanquished enemy, who had sought this miserable solitude in which to bear his degradation.

Kneeling beside him, she looked into his face, blackened by defeat and disease, and he turned away from her, fearful to see the revulsion she might display upon viewing him.

"You have come to comfort me, Sarai?" he said sadly.

"Oh, sir," she pleaded. "How I wish I *could* comfort you."

At those words, the half-blind monarch strained to see her. "Is that pity or love I hear in your voice?" he whispered.

Tears flowed quietly down her face, and she lifted his hand to her cheek. "Both, sir," she said soothingly. "I pity you for the shame which has come upon you, and I love you—as a human being."

Pharaoh sighed. "I see—and I begin to believe I am no more than that, as well, for though they say I am di-

vine, I have no power over this," he said, feeling his
face and arms. "Even the magicians of the court cannot
help me."

Sarai stood, searching for words with which to tell
Pharaoh of her secret.

"You leave me, Sarai?" he cried. "But who will comfort me? A Pharaoh has no true friends, you know."

"I do not leave you, sir," Sarai said comfortingly.
"But when I speak my heart, you will regret the day you
brought me here."

"No," he interrupted.

"Sir, let me speak," she insisted, hesitating, forming
the words in her mind. And at last she said, "Your
plague, my lord, will not be remedied by the magicians
of Ra or Osiris or any other god, for it is the doing of a
god unknown to you, the God of Abram, the One True
God, whose name is Unknown."

Pharaoh started.

"Abram lives in tents," she continued, "not because
the Guti overthrew his home, but because this God revealed Himself to him and called him out."

Pharaoh's face bore a trace of incredulity. "Sarai, I
am not a deeply superstitious or even a religious man.
My own gods are incredible to me at times. I do not
see—"

"Sir, please, be patient with me," she pleaded.
"Whether or not you wish to believe me, the words I
speak are truth. The plague has come because you had
me here against the will of my family, my God, and my
husband."

Pharaoh wrenched painfully in his seat. "Sarai—"

"Yes, Your Majesty. I am Abram's wife. Forgive my
husband and forgive me—but you must see that you
brought this upon yourself, for if you were not known
for your—cruelty—Abram would not have deceived
you in a weak moment."

Sarai stopped speaking, for Pharaoh's eyes showed
his self-rebuke. "You twist the knife neatly, my beauty," he whispered.

Sarai trembled, apprehensive of his reaction, but she stood tall and said, though gently, "I do not fear you, my lord. Whatever recompense you may take, my God is my protection."

Pharaoh sank deep into his chair at this, a pained note of lonely admiration crossing his face. And with a final gesture of resignation, he sighed, "Leave me now—"

Chapter XIII

A meadowlark woke Abram.

He had spent the past five days in prayer, alone, and this morning he rinsed his face in the icy water of the brook which ran through the wadi where he had slept.

He looked up just as Eliezer came running over the ridge toward him.

"Master Abram!" he called. "Men from the Pharaoh's court—they are in camp. They are asking for you!"

Abram threw his cloak over his shoulder and trudged up the slope. "What do they want?"

"They say Pharaoh desires to see you, and they want to take you there—now."

"Did they say anything about Sarai?" he asked anxiously.

"Well, sir, the strangest thing has happened! They say the entire court, save Sarai, has been hit by a plague the likes of which they have never seen, and that no one outside the court was touched."

Abram tingled with the strange revelation. "Eliezer, God is good!" he proclaimed, running up the hill with fresh energy. "God is very good!"

"Sir?" Eliezer smiled in bewilderment. And shrugging his shoulders, he followed his master.

Sarai was called to the receiving hall.

When the Pharaoh entered, his swollen face and arms covered with linen strips, he bore himself with the royal dignity which could never be broken. Sarai could not help admiring the man who had been her enemy.

He said nothing but pointed toward the door of the hall. There stood Abram.

Pharaoh studied her radiant face and then called her husband forward, the Man of God confronting his old friend with some trepidation, but without fear.

Pharaoh sat in deep silence for some time. Through the inflamed eyes shone a look of respect for his conqueror. The man who ruled the world's greatest empire was a sight to pity now, but as he looked about him at the people of his court, beleaguered with disease, and then looked intently at the man who had once been his companion, he spoke unbrokenly, simply and with dignity, words which strangely pierced Abram's heart.

"What is this that you have done unto me?" he queried. "Why did you not tell me she was your wife? Why did you say she was your sister? So I might have taken her for my wife? Now—" he paused, looking at Sarai with sad eyes. His voice softened and seemed to tremble, but he recovered it. "Now—behold your wife; take her; and go your way."

PART IV

The Desire and the Discontent

Ye have need of patience, that after ye have done the will of God, ye might receive the promise. But let patience have her perfect work, that ye may be perfect and entire, wanting nothing.

Hebrews 10:36 and James 1:4

Chapter I

Abram came away from Egypt a wealthy man, far wealthier than when he had left Haran with the inheritance received from his father. Partly in payment of bride-price for Sarai and partly to placate Abram's angry God, Pharaoh had endowed him with much gold, silver, cattle, sheep and goats, and goods of all kinds. In addition, he had given him people—menservants, maidservants, and slaves.

All in all, Abram came away from Egypt with well over three hundred people in tow, in addition to those he had brought with him, but this was a mixed blessing.

It was expected of all his followers that they would adopt his God as theirs. This, however, was an ideal of custom and not a real hope. The Egyptians did not easily transfer loyalties. Though as bondmen and bondwomen they were obliged to please their master, their worship of the One God took shape in outward form only and not in heartfelt conviction.

This, added to a number of Abram's first followers who had turned from him, laid the ground for seeds of schism ready to spring to life.

Indeed the ordeal of the famine and the Egyptian episode was over when Pharaoh's men led Abram and his people to the border with all their goods, telling them never to return. But the true results of the testing period would be fully felt only when they reached Canaan again.

For the winnowing floor of the famine had left much chaff among the people of Abram's original tribe, who, with time, would be shown for their true character. Those who were strong, though they may have wavered with the first wind of adversity, as Abram had, were even stronger for the trial when it was passed. But those who were weak would be blown away, because their faith had lost its roots with the trial despite the fact that God had shown His power and providence in a spectacular and miraculous way by sending the plague.

And there were those who had been so swayed by the predictive powers of the Wizard of Shechem, that they could never again fully trust in Abram's God. Even when news came that the seer had died of starvation in the wind-swept hovel of his tent, refusing to leave with the advent of famine—even then, some of Abram's followers returned to the worship of Baal.

And there were those who were impatient with their lot as homeless wanderers, as keepers of sheep and goats; those who zealously clung to the idea of a glorious Semitic heritage which was all too slow in coming; those who had lost their idealistic worship of Abram; and those who simply wanted out of what they considered a poor choice of followings.

Whatever their reasons, a large number, not a majority but a sizable group of Abram's people, had turned from him. And the presence of the Egyptian idolators only added fuel to the fire.

It took several weeks to reach Beth-El again, but when at last they came to the pastures of their old home, Abram took his people to the mountain where he had erected his second altar to God.

As he trekked up the slope, many emotions nudged his soul. Joy at returning, relief that the harrowing trial was over, great regret for his foolish mistakes, enormous shame for his loss of faith, gratitude, and devotion —all these were his.

In familiar ceremony he resurrected that altar in front of the congregation, and his many loyal followers felt the thrill of the homecoming with him.

But this time, as he raised his arms in contrition and praise, many others looked on with faithless and dreary eyes.

Chapter II

As the months passed, Abram's wealth and reputation became legendary throughout Canaan. Though still a nomad, he had returned to his former position of Hebrew caravaneer. Following the edicts of his God, he was not stationed in any particular city, but he still enjoyed a prosperous trade.

Abram's tribe had become so large, however, that it was increasingly difficult to manage, especially with the incessant feuding between its factions. He needed a partner, and the logical choice was Lot. His bright, adaptive nephew, who had proved himself capable as a businessman in dealings with contractors throughout their journeys, would surely serve him well. More importantly, Lot was his kinsman, his logical and customary partner.

One thing only withheld Abram's immediate decision. Lot's attitude toward his uncle had improved little since Egypt. It hurt Abram more than a physical blow whenever he realized that Lot, the one he loved like a son, had not yet forgiven him his all too human frailties.

Rejection was in Lot's eyes whenever Abram spoke with him, and it ate at their relationship like corrosive acid.

But, Abram thought, perhaps a distribution of the wealth was exactly what was needed to bring them together again. It was with this in mind that he finally called Lot to his tent several months after settling at Beth-El.

Lot was uneasy. "You wished to see me, Uncle?"

"Sit down," Abram smiled. "I want you to help me."

His nephew looked at the tent floor. "Yes, sir?"

"I wish to turn a third of the property and a third of

the tribe over to you," his uncle said generously. "I will remain the principal owner, you understand, but it will be under your management, and," Abram studied Lot's face, "whatever profits you realize from your management will be yours to do with as you wish."

Lot was speechless.

"Does that meet with your approval, son?" Abram asked.

"Oh, Uncle! Yes, sir! It does! It does!"

Well into the night the two men calculated and discussed their arrangement, and Abram went to sleep satisfied that his decision had been a sound one.

The third Abram turned over to Lot included four hundred tribespeople, so quickly had Abram's tribe grown. Within a year of his journey out of Egypt his people numbered over one thousand. Bondmen and bondwomen, servants and free hired employees were among this number, as well as a good many who had contracted to join with Abram as tenants, serving him in return for the securities which such a large household afforded.

The tribe of Abram, then, was immense, one of the largest of its day, and Lot was indeed fortunate to be the junior partner.

With their responsibilities, however, Abram and Lot did not see each other often. Several days at a time might pass and they would only occasionally meet around the fire of the central tents in the evenings.

Prosperous trade demanded dealings with those of many different cultures, and the shrewd businessman of Abram's day quickly learned international diplomacy. Lot was no exception, though it troubled Abram to see how entangled his nephew became with dealings in the large cities nearby.

Jericho, famed for the brilliant beauty of its Fire Trees, satiated with such natural resources that the water literally flowed in the streets—Jericho, which lay a mere ten or fifteen miles from Beth-El, was indeed a bountiful trade neighbor. Yet, as a center of moon worship, it was one city Abram most avoided. But Sodom and its sister cities, Gomorrah, Admah, Zeboiim and Zoar, located about sixty miles from the camp, were of even greater concern.

The Vale of Siddim, which encompassed these city-states, was the most fruitful and beautiful of all the areas near the Salt Sea. Lot was drawn there often, much too often to suit his uncle. Sodom and Gomorrah were the vilest, most depraved cities in the eastern world. Orgies of unspeakable proportion, perversion of the worst sorts were fair play in these cities of ill repute. And Abram feared immeasurably for Lot should he become too familiar with their cultures. Frequently Abram would see him making preparations to take his train in that direction, and it became more and more difficult for him to restrain his tongue, which would have detained his nephew if possible.

A trip to Sodom, the largest of the five cities, took at least a week, but often Lot was gone several weeks at a time.

Abram stood with his flocks on the green slopes of the mount one afternoon, watching as Lot led his huge caravan out of Beth-El. The rough terraces which led down toward the Arabah and the Vale of Siddim required pack trains, and Lot's donkeys were laden with rich treasures. Often Abram had led such trains through Mesopotamia for his father, when they went to cross the Syrian range.

His mind wandered back to those pleasant days of ease and adventure. A slight twinge of nostalgia coursed through him as he remembered the home and family he had left behind, and the comfort of city life.

As he looked about him at the flocks and tents— though wealth was here beyond what he had ever hoped to regain—he was a city dweller at heart, and that old fear of eternal wandering still sometimes touched him.

But then, thinking again of the plain, the incomparable degradation of Ur, of Sodom, of Gomorrah, he remembered the promised land and the inheritance which was to be his son's one day.

"God," he thought, "forgive my foolishness. Your will is my only true desire—but, Lord, help my nephew to desire it with me."

Abram met Lot when he returned from Sodom, and that evening as they supped together, he formed the words in his mind he wished to say to his nephew. Lot sensed that Abram was about to advise him and was perhaps preparing his own defense when his uncle asked, "What takes you into Sodom so frequently, son?"

"Business, sir."

"Yes, I see you are doing well with the trade you've established," Abram paused, motioning Sarai's handmaid to bring more wine and cheese. "But how did you happen to begin such strong trade with the Sodomites?"

That last word hung rancidly on Abram's tongue, full of connotative references to the sin of that city. Lot knew Abram was fishing, leading up to the true issue at hand.

"I knew wool was bringing a good price there, to begin with," he said, somewhat guardedly. "And, then —one thing led to another, and—"

"And now you find it necessary to go there every few weeks?" Abram interjected.

"I see you disapprove, Uncle?" Lot said tensely.

Abram rose and paced the large, luxurious tent, his arms folded across his chest, an intent, furrowed look on his face.

"I do not disapprove of your trade, Lot. I also have traded among the cities of the plain and have even had dealings with Sodom. It is not the trade of which I disapprove."

"Then I do not understand, sir," Lot said weakly.

Abram was suddenly reminded of the time his nephew had used those same words when he wished to go with the harlot of Damascus. Turning to him, his eyes snapping with anger, he demanded, "Lot! You know very well what my concern is! You only feign ignorance!"

Lot looked for words with which to combat his uncle but only retorted, "You told me to do with the prospects as I saw fit, and I have done that, Uncle! If you wish to withdraw the share with which you have entrusted me, that is your prerogative!"

Abram shook his head. "What am I to say to you, Lot, to make you see?" His heart and voice were tender now, as he looked at the one he loved as his own. "You are alien to me, it seems, Nephew. I am the one who does not understand your ways. You knew what you were giving up to come with me, to follow after my God, who I had hoped was your God as well." Abram sighed and again paced the floor, Lot watching him intently.

"I remember so well the day I first saw you," he continued, "when you ran to help me with my brother the day of the Guti battle." Abram's eyes were bright with the memory, and Lot looked down in sudden pang of sentiment. "I remember the day you raced toward me from Haran, saying you wished to come with me; I remember how you stood by me when I went before the high priest in the Damascus court; I remember how you encouraged me when I watched the dying grass at Beth-El." Then, looking at Lot, he said softly, "All this floods my memory with joy—but something is now between us, Nephew. There is a gulf so broad I cannot seem to leap it, though I have tried. God knows, I have tried!"

Abram awaited a response, but Lot only sat in dejected silence, pondering something Abram could not touch. "Please forgive an old man's preaching," he began again. "You knew the road would call for certain sacrifices. We are not city dwellers, you and I. We are strangers in this land, awaiting the promise." Abram smiled, looking out at the lights of the most wealthy encampment in Canaan. "But we can hardly complain of the way in which we have been destined to live that life."

But now Lot grew restless. Following Abram outside, and after some period of silence, he said dryly, "Will that be all, sir?"

Abram knew he had not reached him, but with a final effort he placed his arm around his nephew and said, "Seek wisdom, for she will never fail you."

At the sound of those seemingly pedantic words, a sudden surge of the resentment which Lot had withheld throughout the discussion now sprang up in him. The antipathy which he had harbored against his uncle, which until now had only shown in his eyes, poured out in a geyserlike retort. "Uncle Abram!" he cried bitterly, "Do not speak to me of wisdom! For once I thought I had found it in you—but you have not always been the embodiment of that most precious of gifts!"

At this he ran from Abram's tent, down the hill toward his own, leaving the Man of God in speechless solitude, the memory of his folly in Egypt pressing freshly upon him like a burden which had never been removed.

During Lot's estrangement, the seed of discontent had reached maturity and had chosen to sprout in the fields of the shepherds.

Lot's flocks had grown to overriding proportions, and it seemed the land grew less and less sufficient to contain both his and Abram's. Added to the schism already evident in the tribe, this set the scene for quick-flaring rivalry of any kind.

Nearly five years of intense feuding was to ensue between the herdsmen of both parties.

Though Abram's total land area now covered many square miles, it appeared that there never was enough to keep the rivals separated. Ceaselessly they vied for streams, pasturage, and flatlands. The first to arrive on a spot was often challenged by a newcomer claiming he had rights to the land as he was of Abram or Lot, and especially during hot seasons, tempers were sharp and bitter.

However, what began as squabbling over property rights, taking the form of verbal debate, advanced to more frequent incidents of rage and even physical tangles between the herdsmen.

It was during the early stages that Abram could have best used Lot's help in squelching the uprisings, but the young man was less and less frequently available. His journeys to the Vale of Siddim were no longer disguised as business trips. He went for the increasing involvement he enjoyed there, nor did he hide his intentions, for the discussion Abram had had with him several months before had only further alienated him from the man who had failed to meet his expectations.

But if the now minor uprisings were to continue, they would surely develop into border skirmishes of a warlike nature. For long months Abram shouldered his burden to the best of his ability. But the Hebrew's empire was now so vast that little short of an armed policing of the shepherd districts would cope with the predicament.

It was a strange, unnatural dilemma which the wealthy Man of God now faced. He could put down the rebels of Lot's tribe if he so desired. His power was great enough. But this was not merely a question of force. It was a question of priorities.

The problem centered on Lot, his beloved nephew. It was his attitude toward Abram which had really fanned the flames of rebellion. Lot's people were not blind to the bitterness their leader had for his uncle, and as much as he might have considered it a matter of too little land and too many flocks, Abram knew that if Lot were to rejoin him, his people would more easily follow.

As it stood, however, they took advantage of their leader's frequent absences to advance themselves, assuming that his belligerence toward Abram made fair play of their own divisiveness and discontent.

The question of values plagued Abram. Should he wait for Lot to see the necessity of coming back to him, and thus risk the possibility of losing his people in chaos? Or should he forcibly intervene in the civil strife and lose his nephew forever?

His father's heart told him to do the first, but all that was practical told him the latter step was imperative.

Through the third and fourth springs matters reached a near climax. Though the streams were swollen, the valleys ripe with emerald blades, still the quarrels continued.

Eliezer, who had borne it all alongside his master, who had seen Abram age under the strain, walked with him now into the hills surrounding the camp.

"I am very tired, friend," Abram said.

"Yes, sir, I can see you are. Is there anything I can do for you?"

"Yes, Eliezer. You may tell me: am I an old man—as old as I feel?"

The faithful servant smiled admiringly at his rugged, muscular master. "Oh, no, sir. You are in your prime, an example for any younger than yourself!"

Abram sighed. "I knew you would answer that way, Eliezer. But I was in my prime when I left Ur. And not by any means a colt even then, you know."

"But not by any means ready for pasture now, sir," Eliezer smiled.

Abram laughed. "You invigorate me, son. But, tell me," he said, his voice betraying a solemn note, "now that we have discussed the health of my body—how do my people fare?"

Eliezer was silent with thought. "Not well, sir," he finally answered.

Abram looked at his servant intently. "And to what do you attribute that?"

"Well, sir, if it were my decision to make, I would . . ." he paused, fearing lest his advice be considered presumptuous on his part.

"Go on," Abram urged, eager for counsel.

"I would take more decisive steps—"

"Call out the forces?"

"Yes, sir."

Abram paced the slope. Then, oddly changing the subject he said, "Do you not find it strange that so long after being given a divine promise, I should not yet have received it? And isn't it strange that at this point I should even be pondering the collapse of all that I hold dear?"

Eliezer rose and walked to Abram. "But, sir, we have been through worse before."

Abram stopped. "Yes, I know. And that has kept me going thus far." Looking toward the distant plains, the site of his nephew's camp, he stood silently for several seconds. "One thing only is the foundation of my troubles," he said at last.

Eliezer contemplated Abram for some time. "You think of Lot, sir?"

"Yes," he whispered. "He has never forgiven me, Eliezer."

The young man at Abram's side swelled with anger at the thought of Lot and how he had pained his dear friend, and with burning ears he listened as his master attempted to rationalize the abusive character of his unfaithful nephew.

"Perhaps," Abram thought aloud, "perhaps Lot feels as his father, my brother Haran, must have felt when trapped in Ur. When my father could not meet his longings, he ran away. And now, Lot has seen his reliance on me bring little fruit. Perhaps there is something borne in his blood, as there was in my brother's, which will one day tear him from me completely."

And then, thinking of his father's aging sorrow over the loss of Haran, Abram said, "And if he goes, he will never return."

Eliezer could not bear to hear Abram further torment himself, and in a burst of indignation he said, "But you needn't sacrifice all you have to regain him! He is not your son!"

Abram turned to Eliezer, sensing his deep devotion, but the tactless reference to his lack of an heir had stung him to the quick.

"Still, he is all I have, Eliezer," he retorted, beginning down the hill.

But Eliezer called to him, "You have the promise, sir—"

Abram did not respond.

Chapter III

The lights of Sodom were riotous, like an illumined array of gems. The evening streets were, as always, crowded and unruly, flooded with the sounds of cart wheels, laughter, wild, erotic music, and drunkenness.

Lot's pulse pounded as he and his men pushed their way through the plaza. Every night was like a festival here. He had never known such pleasurable freedom, such revelry anywhere else in his travels. How he loved it!

Toward the far side of the wide, elaborate marketplace was a small cafe, not very impressive to outward appearances, but one of the most fashionable nightspots frequented in the city.

This lowly building was Lot's objective. Day and night in the hills of Beth-El, his thoughts centered on this place, and whenever opportunity warranted, he made speed for the gates of the city which harbored it.

Inside the cafe the light was dimmer. The noise from outside was hushed as the small door closed on it, and was replaced with the sensuous vibrations of eight-stringed lyres played by the hired musicians.

Such a spirit of license and abandon dominated this little place that all who entered felt released from anything which might otherwise inhibit them.

The small main room of the cafe was packed from wall to wall with men and women who came from all parts of the city and outlying areas to find that release. Somehow this remote, unattractive hovel was the most successful of the many centers in Sodom which devoted themselves to freeing their clientele.

Perhaps its popularity was due to the management,

which brought in the loveliest women and the most winsome young men to ply their trades.

Lot smiled to think how clever the owner of this establishment was to pour capital into the quality of his employees, rather than into the external appearance of his building. It had paid off handsomely indeed.

Nor was Lot slow in being caught up in the spirit of the tavern. Looking about at the revelers who flocked here, he thought his poor uncle would never be able to understand his friends. He did not even try to communicate to him the meaning of the liberation he enjoyed on his trips to Sodom. Abram was so inextricably linked to the narrow confines of his dreams and to his meaningless taboos, Lot reasoned, that his uncle could never be educated to the more humane, realistic school of thought Lot now espoused.

When his uncle had spoken to him years before on the temple steps in Damascus of self-esteem, chastity, and the narrow way for the sake of righteousness, purity, and wisdom, Lot had not debated. The words had frightened him, and they had sounded true. When Abram had insisted that Man had another side to him, a side which separated him from physical tyranny, Lot had been convinced.

But he had been freed of that old way now. The bonds of rigid prohibitions had been broken for him. He saw that system now as the symbol of all which would distort and confine a man's true spirit.

"After all," the Sodomites reasoned, "what is truly provable or real but what Man senses and perceives with his impulses? What is more noble than nature, than the way in which we are created?" they asked. Yes, there were deities, supreme beings, but this was all the more reason to live according to the natures with which they had endowed us.

If it was a man's nature to have many women, let no one question that, and if it was a man's nature to lie with another man, let no one, himself least of all, question that.

Certainly the Sodomites saw no need to distinguish between the physical and the spiritual. If there were such a spiritual side, it was all bound up in, and not separate from, the physical.

True love between humans, they reasoned, did not ask for or demand limitations. Freedom and love were brothers, they said. To say no was to rob another, as well as one's self, of the freedom and love so cherished.

Lot shook his head. Such a liberal, humanistic viewpoint his uncle never could have fathomed, he smiled condescendingly, a note of pity in his expression.

But now his attention was drawn to the far side of the room, where a narrow, modest staircase descended from the top story. The women of the cafe were coming down to entertain, and Lot's heart sped involuntarily. The object of his trips to Sodom would surely be visible at any moment.

Lot's eyes brightened. There, at the top of the stairs, stood a beautifully garbed woman awaiting her entry, and Lot, rather boyishly, pushed his way through the crowd to the foot of the steps.

"Mala!" he called through the din, "It is I, Lot!" He waved anxiously at her, but she pretended not to hear. At the sound of his voice, an indefinable look, a mixture, half of pleasure and half of disgust, worked its way across her haughty face.

But at last, after much waving and gesticulating, Lot managed to attract her attention. She moved slowly through the crowd toward him, her face taking on a more pleased aspect, though it required all her native charm to manage even a coy smile.

"Why, Lot!" she leaned next to him. "I was so hoping you'd come tonight."

Lot had traveled more than most men of the day did in their lifetimes and had acquired more material goods than most dreamed of, but still despite all this, when he was near Mala, his crude shepherding origins, his nomadic tribesmanship seemed to creep up from the recesses of his past and rob him of all the suave assurance he would have displayed.

He became addlebrained, speechless, the subject of her every whim. He stood now gaping at the flashy beauty before him. Mala's thick, red-black hair fell in a myriad of waves far down her back and shoulders. No braids or ornaments confined it. It moved resplendently as she moved, and caressed her ample body like the robes of a queen.

Within this frame her dark face was set like a polished jewel, all aflame with color, some natural, but mostly the product of an artist's brush. Her large, dark eyes flashed brilliantly, encircled by a camouflage of dark paints, her cheeks and lips stained the same vivid scarlet as her flowing gown.

Deep, brilliant red was Mala's color. It radiated from her garments like the blood of the hundred men she had slain with a glance. Her presence was hot, vibrant with life, dangerous to be near, and all too lethally primal.

Lot had been bewitched by her powers for months, sleepless with the thought of her.

"Oh, Mala, I had to come again," he said, reaching for her.

But Mala quickly pulled away and motioned for the wine to be brought.

"How is your trade here now, Lot?" she asked, handing him a heavy goblet.

"Very prosperous," he answered absently. Why must she always talk of trade? he wondered. "Oh, Mala, come out to the courtyard with me," he petitioned furtively. "We can be alone there."

Mala feigned temporary loss of hearing, smiling at a group of customers who had gathered near her.

"Mala?" Lot said. "Did you hear me?"

"Oh," she turned to him, "I'm so glad to know it goes well. That will bring you here more often then."

Frustrated, Lot shrugged his shoulders and gazed at her. She seemed to sense his hurt, and the tricks of her trade told her she had better not wound him too deeply or she would lose him. Putting her arm through his, she warmed him with a smile.

Lot grew limp and pliable again. And then Mala drew the net closer by sauntering off to speak with other men about the room.

Lot was about to follow her but stayed behind instead, watching her with the pout of a neglected child. Why must she torment him so? he asked himself. For months now he had come here, never knowing what response would be hers. She came to him eagerly, it seemed, many times. But just as often, she kept her distance, like a toy on a string let down only often enough to keep its interest.

She was a master at making confused fools of her admirers. And yet, Lot told himself, "When I am here, she seems more caught up in tormenting me than she does the others." But a new question plagued him as to whether this was a positive or negative omen.

It was just such a quandary Mala sought to create for him, and as the temptress wound her way through her audience, Lot watched in feverish admiration.

Mala's manager motioned her aside, and she stepped into an antechamber with him, the fat, heavily bearded man ordering her to sit down.

"I see your shepherd boy is down from the hills again," he snorted.

"So he is!" she tossed her head angrily.

"Shhh," he silenced her. "Don't let the customers hear you."

Mala stood up defiantly and started for the main room again.

"One moment, my scarlet beauty!" he warned her. "Let's not cozy up too much with one partner. Not good for business and besides," he snorted again, garlic breath reeking, "a sand rambler? a sheep trapper? Ha!" he exclaimed. "Surely, Mala, you could show more class!"

Mala turned violently on him, her black eyes sparking. "Show me a wealthier man in Sodom! His uncle is the Man from Ur, you know."

The manager looked disbelievingly at her. "Not the one camped by Hai—the one they all talk about?"

"Abram, to be sure!" she lashed at him.

The proprietor rubbed his bearded chin in contemplation.

"You won't be seeing me wasting my life in this flea hole forever," Mala laughed bitterly as she started for the door. But turning again to him before leaving, she smirked, "He's a sand rambler, true, but a more moneyed man in the courts you'll never find. And," she said haughtily, "you'll be seeing me ride the streets of Sodom in a handsome carriage soon enough!"

The manager grabbed her arm and sneered, "You think you can take a sand flea out of his hole and put him in a fancy nest? He'll never consent to be a city dweller!"

Mala smiled triumphantly. "Ah, but his heart is already here—his feet will follow!"

Chapter IV

The seed of discontent had fully blossomed.

Abram had spent three days in the hills conferring with the herdsmen, but it seemed no use. A confrontation in one quarter or another was inevitable, and Lot had still not come home.

Sarai looked helplessly at her husband as he sat dejectedly over his supper that night. From the look of him, she realized it would be best not to speak until spoken to, but she could guess the content of his thoughts anyway. Their childless state had been the topic of their conversation many times, for since the withdrawal of Lot, they had spoken of it often.

A sorrow inexpressible in words had grown year by year as they had waited, hoping for the signs of conception, but lately they had discussed it little. It was too painful.

Abram pushed his food aside and walked out into the cool evening. The Egyptian handmaiden, Hagar, whom Abram had given Sarai, cleared away his place and then studied her mistress's face. It was not the place of a servant to question or inquire into the private lives of her superiors, and so she kept silence.

Hagar was young, with an inquisitive, perpetually secretive expression on her adolescent face, as if she harbored thoughts too personal to be expressed. Sarai paid little attention to the girl, whose young womanhood had only recently shown signs of flowering. She was but a child in her mistress's eyes, and a rather lightheaded one at that, too caught up in daydreams to be of much practical worth. Sarai laughed a little to herself when she saw her handmaid's perpetual concern for her appearance. She wore an Egyptian body dress of colorful stripes, two broad straps forming the bodice as they crossed her torso. A long fall of deep chestnut hair flowed down her back, and her bare arms sported too many rings and bracelets.

The wide-eyed girl continued to stand in silence, staring toward the tent door where Abram had last been seen.

"Don't gape, Hagar," Sarai said impatiently. "What is it? Speak up."

Hagar blushed slightly and then, regaining her composure, said, "The master is a solitary man, is he not, mistress? He often likes to go out alone, doesn't he?

Sarai was surprised at this topic of discussion. "Well, yes, I suppose he does. Why?"

Hagar spoke softly, as if dealing with a most sacred subject, and still holding back the tent door, looking out at Abram, she said, "He must have a most heavy burden."

Sarai did not know how to respond to this, being somewhat surprised at Hagar's girlish insight. She could not chastise her for delving into their affairs, as she had asked no personal questions, and indeed, the young woman appeared to be showing genuine concern.

"Perhaps, Hagar. But that is no problem of yours," she said gently. "Go about your work now."

The maid was rather slow to move, still peering out the tent door. But at last sensing her mistress's growing impatience, she stepped in again. Before busying herself, however, she asked, "You have been the master's wife almost eight years?"

Sarai was astonished at her maid's forthrightness. "That is no concern of yours, girl!" she reprimanded. "Go now!"

Hagar took up a water urn and left the tent, but as Sarai watched her cross the yard, she noticed a strange new self-importance in the girl's gait.

Chapter V

It was another week before Lot returned from Sodom, and what greeted him was blood-chilling.

Drawing within a few miles of Beth-El, his hands and feet grew suddenly icy with fear. The hills which harbored the encampment were alive with flames. Scattered throughout the rolling meadows of the property, for miles in every direction, were low brush fires set by the vying enemies of each faction.

In a panic, Lot shouted, "Make speed for Abram's tent!" And running with savage haste, he and those accompanying him left their animals and goods and rushed for the distant flat within the valley.

As they neared the wadi which fed the camp, they were met by an onslaught of stampeding cattle, sheep, and goats frantically fleeing the conflagration. Lot and his men stood flat against the steep walls of the gorge until the first rampant herd had passed and then breathlessly climbed to the top of the ravine.

What met their eyes froze them with terror. The inevitable had finally come. Abram and his trained soldiers had at last been forced to go against Lot's many rebellious herdsmen, the resultant bloodshed and holocaust leaving hundreds wounded.

Abram had given strict orders that his men were to injure and stifle the rebels only, and not to kill. So the fatalities were minimal, though the scores of wounded men before Lot forestalled all consolation.

Horror etched on his paper-white face, Lot ran to Abram's tent. "My God! Uncle Abram, what has happened? Where are you?" he screamed, pleading for someone, anyone, to explain the meaning of the nightmare he saw about him.

He tore back the flap to his master's tent, but the dim light offered no sign of Abram. Sarai sat in the middle of the dwelling, attempting to comfort a wailing crowd of women and children who sought sanctuary there. She had not heard him above the noise of the moaning and crying, but he stood helplessly in the door, his head swimming, and called to her, "Madam, where is my uncle! Where is Abram? My God, what has happened?"

Sarai looked up at him in surprise, and her face filled with disgust and bitterness such as he had never seen. She stood up and rushed at him, an unearthly shriek issuing from her soul. "Get out! Get out, you worthless infidel! How dare you claim kinship with one called Abram! How dare you refer to his God as yours? Get away from his tent!" she cried.

Lot fell back from the door, but still she came at him. "You ask where he is?" she cried. "He has asked for you a hundred times—but you were rolling like a hog in the mire of Sodom! Go now and see your uncle!" she jeered, pointing to the hills where he had gone with his men. "Go and see how he labors to bring order out of the chaos your lechery has left him—he who gave you his honorable name and showered you with all your wasted substance!"

For hours, Lot wandered aimlessly through a blur of hot tears among the cindered hills of Beth-El. Dragging himself from one group of weary fire fighters to another, "Where is Abram?" was his ceaseless question. But always the answer was, "The next hill."

Lines of men and women passed wet blankets and switches of damp green brush up the steeps from the streams and wadis deep into the pastures raging with fire.

And for several hours, hundreds of workers beat and doused the flames with blankets and wet swatches of brush.

Slowly, painfully, the fires were one by one contained

and extinguished and one by one the crews lay down from their work in exhaustion.

At last, several miles from the central tent, Lot came upon his uncle still working and overseeing the control of the last blaze.

For some minutes he stood back watching him, the well-developed muscles of Abram's upper body glistening with sweat in the red hot glow of the leaping flames. Lot shielded his face from the heat and cowered in the relative darkness of the shadows—now, after finally finding Abram, hoping his uncle would not recognize his presence.

Tears of remorse and self-hatred flowed down his cheeks and into his beard. He remembered how he had admired his master on many occasions before, and that old feeling came again, only this time bringing with it such self-condemnation that he could not face his own soul.

Bitter guilt for the pain he had brought Abram tore at him. All the past stood clearly before him now, the good and the bad, but most of all, his boorish idiocy.

Coming out of the hills, he at last ran to Abram and threw his arms about his tired, perspiring shoulders.

"Uncle, let me help you!" he pleaded.

Abram felt a surge of anger well up within him at the sound of that voice—that untimely, inadequate petition, and he wheeled about to face Lot with hot, contemptuous eyes.

He raised his blistered hand in his anger, and with one mighty, crashing blow, he laid Lot prostrate on the ground.

So overcome, the prodigal in mixed pain and shock, stared up wildly at his master.

But Abram said not a word, only glaring down on his young betrayer before he walked away toward camp.

Chapter VI

Dawn arrived as the fire-fighters made their way back to their beleaguered families.

Their unrelenting efforts had saved the greater part of the fields; the animals and household goods had also, for the most part, been spared the disaster.

The exhausted people of the tribe rested as best they could until the heat of the day made it impossible for them to sleep.

And when the waking workmen had voraciously downed a huge meal, Abram rose before the congregation and walked to a high point where they all might see him. His face was intent, furrowed with sorrow and deep thought, his body bearing the aspect of one tossed about on the harsh sea of a most difficult decision.

The vast crowd was silent, wondering what the master was about.

And after what seemed an eternity, Abram raised his arms, motioning the people to follow him.

All except the badly wounded and their attendants rose and walked high into the vast ridge which hemmed the western side of the Salt Sea valley. They drove their weary legs relentlessly onward, in mass curiosity sensing the mysterious crescendo to which this moment was leading them.

Nearly half an hour of laborious progress brought them to the summit of a high hill overlooking the Jordan Valley and the great body of dead water which marked its end.

The many people crowded into the flat space which provided the view. Those who were too weary sat on the grassy slopes, but most could not bear to be cut off from the witness of whatever Abram would present, for they sensed that the end to their civil strife was at hand.

Down the mountain toward the camp, which now lay to the right of the view, were vast acres of scorched, barren ground. There was free running water to be sure, but the land Abram had contracted from the Canaanites and Perizzites of the vicinity would require many weeks before regaining its pleasant condition.

Far to the left, however, and running some sixty miles southeast of Beth-El was the verdant, alluvial expanse of Zoar, where the Vale of Siddim and the cities of the plain were harbored.

As far as the eye could see to the right and left, Abram and Lot had trafficked.

But today, as Abram overlooked this hushed scene near Beth-El, which the night before had been a scene of terror, he saw the lush valleys near Sodom and Gommorah, and for long moments he pondered it all.

Finally, turning about, he looked through the crowd for his nephew, and pointing toward him, motioned for Lot to step forward.

Lot had been rather anonymously standing far from the front of the audience, and a chill went through him at Abram's commanding gesture. Sheepishly he made his way through the assembly, which murmured and whispered about him.

Feeling extremely small, he walked haltingly up to the elevated point where Abram waited.

His uncle's great, cloudy eyes stared down on him, and Lot hesitated to take a step nearer. Following Abram's gaze, he looked over the fields and valleys at their feet, shuddering with the wind which blew up the steep incline.

A thrill of incredulous wonder went through him as he took it in. What did his uncle mean to do?

Looking at Abram apprehensively, he recognized something familiar in the sad, stormy eyes which greeted his—something which spoke of the yet unbroken love the aging man had for him.

And then Lot trembled with disbelief as his uncle said in slow, thoughtful, but determined tones, as if the climax of many months of deliberation was about to be reached, "Let there be no strife between us, I pray, and between my herdsmen and yours, for we are brethren— Is not the whole land before you?" he said, faltering only slightly, and then going on as if to hesitate would rob him of the necessary resolve to say the rest. "Separate yourself, I pray you, from me: if you will take the left hand, then I will go to the right; or if you depart to the right hand, then I will go to the left."

Lot faltered beneath the weight of the position in which he had been placed, and, staring incredulously at his beloved uncle, his young body shivered with the unexpected dilemma placed before him.

Surely, there was some compromise they could reach, he thought. Surely his uncle did not truly mean to part from him.

But a strange feeling now overtook him, a devious, inexplicable tingle of potential liberation, of the ability to select purposely what his heart most yearned for.

And then, lifting his eyes, he looked toward the Plain of Zoar, the Vale of Siddim, the cities of the plain, gleaming with the beauty of the lush green which was there. Memories of the woman Mala flashed into his mind, of the riches and glories to be had there.

And though a twinge of guilt haunted him, though he could barely believe his own heart, though he did not look at Abram—both men sensed his decision.

Then, as if quick movement might ease his conscience of the murderous blow it had just been dealt, Lot stole away down the left side of the mountain, his stunned followers standing by for some moments and then gradually dispersing to join him.

The Man of God sat solitary on the mount well into the cool of the day.

The sun was setting now, and far beneath, the caravan of the one he loved like a son wound its arduous way toward the Salt Sea and the environs of Sodom and Gomorrah.

Through the hazy consciousness of a broken heart, Abram kept vigil on the brow of the hill, not knowing how many hours passed before his Redeemer came to him, saying:

"Lift up now thine eyes, and look from the place where thou art northward and southward and eastward and westward, for all the land which thou seest, to thee will I give it and to thy seed forever. And I will make thy seed as the dust of the earth, so that if a man can number the dust of the earth, then shall thy seed be numbered."

Chapter VII

These were troubled days for Sodom.

When Lot had left Abram a year ago, he had considered the political tenor of his new home of little concern to him.

Twelve years before he had come to live here, the five cities of the plain, or the Pentapolis, of which Sodom was the most notorious member, had been subjugated by outside force. Since then they had served a great Mesopotamian confederacy under the dictatorial rule of one Chedorlaomer, king of Elam, east of Babylon. His allies were the famed Amraphel, king of Shinar in the alluvial lowlands of the fertile crescent; Arioch, king of Ellasar in southern Assyria; and Tidal, king over a broad area of land in northern Canaan.

This generally eastern dominance of the cities of the plain extended over much of the then-known world, from inner Asia to the Negeb.

And the five cities in the Vale of Siddim were among the wealthiest possessions of the Confederacy. For twelve years they had labored under the oppressive hand of Chedorlaomer, and in the thirteenth year they rebelled.

It was on the very eve of this civil upheaval that Lot had entered the plains to make his home. Being prosperous enough to leave his people under the management of his many officials, Lot visited the city as frequently as the plain, and shortly became a virtual city dweller, which pleased Mala extremely.

On the night of the wedding feast which followed Lot's taking of his bride, news came of the long-awaited alliance of Sodom and her sister cities to challenge the oppressors.

A general furor of gaiety grew out of this announcement, and long into the night the wedding guests danced and caroused in joy, as much for the marriage of the cities as for the marriage of the young couple.

But the weeks which followed were uneasy. The first step of rebellion was in the area of finance. Under the authorship of Bera, their king, the Sodomites no longer took a third of their profits in grain and produce or a third of their profits in cattle and gold to the tax collectors who sat at the gates.

No longer did they pay obeisance to the Assyrian governors who rode through their streets in gaudy chariots, and no longer did they watch indifferently as members of their community were taken as slaves to the court of the emperor.

Nor was the Pentapolis ignorant of the consequences of such action. They knew the Confederates would not long withhold judgment from them. But their courage lay in the knowledge that many other subjected city-states were similarly rebelling. The entire empire, in fact, groaned with discontent. And so, they reasoned, there was strength in numbers.

What they did not anticipate was the strength and speed with which their conquerors would retaliate. Before the rebels of all the nations had sufficient time to organize themselves into a cohesive body, the four kings of the east were prepared to quell them.

It was with fear that chills the marrow in a man's bones that the sister cities received word of the imperial response.

The armies came, moving along the great three-hundred-mile military highway which led from central Asia to Damascus and down the eastern side of the Ghor. Marching, plundering, massacring, and then moving on, they subdued city after city.

Beginning with the gigantic Rephaim south of Damascus and working their way through the Zummim of Ham and Emmim of the hills one day to be called Moab to the Horites who dwelled in caves near the Dead Sea, they marched until they came to the wilderness.

Turning their attention northward, they next came into the land of the Amalekites and Amorites southwest of the Dead Sea. This was dangerously close to Sodom and her sisters, and the people of the Pentapolis, knowing the kings were saving them for last, felt the day of imminent and costly battle pressing them.

Lot realized it would be unwise to stay inside Sodom if his people and possessions were at the camp some miles away, and so the young husband had to take his bride there despite all her protests, or else be separated from her indefinitely, or permanently.

Convinced the hills were safer than the target city, he at first pleaded for and finally ordered Mala's obedience. But, shocked at her husband's turn of dominance, she at last complied only amid much hysterical wailing.

For days the camp carried on as usual, trying not to let the growing tension of the hour weigh them down. But, never knowing from one day to the next if they would go to bed and wake safely, if they would still see Sodom on the horizon with sunrise, their nerves were ready to shatter like thin ice.

The news from the city was never encouraging, and often the shepherds could see scouts of the invading armies surveying the valley from the hills above.

The land of the Amorites lay only miles away to the west. It would be merely a matter of time before the armies which had subdued that stronghold came to take the Vale of Siddim, and waiting for this was like waiting for a deadly plague to creep into one's body with the bite of a fly which hovered overhead.

The city dwellers as well as the caravaneers faced this fear. At last the bowstring was drawn to the breaking point, and rather than wait in mental anguish for the Confederates to come to them, the allies of the plain took the initiative. At least, they reasoned, they would have the element of surprise in their favor if they struck first.

It was at the southern tip of the Salt Sea that the five kings of the Pentapolis met their foe. Beneath a scorching sun which drew steam from the very desert itself, they first glimpsed their enemy.

Robed in scarlet tunics with shining brass helmets, the advancing horde from the east was an awesome spectacle. Chedorlaomer and the mightiest of all warriors, Amraphel, did not direct the war from the sideline as many generals did. Instead they led their cavalcade, thousands upon countless thousands, through the treacherous lowlands of the sea, riding in front of them, their banners fanning the breeze, their chariots gleaming in the bouncing glare of noonday.

Bera and his four allies knew the cause was hopeless before it had begun. Yet they were determined to do their best in stifling the enemy which came in an unending wave across the valley floor.

The valiant little alliance which waited for them did not stand long. In a battle which was to end before the heat of midday, Bera and the king of Gomorrah, Birsha, attempted desperately to salvage what little of their dignity was left, but they would have done better to surrender.

Their armies were pushed far up the Arabah to the extreme southern tip of the sea, which was notorious for its infernal slime and asphalt pits. No longer able to fight back, the five forces were easily divided, Bera and Birsha fleeing with their men toward the pits and the remaining forces racing for the dry, craggy mountains which bordered the sea.

And as they ran, they were only faintly conscious of their bearings. Pushed to the extremity of their endurance, the forces of Sodom and Gomorrah stumbled through the black, volcanic rubble which hemmed the Vale, many of them falling in exhaustion to await their conquerors, others continuing until they could go no further because of the bituminous pits.

The sulphurous mass, spewing and bubbling below them, sent a deathly, reeking odor into the air around the salt flats. But, many, when they saw the final approach of the enemy, did not surrender but leaped over the sides of the jagged pits to die.

Bera and Birsha were among them. Not necessarily nobly, but determined not to be captured, they flung themselves into the pits and were sucked under by the scalding, black, soup.

After their victory, the invaders spared no time in heading for the spoils of the Pentapolis. The very evening of the battle, Lot's people stood in their hilly home, watching as Sodom and Gomorrah were sacked.

It was an expensive lesson the sister cities had learned about their oppressors, but for Lot, the unexpected was yet to come.

It had been foolish and uncalculating of him to assume that his position in the hills immunized him against a part in the proceedings. His naiveté was a product of his casual, nomadic approach to the politics of his new city life. Living close to an oppressed city was to risk suffering under the same oppression. And certainly Lot's large, wealthy encampment had not escaped the eyes of the conquerors.

That night a small armed band appeared on the edge of the camp, but they need not have come in force. Lot had no army—only the skill of his men, who were best at herding and hunting.

Lot comforted his weeping, frightened wife and, pulling his cloak about him, went out to attempt a bargain.

Unlike the Guti, these "civilized" forces did not kill for the joy of it. Their massacres were calculated to bring the best advantage to the empire, to quell rebellions, to gain land, but not to enjoy a sport. Lot knew what they really wanted was his wealth, for it would profit them little to harm him.

The captain of the band warned him to come no

closer as Lot raised his arm in greeting. Perspiration glistened on his forehead, though he told himself fear was unnecessary.

"Good sir," he called, "whatever you want is yours for the taking, only please do no harm to my people!"

The captain left his chariot and said with a smirk, "You are a very prudent man. Your wisdom may be your salvation."

He then motioned his men to search the tents, and one by one they entered, bringing armloads of goods which appeared useful or valuable to them. The night camp, concentrated in one area, offered immense booty, and the silver, gold, foodstuffs, fine fabrics—all Lot's substance—was loaded into the waiting wagons of the band.

Mala cried incessantly as the riches were hauled off, and Lot's heart ached with the agony of sudden poverty. Each saddle, each skin of wine, each ornament taken from camp was like a piece of himself torn away. But most of all he dreaded the humble words he would have to speak to Abram to be readmitted to the family—if Abram would take him back. And Lot's head was dizzy with the sudden depths to which all his labors had been plunged.

But the nobility which was still inherently his prevented him from thinking solely on his possessions. His distress was somewhat relieved by the thought that the enemy would leave him and his people unharmed.

This supposition, however, was premature. The familiar cries of Mala now came more intensely from the main tent, and Lot turned to run to her, but a wrenching twist of his arm warned him to go no farther. Like more spoils of war, the beautiful woman and her handmaids were thrust from the tent and bound with strong cords. Several of Lot's closest officials were then added to this company as he struggled to free himself from his captor.

"What do you mean to do with us?" he demanded, all his energy helpless against the one who shackled him.

"Your uncle will pay a handsome price for you, Master Lot. Didn't you consider that you and your allies are more valuable than all the gold your camp might afford?"

The captain's large white teeth showed in a cruel smile, displaying obvious delight in the parley.

Lot, thrown rudely into a wagon with his family, could only look lingeringly on those he left behind until they were lost in the enveloping darkness.

Chapter VIII

The armies of the Confederacy had joined one another after the battle in the strange dry hills east of the sea.

Upon arriving here, Lot had found himself and his people thrown in with a mammoth herd of prisoners of war, all selectively chosen for the price they might bring or for the fine slaves they might make. As for the women, many had been chosen for the king's pleasure.

But the children—Lot wondered about them. As he studied their pitiful little faces, some sleeping restlessly on their mother's laps, others wide-eyed with fear, he wondered what cruel design was laid for them.

The prisoners huddled in the icy wind which blew off the sea, stationed far from the many fires which warmed their hosts. Bulky guards in heavy gear traipsed around their enclosure ceaselessly eying the heavy chains which shackled them together, watching for signs of breaks. A large rope fence had been placed about the area where they were now seated, giving much the feeling of a cattle pen.

And were they not cattle of a sort? Captured and tamed to serve their masters? Yes, they were like a siring group, new-bound to slavery, and they would kick viciously against the pricks. But like so many enslaved nations before them, in other places, at other times—Lot thought—several careful generations of breeding would produce a fine crop who would unthinkingly serve and obey, as if born to it by inherent instinct. And, he reasoned, only a miracle of the human spirit would make them rise to pursue freedom.

Lot could not see Mala or the other people of his tribe. They had been too badly mixed in with other prisoners, and though he searched every face as far as he could from his seated position, they were not to be seen.

He settled himself in submissive silence and tried to sleep, but hunger gnawed at his ribs. Nothing but his cloak shielded him from the frigid winds. Grown men about him shuddered violently at each breeze, but more with fear, he thought, than with cold.

He would not fear, he told himself. His naturally stubborn, headstrong heart rose in determination.

Suddenly a new apprehension clutched him. The captain had told him he was captured for ransom, not for slavery, but Lot wondered just how much he could expect from Abram now. What made him think his uncle would willingly offer up his wealth to bring back one who had so belligerently and thanklessly turned from him?

The guilt which had hounded him for so long, the guilt of turning from Abram and his God had been more and more easily put from his mind with passing time. But all the reasoning which told him his choices were wise, that Abram was the fool, now seemed meaningless. Now that Lot had been torn from riches and comfort, the thoughts he had been able to put out of his mind for six years, all he had claimed was irrelevant because his uncle had once failed, seemed suddenly all-important.

Stripped of the conscience-numbing glamor of Sodom, Lot squirmed under this self-examination. It was uncomfortable and he tried to replace it with other thoughts. But still the knowledge that his behavior had been based on wretched excuses pounded its way home with each heartbeat.

So, his candidacy for slavery was just as possible as that of those around him. He shuddered with the realization. Visions of his future children and grandchildren, visions of his little ones being herded about by the demands of a sovereign race, flashed before him.

It was with a sigh of relief that his nightmares were dispelled by the voice of one nearby.

"Dreadful cold, sir, isn't it?" a young man whispered.

Lot, thus rescued from his silent terrors, turned to the fellow captive. "What's that?" he said.

"I say, 'Dreadful cold,' " the prisoner repeated.

"Oh yes, it is." Lot pulled his coat tighter to him.

"You weren't asleep, for your eyes were open, but I spoke three times before you answered," the man said kindly. "You were thinking of your loved ones, no doubt?"

Lot nodded silently.

The young man reached inside his cloak and drew out a hunk of bread. "They didn't find this on me," he whispered. "I've been saving it. Here," he said, offering Lot a piece.

Lot was not too proud to accept the much-needed food. "Thanks so much," he smiled. And after eating, he felt more like talking. "I take it you are an Amorite," Lot said, referring to the man's speech.

"Yes, and you?"

Lot hesitated, not knowing whether to answer that he was of Sodom or Chaldea. "My people are caravaneers," he finally said.

"Oh, Hebrews," his friend smiled. "A worthy occupation." And studying Lot's clothing, he added, "I see it pays well. Where were you when you were—"

"Captured? Near Sodom." Lot's voice was shaky with the memory.

"You have people here?"

Lot's eyes answered for him.

"Well," the Amorite continued, "Do you know why you were taken?"

"Yes—for ransom," Lot said.

"Ah, then you're one of the fortunate few."

But Lot looked at the ground, and the Amorite sensed a problem. "You do have someone to pay it, don't you?"

Lot grew a bit impatient with the man's questions. But rather than lapse into silence, he continued, "I hope so, though I'm not at all sure."

The Amorite's curiosity was whetted by this, and Lot could see he was anxious to hear more. After a long time had passed, he went on:

"My uncle and I do not get on well. A year ago we separated, I with one-third his tribe and possessions. It was the culmination of six years' strife between us." Strangely compelled to continue, Lot felt a freedom in speaking to his new friend. "I must confess," he said, "I didn't do right by my uncle." His voice was soft and almost repentant. "He was more than patient with me, though I never let myself realize how I responded to his generosity."

The Amorite waited to hear more but, sensing Lot's contemplative mood, was patient for some time. Then he asked, "Where is your uncle?"

"At a camp near Hai. Do you know the place?"

The Amorite's eyes were suddenly alive with interest. "You wouldn't mean your uncle is Abram, the Hebrew of Ur?"

"Why, yes! How did you guess?" Lot exclaimed.

"I know Abram!" the Amorite answered. But then, shaking his head, he said, "My, you have been cut off from him, haven't you? He has not been at that camp for a year now. He has contracted near Hebron, in a place called the Oaks of Mamre, after my eldest brother, the owner."

Lot suddenly felt his alienated position more poignantly than ever before. That he, once like a son to Abram, should not even have known his whereabouts for a full year—the thought was lonely and foreboding. A voluntary defector, he should not have been surprised that his self-exile had left him little communication with Abram's doings. Had he thought the world stood still when he left home, that all his relatives became fixed like wax figures until his return?

Still, the thought was unpleasant, a little like an announcement arriving long after an event has occurred. How presumptuous of him to consider himself any part of Abram now, to have thought his uncle might ransom him, or even care where he was.

But while Lot wallowed in self-pity, the Amorite was busy formulating something in his mind, and at last he said, "I haven't told you my name. It is Aner, and you are Lot, aren't you?"

Lot was shocked at this pronouncement, and Aner smiled. "I can tell the news of your uncle's doings is burdensome to you. But how do you suppose I knew your name?" He leaned toward Lot gently. "Don't you see? Your uncle has spoken often of you. He has never said much about why you went from him, as if the thought of it pained him at heart—so we never questioned him." Aner paused in contemplation. "Did you live with him near Hai?"

"Yes," Lot said sadly, looking far away, his thoughts there now.

"Ah, then I see now why Abram left those gorgeous fields and came to Mamre."

Lot smiled. Something in that news comforted him.

For several days the armies and their prisoners marched up the dry King's Highway toward Damascus and the inner reaches of Asia. But the broiling heat and his aching, swelling feet did not daunt the enthusiasm young Aner had for a scheme which had been brewing in his mind.

He spoke of it ceaselessly as they walked, never letting it be heard above a whisper but flailing his arms ecstatically with each new idea.

Aner planned to escape. He said his two brothers, Mamre and Eshcol, had a small army, about three hundred men all together. If Abram would consent to join them, with his three hundred and eighteen trained servants, they would have a good battalion. If Aner could only be freed of this dreary march, he would scurry back to Mamre and give word of Lot's capture. Surely, he said, Abram would then offer his help, and the region of Canaan might be freed once and for all of its oppressors.

Lot paid little attention to Aner's foolishness. Nonetheless glad for his companionship, Lot only laughed at the silly plan.

"Even if you could escape, which is nigh to impossible, and even if Abram did consent, which seems doubtful, what could such a minute force possibly accomplish short of being stomped under the heels of Chedorlaomer?" Lot asked. "Forget this idiocy," he laughed. "I admire your courage, and should you escape, I would be ever so happy for you. But forget the rest."

But Aner paid as little attention to Lot as Lot did to him. "What ever was accomplished by that attitude?" he responded. "Anything is worth a try. Greater things have been done—and, after all, we cannot lie down like dead dogs to be hauled away with no struggle, can we?"

Lot saw it was useless to argue, so he sat by passively as Aner began to carry out his scheme.

The first step was to be freed of the shackles. Since this could only be worked on at night when they were seated, Lot spent many evenings watching as Aner filed away at his ankle hinge with broken rocks, the only sharp implements available.

Since the crowd of prisoners was so large, Aner carried this out in relative obscurity, those around him never breathing a word of his efforts lest it get to the guards.

Those watchdogs, fortunately, stayed around the edges of the pen, only rarely coming inside. At such times that they did come near, Aner always received ample warning of their approach.

The young Amorite was apparently the only one brave enough, or, in Lot's eyes, foolish enough, to try such a plan. "Even if you do free yourself of that chain, how do you expect to get away from here?" he gibed.

But Aner only continued filing and said, "At night the guard changes. The evening my chain is finally broken, we will wait for that moment. You are to lead a small group of men here to stir up a commotion among the prisoners. And while the guards are busy finding the reason for the commotion, I will sneak through the opening left at the instant of the shift."

"And if you get that far, what happens next? There is more than one ring of guards in the event of just such an attempt. Haven't you seen those stationed in the hills?" Lot questioned.

Aner looked at him with a knowing smile. "Don't worry. I have it all planned. There's not a thing you can think of which I have not already worked out." And then leaning secretively toward Lot, he whispered, "Where's the least likely place you would go to find a fugitive?"

Lot shrugged his shoulders, and Aner laughed, saying, "Why, in the tents of his captors, man!"

The Amorite said no more then, but went back to his filing, and Lot lay down in a puzzled sleep.

Three days later, Aner's leg iron, weakened at the hinge by continual strain on the pin-bolt, severed itself from the main chain which joined him to his fellows. The guards did not see the dangling shackle which slapped the ground as he marched in formation all that afternoon.

That night the long-awaited plan was put into effect. Lot, very fearful for his new friend, and feeling rather foolish, gave the signal for the riot to begin, and amid the chaotic noise of the upheaval, Aner did precisely as he had said.

Pushing his way through the crowd, he came to the heavy rope encircling them, and while the guards' attention was diverted, he slipped out of the pen through a vacancy left during the change of guards, just as he had planned.

All was going smoothly, and now the second phase of the plan had to be carried out. As he had told Lot, the most unlikely place for a fugitive was within one of his captor's tents, and so he scurried through the shadows, unnoticed by the armed militia who milled around the noisy pen. He ran in a crouching position until he came to a long barrack tent which housed one unit of the army. With the courage of a fool he threw back the tent door and called in a deep voice of command, "Men, at arms! You are to report at once to the prison camp. A riot is under way. Take time only to gather up your weapons!"

The sleepy men in the tent were on their feet instantly at the sound of the supposed command, having no reason to suspect the imposter. And their eyes, fooled by the darkness, their ears, numbed by drowsiness, told them the figure in the doorway was indeed their captain.

They hurried out of the tent, their heavy gear in tow, not seeing Aner, who had now slipped back from the door. And when they had all gone, Aner quickly crept into the barracks, dressing himself in a full soldier's uniform.

The rest was a matter of timing. He must be gone before the officials realized what had happened. As he did not wish to attract attention, he did not run but calmly walked to the hills above the camp. "I was sent to see if any have tried escaping the prison camp through your vicinity, soldier," he said, authority ringing in his voice, as he came upon one sentry.

"No, sir."

"Good man," he smiled. "Keep an eye out."

"Yes, sir."

His head held high, Aner then worked his way through the dark, craggy hills until he could slip unnoticed over the far side. As he was about to do so, he looked back one last time at the throng below, where the confused captains had finally forced order, and where the guards were counting heads.

"One is missing!" a sentinel shouted, and Aner smiled jubilantly as he raced toward the desert and his brother's home.

Chapter IX

The trappings of nomadic life did not allow for sophisticated armies, but the four chieftains, Abram, Mamre, Eshcol, and Aner had well-equipped forces nonetheless.

With daredevil ambition the small battalion, some on camel but most on foot, worked its way up the long path of desolation left behind by the retreating victors. The large forces from the east were not as fast-moving or as motivated as Abram's, and so it took only a few days of concentrated effort to reach them.

Creeping through the range which hemmed the King's Highway, they finally spied their objective, the huge enemy camp settled for the evening on the shoulder of land closest to the sea. They were near Dan, a small town south of Damascus.

Abram dismounted and walked toward a platform of rock. Scanning the mammoth layout, his eyes fell on the large, penned area which enclosed the prisoners, and his father instincts rose wildly at the thought of Lot's condition. His feeling for the young rebellious one who had turned from him so cruelly had never left his heart, and since the brave, bone-weary Aner had stumbled into camp with news of Lot's capture, Abram's only desire had been for vengeance.

He called to the others to join him, and the four men laid themselves flat on the ledge, studying their adversary for some time.

The mighty armies of Mesopotamia were an awesome sight. Now that the reality of this venture was fully upon them, the men wondered if they had been fools. But Abram, being from the same region as the invaders and somewhat familiar with the habits of eastern armies, told them that after a victory a Mesopotamian force usually spent its retreat in revelry and celebration, paying little heed to its surroundings.

"Their overconfidence robs them of the care they should take in securing their camps," he laughed. "More than once I have heard of such forces, who, letting down their security, have been overcome by a retaliating foe."

His three friends laughed at this. "Why don't they learn?" Mamre asked.

"That is one of the mysteries of the Orient, my friend," Abram smiled. "Vigilance has never been the byword of my countrymen. We are mighty warlords and a proud race, but many times too proud for our own good."

With this encouragement the men set about to plan their strategy.

The soldiers of the Confederacy slept comfortably in their long tents each evening and were therefore not spread widely throughout the camp, but concentrated in small areas. This was the key to Abram's plan.

When darkness finally came, and when the nightly celebrators went to their tents, Abram and his followers crept slowly toward the camp. Splitting into tiny forces of a dozen men each, the six hundred moved down the hills.

Very quietly they set upon the few sentries who were stationed near the borders. Then, encircling the camp in the shadows, each small group headed for a predetermined barrack.

When within a few feet of the sleeping, ill-prepared soldiers, their leaders awaited Abram's signal to begin.

"Go!" he commanded.

And with this they raised an unearthly clamor. Beating upon their shields, whipping the sides of the tents with their spears, yelling vociferously—so they greeted their dreaming foes.

Instant terror and confusion reigned in the camp, the

beleaguered soldiers' own shouts of surprise and fear adding to the chaos of the moment. As they leaped from their pallets, reaching for their weapons in the darkness, colliding blindly with one another—they knew a dreadful host had invaded them. Each shadowy comrade was the foe, any adjacent body the enemy—in mad confusion they lashed at one another.

Some dashed out into the open, and at this juncture, Abram's small army greeted them with its own weapons.

Meanwhile, Aner had entered the poorly guarded precincts of the prisoners, leading them out to finalize the coup. Having witnessed the escape and now the return of their hero to defeat the foe, the captives were more than willing to do what they could to ensure his success.

Though chained to one another, the men rose as a body and proceeded in rows to invade the camp. Forming a stubborn wall of resistance, the trampling waves of prisoners marched on their enemies, unarmed save for the ponderous iron chains, which they kicked mercilessly into the faces of their foes, their heavy shackles biting into their own bleeding flesh at every move.

Trampling through the grounds relentlessly, they continued, despite the bodies of wounded or murdered comrades linked and dragging between them.

A furious vigor gripped this handicapped crew. The downtrodden had risen with that miracle of the human spirit which cries for freedom.

Even the four kings were unable to bring order to their troops before they themselves were greeted by the blows of the nomadic host. At the first sounds of the chaotic invasion, mighty King Chedorlaomer and his closest ally, Amraphel, stood half-dressed on the elevated porch of their portable palace, their drugged eyes bloated and only slowly alive to the madness about them. Arioch and Tidal groped toward the door behind, the nightmare of reality dawning on their sluggish senses.

"Friends—to arms!" the king of Elam shouted frantically. "The Egyptians are upon us!" he cried, assuming that only that mighty empire could have so nobly assailed them.

The four allies, showing little courtly dignity, careened headlong into one another, scrambling for their shields in the dark recesses of the tent.

"Valet! Steward!" roared the king of Shinar, the mighty monarch of Assyria. "Where are you, oaf! Help me with my armor!" he bellowed. But his personal servant was nowhere to be seen, having disappeared into the fray below.

The armies of the Confederacy were divided, helpless to overcome the vengeance wielded upon them. In the darkness the kings watched incredulously as their troops swarmed among their slain brothers and were pursued in droves into the hills.

And now, the predators were upon the kings themselves. Within head-spinning seconds their quarters had been surrounded, their great tent of command an easy target for the fast-flying darts of the enemy.

Like hurtling spikes of a hundred scorpions, the spears and arrows of Abram's allies riddled the heavy goatshair, leaving the once-noble tent secure as a sieve.

In bewilderment the trapped monarchs huddled in the center of the spike-riddled room.

But the secret of their mutual despair was never to be fully known beyond those confines. Defying humiliation, Chedorlaomer turned to his cowering companions and threatened them with their own shame. "Stand up!" he shouted. "Or by the gods I will drive you through with my own spear!"

It was therefore a stalwart group which faced the mortal thrusts of its unknown assailants. And it was with heads held high that the four kings of the great alliance met the end of their campaign.

Chapter X

When morning came, Abram wandered, bone-weary, through the leveled camp of his enemies. Even now the remaining Confederates fled up the valley of the King's Highway, and by this time their pursuers would have chased them as far as Hobah, north of Damascus.

Though exhausted by the journey and the night's activities, Abram's first thought was for Lot. In the grey light of dawn he searched the ranks of the prisoners for his nephew.

But in such a throng the faces tended to obscurity. Each was hunger-ridden, drawn, and weary. The joy of victory was felt here, but the many dead and wounded, the many drugged by the intolerable pain of their biting shackles, cast a gloom even over that.

Abram asked for news of his nephew, for directions to him, but few spoke his language, and those who did had not inquired the identity of those around them.

The poor people gathered here were a conglomeration of captives from all the nations the Confederacy had overrun on this campaign. Long, lanky Rephaim, the dark-skinned Zummim, the hill-dwelling Emmim and Horites, the wealthy Amalekites, Amorites, and the people of the five cities, all blended their speeches and dress in the confusion.

And Abram marveled that such a diverse group had maneuvered so single-mindedly the night before.

Finally, he spied a group of Sodomites in a far corner. Walking quickly to them, he called, "Do you know where Lot the Hebrew is?"

One of them had seen him the night before but could not tell where he was now. Abram went on, looking intently at each face, and he had nearly given up the quest, but at last he saw Aner standing over a low form, waving to him.

The ex-prisoner knew his way about the once-chained figures and had located Lot with ease. Abram ran to the couple, but stopped, miserable at the sight of his nephew.

The one he loved like a son lay in excruciating pain, his swollen ankles more badly battered than those of any other captive Abram had seen.

"Lot," he whispered. "My son, what has happened to you?" He knelt beside him now and cradled his head on his knee.

Lot looked into his master's face, ashamed to speak, with the full knowledge that Abram had risked his life for him. Large, hot tears poured down his face, and he struggled in pain to say, "If I had not left you, Uncle, I would have needed no rescue."

Abram quieted him and held him close. Pointing to Lot's battered, bruised feet and ankles, Abram looked at Aner. "Oh, friend, what caused this?" he asked.

"When I freed myself, Lot says he fought with all his strength to loose his legs from the chains. What took me five days to accomplish, he struggled to do overnight, for when he saw I would go to engage your help, he wanted to save you the need to come." Aner paused and then said, "He knew you would have died for him."

Chapter XI

Happy news, like sad, travels quickly, and so it was that a great celebration had been prepared for Abram and his allies upon their return.

Leaving the Damascus area, they cut north of the Salt Sea, intending to go down the west side to Mamre, and when Abram, his allies, and all the refugees appeared near the lovely city of Salem, they were greeted with a homecoming festival fit for a king.

From miles around people had come, people of all tribes and tongues, hoping their loved ones might be among those returning, or simply wishing to glimpse the ones who had so soundly won back their freedom.

The custom of greeting returning victors was common throughout the eastern world. And so it came as no surprise to Abram that he was met thus, in the King's Dale of Shaveh.

What a wild, clamorous joy broke loose upon first sight of the approaching forces! Women of the various nations, all robed in the festive garbs common to their lands, danced their way before the oncomers, swaying and twirling like so many leaves before the wind, singing of war, triumph, valor, and fearless pride.

And as they marched, Abram's followers searched the pressing crowd for familiar faces, women and children breaking from the ranks of the spectators, running with tears of joy to their safely arrived men and families.

Such reunions there were, everywhere couples and families clasped tightly in the rapture of being once again together.

Abram and his allies rode, as was customary, ahead of the victorious warriors, and the former prisoners who had been freed by their own earnest desire for liberty.

Lot rode beside him, though he felt greatly shamed and unworthy of doing so. And from the height of his large, colorfully decked camel, the handsome, aging Abram eagerly surveyed the crowd.

At last he saw Sarai, waving joyfully to him, trapped in the jostling throng. Dismounting, he quickly forced his way to her, and for one moment they were alone in the embrace of their own reunion.

But a sudden thrill of excitement now coursed afresh through the crowd. Shouts of "Look, the King is here!" and "Hail the King!" rang everywhere. Abram looked up to see the newly crowned king of Sodom approaching with a large train of court princes.

The young monarch, following the defeat of his father, had taken a fallen throne. Little promise of a fruitful reign had been his. And today, Abram thought, he wished to behold the saviors of that kingdom, to make known his inexpressible gratitude.

Seated on a fine, canopied dromedary, he motioned to a man at his side, apparently his prime minister. Bowing low, the official took his instructions, and turning to the crowd, he shouted, "Abram the Hebrew, and his allies, Mamre, Eshcol, and Aner, the Amorites, are requested to come forward."

Abram was not anxious to receive the applause of Sodomites. Nothing in his nature sought the approval of those with whom he had no conversation. Thus, as the applauding crowd stepped aside to let him pass, it was only out of respect to custom that he went forward. Passing row upon row of men and women prostrate before their king, something within him cringed.

The king smiled down on him from his lofty position, much as if giving the blessed benediction of his very presence to a humble servant. He seemed to wait, but Abram did not bow.

The crowd stirred restlessly, and the king, not a little dampened by the independent pride of this shepherd chieftain, slipped quickly on to the business at hand. He knew it best not to enter upon his reign by quibbling over formalities with the hero of his people.

And so, clearing his throat, he forced another masterful smile, raising his regal hands in a flourish of showmanship, and began his first public oration:

"Men and women of Sodom, and others gathered here, this is indeed a great and memorable day for the City of cities. The enemy who would so vainly have warred with us has been vanquished. The noble city has once again seen the approval of her gods."

At this, Abram swelled with indignation, but, continuing to twist the glory of this victory to the credit of his "noble" town, the king pointed to him and went on.

"In their wisdom the gods chose the most unlikely of tools to accomplish their purpose. As if in mockery of our enemy, the gods chose a Bedouin—a plainsman who traffics in sheep—to overcome them."

Abram fought back the torrent of disgust which hammered within him. How dare this infant blue blood deal so with him? It was with numb, disbelieving ears that Abram heard the rest:

"Oh my people, is it not a great day we have seen? Is it not a sign forever to you and to your children that the jewellike city of your nativity is the haven of the gods?"

The king looked now at Abram and with a final touch of drama commended him, saying, "Pass on to your children the tale of the lowly shepherd through whom the gods have forever shamed our foes!"

Then, turning toward Abram, the king said in grave, magnanimous tones, "Abram the Hebrew, you have returned with my people and all our possessions. By the gods, I ask that you give me the persons, but—" and here he paused for effect, raising his voice in tones of abundant self-sacrifice, "but—take the goods for yourself!"

At this a tumult of cheers and applause filled the valley, evident approval of the king's generosity rushing through the roaring crowd.

Abram looked up at the pompous Sodomite who had deftly used this entire episode to focus the crowd's attention on himself. Freedom-loving warriors and death-defying men who had fought in bloody shackles had been neatly deprived of their just reward, the laud and praise of their countrymen. Instead, it had been surreptitiously and underhandedly turned toward an imposter. This babe-in-arms was a brilliant politician after all, Abram mused. How masterfully had he turned love of country into love of king, how magnificently had he made himself the hero, and how strange that no one seemed to notice but the "lowly shepherd" standing before him.

With a well-disguised sneer, Abram asked to speak.

The king obligingly condescended, and applause again broke out as he let Abram step up to be seen by all.

Perhaps mimicking the king's stage play, Abram raised his hands, and the silent crowd waited for his words. It was in a tone of subdued sarcasm that Abram began.

"People of Sodom and all gathered here, King of Sodom and your regal court," He paused and then said very rapidly, "My intent was never the salvation of your foul city!"

At this the monarch started in angry shock, but Abram went on.

"Nor was my intent the promotion of your prosperity or the continuance of a culture for which I have only the deepest antipathy. My intention, Oh King, was the rescue of my brother from the clutches of your political squabbles, and—if in the process I have somehow benefited you—then let my God be the judge of that most questionable result!"

The king was in a turmoil, his eyes a storm of confusion. He could not very well silence the one who had saved him and his city, but, how dare this Bedouin—?

Abram bowed, a sneer of inexpressible disgust evident to all his audience. "Your Majesty," he continued very deliberately, "My allies may take their share, but since your gods have already 'made me a hero,' I cannot accept more from them. For," he said, standing high and speaking emphatically, his words echoing in the hills, "I have sworn to my God, to the Lord most high, Maker of heaven and earth, that I would not take a thread, or a sandal thong, or anything that is yours lest you should also say you have made Abram rich!"

The crowd was dumfounded at the Hebrew's confident wit. An involuntary roar of laughter followed, and the humiliated ruler rose angrily to silence the disorderly throng—but he only glared speechlessly at the proud shepherd before him.

During these proceedings, a small group of figures had gathered unnoticed on a hill to the far side of the crowd, and as Abram was about to leave the king's side, the prime minister came forward, whispering something in His Majesty's ear.

The crowd became silent, and seeing that the monarch's attention had been drawn to the gathering silhouetted on the hilltop, they grew curious as to the meaning of the mystery.

Abram, too, strained to see who the anonymous newcomers might be but could make out little to satisfy himself.

The distant collection of men now moved forward a bit, and the central figure walked down the hill toward the waiting crowd. As he grew closer, some seemed to recognize him, and a muffled undercurrent of whispers spread from person to person.

Abram could not make out the words, but he gathered that the conversation centered on the strange, austere man who approached. Abram now grew apprehensive. The throng seemed not only excited and curious, but almost awed—fearful—as if this man had a mysterious charisma which captivated them.

Uneasily, Abram drew close to the prime minister

and whispered, "What is this? Who is this man and why does he move the crowd so?"

The dignitary looked in surprise at Abram and said, "You don't know?"

Abram shook his head. "Should I?"

The prime minister seemed to brighten at the prospect of breaking in a novice to a bit of what he considered humorous local color. "Well, surely you've heard of the king of Salem," he offered.

This was said with such emphasis that Abram gathered that some deep meaning should be inferred, but he could see none. Salem was a peaceful, quiet little town, set to the northwest of the Salt Sea in a fertile corner of the Jordan Valley. It played no major political role hereabouts, and though Abram had traded with the community, which lay between Mamre and Beth-El, it had never especially drawn his attention.

"I have heard of Salem, and I have known that it, like other cities, has a king. But come, man, what's the mystery?" he said, impatient with the prime minister's deliberate delay.

The official leaned toward him and whispered, "The king—Melchizedek is his name—claims to be a priest, though I've never been clear on what religion he claims. But," and here he laughed to himself, "the peasants and Bedouins around these parts have a legend which says the old fellow was living, as they say it, 'before the mountains were formed.'" And with this last statement, he put his hand to his heart, in mock reverence for the folk tale.

Abram smiled. "I see. But has he no formal history? Surely all this could be cleared up by a look at the record."

The prime minister only shrugged his shoulders and smiled, "Of course, but what purpose would it serve? Let them have their dreams. Besides," he laughed, "the Salemites claim there are no such records on this man."

This answer seemed a bit evasive and unfulfilling,

and Abram could not help being bewildered by the
stubborn superstition surrounding this Melchizedek. As
much as he would have dismissed the tale as a farce, it
had a note of familiarity about it, somewhat like the tale
of Shem.

Abram was caught away from his reveries by the
fresh realization that the crowd's attention was once
again on him, and looking up, he saw the king of Salem
coming his way.

At his approach, even the king of Sodom and his flip-
pant prime minister were a bit uneasy. This stranger,
with his simple, unadorned clothing, his long white hair
and beard, did not look the part of a king. Nor did he
come with a gaudy train of servants and officials; yet
commoners and royalty alike were silenced at his presence.

Whether or not they believed the reports about him,
men and women did not take this monarch lightly.
Their private jokes did not apply when he stood before
them. What they said humorously of his legend in their
homes and among their friends was of little account
now. It stood that the people were strangely respectful
of him.

When Melchizedek drew near, an awesome sensation
overtook Abram. Why did the old man look at him this
way, as if his sad old eyes had long awaited this day, as
if Abram held some special meaning for him? Abram
shook himself, but still an unusual emotion was his, as if
a kindred spirit flowed between him and this stranger.

Echoes of the legend haunted him. He was suddenly
a bit afraid of this king, almost awed by his presence.
But, he reasoned, was this not a man, like other men?
What illusion had hold on him to make him feel as he
did?

Abram reasoned thus in his mind and stood erect, determined that such feelings were foolish, that this was
only a king and not a very great one at that, a king of
Canaanites who dwelled in some obscure little village in
the valley.

He looked at the ground and waited for this "priest" of some equally obscure god to speak.

But the king did not speak immediately. He called to an attendant, who brought a platter of bread and a goblet of wine, and in strange ceremony he broke the bread, handing it with the cup, to Abram. Still not looking Melchizedek full in the face, Abram obliged him and took the offering.

But the words which followed were more surprising than the gift. The old king looked out over the people and then, placing his hands on Abram's head and gazing toward the sky, he said:

"Blessed be Abram of the most High God, possessor of Heaven and earth: and blessed be the most High God who hath delivered thine enemies into thy hand."

The crowd wondered at these words, and the king of Sodom sat rigid on his camel, held by this encounter with the impact of truth.

Abram trembled and stared mutely at this man, to whom he again felt irresistibly drawn. A tingling fear and yet a peace flooded his heart as it had that day on Mount Gerizim when he had seen the Lord. He bowed in humility before the mysterious one, who was not just a man, and an unquenchable desire to know the stranger gripped him. Melchizedek reached down and lifted Abram, and the Man of God speechlessly surveyed the withered face before him, the bewildering legend filling his mind with questions he feared to ask.

Melchizedek seemed to read Abram's thoughts. But he said nothing, only looking at him with knowing eyes, his old, half-sad countenance revealing the long-sought consolation which was his today.

And as Abram studied the mysterious figure before him, it was as if the pages of history could be read in that face. Though the questions were still not fully answered, Abram sensed that the deep secrets of those ageless eyes spoke of the key to the future—that somehow, here stood a "great man" whose name meant "King of Righteousness" and who "Without father,

without mother, without descent, having neither beginning of days nor end of life—but made like unto the
Son of God—abides a priest continually. . . ."

Chapter XII

After he was rescued, Lot went back to Sodom with the promise that as soon as his business there could be consummated, he would return to Abram.

Lot's face had been so intense with devotion, his pleas for forgiveness so real, and his joy at their reunion so evident, that his uncle had been filled with a happiness he had not known in years. Lot, he had told himself, would indeed come home again.

But that had been months ago, and Abram's spirits could not forever be bolstered by unfulfilled promises. The people of the camp at the Oaks of Mamre sensed their master's hopelessness, some understanding it, and others not.

But how could they fully know his feelings, among them the fear of old age and the thought of one day going to his grave without an heir to carry on his name? These were insidious emotions, which, though they spoke of a much later time, were real fears nonetheless.

He and Sarai had spent ten childless years together, and they had not married young. Day after day, as Abram carried on his routine, as he went about his work in the camp and in the fields, as he contracted and bargained for trade routes, as he saw the increase of his wealth and tribe—a growing sense of aimlessness overtook him.

"What is it all for?" he asked himself. What sorrier sight was there than that of a successful man whose work was to die with his death, and whose name was to be buried with him?

Only the promise of his God, which he repeated to himself daily, gave him hope. But how long could that hope remain? Must not even God bring about His will within the spectrum of nature? And for Abram and Sarai, nature would soon close the door to any possibility of that long-hoped-for conception.

All these fears had only been intensified by this last parting with Lot. Though, as Eliezer had said, Lot was not Abram's son and he need not grieve for him forever —still, in Abram's mind and heart, Lot had been a symbol of his dreams and hopes. Irrational though it may have been—and when is love rational?—Lot had served to nearly fill the void in Abram's sonless heart. And Lot's failure to return had once again blackened an already dark and lonely corner of Abram's soul, having dredged up the uncomfortable fears his presence had once served to cover.

Eliezer joined his master one afternoon in the shepherds' field overlooking the Jordan. He knew Abram's thoughts, for since they had left Beth-El years before, Abram had come here often to meditate.

The field was verdant with the oaks which grew so resplendently here. Mamre the Amorite had leased Abram a fine parcel of land, the leafy shade trees such a relief from the sun. But Abram stood in the open, not seeming to care that the sun touched his face so harshly.

The young man stepped up beside his master in silence. No word was spoken for a long time. A hot breeze blew the aging man's hair from his face, and Eliezer studied him but said nothing.

At last Abram turned to his young companion, and with sad, tired eyes he asked, "Will Eliezer leave me as well?"

The younger man smiled and whispered, "Never, sir."

Chapter XIII

Sarai, more than anyone, knew the content of Abram's heart. She knew the fears he tried vainly to disguise, for they were hers as well. A childless man and the woman who bore him no heir—they were objects of pity and ridicule. And Sarai had heard, as Abram had, the whispers passed between strangers; she had seen, as he had, the looks of pity and suspicion which flashed overtly or covertly across the faces of friends and enemies alike.

"Will Abram never have a son?" she could imagine them asking. "Poor Abram, to have married a barren woman! Such a sad thing for one so prominent as he," they were thinking.

And so, while Abram felt sorrow, Sarai felt the even more damaging emotion of shame. For, to the people of her day, the woman was suspect in such cases, and the man only to be greatly pitied.

While Abram mourned for their deprivation, Sarai must, by custom, carry the guilt. And so, for her, it was a double curse—to be without the joy of a child, and to be burdened with the blame as well.

It was not Abram who made Sarai feel thus. It was not even in his thoughts to hold her accused. But because others did, she often thought she read disapproval in his eyes as well.

Added to this was the fear of further burdening the one she loved with her own problems. It was not the woman's place, she was told, to oppress the husband with "silliness." "Bear in silence," she had been taught, and though it was not Sarai's nature to bear buffetings in peace, she was determined not to load a falling man.

Deluged, therefore, with their own separate griefs, few words passed between them. And in their worlds of silent dejection, neither realized the pleas for reassurance the other could not voice. Abram misread Sarai's seclusion as one more ugly rejection of him by a loved one, and in Abram's silence Sarai read the disapproval she had so long dreaded.

But in all this, one looked on and observed. As a shadow on a sundial moves imperceptibly but steadily, as its movements are not fully realized until they have spread a wide arc, the onlooker plotted her course. She was Hagar, Sarai's young but rapidly maturing handmaiden.

Her strategy was subtle, her movements undetectable at first, but the shadow of her impact would cast itself widely before it was realized.

Part of Hagar's anonymity lay in her silences. Except for the time the girl had inquired how many years her mistress had been married, Sarai had had little reason to take note of her.

She was a generally obedient and satisfactory servant. The fact that she seemed to dwell in a secret world Sarai attributed to her romantic youth, and nothing more. If she seemed addle-headed or preoccupied at times, her mistress did not often scold her, for she served well in her capacity. As long as she did not interfere with Sarai's life, her affairs were of little matter.

But Sarai underestimated her young lady-in-waiting. She should have been more perceptive, for Hagar's moody self-contemplations, her obsession with her appearance, and her secretive attitude were more than the symptoms of an adolescent phase. They were evidence of a womanish plot, the plan of an artful seductress's mind in a very young but blossoming body.

For Sarai's handmaiden had long nurtured a dream, and that dream, should it be fulfilled, would alter the course of history. Abram was its object, and it had a twofold end.

Hagar loathed her new life. Egypt was her home. This trackless expanse, this life in tents held no happiness for her. She was a bondwoman, for all practical purposes a slave, neither free to choose her own destiny nor able to make her forced destiny palatable.

She despised it all, and all connected with it, especially the one she was forced to serve: Sarai.

In Hagar's eyes, her mistress was arrogance, the symbol of her subjection. Though Sarai treated her well, she was her overseer nonetheless. And Hagar, born of free Egyptian parents, carted to the Pharaoh's palace, and given to Abram like a piece of livestock, could not tolerate bondage under the most pleasant of guardians.

Every task, every request, every command was a burden. The sweetest foods provided her were bitter, the finest clothing rough wool. And Sarai's indifference to her very existence only added to Hagar's bitterness.

What better way to achieve some respite than to attack her aristocratic mistress at her vulnerable point: Abram and their childlessness?

One objective, then, would be met. But the twofold goal also involved her personal desires. Since the day she had been unloaded with all the other servants and supplies at Abram's camp in Egypt, seven years before, she had longed for the man who was unreachable. The strong, handsome one who owned her also possessed her thoughts and dreams. The man whose hair showed grey in the tentlight did not lose his allure as she reached full maturity. And though he never saw her now, she knew he must one day.

She was a young woman, and Abram was surely not satisfied with Sarai, she considered. Certainly her mistress was beautiful, the most beautiful woman she had ever seen—but growing older. And, Hagar reasoned, Sarai had not fulfilled her husband.

So it was with some boldness that she set about to accomplish her desires. Her growing self-confidence displayed itself more overtly. To Sarai's increasing irritation, Hagar waited on Abram with multiplying attentions. Whenever he entered Sarai's chambers, the lovely young woman with the chestnut hair and flowering beauty catered to him with a zeal becoming obvious in its intentions.

Hagar managed always to be near if the master's cup was empty, if his feet were hot and dusty or his cloak torn. And, inevitably, her bearing was poised, confident —but charmingly humble—her youth and radiance altogether his for the asking.

Abram did not seem to notice her advances, but they did not escape Sarai. Since there was little firm action to accuse her maid of, she had no recourse but to send her from the room when Abram came. And this she did more and more frequently until she had made it plain that Hagar was not to approach Abram again.

But the shadow of the sundial had been formed. It was too late to stop its arc. Already Abram sensed an inexplicable coolness in Sarai. He could not understand why, but he found her going farther from him with passing time.

And though Abram did not yet associate Hagar with the change, nor see her hand in it all, the maid read success for her scheme in Sarai's moodiness. For, she knew, a woman with her mistress's insecurities often loses such contests by default.

The day was overcast. Winter was coming on, and heavy pillars of clouds stood grey and foreboding over the camp at the Oaks of Mamre.

Sarai had worked with the women all that day baking small cakes and making cheese from fresh goats' milk in preparation for the long rainy months ahead. Already the beginning of winter made its way in small drops to the ground, and soon the hills would be robed in water and the steams swollen and fast-flowing with a rich downpour.

Sarai told the women to gather their clay pots and utensils together and scurry to their tents before the worst rains hit. Those were ominous clouds she pointed to, and the women gratefully complied.

The men had been out in the fields all day. Abram would not be home until late that night, and so Sarai invited her closest women friends into her chambers. With them came their little ones, a fine collection of infants and young children cozying in the warmth of the heavy goatshair tent.

They talked of many things, Sarai and her friends, but inevitably the conversation focused on the children. How beautiful they were, Sarai smiled. Plump and red-cheeked, they played together in all the happy spirit of carefree youth, and Sarai looked on with admiration.

The women sensed her secret longings, their pity and sympathy strong for the patriarch's woman. But how could their mistress be consoled?

Sarai sat on a low cushion in the center of the room, and the children were drawn to her silken black hair, now streaked with thin strands of silver. Her beauty was not lost on them, and they clamored to be near the warm, tender personality who welcomed their small voices.

The women were flattered by the attention the mistress shed on their little ones, and so the evening was passed in Sarai's favorite way. As they sat around her, the lamplight casting flickering shadows on the walls of the tent, she told the children marvelous stories of kings and queens, great heroes, and splendid animals. To the accompaniment of the wind, which blew outside, their little souls flew with her to fantastic worlds inhabited by dragons and magical creatures, and as they sat on her lap, watching the mysterious movements of her hands unweave the secret world for them, it was as if her heart beat with their own rhythm and her speech was surrounded by their own thoughts.

Here a curly-headed boy leaned against her cushion, there a small girl held her hand, and a brave little soul who gazed intently at her regal face reached up and dared to touch it.

The men came back to camp very late that night. The children were asleep around Sarai, and as their mothers were awakened by the sounds of masculine voices, one by one they took the sleeping little ones in their arms and went to their own tents, leaving Sarai with her handmaid.

Abram would be in shortly, so Sarai rose to put the chamber in order. A smile lit her face at the thought of the children, and only a little heaviness was hers on such occasions.

Hagar studied her mistress for some moments, assuming one of her typically mysterious moods of contemplation, and at last she spoke. "My mistress is happy this evening?"

Sarai smiled. "Yes, very." Even her handmaid could not trouble her tonight, she thought.

Hagar was again silent; and then said, "You enjoy the children?"

"Indeed," her mistress beamed.

Hagar busied herself and did not look at Sarai, saying in a coy tone, "It is often true that what we cannot have, that we find our chief pleasure in."

A cold chill went up Sarai's back, and she stood in grave meditation a moment, sensing the belligerence in the maid's statement. She looked at Hagar with piercing eyes but could think of no response. Strange, she thought, for one who managed all the women of a train to be somehow always at a loss to handle her own handmaid.

Sarai watched the self-important bondwoman as she went about her work, and Hagar at last turned again to her mistress with a subtle look of triumph.

Knowing she had touched firmly on Sarai's weakness, she took advantage of the moment. Feigning intense sympathy, the maid shook her head and murmured to herself. Sarai seethed with indignation.

"Out with it, Hagar!" she shouted. "Say what you mean to say and be done with the thing!"

But Hagar only concealed a sly, secretive smile and

turned to her mistress as if shocked and distressed at her outburst.

"Why, madam, I was only thinking of your happiness," she pouted. "Yours—and Master Abram's."

Sarai flushed with anger. "Abram?" she queried. "Why do you speak of Abram?" she asked, hesitating now and studying the maid suspiciously.

Hagar gained the boldness of Sarai's indulgence, and with a deep breath she broached the topic of her thoughts.

"My mistress truly loves my master?"

Sarai was speechless at the girl's impudence, her heart pounding madly, and yet she said nothing.

"Of course you do," Hagar continued. "Who could not love Abram?" Now the maid's eyes were gleaming with the prospects of her next words.

"It occurs to me, mistress, that since you love him, you will give him his desires."

Sarai shook with an inexplicable mixture of hatred for and fear of this audacious, spirited girl. What could she be after? she wondered.

Hagar approached her mistress with the fullness of her new-found courage. "Perhaps you should sit down, madam. You do not look well."

But Sarai wrenched her arm from the bondwoman's hold and demanded, "Speak, girl! What are you saying?"

"Madam," Hagar smiled, "it only occurs to me that a man like Abram deserves—"

"A son, a family?" Sarai cried.

Hagar shrugged and assumed a subservient mood. "The mistress is angry with her servant?"

Sarai was confused and frustrated. At last, unable to tolerate a further pursuit of the issue, she ordered Hagar from the tent.

The maid left silently, a meek and docile attitude all too cleverly disguising her victory.

Sarai sat alone in her dimly lit chamber, the wind moaning and whistling through the heavy cloth, as she

contemplated the purpose and intent of Hagar's words.
The lamps flickered and Abram did not come. As she
waited for him, she remembered the faces of the children. She thought of Abram's loneliness, his unfulfilled
dreams. She thought of Hagar and as she did so, scenes
came to her of the attractive girl as she had waited so
zealously on Abram in times past.

The puzzle was beginning to fit together. "Give him
his desires," Hagar had said. Of course—Sarai shuddered. The picture was now complete. She saw the design Hagar had woven, and her heart stopped at the
revelation.

"Lord, no!" she cried. "Surely Abram would not
want that!"

Tears flowed down her face, and the lamp faded with
the darkness.

When Abram arrived, it was nearly dawn. He had
not been able to return with the other men, as he had
stayed behind to supervise the reconstruction of one of
the sheepfolds damaged by an eroding slide of mud and
shale in the hills.

When he entered Sarai's tent, he knew she had been
crying. She lay where she had fallen asleep, on the cushions in the corner.

"Sarai?" he called to her. "Sarai, what is it? Have
you been alone all evening?"

The lovely woman woke and, seeing her distressed
husband, felt shame that he should find her thus. She
roused herself and straightened her hair.

"Oh, Abram. I must have fallen asleep waiting for
you," she said.

But Abram was not persuaded. "Sarai, something has
happened. I know you have been crying. Why, you fell
asleep crying," he said anxiously. And taking her in his
arms, he encouraged her to unburden herself.

Sarai struggled briefly but he held her close, and at
last, unable to keep her feelings to herself, she stam-

mered, "Oh, husband——" and a flood of tears followed. She could no longer withhold her fears from him. The months of silence must be broken, the expression of her longings voiced. Despite the results her openness might have for Abram, she could no longer bear shame and loneliness alone.

"Forgive me, my lord," Sarai sobbed, "but I must speak, or my heart will surely die within me."

Abram looked into her face and began to realize that her months of silent coolness had been no rejection of him, but a shroud for some unvoiced fears of her own.

"Sarai, tell me!" Abram pleaded. "What has made you unhappy?"

His voice and bearing were tender, and Sarai took courage, speaking at first brokenly, but then more freely. "Oh, husband, what use am I to you—to anyone? What purpose do I serve?" she cried.

Abram could scarcely believe his ears. He held her at arms' length and read her expression.

"My darling," he whispered, incredulously, "what can you mean? What silliness is this?"

Sarai, not wanting to see Abram pained, reached for his hand. "Husband, look at me. I grow older. Soon I will lose what little beauty I have ever had, and——"

Abram clutched her close to him half in outrage and all in love, saying, "Sarai! Your beauty far surpasses any touch which the years may endeavor to make. How can you speak this way? What has happened?"

At this he looked about him in anger as if seeking a culprit on whom to place the blame for his wife's agony of spirit. "Sarai, who has given you such thoughts? It is not like you to think so!"

"They are my thoughts, my husband. And they are the truth."

Abram hesitated and smiled down on her. A long moment passed as he gazed on her soft hair and ageless face. "Oh, my love," he whispered, a tremor in his words, "the princes of the world have vied for you, the Pharaoh of Egypt would have taken you for his queen.

And—I have you. No gift any man could be granted would equal the gift my God has given me in you."

Sarai was silent, her head nestling in his arms. A smile worked on her face, and she could not help yielding to it. But still, the nagging fear did not subside.

"My lord, beauty does not make a woman. Don't you see?" she sighed sadly. "A woman who cannot fulfill her husband's dreams is not complete in herself."

Abram quivered with anticipation. He knew Sarai's heart and thoughts, but he could not bear to hear them. He rose and paced the floor, but at last he said in low tones, "What do you mean, Sarai?"

She walked toward him, but he did not turn to her, for he did not wish to read the content of her face. She placed her hand on his shoulder and said, "My lord, you know what I speak of. I know your love for me, my husband, but I can never repay it. You know you have married half a woman. You know you have married a —barren woman!"

Abram wheeled about, his ears burning with those words.

"No!" he shouted. "Sarai, say no more!"

They both shook with the impact of the moment, the terror, the silent fear they had so long carried, now burning them with a force greater than all the months of loneliness they had passed with its secret.

And yet, it was out—a strange, hideous relief, though bitter to the taste. And in convulsive need they clung to one another.

Abram at last looked at her again, and with intense tones he said, "No more of this, Sarai. I will not hear another word. The Lord God has promised us a son, a seed to inherit the land, a destiny beyond all our dreams. We will not lose faith in that, my love!" he trembled, seeking confirmation from her, a nod of acknowledgement, a sign of hope.

But Sarai stood mute, her face expressionless, and she turned from her husband rigidly, as if she had not heard.

He watched for a response, but when none came, he reached for her. "Sarai," he said in a whisper, "I know it is hard to have faith, not only for you, but for me as well."

Cradling her head on his shoulder, he sought words to comfort her. "The thoughts you have shared tonight, why did you withhold them so long? Why have you harbored loneliness when you could have come to me? These are not your thoughts. Some devious, jealous mind has planted them there, and they have grown in your little heart, tended by tears you have cried when I am not near. Is that not true?" He paused, but still Sarai did not speak.

And at last, when no other words would serve, he said, "If only you knew my love for you."

Sarai softened in his embrace. With that simple affirmation, weighty concerns seemed to pale, and two souls touched within the vaulted confines of their desolation.

Chapter XIV

A weary and heavy-hearted Abram faced the new day. No sleep had served to lift the burden of the night from his shoulders. Indeed, it was difficult to have faith when ten fruitless years had yielded no encouragement.

The most difficult heartache for him now lay in the sorrow of his wife. The one who had been his love since youth must be comforted. He remembered her strength, her ability to leave behind her home and family, to venture with him from the comforts of city life and the luxuries of solid walls, to the wind-swept emptiness of the plains and the desolation of the wayfarer's life. He remembered her obedience, her willingness to pose as his sister, risking bondage for the sake of his own cowardly and selfish scheme. He remembered her cries and the terror in her face as she was carried away by Pharoah's men; he remembered the regal, native beauty of the harrowed woman as she stood beside the throne, a smile of love greeting him when he at last came for her. And he considered now her months and years of lonely shame, her silent bearing of the guilt which custom laid to her charge. Why must she be called barren and not he? Abram demanded.

"Oh, Sarai," he groaned. "How unworthy am I of you! My God! You must answer us!"

As had been his custom so many times before, Abram sought solitude in which to plead with his Redeemer. Had any man before him learned to touch the universal Spirit so uniquely as Abram? Had any man before him learned such boldness? Yet something in his simple, childlike faith moved that Almighty Power as nothing else could.

Here he came again, to the seclusion of his homeless

hills; the city dweller turned wanderer, the wealthy son turned voluntary vagabond—here he came again, trudging over the hill, his cloak slapping with the purpose of his stride: here he came—to call boldly, expectantly, demandingly upon the One of whom others denied the very existence.

Without fear Abram came. He walked miles into the plain and sat at last under the shelter of a great rock outcropping. His fists were clenched; his palms wet with purpose. His heart pounded, not with anger, but with insistence. The words he would speak were already formed in his mind, but he sat in silence, his head throbbing with pain. But for some reason he could not voice his prepared words. He could think only of his dejection.

All day he sat thus, until the cold evening came and the winter wind numbed his hands. He pulled them inside his cloak and drew his knees close up under his chin, burying his face in his lap.

The rain descended mercilessly on him, and he nestled back into a niche of the rock wall. He peered between his knees across hills and plains, grey and wet with fog which had come up from the boggy streams. A damp chill went through him. No one was near, and no one knew where he was. And as he studied the landscape, he had never felt so alone.

He was reminded of the street urchins of Ur, the small, pitiful beggars who huddled against the walls at night without shelter or families. A flood of painful memories overtook him, of his city, his family, his fame, his glorious dreams of the future.

Almost laughing within, he looked at himself now but could find no real humor here. His feeling was agony and desolation. What had he come to—an old man now, huddled by a rock in the wilderness of Canaan, a fool with a madman's dreams, a proud warrior, a shield-bearer in battle, a victor who had won nothing?

He reached up and touched his own face. That was not all rain he felt there. As he recognized his condition, humility overtook him, and he sat, not speaking, only listening, waiting.

It was at that moment as if the very air breathed in anticipation around him, as if the proper hour had come. While he had been cut from all human touch, he felt the personality of the loving Almighty descend to sit with him, and Abram shuddered, crying without sophistication, "Lord God?"

"Fear not, Abram," the invisible One answered. "I am thy shield and thy exceeding great reward."

Abram stood and huddled near the wall, covering his face against the icy wet wind of the plains. Tears filled his eyes and mixed with the downpour, but he took courage and with less trepidation came directly to the issue. "Lord God, what will you give me, seeing I go childless and the steward of my house is this Eliezer of Damascus?"

The Lord was silent, but Abram stepped out from the wall into the heavy winter rain, his head uncovered, his hair and garments deluged. And thinking of Sarai's shame, he directed the Lord to look on his own barrenness, crying, "Behold, to me you have given no seed! And see now, a servant of my house is my heir!"

Abram waited for more, but only silence followed. Was that to be all? he wondered. Was his angry, hopeless desolation to be greeted with only a few words? Was one small token meant to placate him, when he cried for a volume of reassurance?

Abram waited but heard no more, and at last, still feeling unfulfilled, he turned again to the shelter of the rocks. There he sat for some moments, wondering if he was to return home or wait for his God again.

"There must be more," he thought.

Suddenly a whistling wind split the night air. An unearthly gale with no forewarning howled out of nowhere above the plain, and in terror Abram clung to the bare roots protruding from the sod, his garments billowing like the sails of a ship.

"God!" he called, "Please, help me!"

It seemed the universe would be torn by the force of that wind, and in dread he shouted, "O God! Will you see me die?"

For what seemed hours, that wind shrieked in his ears, and when it at last subsided, Abram was left like a rag clutching limply at the cliff.

As he looked above him, he saw the rain had ceased, the clouds had been scattered, and only a clear, diamond-studded sky loomed overhead. Abram's hair stood on end. Never had he seen such a thing. It was eerie, unnatural.

In fearful silence, he stepped out from the wall, and as if led by an invisible hand, he walked onto the plain again.

"Look now toward heaven," the Lord said gently. "And tell the stars, if thou be able to number them, for so shall thy seed be."

And Abram believed in the Lord and He counted it unto him for righteousness.

The Lord was not through with Abram. The Man of God was to be taken the next day through a strange journey into the future which would never again allow him to look at the present in quite the same way.

Knowing Abram's frequent fear of wandering, his longing for a home, knowing that the man He had chosen was a city dweller at heart, and knowing his frequent memories of his family, the Lord would begin where Abram's thoughts most often were. Meeting his primary needs, He would not take him into realms which meant less to him, but would answer his heart's cry first. He would speak of a fundamental purpose in Abram's calling, and He would answer Abram's desire to know why he had been asked to sacrifice everything for a dream which he did not even understand.

It was after a second day of lonely waiting on the plain, as the Man of God shuddered in silence once more beneath the shelter of the rock, his face buried in his arms against the chill night wind, that the voice of his Redeemer came to him again. "I am the Lord that brought thee out of Ur of the Chaldees," He began, "to give thee this land to inherit it."

"Lord God—" Abram responded, lifting his face slowly, reverently, "Whereby shall I know that I shall inherit it?" Abram was daring to ask God to seal and ensure His promise with a sign, as was always done in oriental custom by way of covenant ceremony.

And answering Abram's human needs for reassurance, God complied in accordance with human fashion. The Lord said nothing but directed Abram to look over against the rock wall. There stood a strange retinue of animals huddled together in the biting wind, and the Lord said, "Take me a heifer and a she-goat and a ram, a turtle dove and a young pigeon."

Abram smiled, familiar with the proceedings, for this was the customary invitation given by one party to another to join in a covenant ritual.

"Yes, Lord!" he said, carrying out the order. No further instructions were necessary, for he knew what to do. His sling and dagger served to fell the sacrifices, and as custom dictated, the slaughtered animals must be divided, all except the two birds, who were symbols of the covenant makers. The meaning of the tradition had been lost in antiquity, but it was a most solemn ritual, binding and unbreakable in its intent.

After he had divided the animals, he placed the pieces in two rows against each other, leaving a narrow path through which the instigator of the covenant was to pass, thus taking the responsibility of his promise.

Abram now settled back and waited to see how the Lord would perform this, but as he did so, vultures circled overhead, ready to swoop down upon the carcasses. Abram stood and waved his arms viciously in the air, but still they came closer.

Their great wings fanned the air above him, and with lusty shrieks they threatened him. He ran to the sacrifices, but not in time to keep the birds from lighting. Before they could carry the pieces away, however, he tore his cloak from his back and whipped it like a dervish, screaming, "I will have my promise! Away with you!"

The frightened vultures fled the thrashes of his attack and did not return.

The sun was going down. This was Abram's second night on the plain. Hunger gnawed at his stomach, but he dared not sleep. He knew his God was to speak again. The covenant would not be sealed until He passed between the rows of that sacrifice.

Abram trembled. How would his Lord perform that act? Would He appear to him again as He had so many years before at Gerizim? So much had transpired since that glorious event, yet whenever Abram recalled it, it lived as if it had happened yesterday.

But the anticipation that he might again see his God was too awesome for Abram. He drew his garments tight to him and sat in breathless silence, his eyes wide with hope.

Hours passed. The moon rose, and far to the west the last red rays of sun painted the sky in a low, narrow ribbon.

Abram fought the urge to sleep, but he was weak with exposure and hunger. A deep slumber overtook him, and as it did, an unnatural, tangible horror of darkness enveloped him, a terror so powerful it was more than mental; it was bodily, a gloom like that of an eclipse cutting off all touch with the earth beneath.

And then the Lord spoke again. "Abram, know of a surety that thy seed shall be a stranger in a land that is not theirs, and shall serve them; and they shall be afflicted four hundred years."

In this ethereal trance, Abram struggled but could not speak. His spirit was made to look on scenes of bondage and sorrow. Like a spectator in a gallery he watched the panorama of the future flash before him. Thousands in forced labor—where? Was that the Nile he saw there?

"No, God!" he wished to cry out. "The Egyptians are

too cruel!" In his dream he fought the revelation, but no solace came.

He saw his descendants, wayfarers in an alien country, makers of brick and mortar, builders for a despotic and heartless civilization—against their own will.

He saw the overseers, whips in hand! He saw the afflicters of his people, and he cried out against them but they did not hear.

The spectacle faded. Abram's heart pounded erratically in the darkness of his solitude.

But again the Lord spoke, this time in comforting words. "That nation whom they shall serve, I will judge, and your descendants shall come out with great substance."

Now the Spirit seemed to breathe heavily, as if the Lord were in private agony, and without saying more, Abram could sense that there was much more to hear and see, but that his God knew he could not bear it.

At last, the Lord seemed to sigh, and lifting Abram up, He comforted him saying, "And thou shalt go to thy fathers in peace; thou shalt be buried in a good old age."

Abram awoke, a tumult of emotions conflicting within him. So many questions fought to be voiced. Why were his people to be so tormented? And why did the Lord close his eyes to further scenes of their history? Was it to be so terrible that he could not bear the revelation?

He rubbed his eyes and wiped the sweat from his feverish brow. "Lord God! Why?" he cried. "Let me see the story of my people, of my little children, the ones who will call me Father."

Something moved. He saw a flash of light and looked toward the pieces of the covenant sacrifice. He trembled and drew back, blinded by the light of a smoking furnace, a torch, like the flame of a tent lamp, which passed mysteriously between them.

Shielding his eyes, he looked on it. "My God! Deliver me!" he cried. "Art thou a consuming fire?"

His God had bound the covenant in that moment.

Abram's understanding was opened, but he feared what he saw. In that instant he had seen the terror of the future. He knew now why the Lord had said no more. Those pieces were symbols of his seed, his descendants, and the terrible fire was their history—to be tried and afflicted by nation after nation; to be divided and torn again and again.

But Abram still cried, "Why, God? Are they evil in your sight? Are you like Nannar to persecute the innocent for your own glory?"

The Spirit of God was patient but sorrowful. He drew close to Abram and whispered, "See, Abram—I am the purifying fire. Those whom I love I also chasten. You cannot bear more now. Your people will suffer at the hands of others, but their persecutors will be my tools. I will never forsake my loved ones, and they will be a strong and mighty people even in their weaknesses. Torn and divided, they will come together again, making their predators to flee."

Abram was reminded of the scavengers who had swooped down on his consecrated gift. "Even as I drove them away, Lord?" he whispered.

"Yes, even as you watched over your sacrifice, so shall I make it to prosper in your eyes."

Abram looked again on the pieces, and the torch held new significance for him. It was as if the Lord had helped him to see the fire not only as a terror, but also as a Light in the night of desolation, as a Guardian and Hope as well as a fear.

And so, was the fire not God? Though it burned them, would it not be to purify, and would it not thus lead them like a beacon to its final purpose?

"But God, be patient with me. May I know what that purpose is? If You wish to so handle and purify my people, may I see the product of their sufferings?"

The Lord did not speak again, but as Abram pondered the covenant altar, he remembered the words God had spoken when He first revealed Himself in Ur many years before. "In thee shall all the families of the earth be blessed."

All the families? Abram considered this. A design was beginning to emerge in his mind. "All the families?" he thought. "But how?" As he considered the sacrifice symbolic of his people, he thought, "A purified sacrifice, a people eventually torn and united, a race whose end product will be a pure sacrifice to God, a blessing for all the earth?"

Abram could consider no more. His head reeled as it had the day he had looked into Melchizedek's eyes, eyes which seemed to contain the eons of history. "Lord God," he said, rising to return home, "I am brought to the end of my understanding. Show me no more, for I weary with the heaviness of it all. Such thoughts are too wonderful for me, they are high—I cannot attain unto them."

Several days passed after Abram returned to camp, but he could find no way to speak of his experience. Daily his head spun with the impact of all he had seen and heard, and hourly he contemplated its meaning, but he could not fathom it.

One phrase in particular now haunted him, a short phrase which had been overlooked in his concern for his descendants. That phrase concerned him specifically, and now it occurred to him that it might carry more relevancy for him and for all other men than any other statement his God had made.

Had the Lord not said, "Thou shalt go to thy fathers in peace; thou shalt be buried in a good old age"?

How could Abram go to his fathers? Were they not dead? What did his God mean? How, after he was buried, could he go to his fathers?

Abram's flesh tingled. Could it be that death was not the end of life?

Oh yes, every civilization, every religion held that hope. He remembered seeing men's possessions buried with them in the hope that there was something after death.

But now his own God had encouraged that dream. It had become a certainty, not a hope alone. "My father lives?" Abram whispered. "And his father before him? Why, the ancient Noah and Shem yet live! Can it be?"

With this it seemed the entire universe took on a new perspective, as if not only the future but also the past were part of a grand design, one day to be seen in all its glorious purpose.

Of course. It was beginning to fit together now. Though he did not at all understand it, he thrilled at the infinite beauty of the Creator's, the Designer's purpose.

Man was grandly important. God, in all His majesty, had focused His artistry on this one small creature. Unlike the picture drawn of Man in Mesopotamian or Egyptian mythology, he was not a toy, a chess piece to be dealt with kindly or cruelly at the varying whims of the gods.

Abram's heart pounded as he ran to tell Sarai. Such a thought! Every event, every sorrow, every happiness was a thread in the magnificent pattern of God's loving intent.

Abram did not feel diminutive in proportion to these thoughts. On the contrary, he was lifted—exalted.

But, oh, how humbling, as he considered that his seed, his descendants, should be for some reason, for some yet-hidden purpose, the central theme in the artist's unfolding drama.

Chapter XV

When Abram gave Sarai the news of his audience with God and the glorious renewal of the long-awaited promise, she was filled again with hope. And her husband, who had suffered such a severe and silent separation from her for months previous, again enjoyed the communion of her love.

For many weeks and months Sarai dwelled on that hope, and it would have sustained her indefinitely but for the viperous proddings of her handmaid. And Hagar, indeed, wasted no time in setting about to destroy her mistress's new-found happiness.

But Hagar had learned that her mistress was not infinitely forebearing. Since the night Sarai had sent her from the tent, Hagar had determined that she would have to be more subtle. She had found Sarai's vulnerable point, but it would henceforth be from a more underhanded angle that the maid would deal her blows.

Sarai's love for Abram was Hagar's hope. Could her mistress be sufficiently persuaded of his need for fulfillment and again, of her own inability to service him, Hagar was sure she would have scored the winning point.

Her confidence lay in the oriental custom wherein a barren mistress often gave her handmaid to her husband to have children by her. This tradition was employed to give the master an heir and to supposedly take away the shame of his wife, who, because she owned the handmaid, would thereby claim the child as well. The custom, properly executed, involved the mistress's being present at the time of birth to receive the newborn infant onto her own lap the instant it was delivered.

Ideally, no face was lost because the child was not really hers, and ideally, no jealousy was to be felt upon her husband's entrance into another woman's tent. In fact, custom held that the first wife gained status by having a second under her, and it was customarily believed that the first woman was still the best loved of all her husband might take.

But humans of whatever culture are human nonetheless, and their loves, distrusts, passions, and jealousies are the same from continent to continent and age to age. Whatever man-made custom might say on the issue, no woman relished the prospect of her husband with another, and no woman could feel that the child born from such a proxy union was truly her own.

Be that as it may, the custom persisted, goaded on by the prevailing value placed on male children and the desirability of an heir to carry on the family, to give strength to a line dwelling in the most unyielding and demanding of soils and surviving by the sheer energy of its people.

And so, due to custom, Sarai's love for Abram, rather than being an obstacle to Hagar, might be her richest hope.

Once a month Sarai, the young handmaid, and several other women of the household went to the nearby town of Hebron, where they purchased supplies and marketed their wools. This was a very small part of the dealings of Abram's train. It served more to give the women an opportunity to browse through the markets than to bring in profit. It was "women's business" and did not truly relate to the growth of the train.

But the mistress and her servants looked forward to the monthly diversion eagerly.

The way up to Hebron was rocky and steep. Like many Canaanite towns, this hamlet was set on the side of a hill from which invaders could easily be spotted and warded off. Considering its position, not far from the Dead Sea, the lowest point on earth, Hebron's twenty-eight hundred feet above standard sea level was indeed high.

Surrounded by the hilly, oak-studded shepherd land of Canaan, Hebron was a beautiful village. And this day it was crowded with small shops and vendors. Sarai directed her servants to set up their goods while she surveyed the surrounding booths, Hagar accompanying her to do the bartering in the event she wished to purchase something.

Amid the bustle of the marketplace many small children played, hiding from one another behind large crates of produce or mimicking the adult games of shop and trade. Hagar made it a point to direct Sarai's attention to them, and her mistress, unable to resist, watched them admiringly.

"My master should be here," Hagar would smile. "He loves the children as much as my mistress, does he not?"

Sarai looked piercingly at Hagar but said nothing. Holding herself regally, she walked on ahead of her maid, pretending to pay no attention to her insinuating remarks. But the sting was felt nonetheless.

Sarai should have put an end to Hagar's badgerings then and there, but once again the maid had touched on her weaknesses so firmly that she had no immediate retort.

As the afternoon went on, Sarai's resistance wore thin. The old feelings of guilt and shame came again to haunt her. Despite the hope of the promise, she involuntarily found herself comparing her own aging qualities with Hagar's youth and vitality. Would she ever truly have a child, she in her barrenness?

The hideous proposition presented itself again. Perhaps she was not meant to give Abram the promised son. Perhaps that honor was meant for another.

But God could not want that, Sarai told herself.

The women were gathering their purchases together. The sun would be going down soon, but Sarai stood silently by, watching the now quieted marketplace. Her eyes followed a large group of people gathered about a booth to the far side of the square.

Hagar stepped up to tell her mistress that all were ready to depart, but she hesitated, wondering what had caught Sarai's thoughts. Looking to the gathering which had drawn her mistress's attention, she recognized the fat chieftain who directed the party as the sheik of Hobah.

The people milling about him, gathering their supplies and closing shop, were all his family. This man, who had dealt with Abram on many occasions, was well known to Sarai and the others of the tribe. He had among his party fourteen wives, several of whom had borne him sons when his first wife had failed.

As Sarai studied the group, Hagar read her thoughts and a smile of triumph crossed her face.

That night Abram found his wife in a singular mood. Sarai was silent, her face stony and bitter.

Unprepared for this reception, Abram smiled uneasily. "Good evening," he said, reaching for her. But Sarai only turned rigidly from him, torn with the heartache of that afternoon's ordeal. Abram waited anxiously for a response, but when none came he began to fear the strange look she bore.

When at last she spoke, the introduction to the subject was so abrupt that it was as if she expected Abram to be aware of all she had been thinking that day.

"Certainly, my lord, God has promised you a son— and there is no reason you shall not have one!" she cried, turning to him. "But," she said, bitterness marking her words, "He has made me no such promise!"

Abram looked at her in bewilderment. What was she speaking of? He felt as if he had come into the middle of a conversation of which he was expected to be a member.

"Sarai," he stammered in obvious confusion, "please begin again. What happened today?"

Sarai wheeled about impatiently, her arms crossed in indignation. "Oh, my lord!" she laughed scornfully, "I am no fool. Even without your God, men of your status see the customary way out of childlessness!"

Abram studied her incredulously. To his ears it seemed she babbled foolishness, for he did not understand the context of her thoughts. He had not been with her at the marketplace today. He had not seen the children, or the sheik with fourteen wives. And he had not been worn away by the badgering of a young and disgustingly beautiful enemy, one who knew her mistress's susceptibilities. But her words carried a familiar ring. They seemed to echo the conversation they had had months before, when he found her crying in the tent.

He walked to Sarai and turned her face to him. "Woman, make sense," he pleaded.

Sarai glared wildly at him, the pain of her predicament tearing her even from the one she loved. "Make sense, you say? My lord, surely you deceive me! You know very well I speak of custom!"

"What custom, Sarai?" he demanded impatiently. "Make yourself clear! Include me in your thoughts!"

Sarai shook with his words, but in full spirit she retorted cruelly, "Oh, Abram! Why do you insist on remaining the brunt of others' jokes? Why would a man of your wealth and status allow himself to be mocked by those of lesser degree?" She gathered her strength and cried, "You have no son, my lord! And I will never accommodate you. Follow custom, husband—Surely your God created custom as well as the sun and the stars! Let it help you!"

Abram could not believe what he heard. But he knew someone else had set her mind on such things, as he had suspected the last time she had come to him like this. Approaching her, and extending his hand soothingly, he said, "Sarai, what are these words? Who has tampered with you? Surely you are not suggesting—"

"Oh, husband," Sarai sighed, "take another wife! Is that not the custom of a sheik? Do you not see that

God's promise may require your action? Surely you have considered that you may have to assist in its fulfillment! Take another woman! Take the one you desire—she is mine to give you and I will not withhold her from you!"

Abram did not fully comprehend, nor did he care to hear who she spoke of. He only reached for her, hurt and anger written on his face. "I will hear no more!" he shouted, pulling her violently to him. "Tell me who has filled your mind with this poison!"

But Sarai only stood coldly in his arms, unable to be comforted and refusing to answer. Abram waited in silence, but at last he looked at her hopelessly and departed.

As Abram stepped outside, his head whirled with this sudden turn of events. Like a bolt his previous hopes seemed suddenly grounded. He stood angrily in the yard, looking about him like a crazed dog, seeking vengeance.

As he did so, his attention was caught by a figure standing to the side of the tent. Some of Sarai's words began to fit together now. Was this the object of her pain, this young handmaid? Was this the one who for so long had badgered and confounded his marriage, setting Sarai's thoughts on dark things?

He knew Hagar's disposition for flippancy—he remembered now her flirtatious advances—and some of Sarai's past moods began to form a pattern in his mind. Hadn't Sarai said, "She is mine to give?"

A violent anger welled up in him as he looked on the seductive young woman who lingered purposely in the shadows, her chestnut tresses loosened and draped in a shimmering fall about her bare shoulders. With a terrifying face of retribution he glared at her, disgust his only emotion.

But Hagar only smiled demurely at him and then walked to her tent, as if innocent of the drama surrounding her.

Abram's fists were clenched and his face raised to

the darkness above. The universe moved silently overhead, and only Sarai's weeping accompanied his raging
spirit.

Chapter XVI

Hagar's corrosive influence continued to eat the foundations of Abram's relationship with Sarai. The arc on the sundial was reaching its zenith, and the maid became more obvious in her intentions as time passed.

It seemed Abram could not escape her, and yet he wondered if he imagined that she always purposed to be where he was. How was it that she forever managed to be around the corner, to always present herself across the yard when he came out in the mornings? Perhaps he was now overly conscious of her, but he was certain she had never been so often present before.

The sight of her froze him. To Abram she was the symbol of everything which had torn his wife from him, and he loathed her for it. The same feelings of repugnance welled within him at the thought of her as he had felt when he saw the harlot in Damascus, or the priestesses of the royal courts he had visited in his younger days.

But Sarai's attitude of isolation was only forcing her husband to think about the young woman, and despite the nature of his thoughts, Hagar was increasingly their subject.

Torn between the desire to give Abram a son and the desire to know that her husband did not want Hagar for any reason, Sarai transferred her own frustrations to him. Abram was left in a quandary, not knowing which way to turn. When he sought to comfort Sarai, he was rejected, and yet when he turned in bewilderment from her, it only drove her further into her shell of dejection.

Yet forever there was Hagar, the seemingly inevitable object of the rift.

Abram was alone. Eliezer had been gone with a caravan for some time and would not return soon. The shadows of the tentlight drew memories on the walls. The inclement weather emphasized his isolation, and only his thoughts kept him company, lonely thoughts of Terah, Nahor, Lot—all those he had lost—and of Sarai, most painfully.

It had been many, many nights since she had accepted him into her tent. It seemed the gap between them had become boundless, uncrossable. Abram stirred uneasily. How many nights had he sat thus, in self-pity?

As he looked about himself, a sudden fury gripped him. He would not spend the evening in solitary dejection again, the lamp of his tent his only comfort. Tonight it would be different.

A storm had been raging throughout the day, and the violent wind lashed the tents like sails at sea. A knife-like shower of sleet cut through camp, but it was a determined, desperate man who made his way across the yard. He did not call her name tonight but threw back the tent flap unannounced and entered the chamber wet and shivering with the cold. Wiping his streaming hair back from his face, he demanded that she present herself.

"Wife, we will settle this!" he shouted angrily when she obediently entered the room. Abram's heart ached with conflicting emotions—anger, loneliness, dejection—but most painfully, love. And as he looked on the only woman who could satisfy him, as he realized their seemingly hopeless separation, he could not cope with the warring frustrations he felt.

Sarai could tell from his tone that Abram would not be easily put off. She said nothing, fearful to anger him further. It was an awesome face he wore in his agony, and Sarai trembled as he approached her.

He reached out, placing two demanding hands upon her arms, and with feet spread in a mood of insistence, he stared stormily into her dark, fevered eyes. His heart ached. She was so beautiful. His grip tightened on her, sending two rays of sharp pain up her arms.

"Woman," he said in low, angry tones, as if presenting an ultimatum, "if it pleases you, I will not come again. But," he insisted very coolly and deliberately, "I am known as a proud man. You will tell me now how I have lost you and how I will regain you, or I—" he sighed, not knowing what threat to offer, only looking at her with hot, piercing eyes.

Sarai shuddered with her own pride and walked to the far side of the tent when he at last loosened her from his hold. "Or what, my lord?" she repeated. "Shall you go to my maid?"

The wounded couple stood in silence. A violent anger raged within Abram, and in his frustration, he senselessly lashed at her, "Woman, you have said it!"

"Then go!" Sarai cried, tears filling her eyes. And in pain and pride she said sarcastically, "The Lord has restrained me from bearing. I pray you, therefore go in unto my maid. It may be that I may obtain children by her!"

Abram was stunned, senseless, and like a wounded, trapped animal he struggled with the insane world of his heart. Like a catapulting boulder, he was hurtled through groundless space. He wanted to cry, scream, laugh, clutch Sarai to him, knock her to the floor, all at once.

The howling wind whipped the tent like a rag. The frozen rain lashed the sides like a penetrating knife, and thunder pealed across the vaulted heavens.

Abram's mind tumbled within him like the season's storm, and he might have been the lightning for all the fire in his soul.

"My God!" he cried. He must be comforted. Oh, for the warmth of her arms! How could she deny him?

In a frenzy Abram would have forced her love from her—with his hands he would have rung it from her— but it was not to be had so easily.

"God! Sarai! I must be comforted!" he would have cried, but his masculine pride rebelled.

He said no more but only staggered for the door. He threw back the flap and stumbled into the yard, the whirlwind of his soul caught up in the shrieking of the elements.

Like a drunken man, he stood solitary, his bare head deluged with the icy rain.

"Sarai!" he cried, his voice mixing animallike with the howling wind, "Sarai!"

But still she did not come to him.

He looked across the yard toward Hagar's tent.

The human heart is a strange thing. Hatred and love, being both the strongest emotions, are often confused. And when a man is lonely, his own mind may be a kaleidoscope of conflicting emotions—desires, fear, vengeance, need.

But whatever the turmoil within his soul, in that moment flashes of the young Egyptian woman leaped to his mind, a low note of agony and conflict issued from deep within him, and he stumbled toward the only human warmth available.

PART V

The Purge
ᎧᎧᎧᎧᎧᎧᎧᎧᎧ

Be not deceived; God is not mocked: for whatso-
ever a man soweth, that shall he also reap. For
he that soweth to his flesh shall of the flesh reap
corruption; but he that soweth to the Spirit shall
of the Spirit reap life everlasting.

Galatians 6:7, 8

Chapter I

Abram's legs were weary with the hike. Fortunately it was not often he had to tend to the mundane tasks of shepherding in these hills. This was best left to the younger men, but it did him good to get out, to feel the aging muscles respond to such a challenge once again.

The old, familiar pastures were wet with spring rain, but the sun drew up small clouds of wavy steam across the lowlands. Though the years had bent him with soberness, his mind was relatively quiet today.

He rested on the hilltop, removing his mantle to cool his perspiring head, and breathed deep of the cool air. Save for the heavily greying hair, Abram still maintained his look of virile manhood. An expression hardly definable marked the ruddy, tanned face now touched by the years. The look was not so much of contentment, or of resignation, but of contemplation—the eyes which scanned the horizon still well marked with the sorrow which had too evidently marred them in their time.

Eliezer came out from camp to meet him. The beloved steward was not so young either, but still he carried the same zeal of devotion for his master as he had when they had met nearly twenty-four years before. Eliezer, befitting his single-mindedness, had never married, never raised a family, or found a calling higher than that of pursuing his Semitic heritage.

When he reached the brow of the hill, he rested beside his old friend. No words passed between them, but Abram knew his steward would soon tell him supper was ready and they would then rise, as usual, to spend the evening around the fire.

But it seemed Abram's attention had been distracted. Across the plains toward the west, where the large red sun was settling like a lingering flame on the horizon, a rider could be seen speeding toward the Oaks of Mamre.

Something in the spectacle seemed to stir Abram strangely, his mood of contemplation suddenly exchanged for a strong sense of uneasiness, his face bearing a new mixture of emotions.

Eliezer understood. Standing, he looked toward the faraway rider and said, "I will go now, sir. Come when you are ready. We will warm your supper for you when you arrive."

Abram said nothing but gave a slight smile of gratitude, as Eliezer cast one more furtive glance at the rider and quickly headed toward camp.

Abram stood alone, watching as the figure sped like an arrow over the hills toward him. A tension seemed to control his stance; his hands tightened as if in a struggle. The rider moved him. It may have been pride of a sort which marked his face at the sight of him, or something akin to admiration, but whatever the feeling, Abram could not help but be attracted to the dashing figure on camelback.

The rider was a boy really, no more than thirteen, but the ease with which he carried himself, with which he danced his heavy animal over the plains, gave the look of one much older, one highly experienced in the way of self-possession. A camel in most hands, no matter how experienced the rider, was usually awkward, ungainly. But the control this young man maintained lent a magnificence, a grace to the bulky creature.

Clouds of dust rose like thunderclouds behind the speeding dromedary. As the boy reined his charge over the nearby hill, Abram's heart raced. Yes, he was indeed a handsome youth, something of a fierce pride in his wiry, athletic frame. He was not fully grown, but already his sinews responded to every demand with a dauntless, challenging strength.

The boy's leather skirt was soaked with perspiration. The heavy Egyptian beadwork which embroidered it was still intact, despite the weeks of wear it had endured under the most harsh of elements. The boy wore no sandals, his bare feet tough and rebellious against covering of any kind.

He directed the camel to the hilltop where Abram stood, and as if taking only a slight incline, the magnificent animal leaped up it with a bound. Abram stood aside, and the boy brought his camel to a stamping halt, hot breath blasting from its flared nostrils.

Abram grasped the reins, holding the straining animal momentarily in check.

"Good evening," he said, a certain restraint marking his greeting.

The boy wiped his face with his sleeve and reached for the reins, apparently preferring to control the animal himself. "Good evening," he returned, looking toward camp. Already he nudged his camel in that direction, obviously anxious to go on.

But Abram held him back, and the boy's eyes met his for an instant. A strained silence passed between them, as though neither quite knew what to say.

"Good to have you home again," Abram offered, seeming to search the boy's face for a response. Some twinge of thought briefly touched the rider—a painful thought perhaps—but it passed as quickly as it had come.

The boy looked toward camp again and said, "Supper is ready, I suppose?"

"Yes," Abram smiled, studying him.

The boy's face was unique, with its fine Egyptian and Semitic heritage, his gentle olive skin and unusual, dark snapping eyes, his wavy, black hair; he was a fine child. But he was a wild young animal, unpredictable as the wind, rebellious, so difficult to know, impossible to fully understand. And no matter how often Abram looked at him, it was with the knowledge or the regret that he would never truly fathom him.

The bleating animal strained to be moving. Unlike most of the tribe's camels, this one wore no heavily decorated trappings. It was wild like its young master, and close to the earth.

The boy said no more but gave the camel its rein.

"Won't you stay and talk?" Abram said. "You have only just gotten back."

The boy stirred uneasily in his saddle and started anxiously down the hill toward camp, calling over his shoulder that they could talk some other time.

Abram was left alone on the hill, and after some moments he too moved toward camp.

A cool night wind had come up, and he drew his cloak about him. He had wondered where the boy had been for these many weeks, but he had not questioned him.

Abram never questioned Ishmael.

Chapter II

As Sarai served Abram his supper that evening, she said little. Abram knew why, for her moodiness was not new to him, varying like the seasons but present nonetheless for fourteen years.

Tonight she paced the tent floor, looking frequently toward the doorway. At last she peeked through the tent flap and spoke:

"I see the boy is back again."

Abram did not respond but only looked at her with sad, weary eyes. "Please, Sarai, sit and eat."

Sarai fingered her food absently. "Little good it's done Hagar to have a child like that for a comfort," she smirked.

Abram sighed, having heard it all before. "Not again, Sarai—"

But still she continued. "An animal-child like that must be a strange pride for his mother," she laughed. "It's a good thing he stays away as long as he does."

Abram sensed that his wife would not easily abandon the subject she pursued tonight, but oh, how he wearied of it. As he looked toward Hagar's tent, the maid came out carrying a water jug and passed to the well.

Abram's heart ached with the memory of that long-regretted night when he had entered her tent. His life had altered irrevocably, it seemed, with that simple but all too consequential act. The decision made in a feverish moment of loneliness, of passion, had so distorted the intervening years, that it seemed hopeless his future could ever rearrange itself.

When Hagar returned with the water jug, Ishmael met her at the tent door, and for an instant Abram could almost imagine how different the feeling in his heart would have been at such a domestic sight had Hagar only been Sarai.

But such a sad compromise he had attained. Yes, Ishmael was a fine and handsome lad, worthy to be called his son. And yet, even on the day he had been born, in the dimly lit obscurity of Hagar's tent, when Abram had held him in his arms, marveling at his beauty, as he did now—even then Abram had hesitated to call him "son."

Oh yes, love was there—tremendous love. In his life, Abram had never felt such awe in the beauty of a child, and these many years had not cooled the wonder he sensed whenever he realized that such a boy was a product of himself.

Yet, for all Abram's doting on the lad, for all the pride and bond of affection which held him tightly to him, there had always been a restraint in his relationship with his first-born.

Ishmael sensed it; he had always sensed it. What may have been hidden from an outside observer was as tangible as a stone wall to the young boy. And at his tender age he could have written volumes on its nature and effects. He knew whence he had come, and he knew the look which stole across his father's face when he caught his eye. He knew the feelings and memories Abram harbored, which rose up like strangling weeds to suppress normal signs of fatherly affection. He knew why Abram hesitated to call him "son," why he always called him Ishmael.

And yet, though he knew the reasons behind his father's behavior, the results were nonetheless painful to him. They had warped him. It was not easy to be the symbol of his father's guilt. Often he wondered at the nature of his own name. "Ishmael: God hears," he would smirk. "God hears what?" he would ask himself. "What is it my father wants his God to hear, that he should name me so?"

Hagar handed the heavy water jug to the strong boy,

and Abram looked on silently. Ishmael did not see him standing there, but Hagar did, and her eyes met her master's briefly. Abram hesitated only momentarily and then studied the ground beneath his feet until the two had left his sight.

He stood thus for some moments and then walked inside again. "What have they for food over there, Sarai?" Abram asked.

"Plenty, my lord," she answered. "I do take care of my charges, though I'm certain Hagar could take care of herself, as she has done in times past."

Abram sighed. "Sarai, we have gone through this conversation infinitely many times. I weary of it!"

This was said with definite force, and Sarai knew she had best be silent on the subject. Abram looked at her with a heavy heart, longing to hold her as if the lonely years had never come and gone, as if they stood united again, without regrets. Despite their conflicts, his love and desire for her was still unquenchable, battle-scarred though it was, and challenged by her doubts.

But many years of such conflict are wearing, and it was rarely he found it in himself to overcome the vacuum pride had built between them. He walked to her and touched her face gently. Her silken hair was now thick with silver, but her face was still soft, and though she often distorted it with callous looks of coldness, no amount of camouflage could ever truly mask the feminine warmth it contained—or the love which lay beneath the surface.

Abram looked deep into her eyes and pleaded, "The past is behind, my wife. Time and time again I have admitted I have wronged you. Please, let us hear no more of this."

Something in Sarai softened at that statement. Abram took her in his arms and felt her antagonism subside.

"You do care for the lad, don't you, Sarai?"

The beautiful, aging woman looked up at him and said slowly, "I have tried, my lord. I suppose, in a sense

I do. Yes, I do, though you'll never know the agony his very presence brings me."

Abram understood and still held her. "I am taking the boy with me tomorrow."

Sarai looked at him in bewilderment. "Where, my lord?"

"To Salem."

Sarai looked at him incredulously. "For what reason, husband? Do you hope to gain his heart by taking him there?"

"Perhaps," Abram answered vaguely, walking again to the tent door. "Perhaps. I don't know really. But the lad is of age now, and is he not the heir to the promise? When I reached thirteen, my father took me to the priest of Nannar. Should I deny my only son the blessings of the true priest of God?"

Sarai gave no response but only watched her husband's face as it took on the expression it never wore except when he spoke of the old king, Melchizedek—a reverence, a humility nearly akin to the aspect it bore when he spoke of God Himself. And always it told of the mystery Abram felt when he thought of the man he had seen only once but had never forgotten. So profound an effect had Melchizedek had on Abram that Sarai dared not question his awe of him. Doubts did plague her though, and she asked, "But, Abram, do you think he will remember you after all this time? And if he did, what real purpose would it serve to take Ishmael to him?"

"He is the priest of God, the only one who claims that title," Abram answered patiently. "I do not understand his knowledge of my God. I do not know how he comes to be called by that station, but the years will not have altered it. My first-born must be blessed of him." Abram paused in deep contemplation.

"The old man was so wise, Sarai," Abram continued, remembering that day long ago. "I could tell he knew."

"Of the promise?" Sarai asked.

"Yes, I'm sure of it—to this day I am sure of it."

Sarai chose her words carefully as she said, "My husband, why do you torture yourself with such ideas? You resurrect the past when you speak so. You have neither seen your God nor heard His voice these fourteen years. How can your faith persist? The king may have spoken of a blessing years ago, but—my lord, the past is gone, as you have just said, and the promises with it, my husband, are dead. You cannot regain them, no matter whom you employ to help you."

Abram wheeled about, facing her with stormy eyes. How dare she speak so frankly of his disarmed faith? Yes, it was true that his guilt, his burden of self-disgust, had long stood like a great wall between himself and his Sovereign. It was true that little more than blank silences had filled his meditations these past years. And yet, how could she speak so of that which meant more to him than life itself—his faith in the promise of his God?

"I will do as I see fit, woman!" he shouted defensively. "The old king did know. His eyes held many secrets. In all these years I have not forgotten his words, just as I have not forgotten the Lord—whose face is hidden from me." Abram sighed heavily at this thought, and then he said sadly, "Perhaps the king can help me. Perhaps he can bless my first-born, for—I cannot."

Sarai turned from him. "Ishmael will never be a part of your dreams, my lord, no matter what lengths you go to involve him. He is not part of them, don't you see?" But then she paused, looking at the one she loved, pity in her eyes.

"My lord," she said, tenderly, "he is your son. Do with him as you please."

But Abram had been wounded by her harsher sentiments. "Indeed," he said, glaring down on her, "he is my son; and he is all I have, since I have never regained you. I will find a way to make him shine in the favor of the Lord!"

Sarai shuddered and watched Abram leave. "For fourteen years you have sought in vain for God's approval on your sin and its offspring!" she shouted after him. "The wrong done me be upon you, husband! The Lord judge between you and me!"

Chapter III

It was a silent and sultry Ishmael who met his father early the next morning. Since Abram had come to him the night before, he had lain in his mother's dark tent in sleepless confusion. What did his father mean to accomplish by taking him to the obscure Canaanite town of Salem?

Certainly he had heard many legends of its mysterious king. And his father had spoken of him so often, more times than he cared to count. But what interest did Melchizedek hold for him?

Abram saddled the camels quickly, and before the day had fully dawned, he and his young companion were well away from Hebron.

It was a good day's journey to the small city of Salem. As they traveled, many thoughts came to Abram. It had been nearly sixteen years since that unforgettable meeting with the strange monarch who called himself a priest. Yet all that time seemed as a whisper in Abram's memory, for the sight of the old king's face and the sound of his voice had remained indelibly on his heart, though circumstances of the world and endless years had separated them.

It never occurred to Abram that Melchizedek would not remember him. The thought was too absurd. In the instant they had met, though Abram had spoken nothing and the king but little, a marvelous impulse had passed between their souls, a kinship of spirit, divine and inexplicable in its implications.

Abram had thought often of that fleeting sensation, with which, in its wake, all the universe had seemed opened, and the past and future welded into one.

Though he would never fully understand its meaning until some future date, it lived within him.

Many times Abram could have counseled with the king—he could have made the short journey to Salem with ease; but in all these years he had not set out to do so until now.

The desire to see the wise man once more had never taken the form of action. Somehow, whenever he thought to go to him, Abram's intuition, his heart, told him the time was not yet right—the time would come in due course.

And even today, as he set out in desperate search for a measure of unity with Ishmael, he wondered if the steps he took were in the right direction. Perhaps Sarai had been right—perhaps it was wrong to seek God's approval on his folly and its consequences through the medium of a priest.

But Abram knew only one thing: Ishmael was his first-born, and if he were ever to inherit the promise, he must be won to the desire of it first, or all else was superfluous. Perhaps, then, an encounter with Melchizedek would help unlock Ishmael's heart.

These were only Abram's thoughts, however. Ishmael saw all of this quite differently. It was to him only another of the strange evidences of a driving force he had often witnessed in his father, a force which compelled Abram to involve him in a dream he would never fully understand.

The day was cool and damp. A thick fog had risen from the Ghor several miles away. Ishmael huddled close to his camel for warmth and said very little. It was rare that father and son conversed, but Abram was determined that the gulf between them be bridged in some measure today.

"The hunting has been good this year, Ishmael?" Abram opened.

"Yes, sir," the boy answered vaguely.

Abram smiled as if gratified by that response. "I remember you as a small boy," he said. "Why, from the time you could talk, it seems you have carried that bow and quiver on your back. I would often comment to Eliezer how great an archer you would be one day, and you have not disappointed me."

Ishmael, rather suspicious of his father's attempts at conversation, was nonetheless pleased at his praise. "Thank you," he said.

It was difficult for a proud man like Abram to take these steps in communication, but it was out of a sense of genuine remorse that he said, "I am only sorry I have not shared your experiences in those beloved hills of yours, Ishmael."

His first-born was moved at this unexpected overture and could think of nothing to say, but only stared at his father. Prompted to go on, Abram looked at him and said haltingly, "Son—I have never asked much of you, which is not always commendable in a father, but tell me—what do you do when you are gone so long from us?"

Ishmael maintained his independent, confident manner, and Abram did not see the mistiness which crowded into his eyes at such a question. It would have greatly surprised his father had he known the storehouse of loneliness the boy's facade of indifference served to cover.

This was not the first time Abram had asked him the reason for his long absences from home. The question had never been verbalized, but he had read it a thousand times in Abram's eyes.

But what was he to do? It had become easier and easier over the passing years of his young life to leave the tension of the home front for the shelter of the hills.

Life at the Oaks of Mamre had not always been so undesirable for Ishmael. As an innocent child, he had not so consciously sensed his father's fear of him and what he represented, nor had he intellectually realized his rejection by Sarai or his mother's outcast condition. There had been happy and tender moments, and he had grown to love his father in a strange way.

But, always the real effects of his conception had been felt. The scars had been well planted from birth.

As he had grown older, however, he had been able to identify the source and background of his insecurities. It was with his maturing knowledge that the sorrows, the pain grew, and with them, the desire to escape the home which symbolized all his unhappiness.

As a very young boy he had begun to plot his course for independence. Beginning with voluntary treks into the hills to tend his father's flocks, Ishmael began to stay more and more frequently away from home.

As he found his absences rarely questioned, he stayed in the hills days at a time and finally began taking his camel on extended treks farther and farther away from home.

He had become virtually wild, like a young untamed animal, a rover in love with others of his kind, an inhabitant of caves, an expert hunter, a lover of freedom.

Yet when his father now asked him about his experiences, he longed to cry out, "Why did you never question me before? Why did you never hold me to you?"

How could he answer Abram? What *did* he do when he was so long away from home?

He cringed with the raw memories he had stored within himself. Memories of those moments when his too-young independence had not comforted him on cold nights, when in fear he had cowered behind desert rocks and cried more tears of loneliness than he ever dared to admit.

Abram studied his son, awaiting a response, but none came.

And at last, Ishmael shrugged his shoulders as if to say, "Does it really matter?"

Several hours of rough terrain were between them and the Oaks. The sun had burned away a good deal of the morning fog, and the temperature was now more comfortable.

The journey had been passed thus far mostly in silence. It seemed that no matter what topics Abram introduced, Ishmael withdrew further into his shell of isolation. Yet a question burned within the young boy, and
at last he said, "Father, why are we going to Salem?"

Abram glowed with anticipation. Was this the opportunity he had so long sought, to speak to Ishmael of the
promise? Yes, Abram had talked of it before, but his
son had expressed only indifference. Perhaps today
would be different.

"I am taking you to be blessed by the priest of God.
Many years ago my father took me to a false priest for a
blessing. Surely my son deserves the blessings of the
true Priest of the Almighty."

Ishmael was not surprised at this answer, but he
sensed more motive in this journey than his father expressed, and he was somewhat prepared for what followed.

"Son," Abram said, using the word more often today
than ever before, "I have often told you that you are
heir to the promises of my God. One day all this land
through which we travel will be yours. It has been destined for you by the Lord. I have hoped that when you
meet Melchizedek, you might be impressed as never before with your part in the plan of the Almighty."

A certain feeling of antipathy and resentment rose in
Ishmael at these words. He had heard them before, but
never had they welded comfortably with his spirit. At
times he had questioned his father's stability. His
dreams seemed so incredible, beyond the realm of reality. At times Ishmael had even thought his poor father
mad, though he spoke of the promises with such conviction, that they were almost believable. Indeed, Ishmael
wondered if he even knew his father's God, so little did
such visionary statements mean to him.

But today, more than ever, he wrestled with them.

Perhaps he rebelled against the force with which
Abram drove him toward a belief in the promises. Perhaps he feared the unnatural anxiety his father dis-

played in urging him to conform to his own dreams. Or perhaps Ishmael found it irreconcilable that his father had always avoided involvement with him on all points but this. To Ishmael it did indeed seem strange that one who should inherit his father's blessings should also have been alienated from him since birth.

All this made Ishmael doubt. It angered him, and as he had never been treated with the honor due a first-born, he could not think that even Abram truly believed in his supposed destiny.

Ishmael seethed with pain as he considered the conditions of his birth. Even his own mother was outcast from the general fellowship of the camp, due to Sarai's resentment of her.

And with all his native energy he turned on Abram. "Does it not seem strange," he began, "that your God's promises should be attained by the son of a bondwoman?"

Abram was stunned at the boy's question and sat rigidly as Ishmael continued. "Is it not true, Father, that you take me to Salem as much to absolve yourself of your own doubts in this matter as to convince me of my calling?"

The truth of Ishmael's words bit Abram with venomous teeth, but he said nothing.

"Come, Father," Ishmael said bitterly. "Let us be honest with one another. It is said that I am your first-born, and yet if Sarai had ever had a son, tell me, who would be the first-born of your heart?"

"Ishmael!" Abram cried. "Enough of this. It is not true!"

But Ishmael was not convinced. Almost laughingly he said, "Oh, Father, but it is! Even my mother is kept a virtual prisoner of her past, lonely, unwelcomed in the society of the tribe. Don't you think she has told me how she fled Sarai in fear the day she announced I was to be born? Don't you think I know that my mother was forced to flee for her safety from the hands of her jealous mistress!"

Abram was shocked to silence. He should have known Hagar would tell her son about those bitter days before he was born, when such hatred had developed between the two women that Hagar had actually tried to find her way back to Egypt rather than stay near her rival.

But obviously the truth of that incident had been distorted in the retelling. Hagar had undoubtedly made Sarai out to be the villain of the affair, when in reality the maid had so goaded and gibed her mistress that Sarai's patience had finally been strained beyond endurance. The resulting response proved so harsh that the young girl had foolishly sought escape, almost starving in the desert before she returned.

"You do not understand all that happened then," Abram offered. "Those were hard days for all of us, and for Sarai most of all."

"Perhaps, sir. But, it appears my mother was the most abused. My poor, foolish mother—how she loved you, Father." As he said this, he shook his head half in pity of the one who had borne him, and half in disgust.

Abram read his son's attitude angrily. "Don't be so certain of yourself, Ishmael. There is much you do not know."

"But, I know enough, Father, enough to realize that though you may love me in some obscure, indefinite way, you have never loved me fully and freely, nor have you ever really wanted me, for I am too hard for you to think on. I call up too much in your mind which you would rather forget. I was a mistake, a very bad mistake made in a moment of weakness. When you look on me, you see that! I am a very real symbol of your guilt, Father!"

Abram trembled. What power did this small lad have to make him cower so? Now more than ever, he stood in awe of the magnificent boy who was a product of his own creation, a creation which had turned on him from its inception.

"Ishmael, you do not understand. You are young—"

"Ah, Father!" Ishmael bellowed, "Isn't it strange that when the young challenge the old, the old forever claim the inexperience of the younger for their main defense? But that argument will not hold with me, for I have seen too much in my few years to be called inexperienced."

"Ishmael—" Abram faltered.

"No, Father. I will not be rebuked. Your dreams, whatever they be, are meaningless to me. You shall not use me, as you used my mother and—my cousin Lot—to achieve your supposed promises."

At the mention of Lot, Abram turned angrily to Ishmael. "For what reason do you speak of him?" he cried.

"Did he not flee you, too, Father?" Ishmael shrugged. "Why was that? Did he fear your demands as I do?"

Abram felt as if he had been hit full force by some great blow. "Ishmael!" he cried. "You are wrong! You do not know what you speak of!"

"Perhaps not, Father," he said. "But I do know I can never be made to fit a pattern I was not cut out for. I was not cut right from the beginning."

At this Ishmael seemed to halt and tremble sadly. Looking at himself, he said softly, "I was cut from the wrong cloth," and with only a brief hesitation he turned from his father, too proud to let him see his tears. At last, all the angry, agonized words he had dreamed of saying, all the bitterness he had longed to voice and had planned to the last syllable in the caves and hills of his lonely youth—at last it had all been said.

In that moment it was as if Abram could see his son's lonely years of feigned independence for what they really were, the longing to be needed. He reached to touch him warmly, but Ishmael would have no pity, nor would he accept the all too tardy contrition of his father. In a fury he wheeled his magnificent camel about and raced like a lightning streak into the wilderness of the Canaanite hills.

Abram was left mute, stunned, unable to deliver his

soul of the words it longed to cry: "Oh my son!" he would have pleaded, "If only you knew how wrong you are. If only my selfish guilt had not impeded me, I should have told my love for you!"

But it was too late. Only the departing shadow of the lonely boy was visible as he passed over the brow of a distant ridge.

And as Abram stood alone, it seemed the very hills echoed with the prophetic words spoken by an angel of the Lord to Hagar when she had suffered in the desert before her child was born: indeed, Ishmael was a "wild man; his hand against every man."

Chapter IV

The trip to Salem was never completed. Abram stayed in those Canaanite hills in search of his elusive son for many days, neither eating nor sleeping. And when he did rest, it was with a feverish and fearful heart.

He had tethered his camel to a bluff far below, and had, in desperation, gone high up through no-man's terrain for two days, never finding a clue to Ishmael's whereabouts.

The climb through those hills had strained his aged muscles beyond endurance. Ceaselessly, it seemed, his rasping, painful voice had shattered the mountain air as he called the name of his precious son—but all to no avail.

And his heart cried out as loudly as his voice, "My God, am I brought to nothing? Are all my hopes and dreams—is all my life brought to nothing?"

It was a bitter Abram who dragged himself into an obscure cave the last night of that ordeal. Life meant little or nothing to him now. It seemed he would have happily died here, resigned, without a thought of returning home.

"Home!" he laughed. What was left there?

Abram tried not to dwell on this. It was too hard for him. He sat as a small stone among the rocks, and desired that they should fall on him, that his life might end.

But still, somewhere within him, within the shady recesses of his soul, surged that relentless spirit which would not die. Perhaps it was this which had always entwined him close to the heart of his God. Perhaps it was this quality which had won him favor from the beginning. The spirit of rebuttal—the spirit of Man unashamed, facing his Creator in the honesty of human emotions, and in the integrity of the human heart; the spirit of a man who could come close to despair more than once in his life and yet look up undaunted with his fist raised toward heaven and demand, "Why, God? What is it You require of me? I will have my answer. I will not let You go until You bless me!"

Abram was too weak to think concretely in such terms, and yet these were the thoughts which were harbored silently within him. While some might have cowered in fear at the onslaught of such evils as he had faced, it was not and never had been Abram's nature to retreat.

In essence, then, was this not faith? Was his brash and bold relationship with his Sovereign not a truer and nobler sign of love and confidence than weaker men's self-effacement?

And yet his demanding air did not show forth in pleas of self-pity. It was not a sniveling man who thought on his losses, who remembered his beloved nephew's spurning, who thought on his wounded wife, his faraway homeland, or his pitiful relation with his first-born.

It was an angry man who thought on these things, an angry man who cried out, "What was it for, that You called me out from among my brethren, Lord? Was it to end thus?"

The cave was cold and damp. Thick patches of algae hung in clusters from the ceiling. Abram sought some warmth in the debris dragged into the cave from winters of hibernating animals, and he dug his feet deep into the clots of aging moss which grew up from the floor.

He could not help remembering the seemingly endless numbers of times he had found himself in similar surroundings. He need not name them. They came to mind like a parade of wounded ghosts, passing through the corridors of his memory. Since that first night outside Ur, it seemed his moments of crisis were to be spent in the lonely, howling depths of such empty places.

But Abram clenched his fists tightly. In bitter challenge he whispered, "God, I will die here, now. I will not rise again, until You see fit to raise me up. Carry me to my fathers. For life is over, unless You bless me. I will not move before You bless me." He stared into the darkness, determination marking his every word. "Hear me, God!" he cried angrily, his words echoing and rechoing through the tunneled hollows of the cave. "Hear me! I will not go again to my people as I have gone before, with glowing promises! I will not return with the joy of things which are to be, before they are—and then watch my hopes shattered in another succession of fruitless years!"

Abram waited, as if for a response, but when none came, he smirked at the silence about him, and an empty laugh issued from his soul. "Let it be so then, my Lord. Fourteen years have I lived without You. Your servant will ask no more—I close my eyes in death. Do not wake me; do not come to me!"

Abram's eyes were shut tightly. The darkness was impenetrable, and yet dizzying lights flashed troublesome scenes before him. He saw his father lift the whip to beat him; he saw the innocent Dari die before him, and he saw his people starving in the wilderness outside Egypt; he saw Sarai torn ruthlessly away to Pharaoh's court; he saw his nephew Lot as he left the mount for Sodom; he saw Ishmael as a babe in his mother's arms, and he heard his son's bitter words as Ishmael turned from him.

Like a panorama he saw his tortured, unhappy life, and in a stupor he cried out, "Will You trouble me even in my dreams?"

His feverish mind was not calmed, but at last it lapsed into a nightmare token of sleep.

The stupor which had drugged Abram's body and soul seemed to plunge him powerfully into a despair undefinable in human vocabulary. It was as if in answer to

his staunch dignity, in response to his admirable ability
to challenge, he was to be cast into the very pit of hopelessness.

But somewhere between self-possessed glory and
utter defeat at the hands of a triumphant and nameless
adversary, Abram was roused to semiconsciousness by
a rustling outside the cave.

Slowly, painfully, his eyes opened. "Yes?" he called,
his heart pounding apprehensively, "Who's there?" His
voice was hoarse and shaky, and he strained to penetrate the darkness, but his helpless eyes could see nothing.

Again he heard the rustling sound, and his heart
stopped still. There, in the vague light of the moon
which filtered through the fog at the mouth of the cave,
stood the silhouetted figure of a man.

Abram was as solid as stone with fear. He neither
moved nor spoke. Had the man stepped forward to slay
him, he, in his weakened condition, could not have
moved, so sudden and disorienting was this appearance.

The man did not come forward but stood still for a
long moment, and this frightened Abram still more.

At last, with what little strength remained to him, he
whispered, "Sir, if you mean to rob me I have nothing.
If you mean to kill me, I have no defense, nor would I
fight you. Only, be done with it, whatever mischief you
intend."

Still the figure did not move. An eerie sensation crept
through Abram, and he dared not speak, only staring
blankly at the dark silhouette, his body numb with an
indescribable dread. Something in the stance of the man
was familiar. Abram fought off the possibility which
presented itself. "It cannot be," he reasoned.

But almost as if in answer to his unvoiced doubts, the
man stepped out into the moonlight, and Abram could
see his features hazily. Surely his old heart would never
beat again, such a leap it made!

"Abram—" the figure called softly.

All the challenges with which he had knocked so

loudly against the heavens were suddenly meaningless. In an instant his human pride and dignity seemed as cow's dung, his self-importance as so many filthy rags.

Suddenly his finite stature crumbled before him, and his demands stood out as the cries of an idiot, or as the pleas of an ant against the foot of an ox.

"Abram," the voice called again.

Dared he move? Dared he present himself? Who was he to presume?

No longer capable of his previous self-view, he was now only grateful that in mercy his Redeemer had waited, tolerantly, patiently, as he had harangued the golden skies with the ignorance of human arrogance.

Slowly he lifted himself in pain and walked toward the cave opening. He could not look on his God. He preferred to die. Must he present himself? How dared he deal so rudely with his Creator in times past?

But the Lord waited patiently for him, and as Abram came into the moonlight, he dared to look up at the figure clad in a cloth like undyed wool. And in that face he read such compassion that he trembled with its tangibility.

The presence and aspect of the Almighty was too powerful to be tolerated, and His words plumbed the depths of that proud man's guilt-bedeviled soul. "I am the Almighty God; walk before me, and be thou perfect, and I will make my covenant between me and thee and will multiply thee exceedingly."

Abram's knees could not support him now. He could not possibly stand in the presence of the one he loved more than his life. Falling prostrate, he wept convulsively. "My Lord and my God, I am but dust and ashes before Thee. I am as nothing—"

But the Lord stood by silently as Abram knelt before Him and with compassion such as Abram did not know possible, the divine friend continued, "As for me, behold my covenant is with thee and thou shalt be the father of many nations."

At this the Lord ceased talking and walked away

from Abram as if to prepare him for the next thought. Abram did not look up, but in tense anticipation he awaited whatever the Lord held for him.

At last, his Master returned and whispered slowly, "Neither shall thy name any more be called Abram, but thy name shall be Abraham: for a father of many nations have I made thee."

The Chosen Man of God trembled with disbelief and joy. By custom, the receipt of a new name in the eastern world was symbolic of a new life—a rebirth to a new or amplified purpose—and this was the greatest honor bestowed on a man. After fourteen years of emptiness, he was being given a new beginning.

"My Lord—" Abraham groaned, his soul too full to take it in.

But his Redeemer went on. "And I will make thee exceeding fruitful, and I will make nations of thee, and —kings shall come of thee."

Abraham placed his hands to his face to cover the tears of joy which streamed down his cheeks, and he rocked to and fro upon his knees in amazed celebration. Still he could not bring himself to look upon his God, but held out his arms and cried, "Am I, an old man, to know such things in my old age? Am I truly to know such good things as You speak?"

The Lord smiled happily on his Chosen One and said, "I will establish my covenant between me and thee and thy seed after thee in their generations for an everlasting covenant, to be a God unto thee, and to thy seed after thee.

"And I will give unto thee, and to thy seed after thee, the land wherein thou art a stranger, all the land of Canaan, for an everlasting possession; and I will be their God."

Again the Lord was silent, standing close at hand as Abraham wept at his feet. Yet all the man's anxieties were not quenched. Dare he ask more of the Lord? He wished to know how it would stand with Ishmael in the future. He wished to hear that Sarai would be restored again to him. As limitlessly glad as he was to hear again of the future seed of his descendants, and of all that would be theirs, he was still just human enough to long after immediate happiness and personal blessings.

Yet how could he ask? Instead he said, "My God, is there anything You require of Your servant? Surely gratitude will not repay Your blessings."

The Lord gazed on Abraham, knowing the true content of his heart but desiring that he should ask for his personal desires straightforwardly. As long as the man did not have that courage, however, the Lord answered his voiced question first.

And Abraham was not prepared for the Lord's demands:

"Thou shalt keep my covenant—thou, and thy seed after thee in their generations. This is my covenant, which ye shall keep, between me and you and thy seed after thee; Every man-child among you shall be circumcised. And ye shall circumcise the flesh of your foreskin; and it shall be a token of the covenant betwixt me and you. And he that is eight days old shall be circumcised among you, every man-child in your generations, he that is born in the house, or bought with money of any stranger, which is not of thy seed. He that is born in thy house, and he that is bought with thy money, must needs be circumcised: and my covenant shall be in your flesh for an everlasting covenant. And the uncircumcised man-child whose flesh of his foreskin is not circumcised, that soul shall be cut off from his people; he hath broken my covenant."

Abraham took this in with terror in his heart. Did his ears hear right? Such a command! Could his God really require such butchery?

Abraham was frightened beyond words. Did he really know the Lord at all? he wondered. Who was this whom he served? Could he ever approach such a one with the contents of his inner man again? Scenes from the rituals of Baal and Nannar flashed before him. Abraham questioned his own sanity and cried out within himself that the business of this god he served was to deal in bad jokes.

He clung to the ground beneath him, asphyxiated with bombarding questions, and he desired that this god should leave off talking with him.

But as these thoughts came to him, the Lord stepped nearer and, as if having heard his inmost desires, plumbed the core of Abraham's soul with these words:

"As for Sarai thy wife, thou shalt not call her name Sarai, but Sarah shall her name be. And I will bless her, and give thee a son also of her; yea, I will bless her, and she shall be a mother of nations; kings of people shall be of her."

But Abraham could no longer take in all he heard. Something within him rose in rebellion at this. It was too fantastic, and already he had questioned the intents of the one who stood before him.

This last was too much to endure. Surely this being mocked him, Abraham thought. In disgust he fell on his face, laughing scornfully, and shouted derisively, "Shall a child be born unto him that is a hundred years old? And shall Sarah, that is ninety years old, bear?"

But the Lord was patient, and walking toward his doubting child, He bent down and placed two strong hands on his arms, urging him to stand before Him.

At the touch of those hands a surge of strength and power unlike anything Abraham had ever experienced coursed like a white-water cascade throughout his body, permeating it with renewed spirit.

Abraham was compelled to leave off his mockery and found his eyes studying the face of the Master. An inexplicable reverence and shame took hold on him. He had been touched afresh with the tenderness and love of his God. Without knowing it, he was weeping, and as the Lord's eyes met his, Abraham felt his own hand clasped in the hand of God.

With a new ability, he felt his heart opened and his tongue loosed, and he was free to express his inner thoughts and doubts. Though hesitant, for fear of pain-ing the Lord, he said, "Oh, that Ishmael might live before thee!"

But the Lord registered none of the expected anger or surprise Abraham had feared. Instead He smiled benignly and understandingly at his Chosen Man and, reaching up, placed His two hands on Abraham's head, saying confidently and reassuringly, "Sarah thy wife shall bear thee a son indeed; and thou shalt call his name Isaac: and I will establish my covenant with him for an everlasting covenant, and with his seed after him.

"And . . . as for Ishmael," the Lord smiled again, "I have heard thee: Behold I have blessed him, and will make him fruitful, and will multiply him exceedingly; twelve princes shall he beget, and I will make him a great nation.

"But my covenant will I establish with Isaac, which Sarah shall bear unto thee at this set time in the next year."

At this the Lord lowered his hands from Abraham's head, and yet the man clung to them. The Lord's eyes met his for a long moment, and Abraham studied the indescribable One who stood as a man and yet not as a man before him.

Then the Master turned as if weary and without a further word walked away from Abraham into the hills high above.

Incapable of words, the Man of God watched after him with tear-dimmed eyes, and at last the Figure who had come mysteriously to him was lost in the fog of the night.

Abraham studied the mountain of his Lord's departure for a long while, and he clasped his hands in front of him, remembering the touch of his God.

Thinking on his seemingly wasted years of effort and error, he cried out, "Oh, my Lord, had I but run to You when I first saw You on Gerizim, had I but let You touch me then, would I ever have lived my life as I have lived it?"

Chapter V

It seemed nothing could ever again challenge Abraham's faith, for he had reached the summit, having talked with God face to face.

His people sensed his renewed spirit from the instant he set foot again in the camp at the Oaks of Mamre. Those who had been with Abraham from the beginning, from the inception at Haran and Damascus, who had gone through the tribulation in Egypt, and who had followed their leader for these many decades—they sensed in him the spirit of the Abram they remembered having been drawn to years before.

Abraham's mood was electric. There were many at Mamre who had never known him as a young man when his mission had first begun. They had joined his enormous tribe long after his life had turned rancid— but even these began to see in him the man of legend, the man of whom the older ones had often spoken.

Upon Abraham's return, Eliezer, still loyal as always, met him at the edge of camp.

"Master!" he cried. "We had given you up for lost! Welcome home, sir!"

"Oh, dear friend, Eliezer," Abraham smiled.

Something in that face told the faithful steward that the Lord had been with his master, and though Eliezer did not plague Abraham with questions, he read his joy and reveled in it.

And as Abraham unfolded to his old friend the words of God, Eliezer was filled with the returning joy of hope in his Semitic heritage. Perhaps, after all, his life had not been spent in vain endeavor. Perhaps he would yet live to see his dreams fulfilled.

Almost as if by design, it seemed, spring followed

Abraham's return. Life seemed given anew to the once so-long depressed and weary people at the Oaks. How closely knit they were to the soul of their master. Truly, though they may never have realized it, Abraham's joy was theirs. Very few could be happy if their leader was not, and he had been unhappy for so many years.

But all that seemed behind them now. With the lengthening days and the budding grass of the fields, the camp experienced a resurrection of life uncanny in its impact.

Women sang as they ground at the wheel. The men rose more willingly at sunrise to tend the flocks or trade routes. And the ewes bore fine young lambs that spring.

But it was perhaps the greatest miracle of the season that Ishmael was seen returning to the Oaks several long weeks after spring had begun.

Not all the people at Mamre were moved to join Abraham's new-found vision.

Certainly many were repelled when their master instituted the rite of circumcision. Ishmael, for one, had found his homecoming little gratified by what he considered the insanity of his father's gory proposal that he be among the first to receive the mark of the covenant, and it truly had been a sad day for Hagar when her struggling, unhappy boy was taken by his father's servants into the initiation tent.

But perhaps more than anyone, it was Sarah who looked on with doubtful and even scornful eyes, as her husband went about the business of hope. She feared the seemingly senseless enthusiasm with which he had thrown himself into his dreams.

It was a very hot afternoon when Sarah came to her husband with these thoughts. The ritual of circumcision had lasted many days until all the men of the tribe, numbering in the many hundreds, had finally been initiated.

Sarah had endured this lunacy silently, but now that it was over, she must speak her mind.

She busied herself about the mundane tasks of preparing the evening meal and formulated in her mind how she would approach Abraham. There he sat in the tent door, seeking some respite from the fierce sun of early summer. Nearly three months had passed since his return from the Salem venture. She smiled sadly at the thought of the hope he tried so foolishly to renew in her. If indeed, an old woman—for whom nature had closed the door—was to bear within a year of his homecoming, she should have sensed the seeds of life within herself by now.

Poor Abraham, she mused. She could not help loving him, though she feared for his mind.

His dreams, she reasoned, had always been his weakness and would be his ultimate downfall. His obsession with this strange god, in whom she too had once been convinced to believe, had surely robbed his sanity. And now, he was "a shell of a man," she thought, a man who dreamed on, yet persuaded of the saving hand of his imaginary sovereign.

Did she not owe it to him to try once more to bring him to his senses? Let their remaining years together be in the light of reality, at least, she thought.

She laid down her utensils and stepped up to him. Placing a tender hand on his aging head, she remembered the day he had carried her away to be his bride. A fleeting smile crossed her face, but it was a sad memory, for the intervening years had held such disappointments.

Abraham looked up at her and touched her hand, grateful for her attentions, and she read the question in his eyes which said, "Does this mean you feel my joys with me?"

But Sarah could not voice her inner thoughts. His look of hope recalled to her the young dreams which had also been hers many years before—dreams which a lifetime of heartache had all too cleverly taught her the foolishness of. She remembered the night so long ago when he had stood on the grassy slopes between Mesopotamia and Shenir, when they had just begun their journey into life together. She remembered how he had smiled in much the same way as he did now, saying, "We will one day be abundant with good things like the hills of Palestine." And she remembered how she had so innocently believed in him.

What could she say? He had never outgrown those fonder days as she had. He still clung tenaciously, stubbornly to the old hopes with the faith of a child, she mused. Would it be right to bring him away from that vision now?

"Abraham," she whispered, not yet used to his insistence on that name, "may I speak with you?"

He was about to offer the affirmative when suddenly his attention was drawn to the plains far to the west of camp.

Sarah looked in that direction and saw three strangers standing. Abraham rose and motioned to her to go back into the tent, saying, "I will see if they are friends."

Obediently she complied, realizing that her conversation would have to wait until another time.

Abraham was left alone at the door, and he strained to see if he could recognize the newcomers, but his old eyes were too dim. Rousing his tired legs, he walked out to meet them. But when he had gone halfway he suddenly stopped, staring in amazement at the central figure.

All the joy of youth was once again his as he ran now the rest of the distance, his arms outstretched in speechless happiness.

"My God!" he cried. "Pass not away! Pass not away, I pray thee!"

When he reached the trio, he held his hands out to them, smiling with joyful tears, and then bowing down his face to the ground, he pleaded, "My Lord, if now I have found favor in thy sight, pass not away, I pray thee, from thy servant."

His anxiety to talk again with the Lord was overwhelming, and he looked up, daring to take Him by the hand, and spoke very urgently:

"Let a little water, I pray you, be fetched, and wash your feet, and rest yourselves under the tree!"

At this Abraham rose and pointed eagerly toward camp, tugging like a child at the sleeve of the Lord's woolen robe.

"I will fetch a morsel of bread and comfort your heart; after that you shall pass on, if need be," he pleaded. "Surely you will stay, seeing you have come this far to your servant."

The Lord smiled warmly and said, "So do as you have said."

Abraham turned eagerly from them, running all the way back toward camp, turning every few feet to be sure they were following, and when he had reached the tent, he called, "Sarah! Make ready three measures of fine meal! Knead it and make cakes upon the hearth!"

Sarah, assuming the oncomers were tradesmen, quickly complied. Abraham, meanwhile, ran to his herd, scattering them in his haste, and finding among the bawling cattle a tender young calf.

Lifting the struggling, bleating creature in his arms, he carried him to the central tents, calling to Eliezer to dress him out for the guests.

The steward had never seen his master move this quickly since he descended off Gerizim, and without question he sensed that whoever the guests might be, they deserved the best.

Not long after the three visitors had seated themselves, Eliezer brought out the cakes, with butter, milk, and the choice veal. And as Abraham sat close by, his old heart pounding madly from the chase and perspiration glistening on his face, the faithful steward waited on them.

How does one introduce the Lord to one's friends?

Abraham was at a loss to do so, but Eliezer sensed from the behavior of his master that these strangers were not like any other men he had met.

Abraham did not question the nature of his God's physical body. The fact that He ate as well as spoke and walked like a man did not cause Abraham alarm Such questions of theology did not concern him. As he waited anxiously on his Master, he was stimulated only by the beauty and tangibility of the moment.

No word was spoken until the Lord at last looked up from the meal and asked, "Where is Sarah, thy wife?"

"In the tent, my Lord . . ." Abraham pointed, a thrill of anticipation coursing through him.

At this the Lord stood up and looked toward the goatshair dwelling. Sarah, having overheard the reference to herself, stood just inside the tent door out of sight, hoping to catch anything said of her.

"I will leave now," the Lord said, "but I will surely return unto you according to the time of life; and, behold, Sarah thy wife shall have a son."

Sarah stepped back into the shadows, her hands trembling. Who was this stranger, and what did he know of her? She could not help laughing at this lunacy, and yet a nagging fear poured over her. Who was he?

But then she heard the stranger's voice again, and an icy chill went straight to her heart. "Wherefore did Sarah laugh?" the man was asking.

Sarah was numb. How did he know she had laughed? She stood in silent disbelief near the door and listened as the voice took on an insistent, if not impatient, quality. "Is anything too hard for the Lord?" the stranger was saying. "At the time appointed I will return unto thee, according to the time of life, and Sarah shall have a son."

Now her knees gave way under her. Her head spun with conflicting thoughts. It could not be and yet it was —this man knew all her thoughts, though he had never seen her.

Doubts still plagued her, and yet fear was her dominant emotion. Was this Abraham's God in visible form before her?

"Preposterous!" she said. And yet she crept through the door, fearful to look on Him, and said weakly, "My Lord, I laughed not."

The Gentle Stranger turned toward her, His eyes seeming to penetrate her very soul. Sarah could no longer deny His presence. She knew, now, who He was. No one need convince her.

But she could not look at Him. His knowing gaze too easily stripped her of all her hardened disbelief. She stood before Him as a guilty child and could not lift her head.

It was not in bitterness that the Lord walked toward her, taking her hand in His. But His face and voice were sad as He said, "Nay, but thou didst laugh."

Sarah trembled and tears came to her eyes. She could say nothing. She wished He would not look at her so. Her years of disbelief stood before her like so many skeletons. And she despised herself for them.

Yet the Lord lifted her face to Him, saying in a silent word that He knew the lifetime of hopelessness and disillusionment which had been hers—that the past had been much for any woman to bear.

And in that moment peace and hope were imparted to her.

Chapter VI

Abraham sensed that the Lord would be going now. The two strangers with Him, who had remained nameless during their visit, rose from the meal and waited for their Master's orders.

But the Lord seemed hesitant to go on, looking at his faithful servant with compassionate eyes.

"Surely my God will not leave so quickly," Abraham pleaded. "You are only just arrived." And taking hold of His garment he constrained Him, saying, "At least let Your servant accompany You wherever You wish to go."

The Lord smiled on him with understanding, and said, "Are you certain you wish to go with us, Abraham?"

"Yes, my Lord! Anywhere!" he cried. "I am old and tired, but today I have strength enough for ten men."

The Lord said, "Very well," and then paused, looking sadly at his friend. "We go—to Sodom."

An eerie apprehension gripped the aged Man of God. At the name of that city, scenes of his beloved nephew came to mind like sad, twice-told tales. All the sorrow of years past, all the memories associated with that wayward kinsman came back as if they had lived only yesterday. The dreams Abraham had once held for him, so long half-forgotten, had never really been out of mind. And though he had not once seen his nephew since the battle of the kings more than sixteen years before, one word was sufficient to call back all the old longings as if they had never at all departed.

Abraham looked sadly at the ground. "Sodom?"

"Yes, friend," the Lord said softly, looking at the man whose joyful countenance had suddenly fallen at the sound of two syllables, and feeling all his pain with him.

Abraham longed to ask why his Master wished to go there, but he feared the answer. As he stood pondering all this, however, the Lord and his two companions began walking away from the camp.

Abraham followed after them miserably, and at last, catching up to the group, he said, "I will be happy to take you to the city. Let your servant be with you along the way."

The companions said nothing, and the Lord only looked with sad eyes at the one who loved Him so.

The terrain leading down to the plains near the Dead Sea fell in descending terraces.

Howling wind and blistering sun penetrated the craggy, barren wilderness through which the four figures wandered.

Abraham did not question his Lord's choice of travel. He knew very well that if He had wished, his God could have left him in an instant, vanishing like so much air before his eyes and reappearing in that city as quickly as He had left.

Yet he did not suggest such a thing. He savored too selfishly each instant spent at the Lord's side.

God, physically present, in the form of a common man—the thought was too wonderful to debate. One must not question such a gift but handle it with awesome reverence.

And yet Abraham wearied of the journey. Sodom lay sixty miles from the Oaks. Though his strength seemed nearly youthful when he walked with God, he was old, and his muscles grew tired with the hike.

Several days had passed since they had left Mamre. Abraham could go no farther. The sun glared down on the wayfarers, and at last the elderly man stopped in the shade of a nearby rock, removing his mantle and wiping his perspiring face, drinking from the skin of wine which hung along with his food sack on his belt.

"My Lord," he panted, "forgive me, but I must rest again."

The Lord walked back to him and said, "Abraham, do not weary yourself with this journey. There is no need for you to go farther. Return home."

"But, my Lord," Abraham persisted, "I have come this far. Look—Sodom is visible from here!"

The gleaming city could be seen vaguely from this height, but it would take at least another hard day of travel before they reached it.

Abraham had still not asked why his Lord would go to Sodom, and yet the question had never been out of his mind. He knew the Lord sensed this, but he also knew from past experience that he would have to ask it before the Lord would answer. And he feared what that answer would be.

Perhaps he already knew it. Why else would a righteous God go down into that sin-ridden pit, but to destroy it? He had known this all along, and yet he hoped against hope that this was not the Lord's intention.

Abraham seated himself on the ground, and the white-robed Figure stood in the shade with him as he rested. The Lord did not speak but only read Abraham's heart, and the Man of God was surprised when he looked up to see his Master's knowing gaze.

No words passed between them, but in that instant Abraham realized that his fears were justified. He read in his Lord's sad eyes that his mission was indeed one of retribution.

The Lord leaned down and placed a loving hand on Abraham's shoulder, saying softly, "Shall I hide from Abraham the thing which I do, seeing that he shall surely become a great nation, and all the nations of the earth shall be blessed in him?"

Abraham was mute with fear. He wished to hear the Lord's plans, and yet he feared he knew them already. The Lord's eyes were filled now with tears, and He turned from Abraham, walking to the edge of the bluff from where the city could be seen, and as He looked at it, great sorrow was etched on his face.

He directed His words to His companions who stood nearby. "I know Abraham, that he will command his children and his household after him, and he will keep my ways, to do justice and judgment."

The two men looked on silently, longing to resolve their Master's dilemma, yet knowing His struggles must be resolved by Himself alone.

"Oh, Abraham," the Lord cried, his divine voice heavy and constricted, "I shall indeed tell you my heart and my intentions, for you are worthy to hear them."

The Man of God trembled violently and looked on in terror as the Lord walked again to the bluff and pointed angrily but sadly at the city of the plain, saying in deep agony, "The cry of Sodom and Gomorrah is great, and their sin is very grievous!"

Then, looking at Abraham as if His next words were too hard for even Himself to hear, He said, "I will go down now, and see whether they have done altogether according to the cry of it, which is come unto me, and if not—" He paused here and added only, "then I will know."

Abraham knew his Lord had meant to say more than this. He knew his God had only spared him the horror of hearing it all.

He looked on shakily as the two men turned to continue on their journey, knowing they would go to fulfill the Lord's plans. And visions of his nephew, his dearly beloved Lot, flashed desperately before him. "No!" he cried inside, "You cannot mean to harm him!"

His God stood yet before him, and Abraham roused himself, walking to Him and crying out spontaneously, "Wilt Thou also destroy the righteous with the wicked?"

The Lord turned to him, and Abraham put his hands to his lips unable to believe that such words of challenge had issued from his own mouth. Surely the Lord would smite him, he thought. How dare he question Him so? Abraham stepped back in fear, covered his head, and prepared for the Lord's wrath, but there were no words of anger—there was no hand of retribution for his challenge.

Slowly he looked up, and saw not an angry God, but One who seemed strangely ready and willing to hear his pleas.

Abraham could not easily believe this response, but he took courage from it and approached the Lord again, saying softly and humbly this time, "Peradventure there be fifty righteous within the city: wilt Thou not spare the place for the fifty righteous that are therein?"

The Lord stood silently by and looked at the city, apparently struck by Abraham's words. The Man of God grew bolder and proceeded:

"Far be it from my Lord to do such a thing! To slay the righteous with the wicked: far be it from Thee—shall not the Judge of all the earth do right?" he pleaded.

The Lord looked still on Sodom, and after a long silence He answered, "Let it be—if I find in Sodom fifty righteous, then will I spare the city, for their sakes."

Abraham thrilled to his new hope, but then, thinking of the wretched Sodom, he was filled with a new fear. Suppose, he thought, suppose there were not even fifty righteous there?

Again, memories of his rebellious nephew filled his mind. How he loved him! He could not see him destroyed. It must not happen. If he had any influence with the Lord at all, it must be used now. Despite the consequences of his next words, he must risk them for Lot's sake.

Like a leaf in the wind, he approached the Lord again and whispered, "Behold now, I, who am but dust and ashes, have taken upon me to speak unto the Lord. Peradventure there lack five of fifty righteous, wilt Thou destroy all the city for the lack of five?"

The Lord thought again for some time, and then said, "If I find there forty and five, I will not destroy it."

Abraham's heart leaped within him. Could he possibly speak to the Lord again? He did not seem angry with him. The old man took fresh courage, and, breathing deeply, he said, "Peradventure there be forty found there—"

"I will not do it for forty's sake," the Lord smiled sadly.

Abraham was about to cry out with joy, but fearful the hope he held would not stand much more strain, he said cautiously, "Oh, let not the Lord be angry and I will speak: Peradventure there be thirty—"

"I will not do it if I find thirty there."

Abraham nearly jumped with ecstasy, and unable to contain himself, he cried, "Oh, my Lord! Behold now, I have taken upon myself to speak with you: Peradventure there be twenty found there—"

The Lord walked to the rock again and leaned back in contemplation. Looking at Abraham hesitantly, He said, as if He had been constrained far enough, "I will not destroy it—for twenty's sake."

Abraham sensed he must say no more now. The Lord was done bargaining with him, he knew. And yet, as he watched his Master begin the long descent down the hill to the Dead Sea, fear grew again in his heart. Even though the Lord would spare that city for twenty's sake, Abraham doubted He could find that many there.

The aged man knew of no one righteous in Sodom. If the Lord would even number Lot "righteous," which Abraham sincerely doubted, he would be only one and not twenty.

Yet Abraham loved Lot. His soul cried out to preserve the only kinsman left to him, the son of his dead brother, Haran.

Abraham knew the Lord wished to hear no more. He knew the Lord's patience was not infinite even with His chosen, and yet despite the consequences to himself, he must speak again.

The Lord was well away from him now. Abraham would have to run to catch up with Him, and oh, how his legs ached. Still, he must!

Stumbling and nearly falling most of the way, the old man made his desperate skirmish down the hill.

"Master!" he cried, tears pouring down his face. "Wait! Wait!" he called, his arms outstretched pleadingly.

Still the Lord walked on, and Abraham forced his old legs to continue. At last he neared the Master, and stumbling in utter exhaustion, he grabbed Him by the feet, his face buried in the dirt. Hot tears mingled with the dust and formed miniature rivers of mud near the Lord's sandals.

But Abraham could not speak. His throat was dry with the run, and he was only convulsed with sobs.

Even if he were to speak now, what would he say? He knew there were no righteous men in Sodom. What would he ask for? The Lord's patience would not last forever.

What a fool he was, he thought, as he lay there without dignity.

But then he felt the strong hands of his Lord on his arms. He was lifting him to his feet as He had done that night in the hills near Salem.

Abraham stood slowly, but his legs would not support him. He clung to his Master limply and buried his muddy face on the Lord's shoulder.

His God was silent, holding him like a child, waiting for him to speak, and when he had left off crying, he said in muffled tones, "Oh, let not the Lord be angry with me, and I will speak yet but this once—" Abraham paused, formulating his final hopeless words in his mind. "Peradventure there be ten—"

The Lord took Abraham's face in His hands and was not angry with him, but only said gently, "I will not destroy it for ten's sake."

At this the Lord turned, not looking back again, and went His way to Sodom.

Abraham slumped to the ground, grateful for that last hope, but knowing even it was not sufficient.

The white-robed Figure was slowly lost to sight, and as Abraham was left alone, a new sensation came over him. "Lord!" he called again, like a frightened, lonely child.

A panic gripped him, for somehow, mysteriously, he sensed he would never again see and hold his Lord physically before him.

He stood up and attempted to follow, but it was no use. "Lord!" he cried again, sensing his great loss. "Why did I speak of my poor fellow humans when You were present with me? The poor are with us always, but You are gone too soon!"

Chapter VII

Lot slammed the door and walked into the street. He could no longer tolerate the screaming of his shrewish wife.

Rarely, in the past few years, had his homelife been peaceful. Perhaps it was as much his fault as Mala's, but he had grown to despise this city and all it stood for, and this was the source of their quarrels.

He had once loved the city as much as she. But that was when they had lived on the outskirts, in the style of tent-dwelling merchants. Since they had moved inside its walls, the glamor had worn off, and over the past few years, Lot had become increasingly uneasy with the environs of Sodom.

The humanistic philosophy to which Lot had been drawn through association with Sodomite friends as a young man had gradually shown its true colors. He had discovered a certain emptiness in the belief that Man's highest pleasure comes from inside himself and his fellow creatures.

Yes, at first the dream had seemed logical and operative. If there was a god, he had been told, he had made us for communion with one another, and service to him was best rendered through horizontal relationships. But Lot had discovered a certain perversion in that philosophy, which led in its emptiness from one desperate search to another. And so, he had found, the blind, grasping ones of Sodom were not truly happy in their "freedoms."

With this discovery had come a great loneliness. Often Lot found himself at odds with his own wife, with his sons and daughters, and sons-in-law.

Perhaps then it was his fault that his home was in disgusting shape, but he knew he had once had more than he had here. He knew that when he had been with his uncle, there had been a higher purpose in life—and how often he now longed for that.

The horizontal plane could no longer please him. To seek pleasure in others, or to seek pleasure even in pleasing others, did not satisfy him. In fact, rather than lifting him, this philosophy had cast him into a vicious circling pit of despair.

His daughters, with their painted faces and gaudy clothes, his rowdy, perverted sons and sons-in-law, his brawling unhappy wife, could not understand him. They had never known anything else.

Often, he considered, they did not even know their own emptiness, so blinded were they to all other possibilities. And yet they incessantly sought to fill their unconscious voids with senseless human endeavors and pursuits, insisting that they had the resources within themselves to make their lives meaningful.

Lot knew better. He knew better from experience that the horizontal is meaningless without the vertical—for Man cannot raise Man except to his own level.

And so he found himself thinking and speaking often of Abraham.

Of course, it was difficult for his loved ones to understand his change of heart: they would have none of it. Mala, most of all, despised his growing loftiness and discontent. She took it as a direct reflection on herself and beleaguered him day and night with his self-righteousness.

"Since when do you raise yourself up to sit in judgment on us, Lot?" she would scream. "You are one of us, you know! You chose to be. Do not speak to us now, after all these years, of some god we know nothing of!"

Her words still rang in his ears as he walked to the city gate to be alone.

Tomorrow was a feast day in Sodom. The streets were already crowded with people coming into town for

the celebration. Here and there he saw the city prostitutes, male and female, plying their trades, the houses
of enjoyment, and the physicians' offices for the treat-
ment of resultant diseases. On this corner was one of
the many galleries for instruction in sexual acts, and
there was a phallic symbol hanging above the door of a
shrine to Baal.

Something inside Lot rebelled at all he witnessed tonight. More than ever before he felt the anger which
had been growing in him over the years.

He could not stomach another festival, with its
brawling, riotous orgies, and—the human sacrifices.

Suddenly his feet were running, carrying him through
the streets as if to take him away from his thoughts.
People looked at him strangely as he pushed past them,
eager to find the city gate and a measure of relief from
the life of the inner city.

When he reached the city wall, he leaned against it to
rest and then made his way through the gate. He sat,
along with the beggars and urchins, outside the wall,
and turned his eyes to the hills of Canaan. Somehow,
looking toward the environs of the shepherd folk
soothed him. His mind wandered back over the years
and was crowded with memories of his uncle and his
love of the Lord.

With shame he remembered how Abraham had
risked his life to rescue him from enslavement when
Sodom was overthrown. And with guilt he recalled that
sixteen years ago he had promised to return to him.

What had happened to that promise? How had it
been put off?

The return to Sodom had killed it. Mala's influence
had been too great, and Lot's determination to do right,
too weak.

The mundane affairs he had returned to set in order
had led his mind away from his uncle and his God. He
had never returned.

Sixteen years of wasted life had brought four daughters and two young sons, of whom Lot was not at all

proud. His blood curdled at the thought of his flimsy daughters with their senseless values and love of foolish pleasure, or his sons to whom he had not been able to impart the values of true manhood.

Already, at their young age, the boys showed perverted interests, and Lot had given them up, as he had given up hope for all who dwelled here.

But, he chided himself, who was he to judge them? Had he been half the man he should have been, his family would never have been reared in such an insidious environment.

As Lot sat wallowing in his self-pity, crowds of people from the neighboring towns were arriving for the next day's festivities.

He paid little attention to any of them. He had seen them all before—not individually, but by type. He had seen the same empty faces, the same blunted, satiated expressions, the same hopeless but still searching eyes —he had seen them all, hundreds of times, for they were the faces of the world, never satisfied, ever seeking and never finding, ever hungry and never filled.

Though the feast was tomorrow, the music and dancing would begin in the streets tonight and last throughout the sleepless hours until morning, all in preparation for the celebration.

As Lot watched the crowds, he was suddenly drawn by the appearance of two men who had just passed him. Something in their faces was different, clean and pure. How does one recognize wholesomeness? Yet that is what he saw in them.

Somehow they looked out of place, as if they were from another world—a world untouched by the smut of this city.

A strange, inexplicable sensation came over Lot as he watched them, and almost supernaturally, it seemed, he felt compelled to go to them, to warn them that this was no place for them, that they would not be safe here.

Suddenly he found himself pushing through the crowd toward them.

"Young men!" he called. "Come here!"

The men saw him but did not come. Lot assumed they might think he had evil intentions toward them for his own pleasure, for such propositions at the gate of Sodom were anything but rare.

But he motioned again to them, saying, "Please, I am a friend. Won't you come here?"

The men looked at one another, knowing it was Lot, for they were the Lord's two companions, and they went to him, but did not identify themselves.

"My lords," Lot smiled, "I know what I am about to say must seem strange, but please listen patiently. This is no place for the likes of you. You are obviously fine young men, unused to such a city, and my heart breaks to see you set foot here.

"Besides," he continued, "It is not a safe place for you. Surely you know of the wickedness of this city to-ward—such fine-looking men as yourselves." Lot was embarrassed at his own words, but he was gripped in a panic for the safety of these innocents. "Please," he pleaded, "depart! Do not enter Sodom!"

The two companions said nothing but only walked ahead, as if determined to go in.

Still Lot feared for their safety. Somehow they sym-bolized the purity he had lost so long ago, and which he had sought again all these years. Somehow he felt per-sonally involved in their preservation, as if they repre-sented what little goodness might yet remain in the world.

When he saw them walk on, he noticed that some of the more notorious citizens of Sodom had already spied them out, and they stood now against the wall in a large group, apparently plotting their seduction.

Lot's heart ached and he ran after the young men, begging, "My lords, I know you think me a strange man to pursue you so, but I have only good and not evil in mind. Please, turn into your servant's house, and tarry all night, and wash your feet from your journey. Then you shall rise early and leave this city."

Lot knew that what he asked sounded very much like the proposal of a perverted Sodomite with ulterior motives, and so it did not surprise him when the young men said, "No, we will abide in the street tonight."

But Lot grew yet more insistent. He saw the crowd of men by the wall still gazing at the newcomers, and he became most demanding in his pleas. He must have presented a good case, he thought, for at last the young men went into his house with him.

When Mala saw that Lot had brought guests, she was very angry. "Husband," she cried, "the festival is tomorrow! We are busy in preparation. Tell them to leave!"

But for once Lot would not be ruled by her. Ordering her out of the way, he told her to sit and keep still, or go about her own business, that she was not to interfere, for these were his friends.

Mala was not a little surprised at Lot's new-found courage, but though she complained bitterly, she soon learned that he meant what he said, and she went up to her room to sulk in silence.

Lot bade the men be seated and brought them a bowl of warm water with which to wash, while he prepared a good-sized meal for the weary travelers.

He did not question who they were or where they came from but was preoccupied with their comfort. And as he busied himself in this way, he made frequent trips to the window to see if the crowd was still plotting their capture.

Need he have looked?

Indeed, they were still there, and in fact the crowd had grown. Apparently Lot had not been the only one drawn to the strangers, though the people outside the house were attracted for very different reasons.

Within half an hour of their arrival, it seemed that their fame had spread throughout the city, and in the unbelievable perversion of the citizenry, such newcomers were potential targets for sexual conquest.

To Lot, the obvious purity and wholesomeness of the

young men represented goodness; to the gross appetites of the Sodomites, they represented virginity, the most exploitable of materials.

In their love of themselves and humanity, the Sodomites had confused purity with potential and perverted love into conquest.

How incapable is Man to use himself rightly, Lot thought, as he peered through the covered window. How desperately does he pervert himself in his pursuit of happiness! How mundane and wicked is the human view of things, which sullies goodness with the dirt of its own defilement. How low is the human level, he considered. How futile in its claims. These thoughts were very much different from those which had drawn him here years before.

Lot's house was set on a corner, open on all sides, and as the crowd grew, the dwelling was surrounded by the raucous, jostling, drunken mob.

As Lot stepped back from the window, Mala and his daughters came downstairs crying to know what was the matter. And when Lot's wife saw that the two mysterious men were still in the house, her hot eyes snapped and she threw her plump arms in the air, screaming, "Send them out, Lot! Do you want the citizens to break the house down! What a fool you are, husband, to have brought these two here! What were you thinking?"

Lot turned angrily to Mala, the woman he had long since ceased to love, the one whose lusty, youthful beauty had long ago turned overused and old. "Woman!" he cried, "Close your shrewish mouth!" Walking over to her, he grabbed her arm and thrust her into the corner, crying, "I will live no longer seeing the destruction of all that is good and decent in Man. I have done enough in my life to destroy the love of God in my heart. I will not see these young men destroyed as well!"

Mala cowered in the corner, knowing Lot would strike her if she said more, though the crowd outside had grown so loud that he could not have heard her had she spoken again.

Her painted daughters, images of herself years ago, clung to her in fear as the jostling, lusting crowd beat impatiently upon the windows and doors.

Lot, his heart pounding madly, closed the shutters and barred the front door, but still the mob did not disperse.

The incessant beating upon the house grew louder, thunderous, until Mala and the girls were screaming in terror. The young men walked over to Lot and tried to speak with him, but he was too busy listening to the cries in the street.

"Where are those who came into your house to-night?" the crowd yelled. "Bring them out to us that we may enjoy them!"

"Lot!" they called, shaking the door violently, "Why do you do this to your friends? Bring the men out to us!"

Lot was torn with fear and confusion. The entire house shook with the vibrations of the mob. What should he do? These two youths were strangers, and his family was in danger. What was it that compelled him to care for them?

He must do something quickly, for despite the fact that in this crime-ridden city the door was four inches thick, set in a trench and capable of being opened only from the inside, it was about to give way to the pressing crowd outside. Lot looked at his wife and daughters and then at the strangers. He knew his responsibility to his family, and yet somehow he was constrained to protect these men. He did not know why he felt as he did, but something inside him protested their destruction.

His head spun with the weighty decision before him. His family—or these strangers?

The howling, shrieking throng, the danger of the moment, his disgust with this city—it was all too much for him. His heart cried out against the sinful and dreadful pit of his surroundings.

"A little purity!" he cried, his arms in the air.

The family looked on in horror. Was Lot insane?

"Give me purity! Lord God! Destroy the wicked, and not these innocent ones!"

In a frenzy of tumultuous conflict he looked at the young men and then at his daughters. Such a contrast, he reasoned. Who deserved the protection—his own children, already debauched and on their way to a disgusting choice of vocations, or these pure ones?

Like a wounded animal in the pain of his decision, Lot turned toward the heavily barred door.

Throwing it open, he called to the crowd to make room and then stepped outside, shutting the door quickly after him.

Mala and the daughters clung to one another apprehensively. Such a strange look Lot had borne! What did he mean to do?

Lot trembled as the angry, callous crowd pressed in on him and attempted to pass through to the door.

"I pray you, brethren, do not so wickedly," he cried, his voice rasping and strained.

Clinging to the sagging doorposts with both arms outstretched, blocking the entry, he shouted, "Behold now—Listen to me!"

The crowd grew quiet.

Mala trembled and the girls listened in disbelief as their own father said, "I have two daughters, virgins. Let me, I pray you, bring them out unto you, and do ye to them as is good in your eyes: only unto these men—do nothing: for they are strangers under my roof, and guests in my house!"

The girls inside cried out, and Mala ran to the door. But the young men constrained her, saying, "Do not go out there, madam!"

She wrenched her arm violently from the one who had taken hold of it, and spitefully she turned on him. "Who are you," she cried, "to bring this shame on my children?"

But the crowd became more violent still, and with

cries of "Stand back! We will break through!" they persisted until Lot was nearly trampled under their weight.

"Cooperate!" one of the leaders pressed him. The large, bearded man glared down on Lot demandingly and lifted a fist. "Cooperate, or we will deal worse with you than with the strangers!" he threatened.

At this the young man inside opened the door quickly, clutching Lot's robe and pulling him inside.

Somehow they managed to shut the door again against the crowd and then turned to Lot. "Are you all right, sir?" they asked.

"Yes," he answered. "But what do you mean to do?"

"Don't be afraid," one of them smiled calmly. He then walked to a nearby window and threw back a shutter. Instantly, grasping, clawing hands forced their way through the opening to lay hold of the stranger, but the young man only stood quietly out of reach and then, with a strange motion, raised his hand over his head and made a threatening gesture.

Suddenly the tone of the crowd changed. Their jostling, demanding pressure gave way to screams of pain and fear. "Help me—I see nothing!" several cried. "I am blind!" shouted others. "By the gods, where is the light?" cried another.

The helpless, agonized throng clung for support to one another and searched the walls for strongholds, every one of them struck blind by the power of the mysterious young man's gesture.

Lot was chilled with awe. He staggered to the window and gazed disbelievingly on the miserable, sightless citizenry.

"My Lord!" he cried, slumping to the floor. "Have mercy on your servant!"

But there was no time for such talk. One of the strangers walked to him and said, "Bring your family out of this place instantly, for we will destroy this city. The Lord God is weary with Sodom, for the cry of its people is waxen great before him. Therefore hath he sent us to destroy it."

Lot staggered to his feet, and without question he said, "Mala, make ready. The Lord is surely in this place. I will go tell our sons-in-law to gather their things."

With this he ran into the street. Stumbling over the senseless blind ones huddled there, pushing his way along the wall, he came to his elder daughters' homes and knocked loudly on the doors, but they were long in answering.

He knew his sons were here as well, visiting their sisters before the feast day, and so he hoped to convince them all of the emergency at one time.

Finally the sons-in-law, drunk with the evening's pre-celebration revelry, came down and demanded of him why he had come.

"Get ready to leave!" Lot cried. "Get out of Sodom. The Lord is come to destroy the city!"

But the men only looked at him incredulously. "Good, Father! It is good to see you have been drinking too!" they laughed. "Now go home and sleep. Tomorrow is a long day!"

But Lot pleaded, "The Lord will destroy you!"

"Listen to him, will you!" the elder one laughed. "Listen to who speaks of God!"

"Go home, old man. Sleep it off!" the other scoffed, and the two went back inside, bolting their doors against him.

Lot continued to plead below their windows, beating insistently on their doors, but still they would not listen.

At last he slumped against the wall in exhaustion. The dial of his life had come full circle, he reasoned. In helpless fear, scenes of his elder daughters and visions of his teenage sons flashed before him. Had he brought them to all this through his spinelessness? he wondered.

Tears dimmed his eyes as he looked again at their bolted doors.

"My children," he whispered miserably, turning his steps toward home.

Chapter VIII

At dawn, the family was ready to go. The grey morning light was just filtering through the streets, where most of the Sodomites were sleeping in drunken stupor, when the young men opened the door to lead Lot, his wife, and his two younger daughters out.

"Arise!" they ordered urgently. "You must go now lest you be consumed with the iniquity of the city!"

But Mala was hesitant, looking longingly at her possessions and all she must leave behind. What was contained in her satchel was little enough. Must they go without more? she pleaded.

Lot felt for her misery though he despised her for it; but as he lingered over her, the men took hold of them all and nearly pushed them out the door in their haste.

"Don't you understand?" they demanded. "Time grows short!"

They led them quickly now through the streets and beyond the city gate until they were well away from the town.

The sun was about to appear over the horizon, and the young men seemed anxious to be about their business before sunrise.

"Escape for your lives!" they ordered. "And look not behind you, neither stay at all in the plain, but escape to the mountains, lest you be consumed!"

Lot grabbed their hands in gratitude, but they motioned to him to leave immediately; and one said, "Hasten now! Escape! For because the Lord has remembered Abraham, your uncle, we can do nothing until you are free!"

So this was the reason he had been spared. Lot looked at the two strangers speechlessly, guilt shaming his countenance. And then, hesitating no longer, he took his wife by the hand, and the entire family fled across the plain, in fear for their very lives, their legs spurred on by the imminent disaster which lurked at their heels.

They must not be anywhere on the broad plain of Siddim. The mountains were yet miles away, but they could not stop.

Mala's throat and chest throbbed with pain from the run, and the young girls cried out to rest, but Lot dragged them on, screaming, "We must reach those hills! The sun will be up at any moment!"

"Oh, Father!" the youngest cried, her feet blistered and painful. "Please, Father!"

"Keep going!" he called. "Go, if you care for your life—and whatever you do, do not look behind, as they told us not to do!"

Lot's hot cloak bound his legs, and as he ran, he threw it off, wiping the perspiration from his brow. Mala was crying, heavy, throaty sobs wrenching her body, but Lot would not let her stop.

The burro which carried some of their supplies slowed them down, his plodding demeanor and obstinance to their prodding a continual impediment to their progress.

Looking above, Lot saw that the sun would break over the horizon at any moment, and giving one last desperate shove, he stopped attempting to coerce the animal. The poor, ignorant beast, unaware of the danger presently to be upon him, refused to budge another inch, and despite the protests of the daughters, Lot insisted that he be left behind.

"Father, how cruel of you!" the youngest cried, tears pouring down her face as she clung to the beast's neck. "How can you leave him?"

Lot said nothing, only grasping his daughter about the waist and pulling her to him.

"Come!" he shouted.

And on they sped, the doltish, flop-eared creature left braying like a stranded child on the desert floor.

At last they reached an incline, but still Lot forced them on until they came to a small cave, and only then did they rest.

"Enter," he ordered, "but turn your faces to the wall! Do not look out on the plain!"

The women complied, too grateful for the end of the flight to debate with him.

The lonely, frightened family, so long torn in their differences, sat together now on the cold floor of the cave, huddled closely against one another.

And just as they had settled, the first rays of morning sun pierced the black recesses of the cave.

Tension mounted, and they clung to one another, sensing that the moment of destruction had come, knowing somehow that the Lord would move quickly now, before any other Sodomites awoke with the sun or had time to flee the city.

Indeed, as the men had warned, they dared not look back, for suddenly a flash of light split the atmosphere. So blinding was it that it seemed it would melt the earth with its brilliance; and following this came a resounding blast so intense it seemed the very sky must rend in two.

Outside they could hear the helpless brays of the marooned donkey, blinded and staggered by the unearthly blows. But no one could go out to help him. No one dared go out.

The entire mountain reeled under the impact. The women screamed in terror and grasped at Lot, but he was as helpless as they.

The family was tossed like so many pebbles against the cave walls, but still they did not look out to see the valley holocaust.

One after another, blasts shattered the air. Surely the whole earth was being destroyed. How could they endure?

They clung to rocks and protuberances in the cave, bracing themselves against each deafening onslaught.

Arms and legs bruised from the impacts, the four helpless refugees wept in misery for the end of life. But for
some reason they were spared.

At last there was silence, a silence so complete that it
was almost as intolerable as the blasts. The brilliance
of the light which had filled the cave now gradually
faded and was replaced by an eerie darkness, as if the
sun had been eclipsed.

As suddenly as the light had vanished, a strange,
wailing wind seemed to arise out of nowhere, beginning
far away in the direction of Sodom and growing in force
until it seemed it would blow the very mountain out of
place.

The family clung to one another again, the women
too weary to weep anymore, and when at last the wind
died down, they looked about them for some sign of
light.

"Father," the youngest whispered, half frightened to
death of her own voice. "Is it over?"

Lot listened and strained to see through the darkness.
"I think so," he said stiffly, holding her small painted
head to his shoulder. "I think so."

The family nestled silently for some time, but as the
light returned, Mala grew restless.

"Where are you going?" Lot whispered, seeing that
Mala had stood up.

She said nothing but only looked wildly at him, an insanity in her eyes which frightened him.

"My city!" she sobbed. "Oh, Lot, what have you
done—I must see!" she cried.

"No! No! Mala!" he shouted, "Don't look out there.
They told us not to look back!"

But she was on her way to the cave door.

"Mother!" the daughters screamed, "Don't!"

But Mala did not listen. Like a madwoman she staggered outside

"Oh, by the gods!" they heard her scream.

"Mother!" the younger daughter called, running for

the door. But Lot caught her, refusing to let her see the city.

"Do not look, child!" he demanded, ushering her back inside. "I will not lose you as well."

What met Mala's eyes was almost indescribable. Like a great running scab, the plain lay scorched and palsied under the leveling hand of the Destroyer.

Not a blade of grass was left; not a river remained. The valley floor was ribboned with long, deep crevices like the parched lips of a dead man. And in the distance the foaming, boiling sea lifted hot fingers to cover the worthless rubble of the Pentapolis.

None of it was recognizable. Only the slime pits, the salt crops, and the bituminous pits remained on the plain, mute testimonies to the worth of the citizens who had lived nearby.

A powerful, earsplitting wind still rushed along the sea and the plain, a legacy of the holocaust, bringing immense waves inland. And Mala looked on in horror, her mind snapping at the inscrutability of it all.

Like a leaf, she was driven by the wind, helpless to resist, and not really caring. As if led by an invisible hand, she wandered across the plain, babbling incomprehensibly to herself and laughing like a demoniac.

But the hand had led her to an area still active, and as she came near the salt mines of the city, the ground at her feet was bubbling with molten elements.

The heat was unearthly in its intensity. Mala screamed in agony as she slumped to the ground, writhing with the strange, indefinable chemical heat of her surroundings.

It seemed something was happening to her body. It started in her hands and feet, where they had touched the ground. As if by the wand of some alchemist, it seemed her skin was crystallizing, and as she looked at her hands, they were leprous white.

Lot and the children could hear her cries for help, but they dared not go to her. They huddled in helpless dread until the cries were muted, but they did not look out. And so they were spared the sight of the prostrate woman, whose body had altered in its substance as surely as the city had altered.

Nor would they have dreamed, even in their worst dreams, that the earthy woman they had once touched and kissed was now no more than a pillar of salt on the sterile plain of Siddim.

Chapter IX

Abraham had slept through the night before Sodom's destruction in the same place where the Lord had left him.

Nesting in the niche between the bluff and the great stone to the side, he had pulled his knees under his chin and wrapped his cloak tight about him. He was determined to see the end of the drama of which he was already so much a part. And he hoped against hope that the ten righteous he had bargained for might somehow be found in that vile city below.

But at dawn the shattering blows of destruction which hammered the valley floor and reverberated mercilessly throughout Canaan told him the truth.

At the first sonic report the Man of God was ripped rudely from his hazy sleep and tossed like so much gravel to the edge of the bluff. Not yet fully awake, he scrambled to his feet and dazedly turned about as if in search of an illusive enemy.

He looked wildly at the nightmare sky which seemed to split from end to end as far as the eye could see, and below him he saw the ghoulish hand of destruction lifting Sodom like so much dust in a whirlwind, twirling buildings and walls like children's toys in the hand of a bully.

"Oh, God!" Abraham screamed, but he could not hear his own voice, so deafening was the explosion. Spun about and dashed against the rock, he clung there like a wet leaf, burying his horrified face in his arms.

"Lot! Lot!" he cried. "Could you not have remained with me?"

Abraham did not witness the remaining acts in the drama. At the thought of Lot's apparent destruction, his old heart failed within him and he lay prostrate on the ground, unconscious of the conclusion of the scene.

Perhaps this was merciful. Abraham could not have survived more than he had already seen. As it was, hours must have elapsed before he revived.

When he did awaken, the sky was black with the balm of night. Only a dense smoke, hanging like a suffocating blanket over the length and breadth of Canaan, reminded him of the horror he had witnessed.

Stiffly he raised himself and looked about him, his head still ringing from the blasts. The pallor of death in the air was almost tangible, and the atmosphere was so heavy that Abraham could see nothing below when he crawled again to the bluff.

He was badly shaken, deathly afraid, and lonely. A river of hot tears flowed down his face.

But his sad heart fought desperately against thoughts of his nephew, and somehow, as if by design, his mind blocked out what he feared to remember.

Like a blind fish he forced himself through the sea of blackness about him, instinctively turning himself toward home.

Chapter X

Lot and his two daughters dwelled in the mountains east of the plain for many long weeks thereafter. Where else could they go? They had nothing but a few clothes and a small supply of food in their satchels. The whole Pentapolis had been destroyed.

There were cities in Canaan, but there was no way of crossing the blistered plain which lay between. New eruptions festered daily throughout the valley, as if the Lord were not yet satisfied.

Hourly Lot's daughters cried and bewailed their condition, and Lot was at a loss to give them hope.

"When the valley cools," he would tell them, "we will cross over to Canaan. We will return to my uncle and my people—if they will have us."

But this was not sufficient to quell their complaints. As the days passed, they craved more and more the comforts and pleasures of Sodom and continually called up memories of the young men who had pursued them.

The dark-eyed girls were beauties—there was no denying it; and they had fit the mode of life in Sodom well. They were yet virgins, as Lot had told the citizens outside his house the night before the conflagration.

But doubtless their status of inexperience would not have lasted long, all to their delight and to the delight of their mother.

And so it was not only the hardship of their surroundings and the rationing of food which plagued them, but also the loss of perpetual entertainment and mind-numbing pleasure.

Lot struggled to make the cave life palatable, but it had been many years since he had eked a living out of the wilderness. It came to him slowly, but gradually he regained a little skill in hunting, which he had engaged in most enthusiastically as a boy in the hills of Chaldea and along the way with Abraham.

His father, Haran, had taught him well, and he had once been quite adept with a bow. Once again now he carved a crude weapon of hillside oak and supplied his children with meat. This, in addition to roots and berries from the hollows, was enough to live on.

The labor of his hands served as well to still his mind of the sorrows he had come through. The destruction of his home, his wife, his sons, and his elder daughters plagued him less as he hunted; it was balm and he threw himself chiefly into it.

Despite his efforts at survival, and his measure of success, the daughters grew more restless. "See, Father," they would come to him each day, "the valley floor is ready. We can cross over to Hebron or Salem, or to any town."

But Lot was hesitant. Volcanic pits still existed there, hollow spots covered by ash, deceptive to the eye. And so he would motion them to leave him alone. "Perhaps in a few weeks," he would suggest.

But the fear of the valley was not all that held Lot in the mountains. Shame was the root of his indecision. He had nowhere to go but to Abraham, and erroneously he assumed there would be no place for him there. How could he face his uncle with the guilt of the past? he wondered. Abraham would surely laugh him to scorn. And he knew no one else would harbor refugees from Sodom. By now the obviously supernatural overthrow of that city would have labeled its inhabitants as cursed. And were they not?

Let the daughters say what they might; for now, Lot was satisfied to survive by his hands. Day by day he buried his memories beneath his labors, and found a measure of peace.

As the weeks and months passed, however, Lot's daughters saw that their father had no intention of taking them away from these lifeless hills. In their adolescent minds they grew old before their time. Life slipped away, and with each morning's rising in the wasted existence of these mountains, they saw themselves doomed to a future of emptiness.

But despite their protests, each day there sat Father Lot, blankly spending his hours of toil outside the cave, or sitting at the fire in the evening, seeming not to care or feel for their shame.

And a shame it was to grow to fourteen years a virgin.

It was cold when Lot came back from his labors that night. He brought the day's meat into the cave, dressed out and ready to be prepared, and then seated himself near the fire before retiring, as was his custom.

He did not see the strange looks passed between the girls that evening. He did not know the plot which had long been brewing in their minds over the past weeks. He did not know of the conversations they had held between themselves when he slept, nor did he know that their impatience to carry out their plan had selected this night for its execution.

As they served their father his meal, the elder silently nodded to the younger that the time had come. Smiling, she took a skin of wine to Lot and said, "Poor Father, the day has been hard and you have toiled so long. Enjoy what remains of the wine brought from our home."

Lot was rather surprised at his younger daughter's new-found kindness, but he did not question it and smiled, gratefully accepting her offer. He often found relief in his wine, perhaps too often. But when he did not work, scenes of Mala's self-destruction and memories of his dead children haunted him. The sweet glow of the earthy liquid somehow dulled the pains.

The wine went down slowly and smoothly. Lot was warmed by it. "A little more, Father? It will calm you," the daughter offered again. "Try not to think of Mother," she urged.

Yes, he must not think of Mala, he reasoned. The girl was right—the wine would ease his mind.

"Thank you," he smiled.

As he drank it down, the girls continued talking, calling up memories as if they did not really wish his mind relaxed at all. And yet with each old family name or with each unpleasant recollection, they pushed more drink his way.

"Why did our little brothers have to die?" they would wail. "Why were we spared and not they?"

"Oh, Mother—poor mother!" the younger cried. "Do you remember her eyes? Remember the fear in her face? Why didn't we go after her? She did not know her own mind that morning!"

And so it went, one dark memory after another, one drink after another; and soon his daughters' voices and the painful recollections they recalled to him were distant and shadowy.

He did not resist them. He did not wish to resist. The wine and its effects were pleasant and powerful. The wine, the night—soon he would sleep as a child.

Lot did not perceive what followed. His saturated mind was too foggy, too wet to know that his daughters were lifting him, leading him by the hand to the back of the cave. He did not perceive that they undressed before him, or that they would shamelessly use their own father to fulfill their womanhood.

When Lot awoke the next morning, his head spun and throbbed with the satiation of the night before. He must have slept past noon, for the sun had already warmed the recesses of the cave and shone brilliantly outside.

Something was strange. He did not usually see the world from this angle upon rising. When he had awakened sufficiently to recognize his surroundings, he realized, through his red, puffy eyes, that he was not in his own bed.

He always slept at the mouth of the cave to protect his daughters. But the girls were not here, and with a thrill of disbelief he saw that he had slept outstretched where they usually lay.

A panic gripped him. Surely it could not be, he reasoned. Perhaps—perhaps he had only fallen here in his drunkenness and so they had let him sleep. Yes, that was it.

But bits and pieces from the evening before began to fit together in snatches, like returning scenes of a nightmare. Throwing back the heavy pelt spread over him, he saw his naked body, and suddenly all that had been imperceptible to him the night before came back in growing vividness to haunt him.

"No!" he cried, clutching his swollen head in horror. "God of my uncle! Do not let it be!"

Looking about him in disgust, he stood shakily, grabbing the wall for support and covering himself with his garments.

He felt filthy from head to toe, vile and leprous—untouchable.

The damp room seemed to spin before him, and from deep within himself came an animal cry of fear and degradation.

His daughters heard him, and knowing the source of the unseemly sound, they cowered outside the cave.

Stumbling in a stupor along the wall, he screamed repeatedly, as if pursued by the clawing hands of an invisible assassin. When he saw them standing there through the blear of his sotted eyes, an unfathomable revulsion welled within him.

"Out of my way, you filthy dogs!" he roared, rushing at them like a maddened bear.

Terrified, they leaped away from him, watching the gruesome spectacle of their father's wretched spirit.

Reeling and crying, he seemed ready to rip the very flesh from his bones if it would serve-to purge him.

"God forgive me!" he cried over and over. "Forgive me!"

"Father!" the daughters called weakly, but Lot would not hear them. He only glared at them insanely and demanded that they not touch him, as if forestalling the advance of a legion of demons.

"Away! Away!" he groaned, his hands clamped tightly over his ears.

His helpless pleas for God's forgiveness echoed through the hills, and as the daughters watched, Lot staggered limply across the empty waste of the plains.

The younger clutched the elder in desolation, somehow knowing her father would not return, and she whispered, "Sister, what have we done?"

PART VI

The Seed

He staggered not at the promise of God through unbelief; but was strong in faith, giving glory to God; and being fully persuaded that, what he had promised, he was able also to perform.

Romans 4:20,21

Chapter I

The tentlights were bright in the camp at the Oaks of Mamre this spring night. Since yesterday the sound of music and dancing had continued unceasingly, like a stirring nerve of anticipation.

Never had there been such a happy time—surely never in all of human history—and the thousand dizzy revelers who drank and made merry in these Canaanite hills mirrored that emotion.

An old man was about to be reborn. All that he had strived and longed for in his lifetime was about to be realized, and the very soul of the universe seemed to shout in cadence.

Abraham had been asked repeatedly to sit and rest, but to no avail. His heart was in the tent with Sarah, though he could not be beside her. By custom, the tent of delivery was not to be entered by a man, but Abraham knew in his mind's eye that Sarah had never looked more beautiful than she must be looking now.

As he nervously paced the yard in front of her chambers, he ceaselessly inquired of the midwives who came and went, "How is she? When shall it be?" But just as ceaselessly the reply was, "Be patient, my lord; she is well. It will not be long."

And then, like a child waiting for a promised but long-delayed gift, he would restlessly walk away to sit with his joking companions.

"You have worn a path sufficient for the Jordan to pass through," they would laugh. "Women always take their time, you know; as unpredictable as trade contracts, always late in delivering the goods!"

To which Abraham would nod good-naturedly, never

really following the train of conversation, but casting anxious glances over his shoulder toward the tent.

And then he would resume the pacing, the questioning, the rubbing of the hands, the artful glimpses inside the crack of the tent door. But apparently Abraham would be made to abide the whims of nature as all expectant fathers must—though if given the power, he would have taken his child fully grown and developed.

Had there ever been such a change in a man, as there had been in him these past months? The years, it seemed, had peeled away from his once bent and sorrowing visage. Almost as if by the touch of a magician, his face and form had revived, in vitality, if not in substance.

Save for the destruction of Sodom, these nine months since the Lord had last appeared to him, had served virtually to obliterate all the misery of the previous sixteen years. Life had a new purpose now. The child, soon to be born to Sarah in her old age, had ensured that.

But, her old age? Was Sarah old? "Ha!" Abraham laughed. How could an old woman move him as she did, and how could he be considered old when so moved by a beautiful woman? Had any young girl ever been more desirable, more truly winsome than she? And had any younger man ever been so in love?

Abraham's face stretched in a broad, defiant smile. Let the Pharaohs of Egypt contend for her again! She was the model on which all others should be patterned.

Such had been his thoughts and meditations, his source of joy since Sarah had announced conception. Such had been the balm of his troubled soul, the comfort after the destruction of Sodom, his relief from the guilt of past sins.

Best of all, his relationship with Sarah had healed. What they had lacked was fulfillment; what they had shared was a shattered faith, and on this basis they had truly had nothing.

But why dwell on this? They were happy now, inexpressibly happy. And as Abraham hovered at the mouth of Sarah's chambers, his animation, his concern, his questioning countenance revealed his inner joys.

At last, some news was forthcoming. The matron of the midwives had shown her face at the seam of the door to say that Sarah's pains were coming quickly, that the child would surely be born within the hour.

Abraham's heart leaped. The music of the camp became not only merry but jubilant, almost uncontrolled.

The pipers in their band sat upon the rocks and the ridge to the edge of the central tents. Wild dancers, men and women, spun like dervishes to the resounding clashes of tambourines and cymbals. And such a clamorous chorus of clapping and shouting split the deep velvet sky!

The tension was vibrant. Surely the very stars shone more brightly tonight in anticipation.

At the last announcement, Eliezer had left the revellers and run to his master. He now paced the flat, well-worn space alongside Abraham nearly as vigorously as his master; and in fact any stranger would have assumed that he, being the younger, was the expectant one, and not the aged one with him.

Such a sight they made, the two of them, bumping and angling off one another as they traipsed, anxiously looking toward the tent. And as time passed, the crowd nearest the shelter grew like a swelling sea.

The midwives appeared more frequently now, running, not walking, to and fro, carrying steaming pots of water into the tent.

And the crowd grew quieter, tenser, sensing the nearness of the event. Gradually the music was tapering, the exhausted dancers slowing. The people drew as near as possible to the center of interest, some crowding in front of one another, tussling for a view; some lifting children on their shoulders that they might see; adults as well as youngsters perched on the strong oaken branches of the well-wooded confines; many spectators sitting precariously along the crowded ridge which verged the camp.

With silence the low murmurs of the ladies with Sarah were now audible. The travail of the woman in throes of birth could be heard very distinctly, growing in volume and intensity with the nearing of the time.

Was there ever a more awesome sound than that of a woman in labor? To those who heard Sarah tonight the sensation was a mixture of fear, despair, and pity, but equally of wonder, awe, and joy.

To the Oriental it was in fear and reverence that life was to be conceived. In pain it was to be brought forth, but in joy it was to be given. The audience sat immobile, fixed with the terrible happiness of it all, enthralled with nature as only such an earthy culture could be—afraid and yet uniquely in touch with the primal fundamentals of the life process.

Abraham stood like a rock at the door, though feeling very little the part. His set, penetrating eyes almost dissolved the tent with their stare, and his taut expression, his firm lips, his clenched, urgent hands told his heart.

Though he seemed to stand solidly, it was only in opposition to the nearly leveling bolts which charged through him at every cry coming from the shelter.

Though he looked hard and established in masculine endurance, his muscles were coiled like springs awaiting only sufficient provocation to catapult him through the tent wall to Sarah's side.

And what of Sarah? Are thoughts possible under such stress? Yes, for this stress was the thought itself, the very real expression of all the desire that had gone before, the conscious revelation that it was to come to pass at last.

The travail and the agony would, however, be too miserable a prelude to happiness if prolonged. The woman in labor is able to survive only as she knows it will soon be over, that through this brief span of distress, however agonizing, is to come the finest possible extension of her own life and being.

But agony and happiness cannot long abide together.

In the grace of nature, the labor is cut short, for otherwise the product would not be worth the cost.

The crowd outside the tent leaned forward in silent, urgent anticipation as Sarah's sorrows grew in intensity.

At last a loud, painful groan announced the end of her miseries. But in the dread brevity of silence which followed, Abraham still stood mute and rigid near the door, holding himself back, straining to contain his fears and apprehension, teetering like a man on a flimsy cliff, as he awaited the sound of new life.

It was only seconds before it came, and yet it might have been an eternity in Abraham's mind. His head reeled. In that minute span of time it seemed his whole life passed before him in a panorama of full and ultimate clarity. He sensed now that all his years of wandering, of searching, of longing, of wondering and doubting, but always of believing, had been leading to this moment, to this point in time and space.

He did not feel his legs trembling under him, nor did he realize his old, dimmed eyes were misty. Unconsciously he followed his heart toward the door, and touched the side of the tent to hold himself erect.

At last it came, the sounds of the newborn, the frightened, apprehensive cry of the human just becoming. It thrilled like a course of surging primeval energy through the crowd at the Oaks of Mamre. And at that sound, Abraham's heart nearly flew from his breast. He was terrified, amazed, superlatively joyous, and looking at Eliezer with triumph in his eyes, he threw back the door.

Like a streak he flashed into the confines of the delivery tent. "Sarah!" he cried. "My God, Sarah!"

The world spun madly. Abraham sought through the dimly lit chamber for his beloved wife, pushing aside the many midwives who attended her.

"Sir, be careful," one warned, as he stumbled rudely to the bedside.

There in the warm, pale light of the tent, his eyes adjusted to the figure of the chief midwife, who stood before the lantern. In her arms she held a small, squirming, wailing infant, and suddenly the rash, impulsive Abraham stopped short.

He was dumfounded. His eyes fixed on the unbelievable child of a miracle. His lips trembled, and his flesh tingled with a new sensation.

This was it, here in the arms of this woman. Softly and tenderly he stepped forward, almost afraid, and awkwardly reached for the child. The midwife smiled broadly and placed the bawling, wriggling baby in its father's arms.

Abraham's lips still trembled as if to express something he could not even form in his mind. Tears filled his eyes. As he looked incredulously at the bundle he held he knew the seed of hope and faith which had been planted so many, many years before had suddenly germinated.

Still his voice failed him. He could not speak his heart. He stepped to Sarah's side and knelt by her, the child whimpering in his arms.

"Sarah?" he whispered at last, unable to say more. Suddenly he could no longer contain himself but wept like a released prisoner, wept for joy, celebration, and gratitude, the child nestling close to his heart.

For several long moments they remained thus, the child, Sarah and he, sharing the world which was privately and infinitely theirs. At last Abraham sat up, looking intently at the only woman who had ever merited his love, the only woman who had ever satisfied him.

She was truly beautiful, her face only graced by the years, her regal bearing only enhanced by the passing of time. He held her small, warm hand in his and lifted it to his face, still finding no words adequate to express himself.

Sarah studied the careworn face of her husband, still virile and animated despite the years of heartache he had been through. And tonight she understood at last, understood the unexhausted faith she had often questioned in him. She loved him now as never before. And somehow, as she touched his face, as she looked at the child, she sensed the pulsebeat of the heavens focusing on them. She sensed destiny in the moment, and a shudder of awe passed through her.

Abraham smiled at her secretively, knowing that she too was remembering—remembering how the Lord had visited them in this very place, how He had promised to revisit them at the time of life, and how He had challenged Sarah's doubting laughter, saying, "Nay, but thou didst laugh."

Indeed, He had revisited them. He was present at this moment, as surely as if He stood visibly before them, touching them with His hand.

"Oh, Abraham," Sarah smiled broadly, nodding in unison with his thoughts. "Go tell the people! Tell them, and don't be ashamed. God has made me to laugh so that all who hear will laugh with me."

Abraham stood looking at her once more and then turned eagerly, passing through the door into the courtyard.

When the people saw the child in his arms, a spontaneous joy rent the air. Those on the ridge forced one another for a view, and such a jostling competition there was to see the long-awaited fulfillment of their master's dreams.

Proudly as a king might display a newborn prince, Abraham stood there raising the child in his hands for all to see, and as the roaring approval of the crowd reached a crescendo, Abraham looked toward the sky shouting. "Glory be to God! Glory be to the One Who faileth not, Who calls and leads, Who keeps His covenant with those who follow Him!"

And then just as spontaneously as the crowd had responded, Abraham sensed a new freedom, a new exultation welling within him. Holding the child close to him, he looked toward heaven through a veil of tears, and he began to laugh, to laugh so intensely that his knees grew weak with his joy.

Kneeling now in the courtyard, he held the child securely and looked at the crowd which studied him. As custom dictated, the child's name might be given now in the face of many witnesses, and as tradition prescribed, the name would have meaning, meaning important to all who heard it.

A hush filled the air. Abraham smiled happily at his people, holding the child high and saying, "This is my son, the first-born of my dreams. His name shall be Isaac, 'the laughter of God,' for as we once laughed at His possibility, God has laughed last!"

The crowd applauded now with Abraham—laughed joyously and with the pulse of revelry. They broke into song, coming down from the ridge, climbing out of the trees, dancing and celebrating the hour of fulfillment.

The stars would shine all that night on a celebrating crowd; the universe, it seemed, revolved around the father and his new son.

The Lord in heaven was justified, and all was right with the world.

But Ishmael watched from a distance.

Chapter II

Three years had passed since that eventful evening, three years of great happiness. And yet with each of Isaac's successive birthdays, Abraham was reminded not only of God's precious gift, but of the loss of his first-born.

For on the morning of Isaac's birth, Abraham had been greeted with the news that Ishmael had left. Running to his son's tent, the old father had seen the vacant bed, and searching the tethers, he had found that the magnificent camel was indeed gone.

Little he could have done would have persuaded Ishmael he was still deeply loved, that his place in Abraham's heart had never and could never be lost. But the boy had not given Abraham the option of attempting to persuade him.

Ishmael's refuge had always been the wild home of the hills, and on the eve of his seeming displacement, he had responded in the only way known to him. Creeping undetected from camp amid the raucous celebration, he had headed for his harbor of voluntary isolation, and in three years he had not been seen or heard from.

That day Abraham's happy heart had been mixed again with sorrow, in the thrill of new-found life once again reminded of past miseries. Looking to the hills where he knew his eldest sought comfort, a sad pain had wrenched his vacant spirit.

"I will not think on it!" he had told himself deceptively. "My joy will not so soon be frustrated. I will not think on such things. Ishmael has gone before, and he will return."

Squaring his shoulders, he had then walked back toward the tent of the newborn, vainly seeking to obliterate the misery which would forever cling to him, the memories of the past, of his nephew and his eldest who still maintained such obstinate positions in his heart.

Yes, that had been three years ago, and yet he had not shaken it.

But those years had held joy as well. Abraham and Sarah had seen the growth of a beautiful child. Never had two people performed the role of parents more intensely and conscientiously.

Their hearts and souls had become wrapped up in Isaac, and he had not disappointed them. Never, they reasoned, had a child grown so rapidly, so perfectly.

Isaac was truly his father's son, sturdy and rugged, a real grappler in a pinch. Already he could easily take on Abraham's challenging hand, clinging like a wrestler in Pharaoh's court as he was swung to and fro high in the air, the wind whistling about his face, and his father's lively laughter mingling with his own.

"He is a fine lad," Abraham would smile as Sarah laid the sleeping child down each evening. "Strong and healthy, a boy to make a father proud!" he would boast.

"Oh, Abraham," Sarah would tease, "If he were a rascal and a knave, you would see no fault in him."

"True, and neither would you," he would grin.

Day after day the devotion, the pride and pleasure grew. And Abraham was eager to share the manly arts with his fast developing son. In the evenings as he watched the plump, sturdy, pink-cheeked boy walk and run about the tent on his husky legs, he dreamed of the day he would teach him to wrestle, to ride, and to hunt.

Always he would share his dreams with his wife. Tonight as they sat about the fire, Eliezer played with Isaac and Abraham looked on proudly. "Sarah, that will be a fine day," he smiled.

"What day?" she asked.

"When I can take him with me into the hills."

Sarah looked at Abraham, adoration in her eyes. "It will not be long now, husband."

"When he is only five, I will make him a small, strong bow, and a quiver." Abraham mused.

"And when will you teach him to use it?" Eliezer laughed.

"The following day!" the proud father smiled. "I will teach him well, and he will be a ready learner," he went on happily. "When he is seven, I will take him on his first hunt," he dreamed, looking at the hills, "and he will be a fine bowman, as fine as—" Abraham stopped short, a never-forgotten time now filling his mind.

"As fine as who?" Sarah asked.

Abraham gazed at her sadly and then, looking away, whispered, "As fine as Ishmael."

And so it was that Abraham could not forget his eldest, though he despaired of ever regaining him. Another year passed and the boy did not return, but Abraham sought the skyline of the mountains daily for signs of the wandering one, even to the day of the festival of Isaac's weaning.

This celebration was nearly as riotous and joyous as that attending his birth. An elaborate feast was prepared, to which not only the tribesmen and women were invited but to which Abraham's neighbors and trade associates were also welcome.

In Abraham's wealth, no finery was omitted. Game birds and venison, lamb and veal were the staples, but the delicacies of Egypt, Mesopotamia, and the coastal cities, pomegranates, figs, dates, and rareties from the sea, filled a major place in the festivities.

Fine linen and silks adorned the grounds of the camp, and on these was spread the sumptuous fare. Old and young, slave and free-hired partook alike, and the fine wine of Canaan, brought from miles overland, flowed freely.

Isaac was clothed in his first formal attire, a small smock of white and purple linen, symbolizing his father's prestigious position as a merchant prince.

And no one, of whatever rank, spared praise in speaking of the child, for this was his day. Not again, until the rite of initiation when the blessings of his father's God would be invoked on him, would he again be so honored.

The child was comely, and it seemed as he grew that his beauty grew as well. He was the picture of his father, strong-boned and healthy, with a fine shock of jet black hair, much like Abraham's when he was young. But his nose and eyes were his mother's. Already at this young age he showed his aristocracy, and the touch of royalty was evident in his breeding.

Somewhat awed by the proceedings of the celebration, by the clamorous, joyous crowd, many of whom were strangers, the child clung tenaciously to his mother. A large, striped tarp draped the courtyard floor, and piles of soft cushions and pillows served as couches. Sarah and Abraham sat at the head of a long row of leisurely reclining guests who laughed and ate away the day. Dancers, jugglers, and acrobats filled the hours with entertainment, and the festival would proceed thus for three full days.

As the evening drew on, Isaac was restless. The mad world of adult life held few charms for him, and with twilight his sleepy eyes grew dull to the surroundings.

Sarah placed the sleeping child in the arms of a nurse with instructions to bed him down for the night, but as the nurse began to comply, taking Isaac to the mistress's tent, she suddenly stopped, turning to Sarah with inquisitive eyes. "Madam?"

"Yes."

"Who is that?" the nurse said anxiously.

Sarah turned about, impatiently wondering what her maid could be speaking of, and as she looked at the tent, she clutched at Abraham urgently.

"Husband, can it be?" she cried.

Blocking the door to the shelter sat a tall, well-formed figure on camelback, his head held high, his aloof and penetrating gaze passing over the crowd until the celebration tapered to a silence.

Abraham looked wildly at him, his heart in his throat. Standing awkwardly, he stared intently at the newcomer, fearful to approach, not believing what his own eyes seemed to tell him. And yet it was undeniable. He knew him, his own son returned after four years as if from the dead.

"Ishmael?" the old father whispered, his voice cracking with emotion. "Is it you, my son?"

No answer came from the proud, elusive one who sat staring coldly at him.

Had the figure only shown some response, Abraham would have leaped for joy, thinking his wandering one had come back to him again, that the family had at last been completed, the past forgiven, the hollow in his heart filled to its fullest possible extent, much as his own father, Terah, must have felt at the reunion of Haran, his prodigal.

Such was not the case. Ishmael sat mutely, bitterly glaring at the child in the nurse's arms, with eyes full of contempt and disgust.

Facing his father, he moved slowly in his saddle, the fringe of his handmade leather clothes moving imperceptibly with his proud bearing, his haughty Egypto-Semitic head held erect and austere. At last he spoke, with self-confidence and dignity. "Father," he nodded, "where is my mother?"

The crowd was perplexed. Abraham looked at Ishmael incredulously, not expecting this question.

"I see you do not know," Ishmael smirked. "I should not be surprised," he said looking over the crowd. "Neither have you known where I have been, nor have you thought on me all these years," he sneered.

Abraham moved ahead urgently, "No, Son. You are wrong—very wrong," he said desperately.

" 'Son,' you call me?" Ishmael laughed. "Do tell, Father, how often have you thought of me? How often have you considered my whereabouts? How often have you awakened with thoughts of me?"

Abraham pleaded with his eyes, unable to express the frequency with which he had done these very things.

"But no more of this, Father," Ishmael proceeded. "Where is my mother?"

At the edge of the crowd stood the outcast Hagar, to whom Sarah had denied social interaction, and when Ishmael saw her, he looked at her softly. "Mother?" he whispered.

Despite the punishment which might befall her, Hagar broke from the ranks and flew to his side, Ishmael bending down to touch her haggard, worn face as she clung tearfully and joyfully to him.

"Son, son!" she sobbed, unable to say more.

Ishmael held her hand close and again surveyed his father's face.

"I shall not long interrupt the festivities," the young man said sardonically, "I am only come back to claim what is rightfully mine, and then I shall trouble you no further."

Slowly Ishmael climbed down from his camel, still holding his long-lonely, weeping mother close to him, and looking bitterly at the muted, apprehensive crowd.

"Strange," he said acidly, "strange that this celebration should be held for the younger brother. Do you not find it strange that the first-born of such a great man as my father should never have received such a tumultuous welcome upon first entering the world, or upon leaving the breast of his mother?"

He stepped toward the nurse, who stood in awe and fear as he reached for the child in her arms. Taking Isaac, he held him up in front of the crowd and stared at Sarah, who ran toward him in defense.

"Woman!" he cried bitterly, "Do not fear—I shall not harm your child, as you harmed my mother's!"

Sarah stopped short, fearing to come closer, staring angrily at the bondwoman to whom all her heartache could once again be traced.

"My younger brother," Ishmael sneered, displaying the little one like a rag doll in front of the gawking crowd. "So this is the one who has superseded me, who has without question come to replace me."

Ishmael handed Isaac back to the nurse like a heap of refuse and took a stand at the head of the valley over which the camp spread.

"Good people," he mocked, bowing very low, "pardon me, but I have heard such a thing is against custom —to take the right of the first-born and give it to another—unless, of course, that other one is born, however er tardy, to the favorite wife." He strutted now defiantly. "Does it not seem a strange exception that one born fourteen years before another should be thus deposed by him?"

Ishmael now pointed a challenging finger at his father, who stood helplessly by. "I defy you, Father, to tell me my claim is unjust, to defend your choice of heirs on such grounds as these." He paused, now waiting for a response, but when none came, he roared, "So you have it, friends; the answer of my father. Silence is its own response. Well said, Father!"

At this Ishmael laughed loudly and bitterly, his hands on his hips, his strong, limber legs spread in a stance of challenge. Then stopping again and facing his father with a clenched fist, he cried, "I will have my inheritance! I claim it now, and I will have it now!"

Sarah stared at her husband, who seemed transfixed and disabled by the forceful charisma of his brashly resurrected first-born. "Husband?" she cried. "Answer him! Tell him, Abraham! Will you not reprove him, and his mother?"

Abraham looked awkwardly about him, his world suddenly a nightmare of conflicting values. Primary in his mind was the sudden consciousness of his returned son, one whom he had long ago given up as lost. Was he not to be given a chance to adjust to that reality before being catapulted to the conflict of these painful, blasting, hate-filled demands?

"Oh, Son, Ishmael," he cried, "have pity on an old man! Come to me, Son. Let me see you. Let me touch you."

"Ha!" Ishmael bellowed. "Come, Father. Do not try to win me with lies as you did once years ago. I recall that day, O Father, when we rode to Salem. I almost believed you that day," he laughed, flinging his arms toward heaven in a defiant gesture of desperation. "I almost believed you, and I thought on your words of love for many months while I wandered in those hills. Do you remember?" he called. "Remember? I returned that spring—and do you recall how I was greeted? By the fanatic butchery of a father gone mad with delusions of grandeur! On my body I bear the marks of the circumcision!" he cried. "Oh, Father, that was quite a prize for my one-time act of humility."

Abraham pleaded with him again to come down from the hill, but Ishmael only mocked him, saying, "I came down to you for the last time that day long ago, and shortly thereafter I saw the fruits of my faith in you." At this Ishmael looked up, placing his hands to his mouth in imitation of his father the last night he had seen him; " 'This is my son, the first-born of my heart!' " he cried. And looking at Abraham, he pointed to Isaac and called, "Isn't that what I heard you say of the child there? 'The firstborn of your heart'?"

Abraham trembled with the recollection. "But you do not understand, Son," the father pleaded. "I spoke of the dream and the desire of the Lord's Promised Seed, a heritage which you denied."

Ishmael's face contorted in a cruel grin at that reference, and spitting defiantly on the ground to show his disgust of the topic, he laughed and said, "Only give me my inheritance, and I will leave you in peace. Isaac may have whatever glorious heritage your god has in store for him."

Now Sarah grew angry at this. She would not lose her hopes and dreams again. Looking at Hagar, the source of her old disillusionments, she ordered, "Husband, cast out this bondwoman and her son! Her son shall not be heir with Isaac!"

But at these words a fury rose in Abraham, a fury which would no longer tolerate the too quickly imposed insanity of his surroundings. What was this to which he had been so suddenly and rudely exposed, to have those he loved most contending for his heart and soul?

In a rage, in a desperate plea for order and understanding, he wheeled on the crowd, shouting, "No! Away with you all! I will have peace! I will have logic and reason! Has the whole world gone mad? Is this my son, my beloved son Ishmael, returned, as from the dead, not with words of comfort, but returned to haunt and torture me?"

The crowd was frightened, bewildered at Abraham's anger. Moving back in fear, they let him pass through, his hands placed on his ears as if to shut out all the world around him. "Out of my way!" he cried. "Leave me in peace!"

Eliezer ran after him, unable to believe all that had transpired in the past moments. And Ishmael, the one who had appeared like a phantom of the past to demolish the present, stood laughing madly, a mocking clown on the hill behind.

Chapter III

Abraham could not sleep that night. His reeling head was too full of raging conflict to allow repose.

In muffled agony, he tossed away the night, pleading with heaven to interpose its plan for him, for he did not know what to do.

"He has come again, God!" Abraham cried. "He has returned! I will not lose him again. Please let him stay with me. Do not let him leave. Do not make me do such as would send him from me again!"

Long into the night Abraham prayed thus, fearing Sarah's words and the decision with which he was being forced to contend wholly against his will.

Still, he knew that if Isaac gained the birthright which was God's will, Ishmael would be lost to him forever, and that if he defied God, the promise of the land would be taken away from Isaac.

But must the dilemma be solved in this way? Was there not some compromise to be reached? Must Ishmael be lost to him forever, sent away with no claim?

And what of Hagar? Abraham struggled with that. Must she suffer further, to be cast out without home and people?

Nothing made sense. Surely there was another way. Sweat stood in large beads on his forehead. It was nearly dawn when at last the answer came. And Abraham trembled at the reproving of his God.

"The past has come full circle," he heard the Lord say. "And so it must be, Abraham, for much of what a man sets his mind to do brings unhappiness. But let it not be grievous in thy sight because of the lad, and because of thy bondwoman; in all that Sarah hath said unto thee, hearken unto her voice. In Isaac shall thy seed be called. But also of the son of the bondwoman will I make a nation, because he also is thy seed."

Abraham rose up early the next morning and entered the courtyard. No sleep had touched his mind all that night.

His heart ached as it never had in all his life, but he knew what he must do. Only blind faith guided his steps now, and his soul cried out with each.

Going to Hagar's tent, he roused her and called her out to him. "Where is your son?" he asked, trying to contain his sorrow.

Hagar looked at him apprehensively and pointed to the hill. There sat Ishmael in the same place where he had challenged his father the night before.

Abraham looked sadly at Hagar, whose face still betrayed the undercurrent of secret love she had never lost for him, and his heart went out to her for the thing which was about to come to pass. It was a difficult lesson he was learning this day. But somehow he knew this was the only way. He knew the past must be fully rent from the future, that the sorrow and consequences were man-made and had never been the will of God, that no good could come from evil, and that God must not be blamed for this agony.

For the first time since the night nineteen years before, he again touched the lonely woman, the woman whose single error had cut her off so long from among the living. Taking her hand tenderly, he led her to the brow of the hill.

Ishmael stood and took his careworn mother in his arms. Looking bitterly at his father, he assumed an adult and defiant air which was too gravely beyond his young ability, all in an effort to cover the inner fear.

Abraham agonized. He could not speak but only studied the son of his never-forgotten indiscretion, and the woman of his eternal error. Knowing they sensed the inevitable, he felt the universe weep for their condition and would to God he could have turned back time to correct all that had forced them to this point.

Abraham looked at the ground, wanting to form the words in his mind which would soothe the terror of the moment, but none took shape.

He walked toward the camel which roused now from sleep, and secured a skin of water to its saddle.

Turning to Ishmael with tears in his eyes, he said, "But one word—listen, my son, and understand. The human heart is not divided in its love for many. To love one child does not subtract from the love of another."

Ishmael was silent. The world of his life had always been bitter as gall, but now more than ever he felt the poison of his existence. He could not look on his father, whom he loved and despised with equal passion. "And what of me, Father? What is to become of me?" he asked at last, stifling the pleas which he truly wished to voice, holding back the adolescent within which still cried for security.

Abraham walked toward his son and took his rebellious body in his arms, holding him very close and pressing his young face to his shoulder. "Your inheritance is with God," he whispered. "God has promised you a nation, as surely as Isaac will have one."

But Ishmael wrenched violently away from the embrace. "Is that so, my father? Has God indeed promised that?" he laughed scornfully. "Well said, then. Let it be. And be sure the words concerning me will be true. I will be a 'wild man.' Though my seed dwell in the presence of my brethren, my hand shall be against every man, and every man's hand against me!"

Leading his mother to the camel and lifting her up onto it, he made haste to be done with all of this. Turning wounded and disbelieving eyes on Abraham for the last time, he took his camel's reins in hand, and riding off, he shouted, "Be sure that the nation of Isaac and the nation of Ishmael shall ever be at war one with the other; neither shall they ever know peace!"

Chapter IV

Could any more be done than had been done? Had ever a man moved so fully on faith as Abraham?

He had had his times and even his years of doubt, the harvest of his own folly, and the trials of an exacting God. But he had met the challenge. In obedience he had freed himself of the past, clinging now only to the future, which had revealed itself materially in the miraculously conceived life of his son Isaac.

And as Isaac grew, Abraham grew. With each passing day, the aged Man of God grasped the future more certainly, saw the plan of his Master more poignantly and clearly.

The tempest had been safely channeled. A lifetime of commitment, however rocky the shoals, had seen its chart nearly through to the end.

The shore was in sight. Abraham sensed this; he knew it as surely as a seabird senses the land though he cannot see it for the fog which shrouds it.

Daily Abraham spent hours in meditation and conversation with his God, and happily would he have met the Lord on that shore now, but for one thing. He could not leave this side of the harbor without seeing his son fully grown.

Never had he desired life so fully as now, now that it had been fulfilled. Eagerly he awoke to each new day, grateful for another time with Isaac. And how deeply did he plunge himself into the task of rearing him!

When Isaac reached five, Abraham did indeed make him that small bow and quiver. The next day he did indeed begin teaching him to use it, and as he had foreseen, Isaac was a ready and capable learner.

When the lad was seven, his father took him proudly

into the native hills of Canaan, and rapidly the boy came to love and cherish his moments of adventure with Abraham.

Paternal love was not Isaac's only blessing. Sarah and her son were knit with an affection equally strong, for he was her fulfillment in a unique and saving way, her rescue from a life of purposelessness and cultural shame.

But, perhaps Isaac symbolized even more for his father, for when Abraham looked on him, he inevitably drew closer to his Sovereign. This was God's will before him, in human form. And so it was with a sense of awe and destiny that Abraham raised his son.

Though during the years of rearing the lad, God never again appeared to his Chosen Man, never again walked with him or presented Himself as in times past, Abraham grew in faith like a vine in the sun. Isaac was the ever-present reminder of an intangible Presence. No firmer manifestation of the reality of the Lord could have been asked.

So close did Abraham's walk with God become during those remaining years that the neighboring Canaanites began to call him, "Khalil," the Friend of God.

And such an influence he had! The prophets of Baal had never had such a difficult time in keeping a following as when Abraham challenged them. As he had stood as a stranger on the temple steps in Damascus so many years before, proclaiming his "new" God, now strangers came to him to hear the same story again.

And always he would call for Isaac, saying, "See, this is my son, given me in my old age, a sign of the covenant which my God has made with me; he shall be the heir of many nations and through him shall all nations be blessed."

Chapter V

The night settled on the fields in a heavy mist. Winter would surely be here soon. Abraham, Isaac, and several young men of the camp had been on this expedition for nearly a week, and when the hunt was done, they would return with meat enough to see the tribe through the long, dark months ahead.

A fire was quickly built in this niche of the hills, and the small tents were pitched in a circle. It would feel good to bed down for the night. Abraham's legs ached from the day's hike.

Seated with the joking, happy youngsters, Abraham looked on proudly at his son. Isaac had grown nearly as tall as himself now, and already his young body matured toward manhood.

In his bearing and physique there were hints of his relationship with Ishmael. Both, Abraham recalled, had the same proud faces, the same dark hair and eyes. But, while Ishmael had been wild and rebellious, Isaac showed a degree of depth, of sensitivity the elder lacked. How much this variance could be attributed to their different upbringings, Abraham hesitated to guess, nor did he relish dwelling on it.

Abraham's heart was free and easy tonight, and as was his custom, he left the company of his friends, wandering into the hills to commune with God before retiring.

His soul was full as he sought out a quiet place of meditation. Below, he could still see the flickering fire of the small camp, and he could hear the voices of the young men. "Oh, God," he smiled. "Blessed be the Covenant Keeper, praised be my Redeemer, Who hath prolonged my life that I might see the fulfillment of His promises. My joy is full, and I can barely contain it," he said happily. "Praised be the Almighty for the son of my old age."

Abraham waited patiently on the Lord, not really expecting more than the time of silence and worship which had customarily been his these past years. Only one petition was his, and this he voiced after a moment of tranquility.

"Lord, if now I have found favor in Thy sight, prolong my life yet long enough that I may see my son fully grown—but if need be, I am willing to follow when You come for me."

The icy wind of nearing winter whistled through the gorge where Abraham sat this evening. His meditation would be cut short for the cold, and praising God once again, he stood now to leave.

But with the next sharp wind, a strange sensation overtook him, a sensation as if the breath of the Lord surrounded him.

"How much do you love me, Friend Abraham?" the wind seemed to cry.

The Friend of God knew that Presence. His heart was attuned to it and stirred in response, like the strings of a lyre to the touch of a master musician. But at the sound of the peculiar question, an eerie fear crept through Abraham's bones.

Again the words came on the strange, howling wind: "How much do you love me, Friend Abraham?"

The Man of God was terrified, not by the content of the inquiry, but by its import. Somehow he sensed that a moment unlike any other in his life was come to pass.

"Lord?" he quavered. "Is it You?"

Again the wind roared, and Abraham sensed the presence of God in a new and challenging way. He was frightened, confused. Was this the same God Who had warmed his soul with love and light all these years?

More urgently now, the voice demanded, "Abraham!"

"Behold," the man cried in fear, "here am I!"

"Abraham," the voice called yet more insistently, "how much do you love me?"

"Oh, God! My soul and my life are Thine—Thou knowest it! My years from the time of Your call have been in Your hands, My Savior!"

But the wind blew more intensely yet, taking on the wound of a heavy, sorrowing cry, and Abraham cowered in the darkness. Had he said something wrong? Was the Lord angry with him?"

Defensively he wailed, "God in Heaven, You know I love You!"

Now the wind began to slow, to die into a tapering moan, and Abraham's hair stood on end. Like a man teetering on a precipice, he clung to the rocks about him, knowing the Lord was not yet done with him.

And yet, silence followed now, an interminable silence, during which Abraham's skin stood in goose flesh upon him.

Mysteriously, inexplicably he felt an urgency in the air. He knew that the Lord was about to require something of him, that his years of faith and service were to be tried as never before. No voice told him this—he only knew it, and his heart shuddered at the knowledge.

Already he began to form in his mind what that challenge might consist of, but he could think of nothing more to be done in proof of his allegiance than had already been done.

Looking above him, as if to beg the Lord's indulgence, he whispered, "My God, I have left home and family for You; I have traveled as a wayfarer and a stranger for You; I have dwelt in tents of goatshair and on empty plains for You; I have lived homeless, without city or nation, without a name—all, my God—all for You!"

But still there was silence. Abraham strained the skies for a glimpse of his Redeemer, for an acknowledging nod, but no answer came.

He hovered near the rocks, a terror gripping him, as

the wind grew up again, surrounding him with yet the same question.

"Friend Abraham, how much do you love me?"

"Oh, Master!" the man moaned, lifting his hands toward heaven. "Need You ask? What more can I do for You than I have done? Have I not lost my father in Your cause? Did I not endure separation from my dear nephew Lot, in Your cause? What more can I do than I have done?"

But still the wind shrieked and howled in agony about him, as if not hearing or caring for his words.

"Abraham, Abraham, my friend, how much do you love me?"

The Man of God was dumfounded, helpless. "God, hear me!" he pleaded. "I have given my elder son in Your cause, given him and his mother up to Your will. I saw Ishmael torn like an innocent lamb from me, for Your cause!"

He bowed his head in heavy sorrow at the memory and cried again, "What more must I do for You, my Sovereign, to say I love You?"

The wind was deafening now, tempestuous. Abraham sought the shelter of the rocks and knelt out of the way of the wind, which lashed and beat upon him like a scourge.

Nothing seemed to satisfy it, as it swarmed and howled up and down the gorge, ripping up stones and roots in its wake.

"God Almighty!" Abraham cried. "How may I answer You to show my love for You? Have I not given all for You?"

But with these very words, the wind suddenly ceased, leaving Abraham with the terrifying vacuum of his own question. His words seemed to ring like an echo inside his head.

"Have I not given all for You? Have I not given all for You?"

Abraham saw his inner man now, stark and naked before him. The question had resolved itself in the ask-

ing. He knew the answer, and yet never had he dreamed
he still withheld anything from his Master, nor would he
have dreamed it important that he had.

A thrill of indescribable terror filled him. He knew
now God's requirement, though he dare not guess at its
extent. But as he sensed the supportive hand of his
Master lifting and leading him, like a pale ghost he
obeyed, walking to the ledge which overlooked the
camp.

Below were the young men and Isaac, apparently oblivious to the tempest which had raged only moments
ago in these hills above them. Abraham followed the insistent finger of God, looking painfully upon his son,
but something within him cried out, "No, God! Take
my life, for it is worthless without my son, my only son!
Father, he is all that remains to me, besides his mother.
If You take him, I shall surely die. Your servant shall
surely die!"

But he felt now an awesome sorrow overtaking his
Redeemer and sensed it spreading through the universe.
"Abraham, my friend, how much do you love me?"

Abraham bled inside. "More than life, my Lord—"

But this did not suffice. "How much do you love
me?" it came again.

Abraham looked below, clinging nervously to his Redeemer's support. "God, do You wish me to say I love
You more than—more than Isaac? Then, so shall I say,
my God. For I love Thee more than my son, who is
more than life to me. But, Lord," Abraham groaned,
unable to speak his soul, "if You take him, take me as
well! For Your servant cannot live past that!"

"Abraham," the Lord said now urgently, but tenderly, as if the sorrow of His eternal heart would shatter it,
"Oh, Friend Abraham, I shall not take your son, but if
you love me, my friend, *you* take now thy son, thy only
son Isaac, whom thou lovest, and get thee into the land
of Moriah; and—" the great spirit of God paused here,
and Abraham trembled in dread.

"And—what, my Lord?"

"And offer him there for a burnt offering, upon one of the mountains which I will tell thee of."

Abraham was numbed, leveled, overcome; and falling prostrate, he lay nearly dead, his heart broken within him. Protests gathered like war clouds over his spirit, and he desired to cry out, "Merciless, Cruel One! What monstrous thing is this You ask of me? What deviltry is this You set my hand to do?" A blanket of black robed his soul, a fog of misery shrouded his mind. "God!" he roared, "What is this You do to me? Is it not enough that I should be willing to let You take him? Now You deny me even that passive indulgence! Do You say to take him with my own hand? Monster! Who are You?—Ha! So this is the cruel joke of my calling—to find Nannar after a life of sacrifice!"

And yet, somehow, in that instant, he felt the touch of God more surely and plainly than ever in his experience. Vividly the memory of his Lord's eyes, His tender, compassionate way impressed itself upon him. No cruelty, this. Only the ultimate love of his Master somehow to be revealed in its fullness through his surrender, he reasoned. In that instant, the past flashed before him more adequately in its purpose and fulfillment than ever before.

Now he felt the hands of faith mysteriously lifting him like bands of iron. As if by the touch of a wand, a new freedom, an awesome and exultant joy swept like a cresting wave throughout his being.

Was this a time to doubt? Had he come thus far to tremble now, to stumble at the end?

Truly, he had endured much for his Redeemer, he had given much, but had his God not shown equal faith toward him? Had his God not led him step by step, from crisis to crisis with unerring tenderness, for a purpose? Was he to doubt Him now?

"Up, Abraham!" he told himself. "Shall God betray His covenant? Though Isaac were to die, would He not raise him up again? Will God not keep trust with Himself? Will He betray His own purpose?"

Like a drama he saw more clearly than ever now the years of his life. Doubt was washed away in that moment. The Friend of God would trust. Though circumstances howled about him, he would not again doubt his God.

And though it was with a hesitant, shaky hand, he reached out purposefully to grasp the plan of the Master.

"How greatly do I love thee, my God?" he smiled. "Lead me on!"

Chapter VI

Not since Abraham had taken Ishmael on that never-completed journey to be blessed by Melchizedek, had he neared the small town of Salem. At the time he had doubted the Lord's leading, but he had set out for the Canaanite village nonetheless. Today he knew Salem was the proper destination.

"The land of Moriah," to which the Lord had demanded he go, surrounded the town, and he knew now that the time had come for his long-awaited and predestined journey there.

"We will go to build an altar to the Lord," he had told Isaac and his friends.

This was not an unusual custom for the patriarch, and so the young men asked no questions as they started out, though they may have wondered why he chose such a distant town as his point of offering.

From their hunting camp near Beersheba, it was a three-day journey to Salem. The weather was cold and rainy, as it had been on the entire expedition. The mountainous path seemed to rise relentlessly upward. The deluge of rain formed streams like miniature Jordans, which flowed and plunged through the crevices of the Philistine and Canaanite hills.

As Abraham hiked again through the same passes Ishmael and he had traversed, his was a mixture of emotions. He could not help thinking of his eldest son, of the harsh, stabbing words the lad had spoken to him in these very hills years before.

He walked quickly, as if running from the memory. But even more determined was his desire to outrun the thoughts of the present.

Isaac walked close beside his father, and as the village neared, he progressively sensed the urgency in Abraham's spirit. There was no name for the uneasiness which grew in him as he studied his father's tense walk, his steady steps. He only knew that the aged man was deep in thought, that as they drew nearer to Salem, he said less, and seemed bent on an undesired task, as if to slow his pace or to hesitate would lose him to some nameless act altogether.

The trail edged the foot of a great bluff, above which rose rugged and seemingly impassable slopes. The old man stopped and peered high above him, as if searching the mountain for something—or someone.

Isaac could not know his father's thoughts. He did not know Abraham strained the heights for the cave in which he had spent that fateful night so long ago. Nor could he ever know the depths of agony to which Abraham's soul had been plunged that distant evening.

The Man of God thought on the duty now before him and trembled. "I remember You so clearly, Lord. I remember Your touch that night. Surely my son shall rise again. Surely Your promise is everlasting. Surely he is to know You as I have, my God," Abraham whispered to himself.

He looked on Isaac sadly, and the words of his Master returned as they had come to comfort him in these same hills that night years before.

"Sarah thy wife shall bear thee a son indeed; and thou shalt call his name Isaac: and I will establish my covenant with him for an everlasting covenant, and with his seed after him."

Isaac was so much like himself when young, Abraham mused, and smiling, he thought. "He will know You, my Lord. He will know You even as I have known You."

Faith was Abraham's only shield that morning.

As they came over the final rise and looked down on the small city, clean and white under the dreary sky, his heart refused to doubt. He knew he had always been meant to come here one day, though he never dreamed it would be thus. Did Melchizedek know he had arrived? he wondered.

Lifting his eyes, he scanned the hills surrounding the town. He could have chosen any of them as the site of the altar, but he recalled the Lord's command: "Offer him there for a burnt offering upon one of the hills which I will show thee."

His glance landed on one of the far slopes, an unattractive, rough-hewn hill, rather like a skull in its outline.

"There?" he whispered. And the Spirit of the Lord witnessed in his heart that this indeed was to be the place of sacrifice.

From the back of the donkey which had accompanied them, he lifted the pile of prepared firewood and placed it on Isaac's back. Taking a firebrand in one hand and a knife in the other, he turned to the young men and said, "I and Isaac will go yonder and worship."

They nodded but looked hesitantly at one another, wondering how Abraham was to bring down a proper sacrifice with a hunting knife.

Abraham placed his arm around Isaac's sturdy shoulders and directed him down the slope. He looked at the distant, lonely hill, and his old soul trembled; but raising his chin in a determined gesture, he grasped firmly the promise of the Lord and called back to the waiting party, "We will come again to you—both of us!"

The father and son did not pass through the city below but skirted it in silence. Isaac's legs were strong and carried him easily despite the load upon his back. But still his heart pounded heavily. He was apprehensive, uneasy.

Questions grew like a cancer in his mind. This entire journey had been a mystery to him, but even more so now that they neared their destination.

He had never questioned his father. His love and respect were unbounded, and he did not doubt Abraham's wisdom. He had been reared unselfishly, deeply in the love of the Lord, and so he did not challenge the one who had done so well by him. And yet, today, a general fear of the unknown gripped him. What was the strange look in his father's eyes? Why had they come so far? What purpose was in this?

These were not new questions. He had thought on them for three days, since they had left the hunting fields for this place.

He had heard the tales of Melchizedek and Salem. He knew his father's desire to visit the place, and he had attributed Abraham's actions to the Lord's leading.

Yet it seemed the journey had little to do with those dreams.

He wondered. There was more to this than met the eye, and he had hesitated to face the gravest mystery of all: where was the sacrifice?

As they came to the foot of the mount, Isaac stopped to rest, lowering the pile from his back. Abraham stood beside him, sensing the coming inquisition, and wondering what he should answer.

"My father," Isaac began at last.

"Here am I," Abraham said hesitantly.

"Look," Isaac pointed, "here is the fire in your hand, and the wood on the ground, but, Father, where is the lamb for a burnt offering?"

Abraham studied the boy's dark eyes and knew the feeling of apprehension which was symbolized there. What was he to say? Was he to simply, blatantly reveal the inscrutable truth?

As he searched his mind for the proper answer, words which seemed not his own came suddenly and unexpectedly from his mouth, surprising himself as well as Isaac. "My son," he said, "God will provide himself a lamb for a burnt offering."

Isaac looked at his father, perplexed and not a little dubious. But he questioned no further, and the two began the long climb up the rugged, bony brow of the mount.

At the top was a rocky area, convenient for the building of an altar, and here Abraham set about to construct the place of sacrifice.

Isaac's heart pounded erratically. Small beads of perspiration dotted his forehead as he bent over to help his father lift the stones.

He scrutinized the old man's face, hoping to see some assurance there that the horror which presented itself to his imagination was not true.

As he had called Abraham in the night as a child when frightened by some nonexistent monster, he wished now to cry, "Father, tell me it is not so!" But there was no assurance in his father's face this time. There were no words of comfort. The fact that Abraham avoided his glance only seemed to confirm what were surely insane and groundless fears.

The old father placed the last rock on the top of the altar and stood mutely, grasping the sides of the monument with hesitant hands.

The universe seemed to spin wildly about Abraham now. He closed his eyes, hesitating to face the dread questions which now plagued him. Why had God not stopped him yet? Was he to take hold of Isaac now? Was he to explain? Was the Lord not going to reach out to wake him from the nightmare which swallowed him?

Surely this was not really happening. He would find it all a bad dream at any moment. Deep in concentration, he told himself that when he opened his eyes, he would find himself and his son safe at home, and he would thus recognize what was surely only a cruel tale of an overwrought imagination.

But he knew the truth. He knew the reality of his loneliness, the horror of his independence. This decision was his. There was to be no rescue from it. There was to be no helping or saving hand, no burning lamp or touch of Divine Salvation. There was but a choice, a choice to obey or refuse—and never had Abraham felt so alone.

Oh yes, there had been moments of desolation, moments when he would have preferred death to life. There had been the moment outside Ur in the hills of Chaldea; there had been the terrors of the journey to Egypt, the fear of losing Sarai; the fear of going forever without an heir.

But always there had been the distant hope that a Supreme Guardian would make all well for him, that He would reach down to set things straight and bring him up out of trouble, and always He had.

Abraham knew, though, the meaning of this greatest of all trials. He knew that God could not help him this time, for to do so would be to take the initiative of this ultimate decision from His Chosen Man.

This was his test. This was his moment of proof or failure, the hinge on which the door of future human history would swing, though he did not realize it.

All the years of molding, of designing, of rescuing had been meant for this—this moment above all others —even above his Call or the birth of Isaac itself. This instant of human will would design the pages of the future. A man would decide the course of human events at this juncture, for the power had been entrusted to him by the Lord.

"But why me, God!" he wished to cry out. "Why? What is it all for? Is my obedience truly that important to the Omnipotent One? Who am I that You should be so jealous of my affections, that You should try me like this? Surely I am but dust and ashes. Why do You test me so?"

Abraham's heart throbbed mercilessly within his breast. His breath came in heavy, throaty sobs, and Isaac looked on in mute, helpless terror at the nameless agony he witnessed.

"God!" Abraham cried now. "Let me go! I see no purpose in this!" But the words were hollow. The one who had communed with God, who had walked with

Him and touched Him, spoke only empty words when he made such protestations. Somehow he knew the hand of his Master. Beyond explanations or understanding Abraham trusted Him, and when the rebellion had been voiced, he knew he would act on that faith, just as the Lord knew it.

He was in a very real sense separate from God in that instant, and yet, faith in the One who had led him thus far directed his steps as surely as if the Lord Himself had moved him.

Lifting his tear-dimmed eyes, he looked on his son, who stood now, pleading with his very being that the horror he feared be imaginary.

But as his father approached him, Isaac did not struggle. Perhaps he too sensed the magnitude of the moment. Though he did not understand, he did not rebel. He could have denied his father the action he was about to take, but something sustained him.

Abraham stepped gently to his son, turning him about and binding his hands behind him. He could not look into the boy's eyes again but led him to the altar.

Tears poured down the lad's face, though he spoke not a word, turning his face purposely toward the ground that his father might not see his fear.

And now a violent wind dashed over the mountain, bringing a hail of rain and sleet across the two dismal, pathetic figures who stood beneath the watchful eye of their God.

Abraham reached for the knife which lay beside the altar, and trembling violently, he lifted it toward the sky, joining both hands about its neck.

His ruddy, wrinkled face defied the elements, his silver beard and hair lashed in a tormented rage by the wind. His dark, determined eyes—eyes which had seen more sorrow and heartache than ten men in their lifetimes—stared defiantly at the blustering sky.

His clenched fists throbbed with the pulse of decision, and for only one moment did he hesitate, an unearthly, subliminal cry of despair and—yes—ultimate surrender wrenching his soul.

"Oh, my God! How much do I love thee? If it must be, even so, my God, even so—let it be!"

His hand moved the glistening knife to a set position above his son, and he began to swing it with the lightning swift arc of decision—when suddenly the very earth rocked like a drunken man beneath his feet, throwing him to the ground with one jolting but painless blow.

"Abraham! Abraham!" a trumpeting voice split the sky.

In terror, the Man of God looked above him, and there, with an awesome quake, the clouds had separated in a bladelike line of brilliantly descending light. He covered his eyes, unable to look on the blinding ray, and cried, "Here am I!"

The business was done, the trial passed. An unearthly silence ensued, a silence he had experienced only once before, when the universe had seemed to cease all motion in response to the nearing presence of his God.

Again, as at that time outside Ur, his ears strained painfully, expectantly for the saving words of the Almighty.

Dared he looked up once more? Peering cautiously from under his mantle, the Man of God shot an inquisitive glance heavenward, and there, surrounded by ethereal majesty, surrounded by a radiance inestimable in human terms, he saw the God of Glory—not as he had known Him in times past, for never again was he to know Him so—but His appearance was as the light of the sun, as the light of knowledge and love, not to be translated into the words of depraved Man.

"Lay not thine hand upon the lad, neither do thou anything unto him," the Lord commanded, "for now I know that thou fearest God, seeing thou hast not withheld thy son, thine only son from me. By myself have I sworn, saith the Lord, for because thou hast done this thing, and hast not withheld thy son, thine only son:

that in blessing I will bless thee, and in multiplying I will multiply thy seed as the stars of the heaven, and as the sand which is upon the seashore; and thy seed shall possess the gate of his enemies; and in thy seed shall all the nations of the earth be blessed; because thou hast obeyed my voice."

With this the glory of the Lord was taken up from him, and Abraham looked speechlessly at Isaac, who had witnessed it all with him.

Without a word he stumbled to his feet, and ran tearfully, gratefully to the altar and quickly unbound his son.

"Father," the boy whispered, clinging in stunned incredulity to the only anchor he knew.

Abraham buried his face on his son's shoulder and unashamedly wept. "Oh, Son!" he cried. "Blessed be the Lord Who has given you to me twice by a miracle!"

Isaac wiped the tears from his face and turned once more toward the cruel altar, shakily considering the Hand of Salvation which had just rescued him.

"Father, look!" he shouted, pointing to a thick briar which grew nearby. There, its horns caught in the thicket, was a struggling, bleating ram, unblemished and strong.

The two men looked at one another in disbelief and simultaneously broke out in a peal of laughter, running madly toward the bush, shouting and praising God in their hilarity.

And the Lord looked down in nodding approval. His faith in Abraham had been well rewarded.

PART VII

The Fulfillment
ᎧᎧᎧᎧᎧᎧᎧᎧᎧᎧᎧᎧᎧ

These all died in faith, not having received the promises, but having seen them afar off, and were persuaded of them, and embraced them, and confessed that they were strangers and pilgrims on the earth. But now they desire a better country, that is, an heavenly: wherefore God is not ashamed to be called their God: for he hath prepared for them a city.

Hebrews 11:13,16

Chapter I

It was a very old man who stood twelve years later before the lonely sepulcher adjacent to the field of Mamre. Often he came here led by the hand of his faithful servant, Eliezer—came no longer to mourn, but to remember, to contemplate.

Bent with age and dim of vision, Abraham required the guidance of his friend to find a comfortable place beneath the spreading oaks, where he would sit, as was his custom, in the cool of the day.

Surveying the cave where Sarah had been buried, Abraham was peaceful, content.

His wrinkled face formed a wistful smile, and he spoke, as he often did, of the past. "I told her once that we would be abundant with good things, even as the hills of Palestine. And we did have a good life together, she and I," he whispered.

There was such devotion in that voice, such love undimmed by the years. Eliezer looked on respectfully and only listened with the sympathy of a friend.

"I have been greatly blessed," Abraham mused. "I have lived to see my son fully grown, and such a fine man he is," he said proudly.

Then, reaching for Eliezer, he summoned him to sit close by. The servant drew near, sensing a great urgency in his master's spirit. And he trembled, for he knew what Abraham would speak of.

"I am well stricken in age," the Man of God began. "Hear me, Eliezer, for my days are not long on the earth."

Eliezer said nothing, listening intently to his master's voice, though he did not wish to hear him speak so.

Abraham placed a gentle hand on his servant's

shoulder and stared intently at him, his furrowed brow knit in a mood of deep sincerity. "Let us deal in realities, my friend," he said softly. "One thing only I asked of the Lord, and that He has granted. He has allowed me to see my son a man. I am tired now, and my time has come. My purpose is fulfilled, my life is full. But Eliezer, what I ask of you is a great thing. Will you perform it?"

The old friend looked fondly on his master and companion. "Oh, yes, sir! You may trust me!"

"Then take me one more time to Salem," Abraham said, his eyes full of faraway memories. "I wish to see the city once more. I wish to see Melchizedek before I die," he whispered, clasping his withered hands before him.

Thinking that this was no great service to perform, as Abraham had said, Eliezer promised, adding, "But, sir, is that all I may do for you?"

"No, friend; there is yet one more thing," Abraham said earnestly. And leaning forward, he whispered, "All that I have is in your keeping until I die. Even my son Isaac I leave in your charge to secure him a wife fit for God's purpose."

Eliezer looked in surprise on his master. Deeply moved and greatly humbled by the honor, he gladly took up the task. "I will do as you have said, Master," he reassured him.

But moving yet closer and grasping Eliezer's hand firmly, Abraham said, as if to seal the transaction and bind the urgency of it, "Put, I pray thee, thy hand under my thigh, and I will make thee swear by the Lord, God of Heaven, and the God of earth, that thou shalt not take a wife unto my son of the daughters of Canaan, but thou shalt go unto my country and to my kindred, and take a wife unto my son Isaac."

Eliezer was riveted by the intensity with which his aged master spoke, and realizing the nature of the request, that it was Abraham's last injunction for him, he reached forward in sign of covenant, placing an obedient hand under Abraham's thigh, and swore earnestly, "I will perform it."

Abraham looked one more time into the solemn face of his beloved servant, and sighed, satisfied now that his days could end in peace. "The Lord will send his angel before thee," he said. "And you shall return swiftly."

But then, as if to speak more would bring tears to his already dim grey eyes, Abraham left off talking and asked to be alone.

Chapter II

The wind blew softly up the rise from Salem to the brow of the hill where Abraham stood. His heart was easy, like that of a man who had at long last come to the end of some great pilgrimage.

The sun was setting, and though Abraham watched through dim eyes, he could see Eliezer wending his way across the Jordan plain toward Mesopotamia and the city of Nahor. Ten camels formed the small caravan, manned only by his old friend, and piled high on their backs were gifts for the nameless bride.

Abraham watched until Eliezer was lost to sight, and as he considered his old homeland, he looked once more over the progress of his life.

He remembered his father, his brothers, his city.

The vast valley of the Jordan stretched out to his right, and with a trembling heart he recalled how he and Sarah had stood years ago, seeing it together for the first time. Memories of her striking beauty, even in old age, remained indelibly with him. The woman who had been the challenge of princes bolstered him even yet, and as he considered Isaac, his soul communed tenderly with the thought of her.

And yet there were still unanswered questions. There were problems of the heart which even now moved Abraham with their impact. Thinking on Lot, the man forever and mysteriously lost to history, the man whose life had ever been an enigma—thinking on Ishmael, the child of his error and the barb of his soul—he trembled.

Raising his eyes toward heaven, he whispered, "If now I have found favor in Your sight, Oh Lord, let me know the end from the beginning. Open my aged eyes to Your purpose. Let it be made clear. Let me see the fullness of Your will and plan, for my days are at an end. My struggle and my suffering have been long and wearisome, and I have seen only a portion of Your purpose."

Lifting his hands high above him, he pleaded for understanding. The memories of his life were vast and dramatic, and yet he had only a fleeting perception of his place in history.

"Oh, be not far from me, my Lord!" he called out, longing to see his God once more before he died. "Your hand has been gracious unto me all my years, and yet I would understand Your purposes with me."

The Spirit of God was not long in answering His friend. "Abraham," He called gently to him.

Turning about and searching the hillside anxiously, the man cried, "Lord! Here am I!"

"Come up, Friend Abraham, father of the faithful, father of a multitude! Come up, and I will show thee great things beyond your dreams. Come up and find understanding."

Compelled by the unseen hand of his Redeemer, he obeyed happily and came quickly to the pinnacle of the hill. He saw no one, but he was not alone. "Here am I," he said again. "Instruct me now, my Lord, for my days are short on the earth."

The presence of the Lord was gentle as He said, "Behold now, my love is great toward you, Friend Abraham. Be patient but a little longer and you will understand. For I will give wisdom to the simple and insight to the humble of heart. Hold firmly to the hand which leads you and cast your eyes upon the city, for I will roll back the scrolls of witness and pour out before you the ink of stories unrecorded."

The Friend of God reached up and took hold of the mighty promise, and in that moment his spiritual eyes were opened.

Below marched a thousand armies, and from the beginning of time immemorial he saw the pageantry of a hundred civilizations. From across the span of Man's history they came in droves, their faces turned unswervingly toward this city.

The dark clouds of the past rolled back, disclosing the members of humanity, countless, nameless millions pouring like waves of a sea through the gates of Salem, one day to be called Jeru-Salem, "The Holy City, City of Peace." The lowly were uplifted, the homeless ceased their wanderings, the crippled rose to walk, the sick were healed, the hungry fed, and the broken-hearted made to laugh again.

The gates moved back and the walls expanded, and yet still they came, the tired, the thirsty, the oppressed, until the city spread from horizon to horizon, taking in the Promised Land, its walls and towers gleaming like polished gems.

And Abraham saw the faces of its keepers, the guardians of its borders, saw that they were his descendants, the children of a miracle, descendants of the miracle child, Isaac, uniquely the creation of the Lord and owing their existence to no man, but to the faith of the patriarch.

"Lord, instruct me," he cried. "It is too marvelous for me. My heart cannot contain it. How can this be, that kings and princes should come unto these, my little ones, these who You said would be persecuted so in their generations. I am as a foolish and unlearned man; yet I cry for wisdom! Is not this the village of Salem, the town of Melchizedek? What is it, that it should be so glorified, and my people that they should keep it?"

The Lord moved near to Abraham and said, "Behold, the throne of the King is established forever; a nation of priests shall your seed be unto me, and through you shall all nations be blessed. Behold, now, my friend—"

Abraham's eyes were drawn to the far side of the eternal city, where on a hill stood a solitary figure, one of his descendants, a young man, with strangely the same regal bearing and aspect as that of the old King Melchizedek, who had greeted him at the return from battle so many years before. And yet this man was a commoner, unadorned, and dressed—in undyed wool.

As he surveyed the distant figure to whom all the nations now gave obeisance, he recognized the rocky skull of the mountain on which his feet were planted.

Scenes of his only begotten son Isaac carrying his burden of wood up that hill flashed before him, and pieces of a mystery began to fall in place. Large, heavy tears flowed down Abraham's face as he saw the path of pain and selflessness which this man too had trod to its summit. And a cry of agony wrenched the patriarch as he glimpsed the instrument of cruelty erected there.

Understanding now the heart of God, he said, "The mountain of sacrifice—I see, my Lord." And remembering his words of reassurance to Isaac that fearsome day years before, he whispered, "—God will indeed provide Himself a Lamb."

The Friend of God, the Father of the Faithful, stood at the end of his journey, his mission complete, the final shore in sight. As he surveyed the distant expanse of the Jordan, the Ghor, and the hills of the Promised Land, once again silent and untouched by the passing of time, he knew the entirety of his own purpose.

"My wandering is over," he whispered. "How long have I sought for the end of my journey! By faith have I wandered in the land of promise as in a strange country. But I have found a city which has foundations, whose builder and maker is God. I have seen the King, and let it be said of Abraham that when he saw His day, he rejoiced and was glad."

*If you've enjoyed this book,
you'll want to look for other fine*

BIBLICAL NOVELS

from Tyndale House Publishers

The Birth by Gene Edwards. "In the glorious heavenly realm, the angels eagerly strain to understand what new thing God is about to do as Gabriel passes through the Door. . . . The forces of good and evil are about to clash." Here is the tale of the Incarnation as seen from heaven and earth. Trade paper 75-0158, $7.95.

The Flames of Rome by Paul L. Maier. Decadence . . . idealism . . . sensuality . . . cruelty—this was Rome in the time of the Caesars. Into this explosive setting Christianity made a quiet—then shocking—entrance as power and faith met head-on in a clash that would change the world. Set in the time of the early church. Living Books 07-0903, $4.95.

Isaiah: The Prophet Prince by Constance Head. In this richly painted picture of Bible times, readers are drawn into the hearts and minds of Isaiah and his contemporaries—idolatrous, weak, and power-hungry rulers. As politics and idolatry threaten a nation's worship, Isaiah stands as a spokesman for the true God. Living Books 07-1751, $4.95.

John, Son of Thunder by Ellen Gunderson Traylor. A majestic novel that takes you right into the midst of the twelve disciples. Travel with John down desert paths, through the courts of the Holy City, and to the foot of the cross. Journey with him from his luxury as a privileged son of Israel to the bitter hardship of his exile on Patmos. Here is a saga of adventure, romance, and discovery—of the disciple "whom Jesus loved." Living Books 07-1903, $5.95.

Jonah by Ellen Gunderson Traylor. The saga of two nations, two kings, and the man who reached them both. An epic story of rebellion and obedience, *Jonah* tells of God's work in one man's soul to bring his word to those who might otherwise never have heard. Discover the life and times of Jonah. Living Books 07-1945, $4.95.

Mark: Eye-witness by Ellen Gunderson Traylor. This is an account of how a handful of people—Jesus and his disciples—changed an empire by virtue of their simple faith. Mark's story reminds us that the work of Christ overcomes failure, inadequacy, and pride, taking people beyond their weaknesses to a life of usefulness and power. Trade paper 75-4102, $9.95; Living Books 07-3961, $4.95.

Mary Magdalene by Ellen Gunderson Traylor. This gripping novel sweeps into the psyche of the renowned follower of Jesus, a woman whose sorrows rival her beauty. Interwoven with biblical narrative, the story of Mary Magdalene promises hope and healing for all wounded hearts. Living Books 07-4176, $4.95.

Noah by Ellen Gunderson Traylor. In this imaginative novel, Traylor paints a vivid picture of the pre-Flood world in which society's tamperings with nature have abused God's creation. This story of Noah's growth and struggles is a thrilling saga of faith and courage in the face of the greatest darkness man has ever seen. Living Books 07-4699, $4.95.

Ruth by Ellen Gunderson Traylor. Meet Ruth, a Moabitess, as she strives to understand the people of Jehovah and finds herself slipping away from the harsh Moabite religion. Though the pain of separation and poverty would come upon her, Ruth was to become part of the very fulfillment of prophecy—and find true love on her own doorstep as well. Living Books 07-5809, $4.95.

Samson by Ellen Gunderson Traylor. Readers will meet the lovely, patient Marissa; the ravishing, cunning Delilah; and the friend-turned-enemy Josef. In the middle of them all is the dashing, puzzling, and romantic Samson, a man torn between cultures and two women who love him. Trade paper 75-5828, $9.95.

Song of Abraham by Ellen Gunderson Traylor. This richly colorful novel unfolds the tumultuous saga of one man who founded a nation. Traylor's fascinating reconstruction of the life of Abraham portrays a man of strength, will, and purpose who remains unparalleled in history. Carefully researched and superbly told. Living Books 07-6071, $5.95.

These books are available at your local Christian bookstore. If you're unable to find them, send a check with your order to cover the retail price plus $2.00 per order for postage and handling to: **Tyndale Family Products, P.O. Box 448, Wheaton, Illinois 60189-0448.** Prices and availability are subject to change without notice. Allow 4-6 weeks for delivery.

Terah   Hebron Par

NAHOR   Abram   Haron

Milcah   Milcah
Isah   Iscah
Lot   Lot